"I'LL ACT FIRST AND ANSWER QUESTIONS LATER."

Armand stripped the covers from Catherine's trembling body and considered her dispassionately. "Now, do you have a robe or something you can put on? I don't want you contracting pneumonia on top of everything else."

Catherine's hands moved futilely to protect her body as his eyes searched the room. "You can't do this," she whispered. "I can't even walk. If anyone sees us—"

"Oh, I'm pretty sure someone will," responded Armand carelessly, gesturing for her to sit up. "Don't worry. As I told you before, my immortal soul was damned years ago."

It was crazy, but in spite of everything, Catherine knew a treacherous sense of relief when Armand's arms closed around her. It was no use denying it any longer, she thought tremulously. She was glad she was leaving the convent. She wanted to be with people again. And most shamelessly of all, she wanted to be with Armand, and that was unforgivable.

Books by Anne Mather

STORMSPELL
WILD CONCERTO
HIDDEN IN THE FLAME

HARLEQUIN PRESENTS

HARLEQUIN ROMANCE

These books may be available at your local bookseller.

Don't miss any of our special offers. Write to us at the
following address for information on our newest releases.

Worldwide Library Reader Service
P.O. Box 52040, Phoenix, AZ 85072-2040
Canadian address: P.O. Box 2800, Postal Station A,
5170 Yonge St., Willowdale, Ont. M2N 6J3

ANNE
MATHER

HIDDEN IN
THE FLAME

TORONTO · NEW YORK · LONDON · PARIS
AMSTERDAM · STOCKHOLM · HAMBURG
ATHENS · MILAN · TOKYO · SYDNEY

First published June 1985

ISBN 0-373-97014-5

CHAPTER ONE

'HAIL MARY, full of grace—'

Catherine's hands moved along the rosary beads, marking off each one of the twelve prayers of remission Sister Angelica had given her earlier in the afternoon.

'Hail Mary, full of grace—'

Her slim fingers sped impatiently over the beads, and inwardly she knew a growing, and totally ungovernable, feeling of resentment that she should have to spend the hottest part of the day cloistered in the airless chapel.

'Hail Mary, full of grace—'

It wasn't as if she had done anything wrong, she thought indignantly. She had only passed the time of day with the army officer who had visited the convent to see Reverend Mother. She had not been flirting with him, as her superior had accused. She had simply answered him when he remarked upon the perfection of the poinsettia growing over the iron gates. She had not even considered that he might be comparing her with its lush beauty, that he might be flattering her. It had never even entered her head. But it had entered Sister Angelica's, and Reverend Mother's . . .

'Hail Mary, full of grace—'

Catherine sighed. It wasn't fair. She had not asked to lead this kind of life. It wasn't as if she believed she had a vocation. Until the rebels had killed her father, she hadn't given much serious thought to her future, imagining, no doubt foolishly, that she had plenty of time to make that kind of decision. The fact that she hadn't had been thrust upon her in the cruellest way possible, and for a time the shock had numbed her senses. Then, the convent walls had provided a much-needed barrier between her and the savagery outside, and the dedicated nuns had appeared like angels of mercy. But now, as her pain and grief subsided, she was beginning to realise how impulsively she had embraced their order, and the idea of spending the rest of her life in seclusion no longer had such appeal.

'Hail Mary, full of grace—'

The unrest in Surajo had never troubled her father. As an academic, and a scholar of ancient South American civilisations, he had considered himself immune from the various political factions that fought so persistently for power in the country. The school he had founded at Batistamajor was remote from the more heavily populated areas around the coastal capital, Terasina, and there had seemed little chance of the urban violence ever engulfing them. But it had; and her father was dead; and Catherine didn't know what to do.

Circumstances should have been so different, she thought now, as she threaded the beads through her fingers. When she first came to Surajo, she had been enchanted by the little school set on the hillside overlooking the Batista valley. Although she had spent the better part of her life at a boarding school in England, she had looked forward to the time when she could help her father in his school, teaching the Indian children to read and write and do simple sums. She knew the friends she had made in England thought she was mad to want to come and bury herself in a place like Surajo, but if Catherine wanted to be with her father, she had had to accept his way of life.

Besides, for the first few months she had lived at Batistamajor she had been extremely happy. The children were a delight, and Catherine had been flattered at the way they took to her, following her about and admiring the unusual brilliance of her hair. Until that time Catherine had considered her unruly red-gold tresses as something to be deplored. However, she had finally come to the conclusion that curly hair could be an advantage in a place where the nearest hairdresser was several hundred miles away.

Catherine's fingers stilled. It was a little over a year since she had left school, and eight months since her father had been killed and she had been brought here, to the sanctuary of the Convent of the Assumption. The memory of the night her father died was still too vivid to remember with equanimity, and her pulses quickened at the unwanted images it evoked. If she closed her eyes, she could still smell the torches, still hear the raucous cries of men incensed by defeat, still see the broad-bladed knives smeared with her father's blood . . .

Her stomach revolted, and she returned fervently to her prayers, stamping on the ungrateful seeds of rebellion growing inside her. She had been thankful to Reverend Mother then. The flower-studded gates of the convent had opened and let her in, and she had believed she would never want to leave them again. The world outside had become a bloody battlefield where no innocent person could live in peace. Here, there was a healing sense of timelessness, where one day followed another with reassuring familiarity, and even the guerrilla forces respected the sanctity of these religious women.

Catherine allowed her eyes to move over the bowl of lilies on the altar above her. Huge, waxen blossoms,

spilling their perfume into the atmosphere, they gave
the air a heady fragrance that was almost intoxicating.
Beside the lilies, the candle flames scarcely stirred,
their light catching fire in the carved gold cross with its
precious burden of Christ crucified. She was amazed
there was sufficient oxygen in the chapel to enable
them to burn so brightly, and unknowingly her
tongue emerged to circle her dry lips.

What time was it, she wondered. Tea-time
perhaps—only they didn't have tea at the convent.
There were only three occasions during the day when
the nuns gathered together for sustenance—breakfast, the noonday repast, and supper. There were no
cosy cups of coffee, such as Catherine and her father
used to indulge in; no home-made scones or pots of tea
and toast, enjoyed while Professor Loring prepared
lessons for the following day. There were no unexpected menus at the convent; no unconventional hap-
penings, reflected Catherine, grimacing at her own
pun. Its very reassurance, that essence of agelessness
and tranquillity was distilled from a sameness of attitude, an ability to accept the routineness of one's life as
being merely a stepping-stone to God's grace.

Catherine wiped her damp forehead on the sleeve of
her gown. Acceptance, she thought. That was something she still had to find. She hoped it would not take
too much longer. 'Every day in every way . . .' she
quoted ruefully, and then glanced about her anxiously
in case one of the sisters might have overheard her
blasphemy. And it was a blasphemy, she knew that,
thinking such thoughts in this holy place, when she
was supposed to be repenting her sins. If only her
sense of the ridiculous was not so pronounced, she
sighed. If only she didn't find humour in things which
ought to have been so serious.

She massaged her aching spine in sudden frustration. It shouldn't be a crime to seek relief from the discipline of life in the convent by making light of it, she mused. Wasn't that what they were taught to do? To lighten other people's burdens? So why shouldn't they lighten their own? Yet her infectious laughter had brought down more punishments on her head, and she was constantly trying to control the irrepressible side of her nature. Even though she didn't lie awake at night worrying about it—she was usually too tired for that—she did wonder if she would ever achieve the state of grace the other novices had realised. Sister Angelica said it would come. Sister Angelica said that God had sent her to them when her father had been murdered, and God would show her the way when he was ready.

Catherine had refrained from pointing out that someone other than the Almighty had rescued her from the knives of Rodolfo's men. That, too, would have been a blasphemy. And perhaps, when her faith was stronger, she would see that for herself. But right now, she felt she owed her life to Armand Alvares, the Brazilian doctor from Terasina, who had found her huddled by her father's body and had brought her to the convent.

Catherine's head drooped on her slender shoulders. If only she was more like Sister Angelica, she thought. If only she could accept that God's will had guided Armand Alvares's hand, and not the devil's. Her father had once told her it was rumoured that the doctor was a sympathiser of the rebel army, who had their headquarters somewhere in these mountains, but Catherine scarcely knew him. She had only seen him once or twice before the night the school was burned, and it was some time later before she had speculated on the significance of his appearance at the scene. There had not been time to send an emergency call on the radio-telephone, which had been their only link with the security forces. Yet, Dr Alvares had arrived minutes after her father was killed, and he had succeeded in getting her away against all the odds.

She lifted her shoulders now in a dismissing gesture. It was unlikely that she would ever learn the truth about Armand Alvares. He was an infrequent visitor to the convent, calling only when the nursing sisters needed professional assistance in the small hospital they ran for the benefit of the local population. In consequence, Catherine had no actual contact with him. The younger members of the order were forbidden to mix with members of the opposite sex—except Father Donovan, of course—and Catherine guessed that by the time she was old enough to qualify, Dr Alvares would have returned to his lucrative practice in Terasina. She wondered why he had left the capital, why he was expending his reportedly-brilliant skills in an area whose population was for the most part poor and illiterate. It seemed to lend weight to her father's contention that he was involved with the insurgent rabble who had eventually destroyed everything Professor Loring had worked for.

Her knees were stiff by the time Catherine rose to her feet, brushed down her gown, and made her way out of the small chapel. The coarse cotton of her undershift was abrasive against her skin, but she welcomed the mild chafing. It reminded her of the reason why she was doing penance, and banished the disturbing thoughts of Armand Alvares from her head.

With a trickle of moisture making its way down her

spine and beads of perspiration standing out on her forehead, she knew an incipient longing to shed her cumbersome garments and plunge her body into the cooling waters of the Batista river. Born in the mountains overlooking the valley, the Batista's waters were the life-giving force in the area; and while it was often used for activities frowned upon by the local health authorities, it was still inviting. It would be such a relief to wash away the sweat from her body and feel really clean for once. Taking a bath was another of the simple pleasures she had had to forgo. No one could call the all-over scouring of their bodies with pungent-smelling soap that the nuns indulged in a pleasure. It was a necessary evil. They didn't even wash in the nude. The cotton shifts they wore beneath their habits were never removed, except when changing. Instead, soap and flannel were thrust beneath the cloth and they dried themselves in the same way.

Emerging from the chapel entrance, Catherine turned her face up to the sun, feeling its fading heat through her closed eyelids. How long was it since she had sunbathed, she wondered. How long since she had put on jeans or a pretty dress, or even seen her reflection in a mirror? She was having to learn that such thoughts were sinful, and she silently offered two more Hail Marys as she walked with downbent head across the courtyard, on her way to report to Sister Angelica.

'Ah, good afternoon, child. Or should I say good evening? Sure, the sun is on its way to bed.'

The robust Irish brogue was unmistakable, and Catherine lifted her head eagerly to answer the white-haired priest, whose wry good humour provided the only male contact in her life.

'Good afternoon, Father,' she began, risking Sister

Angelica's wrath by allowing a smile to lift the corners
of her mouth. Then she averted her eyes again at the
realisation that Father Donovan was not alone.
Another man was standing beside him, a man whose
tall, muscular frame dwarfed that of the rotund little
priest, and Catherine's heart pounded rapidly at the
realisation of his identity. It was Dr Armand Alvares,
the man whose doubtful reputation she had been
pondering when she ought to have been concentrating on her penance. It was the first time she had seen
him since the night he had brought her to the convent,
and she found herself wishing, quite absurdly in the
circumstances, that he had not seen her like this.

'You look hot, child,' Father Donovan remarked
solicitously, and Catherine was grateful that the sudden colour in her cheeks had been misinterpreted. She
was intensely conscious of Armand Alvares's eyes
upon her; she was disturbed by the dark penetration
of his regard; and she was uncomfortably aware that
instead of ignoring him, she was by no means indifferent to his presence.

Catherine swallowed, and realising Father Donovan
was waiting for some response from her, she adopted
a suitably subdued tone. 'I've been in chapel, Father.
Making penance.' She paused and then added
quickly: 'Are you waiting to see Reverend Mother?'

'Sister Felicia has gone to inform Reverend Mother
that we are here, child,' he replied kindly. 'Now, tell
me, why have you been in the chapel on this hot
afternoon, when I'd have expected you to be in the
garden, helping Sister Teresa?'

Catherine knew she was obliged to answer him, and
allowing herself a covert glance in the doctor's direction, she discovered that her fears about Armand
Alvares had not been misplaced. He was watching

her, with an irony that bordered on insolence, and although she swiftly lowered her eyes again, she could still see his dark, satanic features.

He was a disturbing man, she thought unwillingly, and then condemned herself for thinking such a thing. She didn't need Sister Angelica to tell her the sinfulness of such thoughts, but her self-castigation would not dispel Armand Alvares's image from her mind. His hard, sun-tanned face, his thick straight hair, that fell silkily over his forehead from a side parting, his lean, powerful body, were imprinted on the inner curve of her eyelids, and she could not remove them. Even if she was prepared to reject the world and all its temptations, Armand Alvares was there, he was real—but he was also the man she suspected of having some involvement with her father's murderers . . .

'I—Sister Angelica disapproved of my speaking to Major Enriques, Father,' she admitted now, quelling the indignation she felt in making her confession in front of Armand Alvares. 'If you will excuse me. I'm supposed to report to her now.'

'Go with God, child.'

Father Donovan made the sign of the cross, but before Catherine could dart away across the courtyard, Armand Alvares intervened.

'Miss—Loring, is it not?' he inquired sardonically, forcing her to acknowledge his presence. His English was faultless, with only the faintest trace of an accent. 'I see you have quite recovered from your ordeal.'

'Of course, of course.' Father Donovan turned abruptly to his companion. 'You know this child, do you not? I'm forgetting it was you who delivered her to us, Doctor.'

'I brought Miss Loring to the convent, yes,' agreed Armand Alvares flatly, thick lashes guarding the

expression in his dark eyes. 'I didn't realise she was
still here.'

Catherine's lips parted. Where else did he expect
her to be, she wondered resentfully. Her father was
dead, and so far as she knew she had no other living
relatives. She had had no job, no money; what else
could she do?

'Sure, and where else would she be than thanking
God for her deliverance?' Father Donovan exclaimed
now. 'Go on, child. Be about your business. I wouldn't
want Sister Angelica to see you here talking with us.
She might decide your punishment had not achieved
its end.'

'Yes, Father.'

Catherine was not sorry to receive her dismissal, but
as she hurried across the courtyard, she knew Armand
Alvares's eyes were still upon her.

A week later, Catherine encountered Dr Alvares
again.

It had been a strange week, a hectic week, during
which she had found herself doing work she would
not normally have been permitted to do. The hot,
humid weather had continued, and with it had come a
sudden epidemic of sickness and diarrhoea caused,
Reverend Mother maintained, by the polluted waters
of the lower Batista. The small hospital was soon
filled to overflowing with patients; mothers and children alike, sharing the same bed and overloading
a ward only capable of accommodating a dozen
people.

Of course, it was inevitable that several of the nuns
should themselves succumb to the infection. It wasn't
easy to maintain hygiene in such temperatures, and to
begin with Catherine had been kept busy washing

sheets and sterilising eating utensils so that the disease should be contained.

But, eventually, much against her better judgment, Sister Angelica was obliged to allow her to help in the ward, although she was most adamant that Catherine should not enter the male annex next door. Catherine didn't mind. Her arms ached from sluicing sheets and scouring pans, and even making beds or emptying bedpans was a relief.

Even so, by the end of the first day on the ward, she was drooping, and she didn't even have the strength to take off her habit before collapsing on her cot that night. Morning came all too soon and, after dragging herself to the chapel for mass at five thirty, she faced the day ahead with grim determination.

Breakfast was usually a simple meal of cereal, with hot or cold milk depending on the vagaries of the cooking facilities. The refinement of electricity had not yet reached the convent and lights, heating and ovens depended on bottled gas or oil, whichever was available. Reverend Mother said they should consider themselves lucky that they had facilities for either, and when they had oatcakes, prepared in the convent's kitchen, Catherine agreed with her. Even so, she missed the butter or honey she and her father used to spread on their toast, and today she had to content herself with a bowl of lukewarm oatmeal before making her way along the stone-paved cloister to the small hospital.

Beneath the coif, which had started the day crisp and white, Catherine's hair was soon damp and clinging to her neck. So far, she had succeeded in evading any suggestions to shave her head, but she knew that once she had taken her initial vows, no such dispensation would be allowed. Perhaps today she would have appreciated the coolness of being without the moist strands clinging to her nape, she thought ruefully, and her face was soon as pink as the sprays of bougain-villea that grew in such profusion over the convent walls.

Fans turned languidly in the heat, propelled by the small generator Father Donovan had provided for their use, and which served a useful purpose when the ward was in normal use. But today, the fans made little impression on the humid atmosphere, and the scent of humanity was almost overpowering.

There was little anyone could do to relieve the patients. An infection of this kind could only be con-tained, not cured, and Catherine felt a terrible sense of helplessness when Sister Francisca carried a still little body out of the ward to be prepared for burial. The baby, for it had been little more, had not even reached its second birthday, and its mother lay supine staring at the ceiling, her stomach already swollen with a new pregnancy.

Farther down the ward, another woman was suck-ling her new-born child. How it hoped to survive in these conditions, Catherine could not even begin to guess, but it laboured away hungrily, tugging at its mother's breast with avid lips. Life was so precious, she thought, drawn almost compulsively towards the suckling child, and something stirred inside her as she watched its eager, seeking mouth. What must it be like to have a baby, she pondered, unwillingly aware of a quickening in her own body. What must it be like to bear a child, to carry it around inside you for nine months, and then eject it into a world so full of violence and uncertainty? What kind of responsibility did one feel towards one's own offspring? Or indeed towards the child's father . . .

'Dreaming, Sister? I thought you people considered such things an unforgivable indulgence!'

Catherine started, jerked out of her reverie by the deep mocking tones of the male voice. It was so unexpected, so unlikely, that a man should speak within these walls that for a moment she could only gaze at him. It was Dr Alvares, as she had known the moment she heard his voice, and he stared at her, his lips twisting as he acknowledged her identity.

'Miss Loring,' he said, inclining his head politely. 'Forgive me, I thought you were one of the good sisters of mercy. My apologies.'

'I—am one of the sisters,' Catherine answered him tautly, unwillingly aware of how disturbingly attractive he looked. In a cream shirt, opened halfway down his chest, and exposing a liberal amount of fine dark hair, tight-fitting denim pants, and a white coat with a stethoscope pushed carelessly into the pocket, he exuded an aura of raw masculinity that was as pungent as incense in the moist, clammy air. When he lifted his hand to push back the hair from his forehead, another of his shirt buttons slipped its fastening, and Catherine averted her eyes swiftly from his totally disruptive presence.

'You are?' he said now, and she managed a positive shake of her head. 'Well—you surprise me.'

'Do I?' Unwisely Catherine lifted her chin and faced him, and was immediately ensnared by the dark gold brilliance of his eyes.

'You just proved it,' he advised her drily, and although she dragged her gaze away from his, the blood thundered heavily in her temples.

'What do you want?' she asked, making an effort to recover her composure, and his lips twisted.

'Better and better,' he commented, infuriating her

with his mocking arrogance, and she knew a most unvirtuous desire to slap his face.

'I mean—' she controlled herself with difficulty '—what can I do for you?' she amended stiffly.

'That depends.' He glanced round at the nursing mother. 'You didn't seem to be with us just now.' He paused. 'What were you thinking? I wonder. I assume that look of intensity you were wearing was objective. In my experience, females who take the veil, as it is called, seldom fulfil themselves as women.'

Catherine's cheeks burned. 'I don't know what you mean.'

'Oh, I think you do.'

He drew his stethoscope out of his pocket and walked to the next bed as Catherine struggled for a reply. 'I—I don't think you should say such things to me,' she got out at last, and the lazily amused eyes surveyed her indignation without remorse.

'Things like what?' he inquired, as he bent to take a limp wrist between his finger and thumb.

'There are different kinds of fulfilment,' declared Catherine tensely, realising she was arguing a case she had doubted on many occasions. She leaned on the rail at the end of the narrow bed. 'How—how is she?'

Armand Alvares straightened after taking the girl's pulse, and regarded Catherine tolerantly. 'She'll live,' he replied dismissively. 'But since when did you lose your amateur status? Or doesn't Reverend Mother know you're in here?'

Catherine's hands curled into fists. 'Dr Alvares—'

'Yes.'

'Exactly—exactly what makes you think you have the right to speak to me like this?'

'Like what?' He shrugged. 'In some religions,

the saving of someone's life makes them your responsibility.'

'But not in Christianity.'

He conceded the point with a careless shake of his head and, following him along the ward, Catherine added, not altogether truthfully: 'And you didn't save my life. I—I was in no danger.'

'No?' He turned to look at her, and she was glad that to most of the patients in the ward their conversation was incomprehensible. 'I was under the impression that you were.'

'They would not have killed me,' Catherine insisted, pushing her trembling hands inside the folds of her robe, and Armand Alvares once again made no demur.

'Killed you, no,' he agreed smoothly. 'There are other ways to die.'

Catherine's face flamed. 'You don't know that.'

'Oh, I do, believe me.'

He bent to speak reassuringly to a young Indian girl, who had been brought in the night before. She was very sick, and she was also in the latter stages of a pregnancy. Dr Alvares spoke to her in the local dialect that Catherine had learned only a few words of before her father died, and the girl responded with gratitude. She had been in pain throughout the night, but her faith in the doctor was touching. Catherine turned away from the sight of his lean brown hands pushing back the matted hair from the girl's forehead and smoothing her fevered temples with a cool cloth.

'I suppose you're one of them!' Catherine accused, as he moved away from the bed, and Armand Alvares stopped to massage the muscles at the back of his neck with a weary hand.

'Are you still here?' he inquired, regarding her

impatiently. 'But yes, I am a man, as you may have noticed. If the veil you have drawn over yourself has not blinded you to all the facts of life.'

Catherine caught her breath. 'I—I shall tell Sister Angelica what you've said.'

'Be my guest.' His mouth hardened suddenly, and her skin prickled beneath the enveloping robe. 'But first, I suggest you come and help me dress a rather ugly knife wound. It will enable you to do some real nursing for a change. And perhaps convince you there is more to life than chanting psalms and prostrating yourself before an unforgiving God!'

Catherine gazed at him. 'A knife wound?'

'A casualty in General Montoya's fight against the rebels,' he stated flatly. 'Not all diseases are inflicted by God, *novica*. Some flourish quite successfully all by themselves.'

Catherine glanced round the ward. Apart from themselves, and the patients, the room was empty. Elderly Sister Cecilia, who had been in attendance when Catherine arrived, had taken the opportunity to go and take some sustenance before Reverend Mother made her daily tour of inspection, and that was why Catherine's conversation with the doctor had gone unremarked.

'You mean—a man, don't you?' she stammered, and Dr Alvares's expression grew sardonic.

'A man, yes,' he conceded, watching her with those intent golden eyes. 'Don't tell me after what you have said that you are afraid.'

Catherine was not afraid. Although she had not forgotten there were men like the animals who had killed her father in cold blood, she no longer believed that all men were the same. But Sister Angelica's instructions had been quite unequivocal.

'I—I'm not allowed to enter the men's ward, Dr Alvares,' she answered carefully. 'I'm sorry. You'll have to ask someone else to help you.'

'Who?' he inquired incisively. 'Who else is there? Look around you, *novica*. Sister Felicia, Sister Maria, Sister Francisca? They are confined to their quarters, too sick to help anyone. Sister Angelica? She is attending to them at this moment. Sister Lucia, Sister Margarita, Sister Cecilia—'

'Oh, all right.' Catherine took a deep breath and halted his catalogue of the nuns who were either too sick or too old to be of any assistance. 'All right, I'll help you. But if Reverend Mother finds out—'

'Leave Reverend Mother to me,' he retorted, and strode towards the double doors that opened into the corridor that connected one ward with the other. 'Come. I do not have all day.'

Catherine followed him more slowly, glancing back anxiously at the ward behind her. But no one was watching her orderly departure, and wiping her damp palms down the seams of her habit, she walked determinedly through the arched doorway.

The air in the corridor was so sweet after the cloying atmosphere of the ward that Catherine wanted to stand and inhale its fragrance. With all the shutters standing wide to admit the scent of the vines growing round the windows, she paused a moment to rest her hands on the cool stone-work. How she longed to be out in the garden, working with Sister Teresa in the vegetable plot. It was back-breaking toil, it was true, but satisfying for all that, and she turned with some reluctance at Dr Alvares's summons.

She tried not to think of what Sister Angelica might say if she discovered where Catherine had been. It was one thing to justify the need for her existence to this

man, and quite another to justify her actions to her
superior. None of the younger nuns were ever
allowed in the men's ward. Attending to male
patients was left to Sister Maria and Sister Helena.
But Sister Maria was sick, and Sister Helena—

'Are you coming?'

Armand Alvares's harsh voice from the open doorway quickened her feet, and she followed him
obediently into the room beyond. The men's ward was
less congested than the women's ward, she saw with
some relief, but the smell was fetid, and it didn't take
Catherine long to understand why. There were abdo-
minal cases here, but that was not all. At least three of
the men wore bandages, and the patient Dr Alvares
was here to attend was one of them.

The appearance of a young woman in the ward
aroused a buzz of speculation, and it took some determination on Catherine's part to walk between the row
of beds. For the past eight months, she had been
confined to the company of her own sex, and to be
confronted by so many inquisitive male faces was a
little intimidating.

Dr Alvares awaited her beside the injured man's bed
with some impatience. 'I've told them your presence
here is not to be remarked upon,' he said. 'As you can
see, you're the only female around.'

Catherine held up her head. 'I don't keep secrets, Dr
Alvares,' she declared, and his hard features grew
mocking.

'I'm sorry. I understood you to say—'

'I shan't go out of my way to tell Sister Angelica or
Reverend Mother. If—if they ask me—'

'—you'll confess, I know.' He expelled his breath
resignedly. 'Can we get on? I do have other patients to
attend to.'

Catherine pressed her hands together. 'Shall I get the trolley?'

He nodded, sitting down on the side of the bed. 'That might be a good idea.'

By the time she came back, he had unwound the bandage swathing the man's chest and shoulder to expose a wound perhaps three inches in length. It began below his collar-bone and ran in a ragged curve to a point just above his rib cage. Someone, Dr Alvares perhaps, had stitched the wound, but it was obviously not healing and the flesh around the gash was puffy and inflamed.

'Well?' Dr Alvares looked up at her from the bed. 'Not pretty, is it?'

Catherine looked at the man in the bed without answering him. He looked about twenty years of age, no more, and she guessed from his expression that he was apprehensive of what the doctor was going to do. There was pain in his face and the grey pallor of exhaustion, and she wished she could communicate her sympathy to him.

'Who is he?' she asked, moving out of the way as Armand Alvares got to his feet to examine the contents of the trolley. 'Is he in the army? Is that why Major Enriques was here?'

At the mention of the name, Enriques, the man in the bed uttered a strange sound. Catching his breath, he cringed back against the iron bed-head, as if in fear. Then, his uninjured arm gripping the doctor's with unexpected strength, his dark eyes sought reassurance in Dr Alvares's unsmiling face.

'*Calma, calma*, Julio!' Dr Alvares removed the boy's clutching fingers with restrained gentleness, turning a furious face in Catherine's direction. 'Keep your mouth shut, why don't you?' he snarled, caring little

for her sensibilities, and she gasped indignantly as he
thrust her aside. 'You're here to do a job, now do it.
Don't involve yourself in matters you know absolutely
nothing about.'

Catherine quivered. 'How—how dare you—'

'I dare because I'm the only doctor in these parts,
and your opinion of me is not important. Now—stop
looking at me as if I'd physically assaulted you, and
help me!'

Catherine moistened her lips. 'How?'

'The wound has turned septic. I'm going to have to
open it up. If I don't, he'll die.'

He said the words without emotion and Catherine
shook her head. 'You're so—so callous, aren't you?'
Her voice wobbled a little as she spoke. 'You stitch him
up with infected instruments, and then calmly
announce he'll die if you don't repair the damage
you've created!'

Armand Alvares's golden eyes glittered. 'You think
I did this?'

'Didn't you?'

'No!' He cast an impatient look at the young man,
and then added in a low savage voice: 'This was done
by some amateur paramedic. It was probably done in
the open, without the benefit of either antiseptic or
anaesthetic. The boy must have been in agony for days
before they were forced to bring him here. They trust
no one, and my guess is he's been hiding out in the
mountains, too afraid to travel in daylight. Your mindless chatter concerning the army major is exactly what
he needs to scare him to death!'

Catherine was shocked and showed it. 'You mean—
he's a rebel? A *guerrilla*!'

'He's a patient,' said Dr Alvares harshly. 'Love thy
neighbour—remember?'

Catherine breathed shallowly. Never in her wildest dreams had she imagined he might expect her to help one of her father's killers, but it wasn't just that. Armand Alvares had narrowed the space between them to deliver his biting message, and suddenly he was too close in the airless confines of the small ward. She could smell him. She could smell his body. It was not an unpleasant smell, compounded as it was of some tangy lotion he was wearing and the heated scent of skin, but it was disturbing to someone who ought not to notice such things.

'I need a scalpel,' he said, as she put the width of the dressings trolley between them and thrust her sticky palms behind her back. 'Can you get me one? And sterilise it?'

'I—I—no—'

'Of course you can.' The golden eyes were incisive. 'For God's sake, if I've bruised your tender susceptibilities, I'm sorry, but you shouldn't make reckless statements without assessing all the facts.' He sighed, pulling a handful of keys out of his pocket. 'You'll find what you need in that room at the end of the ward. The instruments are kept in a locked cabinet. This is the key you need. There's a small steriliser, run off Father Donovan's generator. I'll come and check on you as soon as I've explained to Julio what I intend to do.'

He came into the sluice room as Catherine was removing the instruments from the steriliser, taking off his white coat and rolling back the sleeves of his shirt. He washed his hands at the small sink, using an antiseptic soap to cleanse his skin, and then had Catherine turn off the tap for him as he dried himself on a square of gauze. He had hairs on his arms, too, Catherine noticed unwillingly, his shoulders broad beneath the thin cotton of his shirt. The shirt was sticking to him down the hollow of his back, exposing the darkness of the skin beneath. Like the skin of his arms, and the bronze column of his throat rising from the neck of his shirt, it was deeply tanned, and she guessed he spent long hours outdoors. She supposed he swam when he was hot. She doubted he had any inhibitions about taking off his clothes and plunging into cool clear water. He seemed totally self-confident, totally in command of his own destiny, and he didn't give a damn about her feelings.

'Ready?'

She came out of her reverie with a start to find him regarding her with quizzical eyes, and infuriating colour flooded her cheeks once more. She was tempted to say no again, to deny him the use of her inexperienced services, but the memory of the boy in the bed was stronger. Lots of people got caught up in wars that were not of their making; lots of innocent people died for causes they hardly understood. How could she refuse to help someone who was so vulnerable? Whatever her innermost feelings, Julio did not deserve to die.

'Ready,' she agreed stiffly, picking up the tray, and with a wry movement of his shoulders, he preceded her into the ward.

'I'm afraid we can't use anaesthetic to make this easier,' he remarked, as they approached the bed. 'We don't have sufficient supplies of nitrous oxide or oxygen to warrant their use in a case like this, and the flesh around the wound is too infected to use a local agent.' He paused. 'I shall need you to hold him as I make my incision. I suggest you find him a piece of cloth to bite on. This is going to be painful.'

Catherine felt a little sick, but she quickly found a

wedge of towelling and, using hand signals, she indicated to the boy what she wanted him to do. He was terrified, that was evident, and no obvious attempts to distract his attention could turn his eyes from the blade in Armand Alvares's hand. It was not a thick blade, just a narrow sliver of steel, but with a dangerously sharp edge that caught the sun's rays as the doctor's hand descended.

It was all over quite quickly, and to Catherine's relief the young man lost consciousness almost immediately. He saw the initial incision, but he was too weak to fight her and his teeth bit agonisingly into the wedge of towelling in his mouth. But then, the pain, and the amount of blood he had lost, proved too much for his exhausted constitution, and he sank into a dead faint.

The smell from the opened wound was repulsive and Catherine swayed a little as she watched Dr Alvares drain the cavity. It was her first experience of any kind of surgery, and although she kept telling herself it was only a cut, she couldn't help the comparison between what she was seeing now and what had happened to her father. There had been knives then, and blood, and she had to steel herself to remain stationary when Dr Alvares requested her to hand him a sterilised needle.

But, eventually, it was the scalpel that did it, lying obsolete now on its metal tray. There was blood on the blade and in the dish that held it, and although Catherine had witnessed how it had got there, a wave of faintness swept over her. She had never lost consciousness before. She had never fainted, not even when she found her father's body lying in a pool of his own blood. But the scalpel—*the knife*—with its cruel associations, brought it all back to her in vivid detail, and because it was no longer necessary for her to remain at her post, she stumbled away from the trolley and down the narrow aisle between the rows of beds.

She didn't make it to the door. She knew she wasn't going to, even without Sister Angelica's horrified appearance in the open doorway to deter her. The floor was rising up in front of her, rising up and falling away like a heaving ocean, and the ability to keep on putting one foot in front of the other became too much for her. With a helpless cry, she gave up the struggle, and pitched her length at Sister Angelica's feet.

CHAPTER TWO

THE phone rang as Armand was stepping out of the shower. Without bothering to pick up a towel, he went to answer it, his feet leaving damp marks on the tiled bedroom floor. The air was cool against his moist skin, but he welcomed the chill. It had been a hot and tiring day, and it was good to feel refreshed again.

'Alvares,' he said flatly, in no mood for polite conversation after the words he had exchanged with Mother Benedicta at the convent, and felt anger tightening his stomach at the female tones that, though distant, were nonetheless unmistakable.

'Armand! So, there you are at last. I have been trying to ring you all day. Could you not at least leave a number where I might reach you? It could have been something urgent.'

'And is it?' Armand's inflection did not alter, and the female voice at the other end of the line grew petulant.

'You are so unfeeling,' she complained. 'Do you care so little for your wife and your son that you can simply ignore their existence?'

Armand's mouth tightened. 'I have no wife, Estella, and there are no convenient phone numbers to leave here,' he retorted, without expression. 'We have an epidemic on our hands, as I wrote you a week ago.' He paused. 'What did you want?'

'Do you not have the time to ask me how I am—how Ricardo is faring?' Estella's resentment was evident. 'Do you know how long it is since you have seen

29

him? Don't you care that he may forget he has a
father?'

The barb was deliberate, and no less painful for
being unjustified. Yet it was almost three months since
he had last visited Terasina and, to a boy of Ricardo's
age, twelve weeks could seem a lifetime.

'Is that why you rang?' Armand inquired now, his
tone clipped. 'Is the boy unhappy? Is he asking for
me?'

Estella snorted. 'Do you care?'

'Of course I care.' Armand's fingers were gripping
the receiver so tightly his knuckles were white. 'There
is nothing wrong, is there? Ricardo is not ill?'

'Well—' Estella subjected him to an infuriating
hesitation before continuing '—he has had a cold
recently, and a little fever.' Again, the pause. 'But
nothing serious.'

'Thank God for that.' Armand's gratitude was
barely audible. 'So—why did you ring, Estella? Not to
enquire after my health, I am sure.'

'You do yourself an injustice,' Estella countered
quickly, her voice softening suddenly to a husky
drawl. 'I have feelings too, Armand. Surely you have
not forgotten that.'

Armand sucked in his breath with suppressed impatience. 'Estella!' He exhaled harshly. 'I am getting
cold. I was in the shower when you rang, and I have
yet to dry myself—'

'You are naked?' The words came softly to his ear.
'How provocative, dàrling. I wish I was there with
you.'

'*Estella!*'

The evidence that his patience was running out was
audible in the grim weariness of his tone, and Estella
sighed regretfully. 'All right, all right,' she conceded

irritably, 'it was not about Ricardo I rang. Estéban wants to see you. He wants to talk to you about your work in Batistamajor. He wants to know if you have any information—'

'No—'

'What do you mean, no?'

'I should have thought it was quite simple to understand,' Armand retorted harshly. 'I have nothing to say to Estéban Montoya. Not now. Not ever. You, at least, should know that.'

Estella uttered a sound of protest. 'I can't tell him that, Armand. Estéban has the ear of the *presidente*. If you refuse to speak to him—'

'—he will get over it,' Armand finished for her flatly. 'I suspect Montoya knows my feelings for the regime as well as you do.' He paused. 'But in the circumstances, he is unlikely to stir up this particular hornet's nest, wouldn't you say?'

'You *bastard*!'

Armand's lips twitched. 'It was a pleasure talking to you, too, Estella. *Adeus.*' And before she could respond, he lowered the receiver.

He had towelled the remaining drops of moisture from his hard body and was pulling on thin cotton trousers when there was a knock at his bedroom door. At his response, a black head appeared round the door and Santo, his Indian servant, shuffled deferentially into the room.

'Supper is ready, *senhor*,' he said, speaking in the native patois of the area. 'And there was a message,' he added, pulling a scrap of paper out of his pocket. 'It came a few minutes ago.'

'A message?' Armand jerked a clean shirt over his shoulders and, leaving it loose, he took the grubby piece of notepaper from Santo's hand. Smoothing it between his fingers, he quickly read the words it contained, and then looked up again to meet the old man's eyes. 'Do you know what this says?'

Santo shifted a little uncomfortably. 'I don't read, *senhor*.'

'That's not what I asked.' Armand looked at the man intently. 'I asked if you knew what this said.'

Santo bent his head. 'I know who the message is from, *senhor*.'

'And do you also know that if I show this message to Major Enriques, I will have his undying gratitude?'

Santo's head came up. 'You wouldn't, *senhor*.'

'Wouldn't I?' Armand regarded him dourly. 'How can you be so sure?'

'You have—helped—the resistance forces before, *senhor*,' exclaimed Santo, and then glanced apprehensively over his shoulder, as if afraid his words might be overheard. He lowered his voice. 'You are a good person, *senhor*. You would not let a man die.'

'Not even José Rodolfo, is that what you think?' inquired Armand sharply. 'But I have never been asked to attend the leader of the guerrilla forces before.'

Santo blinked. 'That is not what it says.'

'No?'

'No, *senhor*.' Santo gazed at him defensively.

'I thought you said you didn't know what the note says,' Armand countered smoothly, and the Indian's shoulders drooped at his master's unassailable logic.

'It—it says someone has need of your professional services, *senhor*,' he insisted at last. 'The man who brought the note is waiting to guide you to your patient. Your supper is ready. After you have eaten, if—'

'But what of this tiny circle, like a flower, at the corner of the page?' Armand inquired softly. 'With petals striped, like the skin of a tiger. The sign of *O Tigre*, no?'

Santo started, his angular features taking on an expression of horror. 'How did you—' he began, and then, biting off his words, he was silent.

'Never mind how I know,' Armand replied shortly. His mouth compressed as he stuffed the note into his pocket and started towards the door. 'Fetch me a cold beer while I collect the things I may need. Is it far, do you think? Will I need a sleeping pack?'

Santo regarded him anxiously. Then: 'No,' he muttered in a low voice. 'No, I do not think it is so far.'

Armand studied the old man's troubled face for a few moments, and then nodded. 'Good,' he remarked, passing him and emerging into the narrow hallway of the building. 'Give me five minutes.'

Santo followed him, wringing his hands. 'And your supper, *senhor*? You have not eaten!'

'Later,' said Armand, his mind on the medical requirements he might need. 'I'll eat later, Santo. If José Rodolfo has contacted me, it must be an emergency, wouldn't you say?'

In the small surgery that adjoined the living room of the house, Armand loaded gauze and bandages into his bag. He had no idea what kind of wound or injury he might have to deal with, and realising it could be a matter of life or death, he unlocked the cabinet beside his desk, and took out the precious bottle of morphine he kept for such emergencies. Unwilling to take the bottle with him in case of mishap, he filled a hypodermic and installed it safely in a padded case before putting it at the bottom of the bag. It would only be used if it was absolutely necessary. He had patients at the convent hospital who were constantly in pain, and he was unable to give them any relief.

Santo appeared as he was buttoning his shirt and thrusting it into the waistband of his pants. 'Your beer, *senhor,*' he said, holding out a can still dripping with ice from the small refrigerator. 'And your jacket.' He assisted Armand to put on the soft black leather jerkin. 'You are ready?'

'As I'll ever be,' remarked Armand drily, swallowing half the contents of the can at a gulp. 'Hmm, that's good,' he commented, wiping his chin with the back of his hand. 'Did you give our visitor a beer also?'

Santo hesitated. 'He didn't want one, *senhor.*'

'No?' Armand's dark brows arched. 'No matter.' He emptied the tin in his hand. *'Obrigado. Adeus.'*

'Adeus, senhor.'

Santo accompanied him along the passage to the rear entrance of the building, but when the man who was waiting emerged from the clump of trees planted by the outer door, the old Indian shrank back out of sight.

It was very dark outside. Armand, his eyes not yet adjusted to the sudden change from brightness to shadows, came down the three wooden steps on to the dirt path with some caution. A low wind moaning through the branches of the string-bark eucalyptus blew its hanging fronds into his face, and he brushed them aside impatiently as the other man moved forward.

In the faint illumination cast from the uncurtained windows of the single-storied dwelling, Armand could see that his guide was dressed in the khaki fatigues and pulled-down beret of a paratrooper. His features were daubed with mud, however, making them virtually indistinguishable, and as he moved away from the protection of the trees, the gun he carried loosely at his side was clearly evident.

'Doutor?'

The hissed word was scarcely a question, but Armand nodded. 'Alvares,' he agreed tautly, his fingers tightening around the straps of his medical bag, and the man gestured that Armand should follow him.

Together, they made their way across the scrubby stretch of land behind the house that backed on to the village square. They did not enter the village. Instead, skirting the walls of Auguste's bakery, they struck out across a field of rough corn stalks that sloped down to the river. Keeping close to the fencing that divided the field for protection, they climbed the uneven hillside, until the lights of Batistamajor were far below them, pinpricks in the darkness. To the west, the high peaks of the sierras thrust their rugged fingers at a sky glittering with diamonds, and the wind that had moaned in the valley, swept more confidently around them.

By the time they reached the bleak isolation of the mountain pass, Armand's legs were aching, and he was more than a little relieved to see the dust-smeared Land-Rover half hidden in the rocks at the side of the road. It was wonderful to climb on to the worn leather seat and allow his tortured muscles to relax, and the man with him watched with reluctant amusement.

'It would have been too dangerous to drive into Batistamajor,' he said, speaking for the first time since his muttered identification outside Armand's house.

'I realise that.' Armand expelled his breath heavily. 'Just give me a few minutes to pull round. I'm not used to climbing mountains in the middle of the night.'

'It is not the middle of the night.' The man showed

Armand the watch on his wrist. 'It's barely ten o'clock. Do you usually retire so early, Dr Alvares?'

Armand grimaced. 'Okay. So it's not the middle of the night. Let's go, shall we? Is it much farther?'

Fifteen minutes later, Armand was beginning to wonder whether continuing the journey on foot would not have been more sensible after all. Being tossed about in the front of the Land-Rover, as it bucked and bounced its way over the rough and rocky terrain, was jarring every bone in his body, and it wasn't easy holding on to his bag and trying to keep his seat all at the same time. He had great admiration for the tenacity of his driver, and for the sturdy little vehicle that stood up to such a battering without faltering, but he couldn't help thinking that if José was badly injured, how the hell was he going to get him out of here?

A change of gear indicated that they were at last descending into a narrow canyon. In the light from the dipped headlamps, Armand could see walls of iron-grey rock closing about them, and hear the distinctive sound of water falling against stone. He also had the distinct impression that they were being watched, that their progress was being monitored by more than one pair of eyes, and the feeling was not a comfortable one. No matter how friendly those eyes might be, they were doubtless looking down the sight of a gun, and Armand had no wish to be the victim of any trigger-happy recruit.

Below them now, he could vaguely see the lights of an encampment. Cooking fires flared red against the stark walls of the gorge, and the irresistible smell of roasting meat drifted up to them. He could see men, attending to their duties or gathered in groups together, sharing their evening meal, the air of alertness and observation giving way to one of relaxation and domestic harmony. He could smell paraffin and cordite, and even the acrid stink of horse manure, and as they reached the floor of the canyon and drove between the rows of tents, he heard the unmistakable crowing of a cock.

Their passage attracted a lot of attention, and Armand sensed the feelings of uncertainty evident in each carefully-voiced greeting. They knew who he was, these men with hollow eyes and gaunt faces. They knew why he was here. And now that he was here, they had to face the fact that José Rodolfo was just as vulnerable as they were. They were young men for the most part, yet already many of them were hardened fighters, the survivors of a dozen or more bloody skirmishes in the past year.

Since Miguel Ferreira's accession to the presidency, more and more of the nation's young men had joined the guerrilla forces, and the country was being torn apart by civil war and poverty. Too much money was being spent on the army. Too many warehouses were filled with arms and ammunition to service a military regime that was both cruel and corrupt. The army officers living in Terasina enjoyed an existence totally alien to the rest of the population. Expensive houses, expensive cars, expensive parties—the list was endless; and so long as Ferreira continued to pay his army well, he could rely on their protection.

There had been some initial opposition from the more compassionate members of the government, and Armand himself knew of one university professor who had spoken out against the regime during a lecture tour in the United States. He, like the others, had eventually disappeared without trace, his family left to survive as best they could without either home or income. Ferreira's power was complete, and only the resistance forces fighting for survival held out any hope for the ordinary people of Surajo.

The Land-Rover came to a halt beside a tent larger than the others, lit from within by the glow of a paraffin lamp. Realising he had reached his destination, Armand climbed down somewhat stiffly from his seat, and nodding to the guard who stood on duty at the entrance, he pushed aside the flap and, bending his head, stepped inside.

The tent seemed full of people. A crate in one corner served duty as a desk and a handful of men were gathered about it, studying the map spread out on its surface. They were being directed by a man lying on a pallet bed close by, who in turn was being attended by a boy of no more than fifteen years. The boy's features were worn and anxious as he tried to wipe the sweat from the man's face with a damp cloth, and he flinched away as his superior swore at him.

'Judas, Luis, take that rag away from me!' the man on the pallet exclaimed peevishly, and then his expression changed as his eyes met those of the man who had just come in. 'Armand,' he muttered weakly. 'Thank God you've come.'

It was after two o'clock when Armand at last let himself into his house and, turning, locked the door behind him. Leaning back against the wooden panels for a moment, he allowed his breath to escape on a low sigh, and then, straightening, he walked along the dark passage to his living room, stepping inside and turning up the lamp Santo had left burning. The old man had also left a tray of supper for him. A flick of the spotless cloth that covered the tray revealed cold meat and salad, and some of the crisp pitta bread he liked to spread with goats'-milk butter. There was a carafe of red wine, too—the domestic variety which was all that was available in the area—and it was to this that Armand turned, filling a narrow glass and raising it gratefully to his lips. He wasn't hungry. José had insisted he share what food they had, and the sirloin steak had been all the sweeter in the knowledge that it had originally been part of a consignment on its way to General Montoya's headquarters.

Refilling his glass, Armand carried it to a chair and allowed his weary body to subside on to the cushioned squabs. God, he thought, he was tired. It had been a long day, and by rights he should be climbing into bed right now. But in spite of his physical exhaustion, his mind was still too active to sleep, and he kicked off his boots impatiently, and propped his feet on the low table close by.

Concern for the man he had visited that evening filled his mind to the exclusion of all else. José Rodolfo was sick, very sick; and if he didn't do something quickly, the man would die—and with him the cause for which he was still fighting. Other leaders might be found, of course, he reflected bitterly. Other martyrs to the cause of Surajo's liberation. But it was unlikely they would inspire the same loyalty and affection as José Rodolfo, and the disparate factions already evident in the movement would go their own way and be defeated. Divide and conquer, thought Armand broodingly. There was never a truer saying, and without Rodolfo's charisma to bind them together, the people of Surajo might easily end up fighting themselves. They needed a man whose courage was legendary, whose aims were their aims, a man of the people, yet more than a man—a Messiah, almost, conqueror, deliverer, and friend. José Rodolfo was that man. He had founded the resistance movement, he alone had given the people hope and courage; but in so doing he had created an image of himself that was close to immortality, and if he died now their hopes would die with him.

Armand finished his wine and pushed the empty glass on to the table beside him. He was haunted by the look in the boy's eyes, as he had stood beside Armand and watched the doctor expose the ugly bullet wound in José's chest. Luis; that was the boy's name. Only sixteen years of age, so José had told him. They got younger all the time, reflected Armand, his lips twisting. But Luis was different from the rest. Luis was José's son. A gangling, fumbling wraith of a boy, only eight years older than Ricardo.

Armand hadn't even known José had a son. It was years since they had talked together. But that frail youth, whose trembling lips and shaking fingers had reminded Armand more of a schoolgirl than a boy striving desperately to be a man, had aroused his sympathy. Those huge doe eyes turned on Armand's face, begging for the reassurance Armand could not give, had been reminiscent of another pair of eyes he had looked into that day: green eyes this time, not brown ones, flecked with little yellow lights, and shaded by long, curling lashes, sun-bleached at the tips. Wide eyes, anxious eyes, eyes filled with fear and consternation: Catherine Loring's eyes, or should he call her *Sister* Catherine, he mused harshly. And why should her eyes have affected him so deeply? She was just as much a fool as her father had been. What else could he think when she was willing to remain at the convent, allowing her own will to be governed by the will of those old women?

Oh, he had a certain amount of admiration for

the nuns. Those who had a vocation, that is. But Catherine Loring had no vocation. He could swear it. Her father had brought her out to Surajo to live with him, and had he still been alive, she would doubtless have been caring for his needs at this moment, not immersing herself in the incense-laden atmosphere of a religious order. He blamed Loring for fetching her out here. Batistamajor was no place for a young girl. Terasina was bad enough, but at least there was peace there at the moment, albeit an uneasy one. Here, miles from friends or compatriots—Loring had to have been either a fool or a saint, and Armand had yet to find any individual to fit the latter category.

But it galled him to think that Catherine was so willing to submit. To a certain extent he did feel responsible for her, and discovering she was still at the convent had been a shock. He hadn't given a lot of thought as to where she might have gone, of course. He had assumed, foolishly now he realised, that she would have returned to England, to her relatives there. It was months since British residents in the country had been advised to leave, and although overland communications between Batistamajor and the capital were not good, the rail link between Ribatejo and Terasina was still open.

Shaking his head, Armand got abruptly to his feet, putting all thoughts of Catherine Loring aside. He had more important problems at the moment, not least how he was going to perform a delicate operation like the removal of the bullet from José's chest, without any of the refinements of an operating theatre. It had to be done, and soon. José was losing far too much blood. But the dangers present in the removal of the bullet made the execution of the operation almost as perilous as leaving it where it was.

José had hoped he would do what was necessary tonight, Armand knew that. But without sterilising drugs and anaesthetic, he had not been willing to take the risk. José would die if the bullet was not removed, this was true, but Armand was determined that when he did make the attempt, José's chances were going to be as great as he could humanly make them.

Which meant he needed to take one of the nuns into his confidence. He needed assistance for an operation of this kind. Someone had to help him with the anaesthetic, someone had to keep a check on José's heartbeat and blood pressure, and someone had to be able to exchange the instruments in his hand, when he needed to keep his eyes on what he was doing. None of the men at the camp was suitable. Their hands were too thick and clumsy, too ingrained with oil and cordite ever to conform to even a minimum standard of hygiene. Besides, like Luis, they were too closely involved with this man who was their leader. They had no detachment, a quality which might be vital if José began to fail beneath the doctor's hands.

Armand grimaced. His own chances of survival might be severely limited if José did die. But it was not this which caused the deep lines of worry to etch his lean mouth. It was the realisation that finding someone to help him was not going to be easy with half the nuns laid low by the gastric epidemic. There were only a handful he could rely on. In spite of their dislike of the Ferreira regime, most of the nuns, including Reverend Mother, would not work actively against it. And assisting in an operation on the man who was the leader of the radical opposition might be regarded as unethical. Besides which, he wanted someone who could be relied on not to talk about it afterwards. The last thing he needed was for Major Enriques to start being suspicious of his activities. So far, his presence in the district had gone virtually unremarked. If Enriques suspected his being here had anything to do with the rebels, his permit to work in Batistamajor would be withdrawn forthwith.

Frowning, he turned out the lamp and left the living room, crossing the hall to enter the bedroom opposite. Moonlight illuminated the room through the undrawn blinds, and without bothering to put on a light, he stripped off his clothes and flung himself on top of the bed. Maybe he would sleep now, he thought, pulling a light quilt over his lower limbs. There was nothing he could do until the morning anyway. Maybe in daylight Rodolfo's chances would not seem so bleak, his own involvement so futile. If José was intended to survive, he would; fate—and experience—had taught him that. There was no point in worrying over something that might never happen. But his old maxim seemed so much less convincing now that he was faced with such a daunting prospect.

CHAPTER THREE

CATHERINE was feeding one of the babies when Reverend Mother sent for her. Her back was aching after several hours spent weeding the rows of beans and sweet potatoes Sister Teresa had neglected since the infection had affected her, too, and she had been enjoying the few moments of relaxation away from the crippling glare of the sun.

Not that she had not been expecting the summons. Ever since her unfortunate collapse two days ago, she had been waiting for the call to Mother Benedicta's study, and the nerves in her stomach fluttered anxiously as she handed the hungrily-sucking infant into Sister Angelica's arms.

'I should tidy yourself before you attend Reverend Mother, *novica*,' Sister Angelica remarked dourly. 'There is hair escaping from your coif and you have dust on the skirt of your habit.'

'Yes, Sister.'

Catherine nodded obediently, and bent to brush ineffectually at the hem of her skirt. But when she then raised her hands to push the errant strands of red-gold silk beneath her cap, she left smudges of dust on her cheeks and Sister Angelica clicked her tongue irritably.

'Just wash your hands, *menina*,' she ordered, taking the teat of the bottle out of the baby's mouth in her impatience and causing the child to set up a sudden wail. 'Go along, go along. Stop wasting time.'

In the cooler shadows of the cloister, Catherine

44

paused to take a steadying breath. It was foolish to allow a summons to Reverend Mother's study to upset her so badly, but for so long now she had grown accustomed to obeying every command. And whatever the justification, she had known what would happen if she was discovered in the men's ward, and she should not have allowed Dr Alvares to override her objections.

Dr Alvares.

Her tongue appeared to moisten her lower lip with unknowing sensuality. She had thought about the disturbing doctor far too often in the past couple of days. In all her quiet moments—when she was going about her duties, when she was eating her meals, even in the private moments supposedly devoted to her own prayers—she found her thoughts turning constantly to the time they had spent together. It was unforgivable, when she found it so very difficult to memorise her catechism, that she had no difficulty at all in remembering everything he had said to her. Moreover, she had gone through their conversation time and time again in her mind, trying to find meaning behind every nuance he had uttered, discovering within herself an urgent, and totally reprehensible, desire to justify herself to him.

'What? Still dawdling, *novica*?'

The unwelcome tones of Sister Angelica interrupted Catherine's reverie, and her cheeks filled with colour at the realisation of what her tutor would think if she could read her mind right now.

'Just catching my breath, Sister,' she murmured, avoiding the nun's eyes and, pressing her palms against her thighs, she hurried on her way.

One of the other novices was just leaving Reverend Mother's study as Catherine approached the heavy oak door that gave access to the dimly-lit ante-room, and her spirits lifted. Maybe she was wrong. Maybe this summons had nothing to do with her ill-advised encounter with Dr Alvares. Perhaps all Reverend Mother wanted to do was assure herself that her youngest recruit was not suffering any ill-effects from her feeble loss of consciousness.

Her knuckles stung against the hard wood as she tapped on Reverend Mother's door. The door was so thick she had often wondered how Mother Benedicta heard anything through the wood. But evidently the senior nun's ears were sharp, for after only a moment's hesitation, Catherine heard the peremptory: '*Entre!*'

Sunlight slatting between the ribs of the blind cast bars of gold across the square wooden desk that dominated the room. An aroma of jasmin issued from a vase of the sweet-scented blossoms that stood on a small pedestal to one side of the windows. The air was stirred by a single fan that circled the ceiling, and this was the only sound that came from the room. Catherine was very conscious of these things as she moved to stand in front of the desk, in front of the elderly woman, whose sense of order and discipline ruled the lives of all the inmates of the convent. Outside there might be sickness and aggression, but within the walls of Reverend Mother's study there was an air of unalienable calm. Yet, for all that, there was dissatisfaction here, a distinct feeling of disapproval and disappointment, that pulled down Reverend Mother's mouth as she bid the girl facing her to sit down.

Catherine sank weakly on to the high-backed chair facing the desk, folding her hands in her lap in a deliberate effort to appear composed. It was the only way to disguise their trembling, and she was glad when her superior took a few moments to adjust the shutters behind her before addressing herself to her task.

'*Pois bem, novica,*' she said at last, resting her hands on the hand-tooled leather surface of the desk. And then, reverting to English for Catherine's benefit, she continued: 'I suppose you know why I have sent for you, child. I would have summoned you sooner, but Sister Angelica suggested you might benefit from the delay. It may have given you time to—*como se diz?* how do you say?—reflect upon your behaviour, *não*? To realise that in your weakness was the proof of your inadequacy.'

Catherine bent her head. 'Yes, Reverend Mother.'

'*Muito bem!* Very good! You agree you were wrong.'

'I disobeyed the rules, Reverend Mother,' Catherine admitted cautiously.

'And suffered for your pains,' her superior put in sharply. 'I trust you are quite recovered from the experience.'

'Oh, yes, Reverend Mother.'

The senior nun nodded. 'That is good.' She paused. 'And you will be happy to know that I do not entirely blame you for what happened. I am not at all impressed with Dr Alvares's attitude in the matter, and it is he to whom I attribute most responsibility.'

Catherine lifted her head. 'Yes, Reverend Mother.'

Her superior frowned. 'The man is a barbarian, *novica*. He makes no bones about the fact that he has little time for our devotions, and only the knowledge that he seems to have the confidence of the patients persuades me to continue accepting his assistance.'

It was on the tip of Catherine's tongue to point out that without Dr Alvares's help during the past emergency, many of their patients would have died, nuns included, but discretion fought and won the battle for veracity. In her position, Catherine was not expected to comment, and Reverend Mother continued undeterred.

'I realise you must feel a certain amount of misguided loyalty towards him,' she declared tolerantly. 'After all, the man did rescue you from the schoolhouse, the night your father was killed. But anyone would have done the same in the circumstances, and it is by no means certain that Dr Alvares does not have positive sympathies with the rebels.'

Catherine said nothing. Once again, she could have remarked on the presence of the boy, Julio, in the men's ward, but this time it was caution and not discretion that kept her silent. In spite of what the rebels had done to her father, she could not in all conscience betray his identity, and she wondered with some resignation whether lying by omission was regarded as a venal sin. If it was, then she was guilty. There was no doubt about that. But, she could not report Julio to Major Enriques, not after seeing the terror the army officer's name had evoked.

'Politics have no place in the hospital ward,' Reverend Mother was saying now, and Catherine realised in dismay that she had not been paying attention for the past few minutes. 'One regime is much like another. This constant striving for equality is not what life is all about, is it, child?'

'I—no, Reverend Mother.' Catherine shuffled a little uneasily in her seat, and her shifting gaze was caught and held by her superior.

'I trust Dr Alvares did not attempt to persuade you to share his views, *novica*,' she inserted softly. 'You must remember that it was because of this—unrest in the country that your father lost his life. I realise that to speak of such things may still be painful for you, *minha filha*, but although we may forgive, we must never forget, *não*, my daughter?'

'No, Reverend Mother.'

'Your father was a good man,' Mother Benedicta continued, with a sigh. 'An honourable man. I admired him greatly. As I am sure you did, also.'

Catherine bowed her head. 'Yes, Reverend Mother.'

'Is that all you can say, *novica*? Yes, Reverend Mother; no, Reverend Mother?' The woman's eyes glittered with sudden impatience. 'What did Dr Alvares say to you? What caused you to get so upset?'

'Upset, Reverend Mother?' Catherine's eyes grew perplexed.

'You fainted, did you not?' Her superior's fingers were clasped tightly together. 'Something must have disturbed you? Was Dr Alvares impatient with you? Was he rude? Why were you running away?'

Catherine drew a deep breath as understanding dawned. 'Oh—' She shook her head with some relief. 'I was not running away, Reverend Mother. At least, not from anything Dr Alvares said.' She paused. 'It—it was the knife, you see. The scalpel Dr Alvares used to ventilate the—the wound. It reminded me of—of the night my father died.'

'Ah!' Her superior expelled her breath on a long sound. 'Of course. I should have thought of that, particularly after our present conversation. Forgive me, child; sometimes I can be obtuse. Naturally that young man's injuries would remind you of your father. *Rapariga pobre*, poor girl, it must have been a gruelling experience, and one, I am sure, you would rather forget.'

'Yes.' Catherine's response was heartfelt, but Reverend Mother wasn't quite finished with her yet.

'*Bem*. Good. And now, only one thing more.'

'Yes, Reverend Mother?'

'*Sim*, yes. I want you to promise me that you will not allow such a thing to happen again. I want you to assure me that if Dr Alvares asks again for your assistance, you will refer him to me. Most certainly, I can handle our so-arrogant doctor more efficiently than you, and I venture to say he will not ask again in those circumstances.'

'Yes, Reverend Mother.' Catherine bit down hard on her lower lip before rising abruptly to her feet. 'May I go now?'

Mother Benedicta rose to face her, her stern features relaxing into a faint smile. 'Of course,' she replied, holding out her hand for Catherine to make the customary obeisance. '*Vai com Deus, novica*. God be with you. *Adeus*.'

Outside again, standing in the shade of the cloister, Catherine's shoulders sagged. It was over. The interview she had been dreading was past, and she had emerged virtually unscathed; so why was she feeling so depressed suddenly? For goodness' sake, she hadn't wanted Reverend Mother to chastise her, had she? Another stint of Hail Marys in the chapel was the last thing she needed, and yet she had the distinct feeling that that was what she really deserved. And why? Not because of her abortive efforts in the men's ward. She had done nothing there to be ashamed of, except make a fool of herself. No one would convince her that helping someone who was sick was wrong, whatever her orders had been. No. It was the knowledge of the disturbing thoughts she kept having about Dr Alvares that made a mockery of this life which had been chosen for her, the realisation that if Reverend Mother had learned of those secret fantasies, she would not have escaped lightly at all.

Sighing, Catherine made her way along the paved passageway to where a vine-hung arch gave on to the herb garden. Beyond the rows of carefully-nurtured plants, a low stone wall, topped with iron railings, formed a barrier between the corporal life of the convent and the spiritual one. Beyond that iron fence was the convent's small cemetery, where the nuns who had died in the service of God were laid to rest. A stand of cyprus trees formed a guard of honour along the western boundary of the cemetery, protecting the weathered stones that marked each grave from the seasonal winds that blew down from the mountains.

After only a moment's hesitation, and an anxious glance to ensure she was not being observed, Catherine quickly made her way through the herb garden and let herself into the small cemetery. The little iron gate clanged behind her, and she glanced round apprehensively, half afraid the sound might have been overheard. But the only sounds there were came to her from a distance, and around her, the heat of the day cast its somnolent shadow.

Each headstone in the graveyard was clearly engraved with the nun's name, her age, and the date she had died. Catherine paused to acknowledge each one with a downbent head, as she had been taught to do, thinking, as she had thought so often in the past, how terribly young some of the nuns had been. It was a mercy that the present epidemic had not claimed more souls to add to their numbers, creating more neatly-tended plots for Sister Luisa to maintain.

But it was to a grave set apart from the others that Catherine was making. The skirt of her habit brushed

dustily against the pebbled path as she came to a
standstill beneath a stooping cyprus, looking down
rather emotionally at the rectangular slab of granite
that marked the spot. Thomas Loring's final resting
place was on the hillside he had loved, overlooking the
tumbling waters of the river in the valley below, and
Catherine knelt to touch the stone, and run her fingers
over its weathered surface. A breeze constantly stirred
the leaves in the branches overhead here, sighing like
so many whispering ghosts, and she had spent many
hours here in the early days, pretending that her
father's spirit was one of them. The nuns had granted
Catherine the privilege of burying her father here,
realising the stricken girl would need the solace to be
found in visiting her father's grave, and Professor
Loring had been given a Christian burial, even though
he had seldom set foot in church throughout his life.

'Oh, Daddy,' Catherine breathed now, resting her
hot forehead against the slab. 'What am I going to do? I
wish you could tell me.'

The betraying sound of the little iron gate opening
and closing brought Catherine up with a start, her
cheeks colouring guiltily as she scrambled to her feet.
No matter how justifiable she might think this visit
was, to Sister Angelica it could only be regarded as
wasting time, particularly when she had already had
to neglect her duties to report to Reverend Mother.
Turning, she mentally prepared herself for the
dressing-down she was sure was to come, and caught
her breath sharply when her troubled eyes met the
disturbing gaze of Dr Alvares.

Immediately, she felt the sense of discomfort she
had come to associate with him, the disruptive feeling
of awareness that made her doubly conscious of his
height, of the darkness of his skin, of the muscled

hardness of his body. She knew it was wrong. She knew she shouldn't notice such things. But it was impossible to ignore the width of his shoulders, or the fact that his shirt, unbuttoned at his throat, exposed a smooth expanse of golden-brown skin, only lightly spread with hair. He was wearing his white coat as usual, the kind of coat doctors invariably wore to denote their status, but his pants were hardly uniform, made of cream denim, and closely moulded to his powerful thighs.

Realising her gaze had dropped quite shamelessly over his body, she lowered it even farther, folding her hands together in front of her, and hoping by this stance to convince him that she was not at all disturbed by his presence. Then, clearing her throat, she said politely: 'Good afternoon, Doctor.'

'Good afternoon.'

His low attractive voice caused the hairs on the back of Catherine's neck to prickle quite alarmingly, and she moved her shoulders impatiently to get rid of the annoying itch. She couldn't imagine what he was doing here in the cemetery. He had never visited the graves before, to her knowledge, and her breathing quickened as she started towards the gate.

'One minute . . .'

As she went to go past him, Armand Alvares's hand moved to detain her, his fingers fastening about her arm, just above the elbow. It was the first time he had touched her. It was the first time any man had touched her since her father died, and even before that, her experience of men had been limited to the overtures of boys of her own age. But Dr Alvares was different; *she* was different; and he must know that what he was doing was wrong just as well as she did.

'Dr Alvares!'

Her eyes darted to his face, their outrage evident in the wide-spread transparency of the irises, the aquamarine depths liberally laced with stormy yellow. She was doing her utmost to break free of him, but his hold was unrelenting, and his own expression mirrored his impatience at her futile attempts to thwart him.

'Cool down, will you?' he exclaimed harshly, his hard fingers bruising her soft flesh. 'I know that if Sister Angelica sees me, she'll burn my guts in the fires of hell, but surely we can have a conversation without your behaving as if I'm threatening your chastity?'

'I don't think we have anything to say to one another, Dr Alvares,' Catherine insisted, her voice husky with emotion. 'You made your opinion of me quite plain the last time we met, and after what happened, I'm quite sure you consider it was justified.'

Armand Alvares sighed, looking down at her with eyes more dark than gold, their perplexity evident even to her confused gaze. 'What are you talking about?' he demanded wearily. 'What did I say the last time we met. I don't remember. Enlighten me.'

Catherine held up her head. 'You were rude—'

'I invariably am. It's born of frustration. Go on.'

Catherine took a deep breath. 'If you're just going to be sarcastic—'

'I'm not.' He expelled his breath evenly. 'Please: continue.'

Catherine hesitated. 'Well, you accused me of trying to frighten your patient.'

'So what? You did. You know it.' Armand Alvares's lips compressed. 'Am I to apologise for your incompetence?'

'Incompetence!' Catherine gazed indignantly up at

him. 'If you're referring to my—to my feeling ill, that was hardly incompetence!'

'I wasn't.' Releasing her suddenly, so that she was almost unbalanced, he thrust an impatient hand through the thickness of his hair. 'Look, as a matter of fact, I feel a certain amount of responsibility for your collapse. It was—a little gruesome, I guess, and you were unprepared. But don't confuse sympathy with approval. We all make mistakes; some greater than others.'

'Thank you for your confidence.'

Catherine's tone betrayed her feelings, and Armand Alvares's lips twitched. 'Now, who's being sarcastic?' he countered, causing hot colour to flood her cheeks. 'Forgive me, but is such freedom of speech sanctioned by Mother Benedicta, *Sister*?'

'You—'

Catherine caught the epithet back just in time, but his mocking expression revealed he knew exactly what she had been about to say. Folding his arms across his broad chest, he stood regarding her with unconcealed amusement; like some profane spirit, she thought savagely, falling back on religious similes.

Gathering up her skirts, she would have left him then, but his next words arrested her. 'I'm pleased to see you still have a mind of your own,' he commented drily, shifting his weight from one foot to the other. 'After that litany you spouted the other day, I was half afraid you were beginning to believe in all this rubbish—'

'Dr Alvares!'

'Oh, for God's sake, stop behaving as if I'd shocked you! This is the real world, remember? Now, can we stop arguing long enough for me to tell you why I came looking for you?'

Catherine stared at him. '*You* came looking for *me*?'

'I've said so, haven't I?' Armand Alvares's hands fell to his sides. 'I need to talk to you.' The golden eyes probed hers. 'I need your help.'

'Oh—no—no—' Catherine backed away, shaking her head, and saw the revealing hardening of his mouth. 'I mean—I can't. Whatever it is, please don't ask me. Reverend Mother was most insistent—'

'A man is dying,' Armand Alvares informed her expressionlessly, almost as if she hadn't spoken. 'He *will* die if I don't do something soon. He's got a bullet—lodged here,' he added, his long fingers jabbing at a point just below his rib cage. 'It needs to be removed, but I can't do it on my own. Do you want this man's death—or any part of it—on your conscience?'

'That's not fair!' Catherine halted abruptly as she felt the barrier behind her. 'If—if men choose to get themselves shot—'

'He did not *choose* to get himself shot,' Armand Alvares interrupted softly. 'And I know it's not fair. Nothing ever is. But you're the only person who can help me. I thought Sister Helena might, but—' He broke off to lift his shoulders in a dismissing gesture, and Catherine remembered that Sister Helena herself had been taken ill only the day before.

'You—you must ask Reverend Mother then,' she said now, feeling the iron railings that edged the little wall digging into her flesh through the rough material of her habit. 'If—if she agrees—'

'She won't,' said Dr Alvares harshly, putting one foot in front of the other, inexorably closing the distance between them. 'You don't understand. I don't need your help here, in the hospital. The patient I am speaking of is—some distance away. In the mountains, to be exact. That's why he can't be moved. Travelling across any rough terrain would kill him that much sooner.'

Catherine gasped, 'And you expect me to accompany you into the mountains? You're crazy!'

'No. Just desperate,' said Armand Alvares grimly, halting a hand's breadth from her. 'Please,' he added huskily, his eyes on her averted face. 'Don't let me down.'

Catherine's breathing felt constricted. As on that other occasion in the small hospital, his nearness was a potent distraction and in spite of the fact that they were out in the open and not confined in the cloying atmosphere of the men's ward, she felt as if there was a suffocating lack of air.

'I—can't,' she said unsteadily, moving her head from side to side, and his sudden intake of breath was audible.

'Why can't you?' he demanded, and to her horror she felt his fingers beneath her chin, forcing her head up so that she was obliged to look at him.

His expression was anything but appealing now. The eyes, which only moments before had been entreating her understanding, were now hard and unyielding, glittering with a savage brilliance that told her more about the feelings he was controlling than any angry invective could have done. His mouth was compressed, and the lines which she had noticed occasionally bracketing his nose in times of stress were deeply evident. He was furious with her, that was obvious, and her knees quaked a little as he continued to glare at her.

'Why can't you?' he repeated, and she had the feeling he would like to have shaken an answer out of her.

'How can I?' she protested tremulously. 'Apart from anything else, I'm not allowed to leave the convent.'

'I'll arrange that.'

'How can you?'

'Leave that to me.'

'No. No, I can't. I'm sorry.' Catherine swallowed convulsively, apprehensively aware of how indefensible their situation was at that moment. 'Please— you're hurting me—' And he was. His hard fingers were digging into her chin, and as she spoke, his thumb scraped deliberately cruelly across the soft vulnerability of her lower lip.

'I could hurt you a lot more than this,' he muttered roughly, his eyes moving scornfully over her embarrassed face. 'Believe me, you have no idea . . .'

'Why are you doing this?' Catherine protested fiercely, and with a determined effort she managed to turn her head aside so that he was forced to release her.

'Why indeed?' he conceded with a muffled oath. And then, as she endeavoured to compose herself, he added contemptuously: 'I should have left you to face your father's murderers! After all, if your father *chose* to get himself killed—'

'He didn't—*oh!*' Catherine broke off abruptly at the realisation of what he had tricked her into saying, and without another word, he left her. As she stood there, touching her chin with a tender finger, he stalked away between the tombstones, passing through the iron gate and disappearing into the convent buildings beyond.

Contrarily, as soon as he had gone, Catherine knew a helpless feeling of betrayal. It was as if, by refusing to help, she had let herself down as well as him, and the breeze rustling through the leaves close by were like so many reproachful voices. Were she to be completely honest, she would have to admit that Dr Alvares *had* saved her life. It was all very well pretending that she might have escaped unscathed, that if the guerrillas had discovered her, they would not have regarded her as a threat, but it wasn't very convincing. They had been desperate men; why else would they have killed her father, who had always worked for the community they purported to represent? Without Dr Alvares's timely intervention, her grave might have been dug here beside her father's, and some other person might have remarked on how young *she* had been to meet her death.

She shivered, and turned to look towards the long row of windows that marked the convent dormitories. What ought she to do, she asked herself. What could she do? If only he had asked someone else and not put this burden on her shoulders. It wasn't as if there weren't other nuns with nursing experience, far more nursing experience than she had had, in actual fact. It was true that many of them were middle-aged or older, but some were quite fit in spite of that, and probably just as willing to offer their assistance. Or were they? Catherine caught her lower lip between her teeth, biting hard. After what Reverend Mother had told her, it was much more probable that such a request would be reported directly to her, and having listened to her superior's opinion of the war that was being waged, she had little doubt that the request would be denied. For heaven's sake—Catherine begged forgiveness for the blasphemy—why couldn't Major Enriques arrange for a helicopter to transport the wounded man to the army hospital in Ribatejo? Just because the two men evidently had no liking for one another was no reason for a dying man to suffer.

Keeping this thought uppermost in her mind, Catherine hurried back through the herb garden and into the refectory. At this hour of the afternoon, the dining hall was deserted, and she was able to make her way into the corridor that led to the doctor's surgery. With luck, she might find Dr Alvares there, and be able to speak with him without incurring the anger he had exhibited in the cemetery. She refused to consider what she would do if he refused to listen to her. The man was arrogant, but he was not a fool, and she could see no reason why he shouldn't approve of her suggestion.

But before she had traversed half the corridor, Catherine met the one person she had least hoped to see. Sister Angelica emerged from the women's ward just ahead of her, and her eyes narrowed as they surveyed Catherine's flushed cheeks.

'Well, well,' she murmured, her solid bulk successfully blocking Catherine's path. 'You've been a long time, *novica*. What did Reverend Mother say?'

'Reverend Mother?' For a moment, Catherine's mind went blank, and Sister Angelica stared at her suspiciously.

'You have been to see Reverend Mother, have you not?' she inquired sharply. 'I assume she is the reason why you are looking so hot and bothered.'

'I am?' Catherine touched her cheeks revealingly, and then, realising Sister Angelica was still watching her in that intent way, she added: 'Why, yes. Yes, it must be. She—that is, Reverend Mother, was very understanding. She—er—she doesn't blame me for what happened.'

'She doesn't?' Sister Angelica looked almost put out. 'Are you saying she sympathised with you?'

'No. Not that.' Catherine moistened her lips with a

nervous tongue. 'But—when I explained about my father—'

'What about your father, child?'

'About—about the knife,' murmured Catherine awkwardly. 'That was why I fainted, you see. The blood—on the scalpel . . .'

Sister Angelica looked sceptical. 'You mean that was why you passed out. Because it reminded you of the way your father died?'

Catherine nodded.

'And Reverend Mother accepted this?'

'Yes.' Catherine was defensive. 'It's the truth.'

Sister Angelica shook her head. 'And Dr Alvares had nothing to do with it, of course.'

Catherine could feel her colour deepening. 'No.'

'Very well.' To her relief, Sister Angelica at last seemed satisfied. 'Then you'd better hurry along, hadn't you? Sister Cecilia could do with some help in serving the evening meal. But I shall expect you to report to me this evening. What with the epidemic and all, I fear I have been neglecting your instruction.'

Catherine drew an unsteady breath. 'Yes, Sister.'

Sister Angelica's lips softened slightly and she inclined her head. It was a dismissal and Catherine was glad to accept it as such. But as she turned obediently into the female ward, she glanced back over her shoulder to find Sister Angelica still watching her.

By the time Sister Cecilia professed herself satisfied with Catherine's services, it was after six o'clock. Although the worst aspects of the emergency were over, there were still beds to be stripped, sheets to be changed, and bedpans to be emptied, and as the junior, Catherine was expected to participate in all these activities. In addition to which, there were supper trays to be handed out and collected in again, bottles to be made for the babies whose mothers didn't have enough milk to feed them themselves, and a hundred-and-one other duties that kept her busy long after Sister Cecilia had retired to put her feet up. Glancing through the narrow windows, Catherine was dismayed to see it was getting dark already, and her hopes of seeing Dr Alvares before he departed for the night seemed as substantial as her chances of avoiding an ecclesiastical debate with Sister Angelica. She had hoped he might come into the ward, and she would have found an opportunity to speak to him, somehow. But, of course, he hadn't. Such a coincidence had been too much to hope for, and by the time she found herself free to leave, the room he used as a surgery was dark and deserted.

Biting her lips in frustration, she started along the corridor towards the refectory. It was almost time for supper, and then Sister Angelica would commandeer the hour between supper and compline. As soon as the final prayers of the day were over, she would be expected to retire, and if what Dr Alvares had said about the wounded man was true, when she woke up in the morning he would be dead.

In desperation, she came to a complete standstill, her heart pounding unsteadily in her ears. She had only two alternatives, she decided, trying to calm her nerves. One, she could confess her problem to Sister Angelica and let her take charge of it; or two, she could risk further punishment by missing supper altogether and going in search of Dr Alvares himself.

It was no real choice, she acknowledged glumly, after only a few moments. She couldn't confide in Sister Angelica; not without first gaining Dr Alvares's permission. And, somehow, she sensed this would not be forthcoming. Which meant that she had to find Dr Alvares himself, or put all thoughts of the wounded man out of her head.

CHAPTER FOUR

ARMAND was getting changed to leave when he heard the insistent tapping at the back door of the bungalow. A swift glance at the watch on his wrist elicited the information that his escort was earlier than he had expected, and his heart quickened its beat at the logical conclusion for this change in their arrangements. José must be worse, he told himself savagely, dropping the shirt he had been about to pull over his head. My God! he wasn't dead, was he? he thought grimly, and realising Santo had not heard the tentative sound, he himself went to answer it.

The slim figure hovering anxiously on the step outside was not the dark-skinned guide, however. As Armand jerked open the door, she stepped back with evident nervousness, and he heard her sudden intake of breath at the sight of his half-naked frame.

'*You!*' His tone was blank for a moment, and then dawning comprehension warmed his expression. 'So you decided to come after all. Thank God for that! You've restored my faith in human nature.'

'No, I—'

Catherine started to protest as he put out a hand and hustled her unceremoniously inside. But Armand could not afford the chance that someone might observe his unorthodox visitor, and wonder why one of the sisters from the convent should be visiting him after dark. Few of the nuns ever left the convent at all, and the last thing he wanted right now was to draw attention to himself.

'I'm sorry,' he said, closing the door behind her, and looking down sympathetically into her wide green eyes. 'I didn't mean to be rough with you, but your presence here, dressed like that, could cause some awkward questions to be asked.'

'Do you think I don't know that?' The girl's eyes were bright with indignation. 'I've committed an unforgivable sin by even coming here. If Sister Angelica or Reverend Mother find out—'

'I do appreciate it.' Armand gestured back along the passageway just as Santo, having heard their voices, appeared from the kitchen. 'Come into the bedroom, and I'll find you something to wear. Obviously you can't go like that. It's pretty rough country we'll be covering, and part of it is on foot—'

'No!' Albeit unwillingly, she had followed him along the hall, but when he stopped to speak to the old Indian, she hung back with evident uncertainty. 'You don't understand,' she exclaimed, overriding his barely audible exchange with his man-servant. 'I'm not—going with you. That's not why I came.'

Armand turned, his dark brows descending. 'What did you say?' he demanded.

'I said—I'm not going with you,' she repeated, with evident discomfort. 'And—and could you put some clothes on, please. I—I find it very difficult to talk to you—dressed like that.'

'Really?' Armand was scarcely disposed to grant her request after what she had just said, and looking down at the dark, muscled expanse of his chest, he said harshly: 'What's the matter? Does my unclothed skin offend you? Or does it remind you too acutely of what you've given up?'

Catherine gasped. 'You're crude—'

'No, just honest,' he retorted grimly. 'For God's

sake, if you didn't come here to help me, what have you come for?'

Catherine looked somewhat pointedly towards Santo as Armand finished, and with a gesture of impatience, he dismissed the old man. 'You have no need to be concerned, you know,' he added, pushing open the door of the room behind him and going inside. 'Santo hardly speaks a word of English, and in any case, anything you say here will not go beyond these four walls. You can take my word for it.'

Catherine made no immediate response, but she came to the doorway of the room, and he saw her avert her gaze from the sight of him pushing the tail of the shirt he had just put on into the waistband of his pants. Even so, he noticed that she did cast a covert glance around the room he used as his bedroom, her eyes lingering longest on the framed photograph of Ricardo on the table beside his bed.

Then, supporting herself with one hand against the frame of the door, she said: 'Have you thought of asking Major Enriques to help you? I'm sure he has a helicopter and he could— *what are you doing*?'

Her words were rudely interrupted as Armand abandoned his activities to cross the room and grab her brutally by the shoulders. Thrusting his face close to hers, he withstood her frantic struggles almost effortlessly, and his voice was harsh and angry as he demanded: 'You didn't mention this to Enriques, did you, you little fool?'

Catherine gulped. 'No,' she got out at last. 'No, not yet, I didn't. Now, will you please let go of me, or I shall regret I ever thought of helping you!'

Armand let her go without another word, and she grasped the door-frame again to regain her balance. 'I'm sorry,' he muttered, raking back his hair with a hand that was not quite steady. 'I didn't mean to frighten you. But, God, I thought for a minute—' He broke off abruptly, making a concerted effort to control his agitation. 'That was stupid of me. Forgive me. You—er—you were about to tell me the reason that brought you here.'

Catherine squared her shoulders and faced him, but he saw the trepidation in her eyes. It was there, too, in the hectic colour rising over her cheekbones and in the tightly pressed tension of her mouth, and his conscience pricked him. He shouldn't have pounced on her like that, he chided himself severely. He must have scared the hell out of her and that was not kind. She had risked a lot by coming here, whatever her intentions, and although for one awful moment he had thought she had betrayed him to Enriques, he should have waited before jumping to the wrong conclusions.

'That—that was why I came here,' Catherine said now, holding up her head. 'To—to suggest you ask Major Enriques for his assistance. After all, you're both on the same side, aren't you? Just because you don't like one another—'

'What!' Armand gazed at her now as if she had suddenly taken leave of her senses. 'You're not serious!'

'Why not?'

'You can't mean you risked excommunication, or worse, just to come and tell me that I ought to ask Enriques for his help!' Armand uttered a short mirthless laugh. 'I don't believe it. You must be out of your tiny mind! My God, you're crazy!'

'Why am I crazy?' Catherine pursed her lips indignantly. 'It's the logical solution.'

'Then, if it is, don't you think I'd have thought of it?'

demanded Armand heavily. 'Grow up, will you? If there was any way I could ask that bastard, Enriques, for help, I'd have done it!'

Catherine winced. 'There's no need to swear, Dr Alvares.'

'Isn't there? Isn't there?' He pushed his hands frustratedly into the pockets of his pants, fearing he would take hold of her and shake some sense into her if he didn't. 'You don't understand a thing about this war, Miss Loring. Your head is so lost in the clouds, you don't recognise the truth, even when you trip over it!'

Catherine's lips parted. 'This man—this man you wanted me to help you with is—is not a member of the army?'

'Not the army of Henri Enriques, no,' Armand conceded drily.

'He's a—guerrilla then.'

'That's a matter of opinion, I suppose.'

Catherine caught her breath. 'And you expected *me* to help you.' She shook her head. 'Dr Alvares, my father's murderers were—'

'—not Rodolfo's men,' inserted Armand harshly, and he saw her sway a little as she tilted her face up to his.

'You're lying!'

'Why would I lie?'

'You must be. You were there—'

'And that's why I can tell you: they were not resistance fighters,' repeated Armand grimly. 'Oh, I can't prove it. I've got no convenient witnesses to support my statement. You'll just have to take my word, as a man, and as a doctor, that José Rodolfo's men would not murder a civilian in cold blood.'

'They murder each other,' she exclaimed tremulously, and Armand sighed.

'There's a war going on, Catherine,' he told her, using her name almost without thinking. 'Wars cost lives, innocent lives. They always have. They're not a solution in themselves, but they are a means to an end, and to some people the end will always justify the means. It's a cliché, I know, but it's true.'

'But why would anyone want to kill my father?' she protested, her voice revealing her uncertainty. 'Not— not Major Enriques. I—I don't believe it. I won't believe it.'

'Okay. Maybe it wasn't anything to do with Major Enriques,' agreed Armand, half wishing he had never started this. 'Maybe I'm wrong. Maybe he knows nothing about it. It's possible it was a mistake.'

'*A mistake!*'

Catherine gazed at him disbelievingly, but Armand could see the horror gathering in her face, and he berated himself fiercely. He shouldn't have told her, he realised belatedly. He should have let her go on believing her father had been the victim of a terrorist attack. It was so much easier to bear than the ugly possibility that Professor Loring's death had been engineered for less heroic reasons. It ought to have occurred to him to anticipate how isolated it must make her feel.

'Men get drunk,' he said, by way of recompense. 'Accidents happen.'

'Accidents!' Catherine stared at him with tear-wet eyes. 'Are you telling me my father's death was an accident now? Am I supposed to feel reassured by knowing that the thugs who broke into the schoolhouse might have been *drunk* at the time?'

Armand expelled his breath wearily. 'No,' he said at last. 'No, of course not. Ignore what I said. I could be wrong.'

'But you don't think you are, do you?' Catherine demanded, dashing a defensive hand across her cheek. 'What do you want from me, Dr Alvares? Praise or absolution?'

Armand's eyes darkened. 'You know what I want from you, Miss Loring,' he countered bleakly. 'The reason why I thought you'd risked Mother Benedicta's wrath. I need your assistance. Nothing else.'

'To help a *terrorist*!'

'To help a sick man,' Armand amended flatly. 'A human being. As Sister Angelica would say, as much God's creation as you or I.'

Catherine sniffed. 'Reverend Mother said you didn't believe in God,' she mumbled unwillingly. 'She said you had no time for religion.'

'I don't care for her philosophy, if that's what you mean,' he conceded carelessly. 'I don't believe in seizing postulants by any means at her disposal.'

'You mean me, don't you?'

Armand shrugged. 'What do you think?'

'I think you're just using that as an excuse,' Catherine responded huskily. 'Perhaps the reason you don't approve of Reverend Mother is because you're too much like her. You're not above using the situation to gain your own ends, are you, Dr Alvares?'

Armand shook his head. She was more astute than he had realised, this slender slip of a girl, whose pale, distressed features had a delicate beauty that not even the severe band of her coif could disguise. But she was wrong if she thought his only reason for objecting to Mother Benedicta's policy was a personal one. He disliked the idea of imprisoning any young creature, and because he had brought her to the convent, he felt doubly responsible.

Before he could reply however, Catherine abruptly stiffened. Before his startled gaze, she froze like a statue, her hands pressed together and raised to her lips in an attitude of prayer. Her eyes didn't close. They remained wide and anxious, staring at some point beyond his shoulder, and he turned automatically to find out what she was looking at. But there was nothing to see, just the usual clothes-press and chest of drawers, the scratched mirror above reflecting nothing out of the ordinary.

'What is it?' he demanded at last, unable to restrain the question, and she raised her eyes to his, her expression full of contrition.

'Didn't you hear it?' she exclaimed, lowering her hands to the belt at her waist. 'It was the bell for compline. Now everyone will know why I missed supper.'

'I see.' Armand felt some of the tension leave his body. For a moment, he had thought she had betrayed him after all, and the blood flowed more freely through his veins at the realisation that it was nothing more than a crisis of conscience. 'Well, don't worry about it. You'll have to tell them you were sick.'

Catherine gasped. 'You say that so glibly, don't you? I don't tell lies.'

'Sometimes we have to,' Armand retorted drily. 'But now, you'll have to excuse me. Any minute now, I'm going to have to leave you, and I still have one or two things left to do.'

'But you don't understand,' Catherine cried, taking an involuntary step towards him. 'I can't go back now. The gates will be locked.'

Armand hesitated. 'Come with me then. You have a saying in your country about lambs and sheep, do you not? That one might as well be hanged for one as the other?'

Catherine gazed at him a moment, torturing the belt of her habit; then she shook her head. 'I can't.'

'Why can't you?' Armand bent to pick up a sweater, and tugged it over his head. 'What have you to lose?'

Catherine bent her head. 'When Reverend Mother finds out where I've been—'

'—she'll probably throw a fit,' Armand agreed, sitting down on the side of his bed to pull on his boots. His eyes surveyed her with reluctant sympathy. 'Don't look so shattered. Novices have been known to fall from grace before. She'll forgive you—eventually.'

Catherine lifted her head. 'Do you really think so?'

Armand had no precedent on which to base his assumption, but he would have said anything to wipe that expression of desolation from her face. His own conscience was not so clear that he could afford to ignore her distress. It was his fault she was here, just as much as it was his fault that she was at the convent, and although the last thing he needed was to get involved with a girl like her, he couldn't ignore her plight.

'Look,' he said earnestly, 'I've got to get ready now. I'd like to be able to help you, I really would, but I don't see what either of us can do until tomorrow.' He hesitated. 'Who knows, perhaps you'll be able to slip back into the convent in the morning without anyone seeing you. You may even be able to convince them that you—got locked in a cupboard or something.'

Catherine pursed her lips. 'More lies!'

'All right, more lies,' agreed Armand, rapidly losing patience. '*Mãe de Deus!* I'm not a saint. Right now, my duty lies with the corporal world, not the temporal one!'

Getting up from the bed, he approached her, and she backed nervously out into the passageway again, only to start violently when there was a sudden rapid tattoo on the outer door.

'Relax,' Armand reassured her swiftly. 'It sounds as though my guide has arrived. I'm going to have to leave you now.'

Santo appeared at that moment, having been summoned by the knock, and Armand nodded briefly at the old man. 'Answer it, will you?' he ordered, speaking in the patois he knew Catherine didn't understand, and Santo nodded. 'Tell him I won't be long. I'll just get my equipment.'

'Sim, senhor.'

With a covert glance in the girl's direction, the old Indian went to open the door and Armand took Catherine's resisting arm between his fingers and compelled her back into his bedroom. 'Wait here,' he said, ignoring her indignant protests, and leaving her alone, he strode off towards his surgery.

When he returned he was shouldering the two canvas holdalls which held the cylinders of ethyl chloride and oxygen required for the delicate operation he had to perform. The haversacks also contained the plasma he intended to use to minimise the shock a transfusion might have on José's system, and he was thankful he did not need to carry pints of blood, too. It was going to be tough enough for two of them to carry the essential implements he needed without adding to their burden.

Santo was hovering in the hall, but there was no sign of Catherine and, frowning, Armand asked where she was. 'I do not know, senhor,' the old man answered apologetically, shaking his head. Then he nodded towards the closed door of Armand's bedroom. 'Did you not ask her to wait in there, *doutor*?'

'Oh, yes.' With some relief, Armand lowered the haversacks to the floor and, straightening, he grasped the handle of the door and pushed it open. 'Catherine,' he said, stepping thoughtlessly into the room. 'I'm leaving now—*oh, God*!'

He came to an abrupt halt, gazing blankly at the girl beside his bed. Catherine had her back to him, but she was obviously in the process of changing her clothes and his startled gaze moved over the downy curve of a spine and the rounded swell of very feminine buttocks. She had been about to step into a pair of his pants, the hem of the rough cotton shirt she was evidently planning to wear with them flapping about her hips, but his hoarse ejaculation had distracted her, and the face she turned in his direction was both flushed and anxious.

Without another word, Armand backed swiftly out of the room again, almost falling over Santo, who had moved up behind him to see what had caused his master to swear like that. '*Perdão, senhor, mas o que é que se passa?*' the old Indian exclaimed, trying to see over Armand's shoulder, but the door was firmly closed and his disappointment was evident.

'Nothing that need concern you, Santo,' Armand retorted quellingly, uncomfortably aware of an unfamiliar tightening in his groin. Thrusting the thoughts of Catherine's creamy flesh aside, he again hefted the heavy cylinders on to his back. 'Is our other guest waiting outside? I wonder if he realises how much these things weigh.'

Santo hesitated, still looking speculatively towards Armand's bedroom door. 'The young lady,' he persisted. 'The *religiosa, senhor*. Is she going with you?'

'No.' Armand's reply was clipped. 'Come on. Give

me a hand with these bags. There's another one still to come.'

Santo hurried ahead to open the outer door, but before he reached it the door behind Armand was jerked open and Catherine stood on the threshold. As Armand had suspected, the drab grey habit had disappeared, and in its place was the shirt and pants he had seen her fumbling with earlier. What was more, without the concealing coif, her hair tumbled loosely about and beyond her shoulders, a glowing curtain of red-gold silk, with a sensual beauty all its own.

'Do I look all right?' she exclaimed, gazing at him anxiously, and Armand suddenly realised how reckless he had been in inviting her to go with him.

'You—you look fine,' he replied heavily, unable to keep the note of censure out of his voice, and her tongue appeared in unknowing provocation.

'You don't mind, do you?' she persisted. 'I mean— you did say I should get changed if I was going with you.'

'What!' Armand stared at her, and Catherine's cheeks grew even pinker.

'I know I said I wouldn't,' she confessed awkwardly. 'But like you said, I can't go back to the convent before morning, and—well, I don't want to stay here alone.'

'Santo is here,' said Armand woodenly, realising as he did so he was arguing against the very thing he had asked of her, and Catherine's shoulders drooped.

'Don't you want me to come now?' she exclaimed. 'Have you found someone else?'

'No.' Armand turned away from the distracting awareness of her rounded breasts outlined beneath the thin material of his shirt. Of course, she wasn't wearing a bra, he chided himself severely. She never had. But in the concealing folds of the nun's habit, her slim young body had never looked so womanly as it did in his man's clothes. He was intensely conscious of the dusky hollow just visible above the unbuttoned neckline of the shirt, and the image he had been trying to banish flashed uncontrollably before his eyes, causing him to speak more roughly than he might have done.

'Look,' he said harshly, flexing his shoulder muscles against the crippling weight of the cylinders, 'I made a mistake. I shouldn't have asked you. I realise that now. I've decided I don't need the aggravation.'

'The aggravation!' Catherine held her head up indignantly, but although she was quite a tall girl, she was still several inches shorter than he was and she had to tip back her head to look at him. 'What aggravation? I thought you said the man would die without assistance.'

Her defensive words brought Armand to his senses. She was right. He expelled his breath impatiently. He was allowing a purely physical response to her undoubted femininity to divert him from his purpose. Dear God, he was no stranger to the sight of a woman's naked body, and just because that unguarded intervention had alerted him to the fact that she was not the child he had been regarding her, was no reason to lose sight of his real objective. He *did* need her assistance, and if José died because he had refused it, he would never forgive himself.

'All right,' he said abruptly, starting along the passageway. 'Find yourself a sweater and follow me. I don't have the time to argue with you.'

She looked as if she would like to have refused his ungracious invitation, but she had gone too far to back out now. With a controlled little gesture, she went

back into the bedroom, and Armand strode aggress-
ively along the passageway to the rear door.

By the time Catherine emerged from the house,
Armand had secured one of the haversacks on the
back of the soldier who had come to escort them, and
was in the process of strapping the other on to his
own. The girl blinked a little confusedly as the door
closed behind her and she was left in darkness, but she
started towards Armand confidently enough and he
steeled himself to meet her inquiring gaze.

'I can carry something,' she said, glancing surreptitiously towards the other man. 'Do we have far to
go?'

'You'll find out,' remarked Armand uncharitably,
ignoring her offer and looping the strap of his medical
case over his shoulder. 'Come on. We're wasting
time.'

They had skirted the village and were halfway
across the first field when he realised something was
wrong. It wasn't easy climbing the rugged field path
with the straps of the haversack digging into his
shoulders. It made his previous expedition seem a
piece of cake by comparison, and he didn't notice at
first that Catherine was lagging so far behind.

When he did, he called a halt to the other man, and
waited impatiently for her to catch up with them.
'What's the matter?' he demanded in a low voice.
'Surely we're not going too fast for you. A girl of your
age should be able to keep up with someone as out of
condition as I am.'

'You're not out of condition,' retorted Catherine
fiercely, resenting his tone. 'But I daresay you might
find it harder in sandals like these!'

Bending, she tugged one of the offending articles off
her foot, and Armand saw to his disgust that it was

little more than a slip-on mule. 'For God's sake,' he
muttered, 'why didn't you change your shoes,
too?'

'To what?' she countered defensively. 'A pair of
your boots, perhaps? Oh, yes, they'd have been very
comfortable, wouldn't they?'

Armand grunted. 'You could have worn plenty of
socks.'

'And rubbed all the skin off my feet? Yes, I suppose I
could have done that.'

'Don't be sarcastic!' His rejoinder was sharp. 'Just
because you've shed the habit, does not mean you've
shed the veil!'

Catherine's lips quivered. He could see them in the
pale light of the moon, and his conscience pricked
him. It wasn't her fault she had no shoes to wear. He
should have thought of it himself. After all, this had
been his idea. He should have been prepared for all
contingencies.

'All right,' he said now, glancing round at his male
companion, who had come to see what was going on.
'We'll just have to take it slower, that's all. *Mais
devagar, por favor,*' he added, for the guide's benefit,
and the young man nodded understandingly, gazing
admiringly at Catherine.

It took much longer to reach the high pass where the
Land-Rover was waiting, and Armand's shoulders felt
numb by the time he swung the heavy haversack into
the vehicle. He was sweating, and he noticed there
were beads of perspiration on Catherine's forehead as
she dragged herself up on to the seat. Her hair was
damp, too, curling in moist strands about her forehead, and he saw the way the young soldier kept
looking at her, as if he couldn't keep his eyes off her.
The boy's behaviour convinced Armand he had made

a mistake in bringing her with him, and it was to this he attributed his growing irritation.

The rough journey to the camp made him glad he had put himself between Catherine and the young soldier. The bouncing motion of the vehicle threw her often against Armand's taut frame, and although she kept apologising, there was nothing she could do about it. It might have been easier if he had put his arm around her and cushioned her against the worst of the bumps, but he didn't. Instead, she was left to protect herself as best she could, her smothered cries constantly attracting their driver's attention.

An ominous roll of thunder echoed about them as the Land-Rover began its descent into the canyon, and a few spots of rain blew in through the open windows. The light shower was quite pleasant, and Armand saw Catherine open her mouth to catch several of the drops inside. Of course, he thought guiltily, she had not had anything to eat or drink since lunchtime. She must be hungry as well as exhausted.

Their progress through the camp was slow, the shower of rain causing obvious difficulties for the men cooking their evening meal over open fires. Catherine's appearance, too, caused them to stand and stare in open-mouthed astonishment, and Armand wondered, somewhat irritably, whether he ought not to have insisted she change back into her habit before any of these men saw her. She was too much of a temptation to men who had been starved of any female companionship, and while they would have respected a nun, in her present attire she was far too distracting.

Realising there was nothing he could do about it now, Armand put these thoughts aside, and concentrated instead on the daunting task ahead of him. He

was impatient to examine José and find out if the delay
had had any dangerous effect on his condition. His
strength was bound to have deteriorated, and
Armand knew he would have to trust to luck that the
critical operation would not prove too much for José's
weakened constitution. It would not take long, but the
bullet was balanced so precariously close to his heart,
the risks were enormous.

'Where is your patient?' Catherine asked unex-
pectedly, her voice low and uncertain, and turning his
head, Armand noticed the grip of tension round her
mouth. She was probably scared stiff, he reflected,
with reluctant sympathy. It was months since she had
been outside the walls of the convent, and the blackened faces of these men must assuredly remind her of
her father's killers.

'Relax, it's not much farther now,' he said, putting a
reassuring hand on her knee, but she dashed it away
nervously, as she withdrew into her corner. There was
fear, as well as apprehension, in the gaze she turned
upon him, and his initial sense of anger was tempered
by compassion.

'We're here,' he said unnecessarily, as the Land-
Rover drew to a halt outside José's tent. 'Let me get
past you, and I'll help you down.'

'I don't need your help,' she retorted stiffly, shifting
to the edge of her seat, and swinging her legs over the
side, she vaulted to the ground.

Her cry of agony was unmistakable and Armand,
vaulting out after her, dropped to his haunches beside
her body huddled on the ground. 'Catherine!' he
muttered, forgetting for a moment his intention to
address her as *Sister* here and, gazing down into her
tremulous face, he demanded: 'What is it? What's
wrong? You haven't sprained your ankle, have you?'

Catherine shook her head mutely, tears glistening on the long curling lashes as she struggled to sit upright. Apart from having jarred her body, there were no obvious injuries Armand could see, but even as he came to this conclusion, another thought occurred to him. Ignoring her frantic attempts to evade his hands, he captured one slender ankle between his fingers and tipped the pad of her foot into the light. The bloody flesh made him wince. The skin had been rubbed raw, and the blisters that had formed had burst, and reformed, and burst again.

'*Por Deus!* why didn't you tell me?' he groaned, staring at the mutilated sole, and then, realising their exchange was causing a crowd to gather, he thrust his hands beneath her, and hoisted her up into his arms.

'I'm—all right,' she protested, but her arms slid obediently around his neck and he was engulfed in the warm female scent of her body.

CHAPTER FIVE

HOURS later, it was over. Sluicing her face and hands in the basin which had been provided for her, Catherine knew an unfamiliar feeling of satisfaction, and even the pain in her feet could not dim the smug sense of gratification she was experiencing. The surgery was over. The bullet had been removed and, so far as she knew, the operation had been a complete success. José—as Armand had called the man—was going to make it, and he was sleeping right now in the tent next to this one.

Drying her hands, she rolled down the sleeves of Armand's shirt—*when had she started to think of him as Armand, and not Dr Alvares?*—and stepped tentatively to the flap of the tent. Peering out, she saw it was still raining heavily, as it had been for some time, the steady patter of the drops on the tarpaulin roof rapidly erecting a barrier between the camp and the world outside. An hour ago, one of the soldiers had come to tell *o medico* that the pass was flooding, and that there was little chance of the Land-Rover being able to crawl its way out of the canyon tonight, but Armand had paid him little attention. At that moment, he had been intent on dressing the open wound in José's chest, and his angry ejaculation had sent the man scuttling out of the tent again. Catherine wouldn't have known why he came at all if it hadn't been for Luis. She liked Luis. He was kind, he was gentle, he had been very sweet to her; and he spoke her language. Armand had said he was José's son, and if José was anything like his offspring, then he deserved to recover.

Allowing the flap to fall back into place, she cast a fleeting glance at her surroundings. This tent was much smaller than the one next door. It was little more than a sleeping compartment, with a padded mattress against one wall, covered with an unbleached blanket. Catherine guessed the tent in which the operation had taken place belonged to the commandant, and she wondered which, if any, of the anxious men who had gathered around Armand on his arrival, was the infamous Rodolfo. Or perhaps, not so infamous after all, she reflected, remembering what Armand had told her. But if Rodolfo's men hadn't killed her father, why had he been murdered? The question was one which would probably haunt her for the rest of her life, she thought unhappily. These men did not seem like cold-blooded killers, but then nor did Major Enriques. Yet, she had few doubts he would carry a gun on occasion, and use it, if necessary.

Refusing to speculate any further, Catherine combed her fingers through her hair and wondered what Armand was doing now. As soon as her services were no longer required, he had had Luis bring her here; but after fetching her some food and water for washing, the boy had departed again. Catherine guessed he was anxious to be with his father, but she wished he could have stayed. Now that she had eaten the savoury stew the camp cook had provided, and drunk a beaker of water, the first flush of euphoria was rapidly disappearing, and she was getting anxious, too, not least because of the punishment she was going to have to face on her return.

Pacing the floor was not sensible in her condition, and coiling her body on to the mattress, she eased off her sandals and flexed her toes. A sharp pain shot up into her ankle at that first experiment, and abandoning her efforts, she ran her fingers over the gauze padding.

Before tackling his real patient, Armand had insisted on bathing and dressing her feet with antiseptic ointment, cushioning the soles with strips of gauze that soaked up the moisture and kept the blisters dry. She had never seen him so angry, not even when she refused his plea for assistance in the convent cemetery; but his hands had been incredibly gentle, and a shiver ran up her spine at the remembrance of his cool, controlled competence.

The flap was pushed aside at that moment, and the object of her contemplation came swiftly into the tent. Armand had a rubber cape about his shoulders to protect him from the downpour, but his head was bare, and in the light from the paraffin lamp, Catherine could see drops of rain glinting on the darkness of his hair. He looked triumphant, but haggard, the revealing lines of weariness etching shadows in the bone structure of his cheeks.

'Don't get up,' he ordered, when Catherine made as if to scramble to her feet. 'We can't go anywhere at the moment. You might as well stay where you are.'

Catherine looked up at him, his height and muscled frame somehow dwarfing the proportions of the tent. In a knitted sweater, and dark suede pants, the cuffs pushed into calf-length leather boots, he looked more like an adventurer than a doctor, and her skin prickled alarmingly when he cast off the cape and lowered himself beside her.

'God, I'm tired,' he said, running a weary hand round the back of his neck and allowing it to rest there. With his legs drawn up, and his elbow resting on his knees, he looked younger than she had ever seen him, and she knew a totally shameless urge to kneel behind him and massage the aching muscles of his shoulders.

But of course, she didn't, and when he looked her way she immediately lowered her eyes, behaving as she had been taught to do in the convent. The past few hours had been moments out of time, but now she had to think about going back there, and the sooner she started remembering Sister Angelica's instructions, the easier that would be.

'How do your feet feel now?' he inquired, and she sensed his eyes upon her, cool and assessing.

'Oh—they're fine,' she murmured, not wanting to arouse his condemnation yet again, and he made a sound halfway between irritation and disbelief.

'You should have told me,' he declared flatly. 'Blood poisoning can be dangerous in any situation, but particularly in this one.'

'I know.' Catherine wished he would let it go. 'I'm sorry. I was foolish, I realise that. But—well, I didn't want to hold you up any more than I had done.'

His expression revealed his impatience at her answer, and Catherine guessed he was controlling his natural response. She should have told him, she supposed, pleating the worn cuff of the woollen pants she had borrowed. But after the way he had spoken to her earlier, she had determined not to ask for his indulgence again.

'Why did you stay on at the convent?' Armand demanded suddenly, his hand gripping the hair at the nape of his neck. 'That wasn't your father's intention for you, was it? Until he died, you hadn't planned on entering the church?'

'No.' Catherine hunched her shoulders. 'I was going to help him run the school. But what with the fire and all, and—and—'

'—and the looting,' Armand finished for her quietly. 'I know. You didn't feel you could go back there.'

Catherine shuddered. 'It wouldn't have been the same.'

'I can understand that.' Armand's eyes were disturbingly intent. 'So why didn't you go back to England? Don't you have any relatives there?'

'No.' Catherine shifted a little awkwardly beneath his gaze. 'At least, no one of importance. Besides,' she coloured becomingly, 'I'm needed here.'

'Needed—or interned?' he suggested drily. 'You don't have any money, do you? I should have thought of that. Your father was hardly a prudent man.'

'You know nothing about my father!'

Catherine was offended, but Armand was not deterred. 'He would never have brought you to live here if he'd had any common sense,' he declared, overriding her indignation. 'Surajo is politically unstable at the moment. You should have found yourself a job in London or some place else. Then you wouldn't have been caught up in all of this.'

Catherine pursed her lips. 'My father was making a study of ancient South American civilisations,' she retorted hotly. 'He could never have lived in England. He'd have hated it.'

'I'm not suggesting he should have moved to England. I'm merely pointing out that had you found a job in your own country, you wouldn't be in this situation now.' Armand shrugged. 'Not that I'm not grateful for your help. I am. I'm simply trying to explain why I find your father's attitude so unreasonable.'

Catherine sniffed. 'It's nothing to do with you.'

'No, it's not.' Armand bowed his head in acquiescence, resting both elbows on his knees and allowing his hands to hang loosely between his legs. 'I stand—or should I say *sit*?—corrected. What you choose to do with your life is nothing to do with me.'

As Catherine drew her knees up under her, she wondered why his statement did not fill her with the confidence it should. Instead, she knew a quite devastating sense of desolation at his words, as if by verbally washing his hands of her, he had robbed her of what little reassurance she had left, and she was anxiously casting about in her mind for something to say to justify her situation, when he abruptly shifted his position. Stretching his length beside her, he yawned wearily and closed his eyes.

'Wake me in an hour,' he told her sleepily, lifting his arm to shade his eyes, and before she could protest that she had no means of adhering to his request, his regular breathing warned her he was already asleep.

The minutes stretched, their isolation made absolute by the steady thrumming of the rain overhead. The camp was sleeping, even the man in the next tent was sleeping, and Catherine's sense of solitariness increased as her limbs grew stiffer and stiffer.

She shifted once, trying to straighten her legs without disturbing him, but he stirred and she kept still. He needed to rest, she consoled herself firmly. So many innocent lives were in his hands. While she had only a harrowing interview with Reverend Mother to face, and the possible threat of excommunication. She wondered what she would do if Reverend Mother took that irrevocable decision. As Dr Alvares had said, she had no money of her own, no funds of any kind to get her back to England and support her until she got a job. And in any case, what kind of job could she find, without any formal qualifications, particularly when so many people were unemployed at present?

Quelling the sense of panic that was rising inside her, she found her eyes turning in Armand's direction. He was soundly asleep, his chest rising and falling in even repetition, his lean frame reclining indolently upon the mattress beside her. He was attractive, she thought unwillingly, her eyes wandering sinfully over his body. His broad chest tapered to lean hips; long legs outlined beneath the close-fitting cloth of his pants. Half-defiantly, her gaze lingered longest on the powerful muscles between his thighs that proved his manhood, before her burning cheeks betrayed her. In heaven's name, what was she thinking of, she chided herself angrily. Weren't the crimes she had already committed enough for her? Horrified, she pressed the palms of her hands to her face and looked away, but her curiosity remained—and with it, her self-condemnation.

Uneasily, her attention was drawn to his face, and she breathed a little less constrictedly when she saw he was still sleeping. She felt she would have died of humiliation if he had apprehended her appraisal, and her hands were unsteady as she returned them to her lap.

What time was it, she wondered. How long had she been sitting here? It felt like forever, but it couldn't be that long. Unthinkingly, her gaze alighted on the watchstrap that circled the wrist Armand was using to protect his eyes, and after a few moments' consideration, she made a sound of exasperation. She *could* have timed his rest, she realised frustratedly. She could have checked the time on his watch and known exactly how long he had been asleep. Now, she could only guess, and leaning forward, she tried to angle her head so that she could read the dial.

He shifted as she was suspended over him, and she froze in an attitude of obeisance, her knees digging into the mattress beside him. God alone knew what he would think she was doing if he opened his eyes now, and her mind shrank from the possibility of having to convince him of her innocence. She looked guilty, she suspected, and after the thoughts she had had a few moments ago, she felt guilty, and her lips parted anxiously as he moved restlessly beneath her.

He didn't awaken, however. Much to her relief, he merely found himself a more comfortable position, and she was about to shuffle away when the arm that had been shielding his eyes descended upon her shoulders. Horror-stricken, Catherine felt his fingers slide possessively across her back, and the weight of his arm compelled her down to him with an ever-increasing persuasion.

She braced herself against the mattress, trying desperately to resist the pressure, but it was a futile exercise. Her face was only inches from the soft wool of his sweater, and the draught of her breathing was causing lots of tiny fibres to rise up into her nose. They, combined with the unnatural strain on her muscles, were making it an unbearable situation, and when the itch in her nose became insupportable, she gave up the unequal battle. With a feeling of impotence, she felt the warmth of his sweater crushed beneath her cheek and the unyielding firmness of his rib cage under her chin.

Armand didn't move. It seemed perfectly natural for him to lie with a woman's body coiled close beside him, but Catherine, who had spent the last hour fighting against the insidious attraction of his body, knew a helpless sense of injustice. It wasn't fair, she told herself fiercely. Just because he was tired was no reason for her to have to sacrifice her conscience like this. Steeling herself not to relax against him, she lay, wide-eyed and resentful, staring up at the roof of the tent, the rain on the canvas beating a mocking retreat to her fruitless hopes of absolution.

Catherine regained consciousness with the uneasy awareness that something was wrong. A pale grey light was filtering into the room where she was lying, but although its opalescence proved that she had not overslept, she had the distinct feeling that all was not as it should be.

Yet, in spite of her misgivings, she was reluctant to move. She felt unusually relaxed and comfortable, and there was an enveloping warmth around her, as if she was wrapped in a rather weighty electric blanket. There was a weight on her legs and another encircling band across her chest, and trying to remove their reassuring security seemed all too much trouble in her present state of lethargy.

Blinking, she gazed up at the ceiling above her, seeing, instead of the beamed roof of the convent dormitory, the pitched canopy of a tent. Rough, stitched canvas spanned a metal frame-work that was secured in the earth beneath, and her eyes quickly assimilated the crude wooden crate and the lamp which had long since ceased to function.

The stunning realisation of where she was brought an unbidden gasp to her lips, and with it the unacceptable explanation of what had happened. With a feeling of horror, she attempted to turn her head, and although the effort caused her some discomfort, her worst suspicions were realised. Armand was lying beside her. It was his head cushioned on her hair that made turning her head so painful, and it was the weight of his legs across her lower limbs and his arm across her chest that had given her that truly wicked feeling of contentment.

'Dr Alvares!' she exclaimed desperately, making a concerted effort to break free of his confining grasp. 'Dr Alvares, it's almost morning! I must have fallen asleep, too. Oh, wake up! I've got to get back to the convent!'

'*Qué passa?*' he mumbled sleepily, coiling his body about her even more closely. '*Qué quer? E cedo. De manhã, pequena—*'

'Dr Alvares, I don't think you realise who I am!' Catherine protested stiffly, understanding that he thought it too early to get up and recognising *pequena* as a term of endearment. She quelled the bitter surge of resentment this evoked inside her. 'Please—let me get up. We've got to leave immediately!'

'*Estou cansado,*' he responded tiredly, moving the arm that was encircling her body so that his fingers slipped sensuously under the curve of her nape. '*Qué horas são?* What time is it?' he added, his lips brushing the silken tangle of her hair and, as she struggled to free herself, his mouth found the peach-soft angle of her jaw.

Blood rushed wildly into her face at that sensual caress, the probing brush of his tongue like a flick of fire against her skin. Dear God! she moaned silently, who did he think she was? But what was even harder to control than her panic was the treacherous wish that he knew exactly what he was doing—and with whom.

'Dr Alvares!' she choked now, disgust at her own duplicity lending a note of anguish to her cry, and as if that desperate appeal had finally got through to him, he opened his eyes and looked at her.

Drowning in their golden depths, Catherine felt the will to go on resisting him drain out of her. Instead, her lips parted breathlessly and she helplessly gulped for air. She had never been this close to any man before, and she was overwhelmingly conscious of his leg imprisoning hers, and of how, when he moved, his thigh pressed against her. She was conscious, too, of his arm across her breasts, and of the unfamiliar hardening of their peaks. The rough material of his shirt was a coarse abrasion to their sensitised fullness, and he surely could not be unaware of her reactions to his appraisal.

'Miss Loring,' he murmured at last, his gaze lingering on the tremulous fullness of her lower lip. 'I'm sorry. I suppose I must apologise. How did we get into this situation?'

Catherine's cheeks flamed. 'It—it was my fault,' she got out jerkily, and his dark brows ascended.

'Yours?'

'Yes, mine,' she continued breathily. 'I—I—that is, I fell asleep, too. D—do you know what time it is? It's almost light.'

To look at his watch, Armand had to remove the arm that was imprisoning her ribs, and as he squinted at the dial, Catherine struggled into a sitting position. 'I guess it's about five thirty,' he told her, following her example and in so doing also releasing her legs. Squatting in a cross-legged position, he blinked at her lazily. 'Did you sleep well?' he inquired, brushing an errant strand of hair from her cheek and grimacing self-effacingly. 'Forgive me if I shocked you just now. But were you more experienced you'd know you don't enter a man's bedroom first thing in the morning. Not

looking like you do,' he appended. 'And particularly
not get into bed with him.'

'I didn't get into bed with you,' countered Catherine
unsteadily, taking her chance and scrambling to her
feet. She winced a little as her bruised soles objected to
such rough handling, but she had to remain standing
to deliver her little speech. 'You—you were exhausted,' she declared defensively. 'I—well, I was just
sitting there, waiting for you to wake up, and—and I
must have—must have—'

'—been exhausted, too,' Armand inserted helpfully, and she let her breath out on a sigh.

'I suppose so,' she conceded. 'I—I don't remember
what happened. Just—just waking this morning and
finding you—'

'—taking advantage of the situation,' Armand
smiled mockingly. 'Like I said—I'm only human.'

Catherine sustained his ironic gaze for a few
seconds longer and then turned and walked pur-
posefully to the flap of the tent. Pulling it aside with
hands which were revealingly unsteady, she gazed
out into the semi-darkness, struggling to school her
features as she tried to come to terms with her emotions. Already the camp was stirring, she saw, en-
deavouring to concentrate on immediate things. In
less than an hour it would be light, and even if they left
immediately, she would still be too late to attend
morning prayers.

She hadn't heard him move, but presently she felt
him behind her, and she flinched away when he laid a
reassuring hand on her shoulder. 'I've got to check on
my patient,' he told her flatly, only the smouldering
glitter of anger in his eyes revealing his irritation at her
behaviour. 'Wait here. I won't be long.'

He was gone about ten minutes and by the time he

came back, this time accompanied by Luis, Catherine was fretting to be off. 'José's going to be all right,' he informed her shortly, smoothing his hair with a careless hand. 'And Luis has come to offer his gratitude. Thanks to you his father is not going to die.'

'I—thanks to Dr Alvares,' Catherine murmured in some embarrassment as the boy warmly shook her hand. 'I didn't do much, honestly. But I'm glad your father's going to get well. He's much too young to die.'

'And much too important,' put in Luis fervently. 'Without José Rodolfo, the movement would falter and die, also. Isn't that so, Armand? My father *is* the only chance for our people.'

Armand made some corresponding comment, but Catherine was scarcely listening to him. Her mind had focussed on the two words, *José Rodolfo*, and she stared at Luis as if he had taken leave of his senses.

'Your—father—is—*José Rodolfo*?' she exclaimed, in disbelief, and Luis nodded eagerly.

'You did not know?' he cried. 'But, yes. The man whose life you helped to save last evening is our beloved leader.' He turned to Armand. 'You had no need to keep it a secret, my friend. Sister Catherine will not betray us. By coming here and helping us, she has declared her allegiance.'

Catherine, exchanging a protesting look with Armand, recognised the silent warning he was offering her. Don't say any more, he cautioned wordlessly. Don't make any foolhardy claims here. Don't accuse anybody of anything you can't prove—unless you're prepared to face the consequences.

Pressing her lips together, Catherine looked away from his stern expression and concentrated instead on the bandages that circled her feet. They were something else she would have to explain, she realised inconsequentially, wondering how sympathetic Reverend Mother would be if she ever learned one of her novices had helped in an operation on the guerrilla leader. Not very sympathetic at all, Catherine surmised, acknowledging for the first time that she would not be able to tell the *whole* truth in this connection. Armand should have told her it was José Rodolfo he was treating, she frowned, and not allowed her to think it was simply one of his men. In those circumstances, she might have found it in her heart to be generous. As it was, he had placed her in an impossible position, and there was nothing she could do about it.

'The driver is waiting,' Armand interrupted her now, and she looked almost blankly into his face. 'I thought you were in a hurry,' he reminded her shortly, gesturing expressionlessly towards the exit, and Catherine hastily gathered her wits and preceded him outside.

The air was cool, a mist compounded by the rain of the night before causing a smoky cloud to rise from the ground around them. Catherine shivered and, without a word, Armand pulled off his sweater and draped it round her shoulders. 'I'd hate you to catch cold on my account,' he responded dismissively, when she made an involuntary protest. 'Keep it. It'll be even cooler when we get moving.'

Swallowing her pride, Catherine drew the loosely-hanging sleeves of the sweater around her, trying to ignore the warm male scent of his body it exuded. It reminded her too strongly of what had happened that morning, and it was impossible to dissociate the mental image of their intimacy from the man standing sombrely in front of her.

Meanwhile, Armand had turned to Luis and

appeared to be giving him instructions in their own language. Listening to their rapid exchange, Catherine couldn't help wishing she understood what they were saying, and when the boy cast a speculative look in her direction, she was convinced they were talking about her.

The arrival of the Land-Rover cut short any prolonged farewells. With a faint smile, Catherine accepted Luis's gratitude once again, and then scrambled up on to the seat for the bone-shaking ride back to the pass. Armand swung up beside her, this time positioning himself beside the door, and Catherine leant past him to wave at the boy as they started off through the rows of tents.

'What about the oxygen cylinders?' she asked suddenly, realising Armand was only cradling his medical bag between his knees.

'They'll be returned later,' he responded carelessly, putting his arm along the back of the seat as they began the slow climb out of the canyon. 'As I may have to carry you for the last leg of our journey, I decided not to push my luck.'

Catherine's head swung round. 'You won't have to carry me!' she declared.

'Won't I?' Armand's eyes were disturbingly intent. 'And how do you propose to explain the blisters on your feet, particularly if they're bleeding again?'

Catherine coloured. 'How am I going to explain any of this?' she retorted defensively. 'I've realised I can hardly tell Reverend Mother where I've been.'

'You reassure me.' Armand was sardonic. 'I'm glad you came to that decision on your own. I'd hate to have had to persuade you.'

Catherine frowned. 'Persuade me? How could you do that?'

'There are ways.' As the Land-Rover started its progress across the rocky mesa, Armand's hand closed firmly on her shoulder, preventing her from being thrown against the driver, but Catherine pulled angrily away from him.

'How would you persuade me?' she persisted, glad the young man behind the wheel couldn't understand their exchange. She paused. 'You weren't—you weren't planning on telling Reverend Mother we—we—'

'—spent the night together? *Slept* together?' inquired Armand mockingly. His lips twitched in infuriating self-possession. 'No, that was not what I had in mind.'

'Well,' Catherine took a deep breath, 'I don't see how else you could hope to achieve my silence.'

'Don't you?' Armand regarded her lazily. 'You know, I could think from that that you wanted me to tell her.'

'You're not serious!' Catherine gasped. 'I just don't see how you hoped to blackmail me, that's all.'

'Blackmail you?' Armand gave a short laugh. '*Sister* Catherine, where do you get your ideas from?'

He was teasing her, but Catherine was in no mood for his mocking cynicism, and she turned her head to stare broodingly through the windscreen, biting her lips in frustration.

'All right.' Armand shifted beside her, his thigh brushing familiarly against hers. 'I'll tell you what I meant. I should have had to rely on your—*como se diz?*—your tender heart, hmm?'

'What do you mean?'

Catherine was confused, and more than that, she was desperately trying to ignore the physical sensations his prolonged nearness was provoking. In spite of her efforts to stay away from him, it was impossible to ignore the warmth of his body beside her, particularly when the removal of his sweater had exposed that he was only wearing a cotton body-shirt beneath. She had a treacherous longing to abandon her self-restraint and allow herself to be cushioned against his chest, to allow the muscled arm resting on the back of her seat to protect her from the buffeting motion of the Land-Rover, but she fought against it. Even though, after the night they had spent together, it was foolish to cling to the conventions, she forced herself to do so realising, though she was hardly aware of its significance just then, that such indulgence could be dangerous.

Armand shrugged now, tolerating her propriety with easy indifference. 'You remember Julio don't you?' he suggested softly. 'Your first taste of real nursing?'

'The boy in the ward?' Catherine forced herself to concentrate on what he was saying. 'Yes, I remember him. Has something happened to him? He's not worse, is he?'

Armand shook his head. 'So far as I know, he's making good progress.'

'Well?' Catherine frowned.

Armand hesitated. 'You—you wouldn't like to think of what would happen if Major Enriques learned his true identity, would you?'

Catherine blinked, and then lunged wildly for the front of the cab as the Land-Rover swayed recklessly over a jutting outcrop. The tyres squealed in protest as the driver was forced to apply his brakes, and they skidded sideways for several yards before he managed to get the vehicle under control.

'*Perdão, senhor,*' the young soldier apologised profusely, his thin face flushed with embarrassment, and while Armand made some sympathetic comment, Catherine shuffled awkwardly back on to the seat.

'Are you all right?' Armand inquired, as she nervously smoothed her hair, and Catherine nodded.

'Perfectly, thank you,' she responded stiffly, folding her hands in her lap once again. 'I—what were you saying about Julio?' She swallowed. 'Surely, you weren't suggesting *I* might be tempted to report him.'

'No.' Armand expelled his breath evenly. 'I might.'

CHAPTER SIX

BEFORE Catherine could voice the protest that sprang instinctively to her lips, the Land-Rover began to slow down, and she saw, somewhat dazedly, that they had reached the pass where they had joined the vehicle the night before.

'I believe this is where we get off,' Armand remarked pleasantly, swinging himself down to the ground. 'Come on. Say goodbye to Manoel. *Até a vista, meu amigo. Adeus!*'

Still puzzling over what Armand had said, Catherine smiled at the young soldier before lowering her feet carefully to the ground. Armand made no attempt to help her, waiting until she was safely standing beside him before banging once on the side of the vehicle and lifting his arm in farewell. '*Cuidado,* Manoel, take care,' he called, as the Land-Rover swung round in a semi-circle to go back the way it had come, and the boy took his hand from the wheel to give them a salute.

Left alone with Armand, Catherine looked about her a trifle anxiously. The night before, darkness had cloaked the rugged slopes below them, and she had been so intent on keeping up with him and their escort that she had had no time to worry about the dangers of the climb. But now, with daylight turning the peaks of the sierras high above them crimson, and a damp-laden breeze whistling eerily around them, she viewed their situation with fading confidence. It seemed a long way down into the valley, the roofs of

Batistamajor barely visible above the swirling curtain of mist that rose from the river.

'Shall we go?' inquired Armand in her ear, and she glanced up at him half appealingly.

'Did we really climb up here?' she exclaimed, trying not to look too obviously at her feet, and Armand nodded.

'It'll be easier going down,' he assured her drily, starting down the scree-strewn track. 'Come on. We're wasting time. Be thankful for the mist. We may be glad of its protection.'

Closing her mind to all the horrible injuries she could sustain, Catherine went after him, concentrating instead on the majestic scenery around them. At this hour of the morning, the mountains had a cruel beauty, and their isolation was such, she and Armand might have been the only humans in an alien world. There was little vegetation up here: just now and then a plant, seeded by the wind, struggled to survive its transplantation. Even the cacti were few and far between, their prickly profiles adding to the illusions of the landscape.

By the time they reached the terraced slopes above the village, Catherine was barely able to put one foot in front of the other, and Armand, whose eyes had frequently observed her studied progress, came to an abrupt halt.

'Whether you like it or not, I'm going to have to carry you,' he declared, loosening his belt and threading it through the strap of the bag he had been carrying. After securing it in front of his body, he turned to Catherine. 'If I kneel down, do you think you could get on to my back?'

Catherine quivered. 'I'm too heavy,' she said, drawing back, and Armand's mouth tightened.

'Can you go on?' he demanded sharply, and she took a gulp of air.

'I'll have to, won't I?'

'Or be left behind,' he agreed, without compassion. 'Look—it's getting late. Do you want Major Enriques to find out where we've been?'

Catherine hesitated. 'You—you could go on—'

'—and have you picked up by one of the patrols, wearing my clothes?' he inquired grimly. '*Por Deus*, Catherine, get on my back, or do you want me to carry you over my shoulder?'

She had little choice but to obey. Her feet were hurting so badly she was not even sure she would be able to perform her normal duties at the convent, always assuming she could go back there. With a feeling of inadequacy, she put her hands on Armand's shoulders, and as he squatted down in front of her, she carefully eased herself on to his back. His hands gripping her thighs thrust her more firmly into position, the hard bones of his hips providing a natural resting place, but even so her arms slipped round his neck in sudden panic as he plunged down the grassy sward. She had never ridden on anyone's back before, and he seemed to be moving so fast. Besides which, she seemed so far from the ground, and unconsciously her groping hands invaded the unbuttoned neck of his shirt.

She knew what she had done as soon as her fingers encountered the fine whorls of dark hair that grew down to his navel and beyond. She had seen him without a shirt the night before, and she remembered only too well her own response to his unclothed body. Now, however, she withdrew her hands to a safer position, though her fingertips still tingled from that unsanctioned intimacy.

The smell of smoke and the lowing of animals warned them they were near the village. As they descended into the valley, the mist had thickened, enveloping them in its damp shroud, but now the walls of adobe cottages loomed out of the gloom. Catherine wondered if Armand would put her down now, but he didn't. Instead, he circled the outlying dwellings to the east and approached the village from the river, giving anyone who saw them the impression they had come from the opposite direction. Not until they were within yards of his bungalow did he allow her to slide to the ground, and she looked up at him rather ruefully as she recognised her surroundings.

'Thanks,' she murmured, stepping gingerly away from him and he stalked past her to open the door.

'*De nada*,' he said brusquely, stepping back to allow her to precede him inside, and she thought it was a sign of his impatience that he spoke to her in Portuguese.

Santo was in the kitchen preparing coffee, and Catherine thought she had never smelt anything so delicious as the pungent aroma of the percolating beans. It was so long since she had tasted anything other than milk or water, and her tongue moved revealingly over her dry lips.

'Are you hungry?' asked Armand, after exchanging a few words with his man-servant, but Catherine managed to find the will to shake her head.

'I—have to get back,' she ventured, trying to evade his searching gaze. 'I'll get changed.'

'I'll dress your feet again before you leave,' he stated abruptly, and at her wide-eyed look of protest, he added: 'Unless you want to get blood poisoning.'

Catherine sighed. 'What time is it?'

'A little after seven.'

'*Seven!*' Her cry was despairing. 'Oh, good heavens! What am I going to tell them?'

'We'll worry about that later,' declared Armand, taking her by the arm and hustling her along the passage to his surgery. '*Dois cafés*, Santo, *por favor*,' he ordered, and although Catherine's knowledge of his language was limited, she knew that he had asked for two coffees.

His surgery was small but quite extensively equipped, and after he had directed her to sit in the chair opposite his desk and start removing the soiled dressings, he disappeared to fill a stainless steel dish with clean water. Catherine tackled the task he had given her with some misgivings. Apart from the fact that she was nervous and that her hands shook as she unwound the grubby bandages, it was a painful operation, and by the time he returned, her eyes were filled with tears.

'I know,' she said, as he squatted down before her and cast a speculative look in her direction, 'I'm a baby.' She sniffed and dashed a smear of dampness from her cheek. 'But it hurts. It really hurts. And—and I'm not much good at hiding my feelings.'

'I had noticed,' he remarked drily, as the old Indian came in carrying two mugs of coffee. '*Cá*, Santo,' he ordered, gesturing at the desk beside Catherine, and the man set the cups down within reach of her hand. '*Obrigado.*'

After Santo had gone, Armand removed the last of the dressings and plunged her feet into the bowl of cool water. It stung abominably, not least because he had put disinfectant into the water, and while she was taking short little breaths to ease the pain, he put one of the mugs of coffee into her hands.

'I'd add something to it, if it wouldn't linger on your

breath,' he remarked, swallowing a mouthful of his own coffee. 'Go on. Drink it. You know you're dying to do so.'

'I—I don't.'

'I know that.' Armand sighed, his expression hardening again. 'But after what you've been through, I think you deserve the small amount of caffeine you're likely to absorb from one cup of coffee, don't you?'

Catherine lifted her shoulders. 'I don't deserve anything,' she murmured unhappily, and his mouth compressed as he got to his feet.

'Look,' he said shortly, 'I'm trying to be tolerant with you, but you don't make it easy. For God's sake, if you're so convinced of your depravity, why don't you go and throw yourself into the river!'

Catherine caught her breath. 'What a thing to suggest!'

'Cruel, wasn't it?' he replied unfeelingly, and then, seeing the wounded look that entered her eyes at his words, he dropped down on to his haunches again before her. 'I'm sorry,' he muttered, putting his free hand on her knee and squeezing her leg through the cloth. 'I didn't mean it. I was only—how you would say?—letting off steam, *não*? I'm afraid I don't have much time for religious paranoia!'

Catherine knew she should protest that she was not paranoic, that the feelings of self-persecution she was nurturing were properly deserved, but she didn't. She was far too concerned with her reactions to his fingers gripping her leg, their hard strength creating a warmth that she could not ignore. Dear God, she thought in dismay, she wanted him to touch her. Her strongest impulse at that moment was to put her hand over his and hold it there. But instead, she stiffened under his caress, and sensing her withdrawal, he put his coffee cup aside and bent to examine her feet.

'This is going to be painful for the next few days,' he asserted, after dabbing her feet dry with a coarse towel. 'I don't know how the hell you expect to walk around. What you really need is several days in the hospital.'

'I can't do that—'

'I'm not suggesting you can,' he acceded shortly, unscrewing the cap of a bottle of white ointment. 'All I am saying is, you may find it impossible to continue as you were before.'

Catherine caught her lower lip between her teeth. 'I still don't know what I'm going to tell Reverend Mother,' she fretted. 'Do you think they'll believe me?'

'I guess it depends what you're going to tell them,' Armand responded indifferently, though his fingers were amazingly gentle as he smoothed some of the antiseptic ointment on to the blisters. 'You could always pretend you'd been abducted.'

'Abducted?' Catherine's eyes were wide, and Armand looked up at her sardonically. 'By whom?' she added and, without thinking, took a doubtful mouthful from the mug in her hand.

Armand shook his head. 'By the guerrillas, I suppose,' he replied carelessly, as she suddenly realised what she had done. 'Unless you want to involve Major Enriques, of course.'

'I couldn't do that!'

'No.' Armand was matter-of-fact. 'That's why I suggested the guerrillas. And you might as well finish that,' he added, nodding at the mug of coffee. 'You're committed now, aren't you?'

Catherine immediately put the mug aside and faced

him. 'Why would the guerrillas abduct me?' she demanded tautly. 'I couldn't help them.'

'You have to be joking!' Armand propped her foot on his knee and, after securing a pad of gauze in place, he started winding a fresh bandage around it. Then he looked up at her quizzically: 'You are joking, aren't you?'

Catherine flushed. 'Even—even the guerrillas respect a nun.'

'Rodolfo's men may,' Armand conceded, fastening the end of the bandage with the use of a small safety-pin. 'But don't imagine your habit makes you any less of a woman to a desperate man.'

Catherine sighed. 'Well—I can't say that anyway.'

'No?'

'No.' She lifted her shoulders. 'It would cause too many awkward questions to be asked.'

'What about?'

'Oh—' She closed her eyes against his discerning stare. 'You know.'

Armand pondered. 'You think they might inquire into your—experiences?'

Catherine opened her eyes again. 'You know they would.'

Armand shifted his attention to her other foot and frowned. 'I gather you couldn't bluff it out then?'

Catherine tensed. 'There's no need to be offensive.'

'What is offensive about that?' Armand repeated the treatment with the ointment, and Catherine's whole leg tingled. Keeping his eyes on his task, he persisted: 'You were—how old, when you left England? Sixteen? Seventeen?'

'I was eighteen, actually,' retorted Catherine shortly. 'What has my age to do with anything?'

'Well—' Armand paused consideringly. 'Correct me

if I am wrong, but aren't English girls of that age usually—quite knowledgeable about sex?'

Catherine caught her breath. 'How would you know?' she countered tautly, and then wished she hadn't spoken so impulsively when his eyes turned up to hers again.

'I have been to Europe,' he commented mildly. 'I know London well, as a matter of fact. I did my initial training there.'

Catherine bent her head. 'I see.'

'So, you understand, I am not merely quoting hearsay.' He shrugged his broad shoulders. 'English girls do have more freedom than their contemporaries here.'

Catherine had no response to make to this, and after a moment Armand completed his task and rose to his feet. Finishing his own coffee, he thrust the mug aside and then regarded her intently, his golden eyes sombre as they mirrored her anxiety.

'Well,' he said at last, when she had made no attempt to get out of the chair, 'you're free to go, if that's what you want!' and she hurriedly slipped her feet into her sandals and got up.

'I have to change,' she said tensely, moving round him to the door, and he inclined his head.

'You know where your things are,' he responded bleakly, and she went out the door and along the passage to his bedroom, trying desperately not to limp.

Her pale features looked back at her from the scratched mirror above a chest of drawers and, on impulse, Catherine moved nearer. It was months since she had seen her reflection in anything more substantial than her washing water, and she gazed with some misgivings at her hollow cheeks. She had lost weight, she saw, and her hair was much longer than she had imagined. With trembling fingers, she threaded it into a single plait that fell a good way towards her waist, and then finding a hairpin in the pocket of her habit, she coiled it in a knot at her nape. At least she looked less abandoned with her hair severely confined, she thought, pushing her hands through the sleeveless armholes of the cotton undergarment she wore beneath her habit. But it had been good to feel like a woman again, she mused, even in Armand's clothes, though her mouth went dry at the implied intimacy. Turning, she saw the sweater he had put around her shoulders at the camp, and after only a momentary hesitation, she picked it up and raised it to her cheek. It smelled of soap and aftershave, and the lingering scent of his skin, and she was suddenly back in the tent, awakening in his arms. She had felt so snug and secure there: so content, until he had awakened, too. Then, when he had looked at her, she had experienced a totally different sensation, a palpitating awareness, that had sent the blood pounding through her veins like liquid fire. It was sinful, she knew, but she hadn't really wanted him to let her go. Oh, she had told herself she did, and when her chance came, she had taken it; but standing here, a prey to her scornful conscience, she could not deny the painful truth that she had wanted him to kiss her.

'Are you ready?'

A sharp tap at the door followed by the handle being turned brought her abruptly out of her reverie, and she called out in panic: 'No. No, I'm not dressed yet. Don't come in.'

'The mist's clearing,' said Armand's voice from outside. 'If you don't want to be observed leaving my house, you'd better hurry up.'

'Oh—Oh, yes.' Catherine dropped his sweater, and picked up her habit. 'I won't be a minute. I'm almost through.'

It was as she was putting on the habit that the first feeling of nausea swept over her. Swaying dizzily, she had to pause until the awful sense of sickness departed, and by the time she was fit to continue, Armand had knocked at the door again.

'Are you okay?' he called, some impatience evident in his voice now. 'Look—if your feet are really painful, I think you're going to have to tell someone.'

'I'm all right.' Tying the cord of her robe about her, Catherine made her way across the room and opened the door. Facing him bravely, she tilted her chin. 'Thank you for your concern,' she added, steadily. 'But I can manage.'

Armand regarded her consideringly for a moment, and then he said shortly: 'I've had an idea.'

Catherine blinked. 'An idea?'

'Yes.' Armand pushed his hands into the back of his belt, the action drawing Catherine's unwilling attention to the gaping neck of his shirt. 'How does the thought of your being a runaway appeal to you?'

'A runaway?' Catherine stared at him.

'Yes.' Armand bit his lower lip thoughtfully for a moment. Then, he went on: 'It could fit the facts.'

'What facts?'

'Your being here, for a start,' declared Armand flatly. 'And those blisters on your feet. Not to mention the dressings.'

Catherine shook her head. 'Why would I be here, if I'd run away?' She caught her breath. 'You're not suggesting I came to you!'

'Heaven forfend!' he exclaimed, the mockery in his eyes not entirely good-humoured. 'No, of course I'm not suggesting any such thing. But I could have found you this morning, when I was on my way to visit a patient, and brought you back here to attend to your—injuries.'

Catherine gazed at him, the simple strength of his argument too fundamental to be ignored. 'You mean—you would say you found me some distance from the village?'

'Yes.'

'I—Sister Angelica would never believe you.'

'Why not? What reason would she have for thinking otherwise?'

'I don't know.' Catherine shifted anxiously in front of him. 'Reverend Mother already suspects you have sympathy with the rebels.'

'But she would never think that of you,' Armand inserted evenly. 'Not with—the men who murdered your father.'

Catherine gasped. 'But you said—'

'And I meant it. José was not behind your father's killing.' Armand breathed deeply. 'However, it will suit our purpose for Reverend Mother—and Sister Angelica—to believe differently.'

Catherine's tongue circled her lips. 'Do you think they might believe me?'

He shrugged. 'As you say, what other conclusion could they come to?'

That you were attracted to me; that you invited me to your house; that we spent the night together, a wicked voice inside her taunted unrelentingly, making a mockery of her pleas for remission. But, thankfully, Armand could not hear her anxiety, and besides, the wave of weakness that suddenly gripped her cast aside all other considerations. Sickness rose like bile in the back of her throat, the bitter taste of the coffee she had swallowed leaving her pale and wretched, and as she struggled to control her heaving stomach, Armand took her arm into his grasp.

'What is it?' he demanded. 'What's wrong? Do you feel ill?'

'No.' Catherine could not permit him to take charge of the situation again, no matter how attractive that proposition might be. 'I—I expect I'm hungry. And—and the coffee—I'm not used to it.'

'You hardly drank enough to upset you,' retorted Armand, allowing her to withdraw from his grasp. 'But you may be right about the hunger. I suggest you change your mind and have some breakfast, after all.'

'No.' Surprisingly, the idea of food was quite abhorrent to her and, shaking her head, she made a determined effort towards taking her leave. 'Honestly, I'll be all right. I—thank you for your professional services. My feet feel much better already.'

Armand went after Catherine as she started down the thinly-carpeted passageway, exchanging an exasperated look with his man-servant before overtaking her. 'Look,' he said, his outstretched arm preventing her from opening the outer door, 'don't you think your story would carry more weight if I drove you back to the convent? I mean, I'm hardly likely to have attended to your feet and then made you walk there, am I?'

Catherine hesitated. 'I don't know . . .'

'Well, I do,' declared Armand tersely, turning her round to face the way she had come. 'And legitimate visitors use the front entrance, don't they? If you'll follow me, I'll show you the way.'

By the time Armand's mud-smeared station wagon entered the convent gates, Catherine was a quivering mass of nerves. How could she confess to Reverend

Mother that she had run away? she asked herself unhappily. What reason could she give for doing so? And how could she tell Sister Angelica she had spent the night hiding out in the countryside when it was supposed to be crawling with Rodolfo's guerrillas? What could she say to satisfy their questions? How could she justify her behaviour? And what was infinitely more troubling, how could she hope to tell so many lies, and still expect the Almighty to forgive her?

'Stop looking so terrified!' Armand commanded in a low voice beside her. Turning his head, he met her tremulous gaze with hard-eyed inflexibility. 'If the worst comes to the worst, you can always blame me,' he added harshly. 'Tell them—tell them I enticed you away because I desired your body!'

Catherine stared at him. 'I couldn't do that!' she exclaimed, blushing anew beneath his relentless appraisal.

'Why not?'

She bent her head. 'It wouldn't be true.'

'None of this is. *Qué diabo!* My immortal soul is already beyond redemption, according to Mother Benedicta.'

'Even so—'

'Even so—what?' He allowed the knuckles of his right hand to graze her cheek lightly and she drew back in alarm. 'Like you said,' he murmured lazily, 'you have shared my bed.'

Catherine swallowed. 'Just because we slept together—'

'We didn't *sleep* together,' he interrupted her softly. 'We may have shared the same bed, but that's not the same as sleeping together, believe me.'

'You would know, of course,' she muttered impulsively, and his mouth took on a mocking slant.

'I do,' he assured her, bringing the station wagon to a halt before the vine-covered porch that marked the entrance to the main building. 'Now, I suggest we go and throw ourselves on Reverend Mother's mercy.'

'*We!*' Catherine gazed at him disbelievingly. 'You don't intend—'

'Why not?' Armand shrugged. 'I got you into this. The least I can do is get you out.'

'I—no. No, it's not necessary.' Catherine put her hand on his sleeve to detain him, and then withdrew it again as the realisation that they could be under surveillance made her glance anxiously about her. 'Please: I'd rather speak to Reverend Mother on my own.'

It was true. The idea of facing her superior in Armand's company didn't bear thinking about. She was sure she would never be able to sustain her story if he was looking on, and her colour would give her away, she was sure of it. Besides which, she was beginning to feel distinctly unwell, and if she was going to be sick, she didn't want him to know about it.

Armand hesitated, the dark golden eyes intent as he took in what she had said. Then, running a lazy hand into the neckline of his shirt, he lifted his shoulders, the dismissing gesture evidence of his decision to let her have her way.

'So be it,' he said at last, and she groped eagerly for the handle of the door. 'But—' his fingers suddenly grasped a handful of her skirt, imprisoning her beside him for a moment longer '—if you need me, you know where to find me.'

Catherine nodded, scrambling gratefully out on to the sun-warmed pavings of the porch, and Armand drove away. She watched until the dusty station wagon had turned out of the iron gates, and then she expelled her breath on a shaky sigh. She was on her own now, she acknowledged, wondering why that discovery no longer seemed so desirable, and then groaning weakly, she turned aside and was sick all over Sister Teresa's flower bed.

CHAPTER SEVEN

IT was very quiet in the tiny cubicle that opened off the main dormitory. Without the sounds that usually accompanied the nuns' waking and dressing, the low, narrow building was unnaturally still, and at this hour of the afternoon, even the birds' chatter was muted.

Lying on her thin mattress, Catherine tried to remember how many days it was since she had been there. Three or four, she supposed. But as no one had spoken to her in that time, she couldn't be absolutely sure. Her brain seemed to balk at any effort to think lucidly, and she had found it easier just to abandon the attempt. It was sufficient to know that it was some time since the nuns had been forbidden—on pain of excommunication—to exchange a word with the offender for a period of not less than twenty-eight days, depending, so Reverend Mother had said, on her behaviour during that time. The fact that Catherine had been so ill since the judgment was made had tempered the blow somewhat, even though her lonely isolation had mentally sapped her strength. If she hadn't possessed such a strong constitution, Catherine had the feeling she might not have had the will to recover at all. But perhaps that would have been easier all round, she speculated now, in one of her increasing bouts of melancholy. She was nothing but a nuisance, it seemed. The removal of her disruptive presence could only be an improvement.

She had experienced the gulf that had opened between herself and the other members of the order this morning, when Sister Margarita had come to change her bedding. Catherine was aware that her sheets had been changed many times since her body had at last succumbed to the infection which had swept through the convent, but never before had she been truly conscious of the resentment that caring for her had provoked. Until now she had been too ill to notice that the hands that sponged her body, and fed her broth, did so under duress; that the nuns, who had been her friends, and who had had sympathy for her, now regarded her as a turncoat, someone who had taken their kindness and thrown it back into their faces.

Of course, she hadn't realised what was wrong with her at first. Being sick over Sister Teresa's flower bed had seemed like an understandable reaction to the coming interview with Reverend Mother, and she had entered the convent superior's study quite prepared to face her punishment.

But, unknown to her, other forces had been working against her. Although she had succeeded in telling Mother Benedicta that she had left the convent of her own free will, she did not have time to explain why, or how, Dr Alvares came to be involved, before another bout of retching seized her. Instead, it was left to Sister Angelica to relate that she had seen Catherine return in the doctor's car, and the discovery of the bandages on her feet had been a silent corroboration. When Catherine eventually recovered herself sufficiently to recite the story Armand had concocted for her, it had been received in stony disbelief, and in spite of her blistered feet, she had felt their condemnation. No one had actually accused her of spending the night at the doctor's house—indeed, Catherine suspected even Reverend Mother had balked at such a conclusion—but her involvement with Armand Alvares had been noted, and she would be watched very closely for any further transgressions.

Even so, all that had had to be forgotten when Catherine's temperature had rapidly risen to a dangerous height. The fever that possessed her slender body left no room for other considerations, and her memories of that period were punctuated by losses of consciousness. She remembered bouts of uncontrollable shivering, when even the addition of several more blankets to her bed had failed to warm her, and other occasions, when even her thin shift had felt intolerably hot against her burning skin. She recollected her shame when she had discovered she was even incapable of controlling her simplest bodily functions, and she knew the smell of disinfectant and the remembered ministrations of ungentle hands would remain with her always.

Of course, her treatment had been overseen by Sister Angelica, not Dr Alvares. Such medication as she was given was administered by the senior tutor, her tight-lipped countenance a mirror to the contempt she felt towards her.

Nevertheless, it had still been a blow to discover the pariah she had innocently become. Until today, Catherine had suffered her punishment without resentment, but Sister Margarita's hostility had not been misconstrued. In fact, it explained other incidents which Catherine had put down to *her* state of mind, and the humiliations she remembered at other hands were no longer a figment of a feverish imagination. She had been judged, and condemned, without a word being spoken, and in her weakened condition, Catherine could not hold back the tears. She felt so alone, so utterly removed from the confident girl who had flown out to join her father less than eighteen months ago. In so short a time, her life had changed completely. She had become a liar and an outcast, despised by her superiors and ignored by the women she had thought were her friends. She was wicked; she had evil thoughts—or so Reverend Mother had told her. She had also been told that when she was able to leave her bed, she would be expected to kneel for long hours in the chapel, begging God's forgiveness for her sins. But not now; not yet. For the present she was too weak to do anything but lie here fretting over what might have been. She could do nothing to assuage the feelings of guilt inside her, and as she lifted her hand to scrub her knuckles across her eyes, its trembling was just another indication of how helpless she was.

'*Por Deus!* So this is where you are!'

The harsh male tones were so unexpected in the quiet dormitory that, in spite of their forcefulness, Catherine thought she was imagining them. Apart from anything else, no man, even the doctor, entered these predominantly female quarters, except in cases of dire emergency—and her illness was hardly that. Yet, as she drew her hands away from her eyes to gaze disbelievingly across the room, she saw it was Dr Alvares standing in the doorway to her small cubicle, his dark face eloquent of his angry intent.

'What the hell is going on here?' he demanded, advancing into the room, and Catherine put an unsteady hand out in front of her, as if to ward him off.

'No! No, you mustn't come here!' she protested weakly. 'You mustn't speak to me! I—I'm in retreat, until Reverend Mother says I can rejoin the order—'

'The hell you are!' Ignoring her feeble objections, Armand crossed the room in two strides and came down on the side of the bed beside her. 'My God!

You've had the fever, haven't you?' His hand swept with delicious coolness over her damp forehead. 'You're sweating!' His golden eyes darkened ominously. 'Is no one looking after you? This bed should be changed at least twice a day!'

'I can't talk to you,' Catherine insisted, as he took her limp wrist between his finger and thumb and checked her pulse. 'You don't understand,' she whispered, half afraid Sister Angelica might be lurking somewhere just outside. 'I'm in disgrace!'

'So what's new?' he retorted carelessly, tipping her face into the light, and she winced beneath his studied appraisal. 'How long have you been like this?'

Catherine shook her head, and then, succumbing to the impatience in his expression, she mumbled: 'Do you mean—here?'

'I mean, when were you taken ill?' Armand informed her flatly. 'I brought you back to the convent a week ago. Where have you been hiding yourself since then?'

'A week!' Catherine gazed at him blankly. 'I've been here a week?'

'Is that a statement, or a question?' demanded Armand roughly. 'For goodness' sake, you haven't been lying here for a week, have you?'

Catherine swallowed, trying to remember. 'I—I suppose I must have been,' she ventured at last. 'I'm not sure—'

The word he said then was not English, but its meaning was plain in any language, and his mouth compressed angrily as he rose to his feet. 'No wonder you look as you do!' he muttered, and Catherine blinked anxiously.

'How—how do I look?'

'Like a ghost!' he retorted savagely, turning towards

the door. 'I'm going to get you out of here right now. Take it easy. I'll be back—'

'No. No, you can't.' Her despairing cry arrested him. 'I can't go into the women's ward. No one's allowed to speak to me.'

'I don't intend to transfer you to the women's ward,' Armand responded tersely, pausing in the doorway. 'Like I said, I'll be right back—'

'But I don't understand . . .' Catherine propped herself up on her elbows, her head swimming with the effort. 'Where are you taking me?'

'To my house,' declared Armand shortly, daring her to contradict him. 'Unless you have an alternative.'

Catherine gasped and fell back. 'I can't go to your house.'

'Why not?'

She moved her head desperately from side to side. 'You know why.'

'Because Reverend Mother won't allow you to? Because it's unthinkable that you should disobey her rules?' His lips twisted. 'Forget it!'

'Rules are rules,' insisted Catherine weakly. 'I've not been neglected. I've received adequate treatment—'

'Adequate treatment!' Armand's fist balled against the frame of the door. 'Don't tell me anyone here cares whether you live or die! For pity's sake, how can they call themselves *Christians* and treat one of their own like this!'

Catherine shook her head. 'It's the discipline they live by.'

Armand stared at her. 'And is it the discipline you live by, also?'

Catherine's tongue circled her dry lips. 'It—it should be.'

'That's not what I asked.' Armand regarded her mercilessly. 'Are you content to sacrifice the rest of your life for a cause?'

Catherine closed her eyes. 'Don't ask me that.'

'Why not?'

'What else can I do?' She opened her eyes again. 'You'd better go. If Sister Angelica finds you here—'

'To hell with Sister Angelica!' declared Armand harshly, abandoning his stance by the door and coming towards the bed again. 'On second thoughts, I think I'll act first and answer questions later.' He stripped back the covers from Catherine's trembling body and considered her dispassionately. 'Now, do you have a robe or something you can put on? I don't want you contracting pneumonia on top of everything else.'

Catherine's hands moved futilely to protect her body as his eyes searched the room, and she groaned. 'You can't do this,' she whispered. 'I can't even walk. If anyone sees us—'

'Oh, I'm pretty sure someone will,' responded Armand carelessly, gesturing for her to sit up. 'Don't worry. As I told you before, my immortal soul was damned years ago.'

Catherine turned her head away from him, but her efforts to try and pull the covers over her again revealed her weakness. With a muffled oath, Armand squatted down beside her. Supporting her, with his arm beneath her shoulders, he managed to wrap a blanket from the bed round her, and then, ignoring her thinly-voiced protests, he lifted her up into his arms.

It was crazy but, in spite of everything, Catherine knew a treacherous sense of relief when Armand's arms closed about her. It was no use denying it any longer, she thought tremulously: she was glad she was leaving the convent; she wanted to be with ordinary people again. And most shamelessly of all, she wanted to be with Armand, and that was unforgivable.

'Can you put your arms around my neck?' he asked, his face only inches from hers, and she nodded. But the effort was tiring, and her head fell back against his shoulder as he carried her out of the tiny cubicle, through the main dormitory, and out into the sunlight.

Three days later, Catherine was strong enough to get up for the first time. She was still very weak, and uncertain of her legs, but with Maria's help she was able to put on Armand's bathrobe over her shift and leave the bed to sit for a while in the basket-woven chair by the window. It was very pleasant by the window, a playful breeze toying with the end of her braid and the scent of bougainvillea drifting to her nostrils. She might almost think she was well again, the beauty of the day encouraging an entirely artificial belief in her own strength. But the journey from the bed to the chair had proved more arduous than she could have imagined, and she was quite content to recline there on the cushions, her hands hanging limply over the arms.

'Is well?' inquired Maria anxiously, her few words of English hardly covering the things she wanted to say, but Catherine understood.

'I'm fine, thank you, Maria,' she murmured, forcing a faint smile to her lips as she met the Indian girl's gaze. 'Really. I'll just sit here for a while. You can leave me.'

Maria hesitated, but she had things to do, and

presently she slipped out of the room. A few moments later, Catherine heard her speaking with Santo, no doubt issuing him with more of her orders backed by Armand's support, and Catherine's lips curved irrepressibly at the thought of Santo's reactions.

Things had certainly changed around the doctor's house since she had come to stay, she reflected ruefully. Maria's intervention must have seemed like the last straw so far as the old man-servant was concerned. He had not been able to hide his disapproval when Armand had brought Catherine to the house, and the subsequent employment of Maria, in the joint capacity of nurse-cum-housekeeper, had really put him out of countenance.

For her part, Catherine had been in no fit state to object to any arrangements Armand might make. She remembered little after leaving the convent beyond being deposited in a comfortable bed and given an injection. By the time she was alert enough to understand the reasons for the bitter arguments that occasionally erupted between Santo and her nurse, Maria had been firmly installed, and more importantly, proud of her position.

It hadn't taken Catherine long to realise she was occupying Armand's bed, however. She recognised the room immediately, even without the photograph of the boy which had previously stood on the bedside table. Armand's identity was imprinted upon it, and when he came the next morning to examine her, she had expressed her concern at dislodging him.

'Where are you sleeping?' she protested, despising the weakness that prevented her from vacating his quarters, and Armand smiled.

'There are other bedrooms,' he informed her, pulling back the covers to her waist. 'Now—how do I get beneath this thing?' He indicated the high-necked shift with gentle irony. 'I need to examine your chest, and we seem to have a problem.'

Her embarrassment at exposing herself to his gaze, professional or otherwise, prevented Catherine from making any further comments at that time, and when next he came to see her, Maria was with him. Since then, he had examined her every day, both morning and night, his touch and manner totally dispassionate. The only time they had discussed anything other than her physical condition was once when Catherine had heard the telephone ringing and questioned its presence. It seemed an unnecessary extravagance in a place where survival itself was at a premium, and Armand had explained it had been installed for the benefit of the bungalow's previous tenant.

'An army colonel by the name of Sanchez used to be quartered here,' he remarked, his hands cool and impersonal as he removed the thermometer from her mouth. 'When I was appointed as medical officer to the garrison stationed in Batistamajor, I was entitled to accommodation.' He shook the thermometer and replaced it in its metal case. 'Hence the luxury.'

For Catherine, still uncertain of how wise she had been to leave the convent, Armand's detachment was strangely disappointing. She didn't know what she had expected exactly, but after his anger the day he had brought her here, she had anticipated he would, at least, talk to her. They had things to talk about, not least what Catherine was going to do once she was well again. Remembering Reverend Mother's words about her selfishness and ingratitude, she had no illusions that she might be readmitted to the order, even had she wanted to be. The Sisters of the Convent of the Assumption had given up on her, and it was hard not to panic when she thought about the future. She couldn't live on Armand's charity indefinitely. Sooner or later, she would have to find a job. But where? And how? And with whom?

These were the anxieties she had wanted to discuss with him, but she had had no opportunity. Armand's behaviour did not encourage confidences. He was considerate, but impersonal; reassuring, but remote. He was gentle, and attentive to her condition, but no more so than he had been to the patients in the hospital. And what did she expect, after all? she asked herself fiercely, blinking back the sudden sting of tears. Just because he had felt sorry for her did not imply any emotional attachment towards her. She was fooling herself if she imagined a man like Armand Alvares would see her as anything more than a necessary encumbrance.

Taking a deep breath, she tried to concentrate on the antics of a small lizard as it ran swiftly up the bark of a flowering acacia. Its movements were sure and determined, and she wished her future looked as certain. Her most sensible course would be to return to England, but in spite of her anxieties, she had no wish to go back. It was crazy when she had no ties in Surajo— when she didn't even understand Portuguese—but she didn't want to leave. Perhaps she wouldn't have to, she thought, with sudden inspiration. Perhaps Armand would let her stay and help him. She knew the rudiments of nursing; she knew how to change a dressing or administer drugs; she could certainly change sheets and sterilise bedpans. There must be something she could do to make herself useful, once she had shaken off this awful feeling of weakness.

The sound of the bedroom door opening brought her head round with a start, but her expression lost some of its animation at the realisation it was only Maria, come to see if she was all right.

'I'm fine, thank you,' she said, forcing a faint smile to her lips. 'I—did Dr Alvares get back yet? Would you—ask him to come and see me when he comes in?'

'*Sim, senhorita.*' Maria bobbed her head. '*O senhor is*—how you say?—giving the *chuveiro.*'

'*Chuveiro?*' Catherine frowned. 'Oh—you mean shower; he's *taking* a shower!' Her pulse quickened. 'He is home, then.'

'*Sim, senhorita.* I will tell him what you said.'

'I—*no*! No, don't bother.' Catherine's nerve had suddenly deserted her. 'I—er—I'll speak to him later—'

She broke off abruptly as Armand himself appeared at that moment. Dark and attractive, the beads of moisture still sparkling on the smooth vitality of his hair, he came into the room behind the Indian girl, immediately silencing both of them. In a black silk shirt and matching suede pants he looked both remote and unapproachable, yet the aura of raw masculinity that accompanied him was unmistakable.

'So—am I interrupting something?' he inquired, pausing at the end of the bed to rest both hands on the iron rail. 'You wished to speak to me, Catherine?' he persisted, his golden eyes definitely guarded. 'Or did I misunderstand what you were saying?'

'I go,' said Maria abruptly, hurrying towards the door as Catherine endeavoured to find an answer. 'I bring tea. Fifteen minutes, *senhorita.*'

The door closed behind her with a distinct click, and while Catherine took several breaths to calm herself, Armand pushed his hands into the pockets of his pants and strolled towards the open window.

'What's the matter, Catherine?' he asked, without looking at her, keeping his eyes on the swaying blossom outside. 'Surely, whatever it is you have to say can be said without so much soul-searching. I'm pleased to see you're feeling so much better. Maria told me you were out of bed, and I came to offer my congratulations.'

Catherine's tongue circled her lips. 'Th—thank you. It—it's thanks to you, as you know.'

'Hardly that.' He turned then, looking down at her with a thin smile, and her colour deepened. 'You're stronger than you look, even if that robe does give you a waif-like air.' His eyes darkened. 'I hope you're not trying to find a way to tell me you want to go back to the convent. If you are, then I must say that I'm totally against it.'

'Oh, no!' Catherine quickly shook her head. 'I don't want to go back there.'

'I'm pleased to hear it.' Some of the severity went out of his expression as he came down on his haunches in front of her. 'I'd hate to think all my hard work had been to provide another pair of hands for Mother Benedicta.'

Catherine drew an unsteady breath. 'You don't like her, do you?'

'I don't like what she did to you,' he amended, taking her wrist between his forefinger and thumb and assuming a professional interest in his watch. 'And why is your pulse so irregular? Surely I don't frighten you that much!'

'You don't frighten me at all,' declared Catherine, snatching her wrist out of his grasp. 'You—startled me, that's all. Coming in here. I—I don't generally see you until after supper.'

'That's true.' Armand regarded her with sustained

attention, making no effort to get to his feet. 'But, as I said before, Maria told me you were feeling stronger, and I wanted to see for myself the progress you had made.'

Catherine averted her eyes. 'Well—you've seen,' she said awkwardly, feeling incapable of entering into any discussion with him at the moment. It was as if he was deliberately trying to disconcert her, and while his nearness was not unpleasant, his attitude confused her.

'Well?' he prompted at last, when she made no attempt to speak to him. 'Was I wrong? Was it Santo you wished to have words with?'

'Santo?' Catherine's eyes darted up to meet his.

'You said, I'll speak to *him* later,' Armand reminded her softly. 'If it wasn't me, it must have been Santo.'

Catherine lowered her eyes again. 'It doesn't matter.'

'What doesn't matter?'

Catherine sighed. 'What I was going to say.'

'I disagree.' With light, yet assured, fingers, Armand captured her hand between both of his, his thumbs brushing delicately over the veins on the inner side of her wrist. 'Something is troubling you. I can tell. Now, why don't you tell me what it is, so we can sort it out together?'

Catherine quivered, his hard fingers sending ripples of awareness from her fingertips all the way up her arms. As he squatted there before her, she couldn't help but notice the taut muscles of his legs, outlined beneath the close-fitting cloth of his pants, and the way the silk shirt clung to his moist skin. The clean smell of the soap he had been using in the shower had mingled with the warm scent of his flesh, evoking an image of his lean body, unclothed, turning beneath the spray. Although he was holding her hand almost absently, his arms resting easily along his thighs, his playful fingers were provoking a devastating response, and her breathing quickened helplessly as he waited for her reply.

'I—oh, please—' she tried to withdraw her hand without success '—it was nothing important. Honestly.' She looked down at his possession of her hand and felt the heat spreading over her body. 'Please: Maria will be back soon. Do you want her to wonder what's going on?'

'I don't particularly care what Maria thinks,' he replied succinctly, turning her hand palm upwards and surveying its smooth vulnerability without compassion. 'So soft,' he said harshly. 'So pale and slender. Who would believe this hand has scrubbed floors and scoured bedpans? It looks as if it's never done a day's work in its life.'

'Dr Alvares—'

'Yes?' He was still contemplating his discovery.

'I—' Catherine broke off to steady her voice. 'I—wanted to ask you about that.'

'About what?'

'About—about my working for you,' said Catherine, with a rush. 'You—you must need some help here. I know I'm not much good, as yet, but I can learn, and I'm willing to do anything I can to be of assistance. I can wash sheets and strip beds. I can even change dressings, if they're not too difficult, and keep records and handle medication—'

'Wait a minute!' Armand's harsh voice interrupted her flow, his golden eyes darkening perceptibly as they lifted to her face. 'What are you talking about? Since when have I given you the impression that I expect you to work for me?'

Catherine caught her breath. 'You haven't, of course.'

'So?'

'Oh—' She shook her head. 'I can't go on—living on your charity.'

'No?'

'No.' Catherine pressed her lips together for a moment, and then continued unhappily: 'I thought that if—if you would let me work for you . . .' Her voice trailed away. 'It was just an idea.'

'Just an idea,' he echoed softly. 'I see.'

Catherine drew a trembling breath. 'You've been very kind to me. I thought—I thought it was a way I could repay you . . .'

Armand's eyes turned back to consider her trapped fingers. 'And this was what you were asking Maria to tell me?' he inquired in a low voice.

'No. That is—yes, it was what I was going to say when I saw you. But, I didn't mention it to Maria. Only that I wanted to speak to you when you came home.' She paused. 'But you were already home—taking a shower.'

'Ah, yes.' Armand inclined his head. 'I enjoy a shower at the end of a hard day.' He lifted one hand and rubbed it reflectively against his cheek. 'And a shave, too, which I regret I did not have.' He paused and then, looking up at her, he deliberately lifted her hand and stroked it against his distinctly roughened jawbone. 'And I need a shave, don't I?' he murmured, holding her palm against his skin, and Catherine's lower limbs turned to water beneath the disturbing sensuality of his gaze.

'I—suppose so,' she got out unsteadily, feeling the faint bristle of his beard abusing her sensitised touch. But it was a sensuous abrasion, and when he removed his hand, her fingers lingered where he had placed them.

She didn't know what might have happened next had it not been for Maria's intervention. The Indian girl came bustling back into the room with the tea-tray after only the most perfunctory of knocks at the door, but even that short delay was sufficient for Armand to get abruptly to his feet and Catherine's hand to fall awkwardly back into her lap. By the time Maria had opened the door and entered the room, Armand was standing by the window again, his back to the room, and Catherine was wondering, with some embarrass-ment, whether he felt as foolish as she did. She doubted it. After all, in its least personal interpreta-tion, inviting her to confirm that he needed a shave was not something to get so worked up about. The foolishness had occurred when she had allowed her emotions to get the better of her, and he must have felt as impatient with her as she felt with herself now when she considered how idiotically she had con-tinued to stroke his cheek.

She half hoped he would depart now that Maria had brought the tea, but the girl had brought two cups, and at her bidding he turned. Taking the high-backed chair that stood near the door, he swung it round and straddled it, facing Catherine across the low table where Maria had placed the tray, and she was obliged to offer him refreshment.

'No milk, only lemon,' he informed Catherine politely, as Maria hovered, assuring herself that they had everything they needed. 'And no sugar,' he added, as her hand went towards the basin. 'Thank you. This is exactly what I need.'

Catherine suspected his comments were for Maria's benefit. She was pretty convinced that he would have preferred something cooler and longer, but his manners were impeccable. The Indian girl smiled with satisfaction that all was well, and then dismissed herself demurely, and left them to themselves.

Catherine poured her own tea, annoyed to see that her hands were unsteady. It was partly due to the weakness of her condition, she knew, but the knowledge of Armand's presence could not be dismissed, and she was glad when she could put her cup down again and return her attention to the lengthening shadows outside.

'You must not stay out of bed too long on your first day,' he remarked, after a few moments' silent observation, an observation she had not been unaware of. 'You must build up your strength slowly.'

Catherine tilted her head. 'I'm all right.'

'If you say so.' His tone was slightly wry. 'But you are still my patient.'

Catherine made no response to this, but as the minutes stretched between them, she had to say something. 'Do you—do you still go to the convent?' she ventured, without looking at him. 'Have you seen Reverend Mother since—since—since I left?'

'Of course.' He finished his tea then and put his cup back on to the tray. 'My morals may be in question, but my professional skills are not. Mother Benedicta may be pragmatic, but she is also practical.'

Catherine cast him a reluctant glance. 'And—Julio? How is he?'

'Better.' Armand shrugged. 'He left the hospital several days ago.' He hesitated, and then went on: 'Are you not going to ask me how *our* patient is?'

'José Rodolfo?' Catherine had been loath to mention the guerrilla leader's name. She was still so uncertain of his integrity. But curiosity got the better of her. 'Have you seen him again?'

Armand inclined his head. 'Did you think I wouldn't?'

Catherine bent her head. 'I don't know what I thought.' She caught her lower lip between her teeth. 'You—take risks.'

'Don't we all?' Armand was sardonic.

'If the security forces found out . . .'

'We'll face that contingency when we come to it.' Armand's eyes held hers. 'Don't tell me you care about my safety.'

'I do. Of course, I do,' exclaimed Catherine, in some confusion, shifting uneasily beneath his gaze. 'I'd care about anyone in your position. Obviously, your loyalties are torn by the oath you took to sustain life by any means in your power.'

'Is that what you think?' Armand regarded her intently. 'That I do what I do and still support Ferreira's regime?'

'Don't you?'

Armand swung his leg across the chair and got to his feet. 'I think it's time you went back to bed,' he declared, side-stepping both the table and her question and coming towards her. 'Come on. I'll help you.'

'No—really. I can manage.'

After what had happened before, Catherine had no wish for Armand to touch her, and rather recklessly she stood up. If she could put the width of the chair between them, she might be able to circle round it and reach the end of the bed without any assistance, she thought optimistically, but her legs wouldn't obey her. When she tried to move away, her toe caught in the hem of her shift and if Armand hadn't taken a swift step forward and grasped her arms, she would have ended up on the floor at his feet. As it was, her anticipated collapse was averted, and his fingers dug into the soft flesh of her upper arms as her whole weight was thrown upon him.

'Crazy little fool!' he muttered, his arms sliding round her to support her. 'So self-reliant; so independent! What is so wrong with accepting my help now? You were glad enough of it a few days ago, as I recall.'

'I know.' Catherine's face was pressed against the silken folds of his shirt, and her words were muffled. The scent of his warm body was intoxicating her senses to the exclusion of all else, and she felt a momentary loss when he swung her up into his arms, and dislodged her from her resting place.

'Bed!' he said harshly, carrying her across the room and depositing her firmly in the middle of the square iron bedstead. 'Here—' He came down on the side of the bed beside her as she endeavoured to unfasten the belt of his bathrobe, and brushing her fingers aside, he unloosened the offending knot. 'I'll help you take it off. You must be hot in this enveloping thing!'

'Maria thought it would be more suitable than sitting about in my shift,' Catherine murmured uncomfortably, avoiding his eyes, and she heard his grunt of derision.

'This thing?' he questioned, his fingers plucking the sleeve of the all-over garment she was wearing underneath. 'I've seen more revealing *mortalhas*—how do you say?—shrouds?' He grimaced. 'I have a pair of pyjamas somewhere. Perhaps they would be more suitable.'

Catherine's face burned. 'I couldn't wear your pyjamas!'

'Why not?' Armand's lips twisted. 'I don't wear them.'

Catherine moistened her lips with a tentative tongue. 'You mean you—you—'

'Sleep in the raw?' he queried, half impatiently, tossing the bathrobe on to the chair he had previously been occupying. 'Don't pretend you are shocked. Believe me, it is quite normal.'

Catherine shook her head. 'It's nothing to do with me.'

'But you do not approve?' he inserted softly. 'Oh, little one, you are so—so—'

'Prudish?' she offered, drawing her knees up to tuck her toes under the single sheet which was all that covered the bed at the moment, and Armand regarded her with some exasperation.

'Not—exactly,' he conceded, drawing back the sheet so that she could shuffle her feet under it. His eyes moved over her flushed face. 'You know—I'll go and get those pyjamas right now. You might just find them more comfortable than this ugly thing!'

Catherine swallowed, and looked down at the shift. 'Is it ugly?'

'You know it is,' he averred, getting up from the bed. He eyed the elasticated wrists and high neckline of the offending garment. 'What happened to your own clothes? Did you ever find out?'

Catherine shook her head, and with a stifled expletive, Armand left the room.

He was back in only a few minutes carrying the promised pyjamas. But they were nothing like the cotton pyjamas Catherine's father used to wear and which she had been expecting. For one thing, they were made of silk, vividly coloured in an exotic shade of peacock blue, and embroidered with a dark red brocade.

'An unwanted gift,' he remarked, dropping them

on to the bed beside her. His mouth took on a mocking slant. 'Believe me, I would never have chosen anything so Bohemian for myself!'

Catherine touched the soft material. 'I—I couldn't—'

'Why couldn't you?' Armand folded his arms across the broad expanse of his chest. 'They're quite respectable. Quite feminine, actually. Indulge me.'

Catherine's teeth dug into her lower lip. 'I can't.'

'Why can't you?' With a muffled oath, Armand abandoned his stance and resumed his previous position on the side of her bed. '*Ouca*, do you want me to strip that monstrosity from you?'

Catherine gasped. 'You wouldn't dare!'

'Don't tempt me!'

'I want you to leave.' She swallowed, pushing the silk pyjamas towards him. 'And—and take these with you.'

'*Basta!* Enough! You would try the patience of a saint!' he exclaimed fiercely, his hand reaching for the buttoned neckline of the shift, and although she struggled to evade his invading fingers, he grasped a handful of the coarse cotton.

The material was cheap and it tore immediately, buttons flying in all directions as he ripped it halfway to her waist. Catherine thought even he was surprised at how easily he gained his objective, but she was too busy gathering the two sides together in an attempt to protect her modesty to notice his rueful expression.

'Oh hell,' he muttered, his anger swiftly giving way to remorse, but Catherine was in no mood to forgive him.

'I hope you're satisfied now,' she sniffed, turning indignant features up to his, and then wishing she hadn't when she saw the compassion in his eyes.

'I'm sorry,' he said huskily, putting his hand against

her cheek, his thumb probing the corner of her mouth. 'I didn't mean to do this.'

'You—you're not sorry,' she persisted, struggling to retain her crumbling resistance, but his thumb was doing strange things to her traitorous body. Almost involuntarily, it seemed, her lips parted to allow that probing pad access to her mouth, and its caress against her teeth brought a curious pain to the pit of her stomach.

'I am,' he insisted, the darkening shadows in the room throwing his face into a relief of planes and angles that no longer looked familiar. '*Meu Deus*, Catherine, I wouldn't hurt you . . .'

His other hand came to cup her head and suddenly it was no longer just a question of arguing over who was responsible for the destruction of her gown. His hand was around the back of her neck, sliding into the neatly plaited braid that Maria had dressed for her earlier, and the intimate touch of his fingers was all and more than Catherine could cope with.

'I—you mustn't—' was all she got out before his lips sought the corner of her mouth where his thumb had invaded, and the hands she was holding her bodice together with gave up the struggle to unfold against the silken covering of his chest.

His mouth moved, fitting itself more possessively over hers, and she felt his tongue circling her lips, seeking entry. The persuasion of that urgent caress rekindled the not-unpleasant disturbance in the lower reaches of her abdomen, and when the pressure of his kiss compelled her back against the pillows behind her, she felt a wave of heat enveloping her. Her hands were crushed between them and she was intensely conscious of the heavy beating of his heart against her fingers. It matched the quickened tattoo of her own heart as he moved over her, and her torn nightgown was forgotten beneath the searching possession of his lips.

'Open your mouth,' he breathed against her lips, and she found herself obeying him and allowing the moist intrusion of his tongue. That sensual exploration was something she had never experienced before, and although all her senses were screaming that she ought not to be allowing this to happen, she could not resist him. She could feel the ridge of muscle below his ribs as his hard body moved along the length of hers, and her hands, freed from their futile efforts at protection, curled into fists, bunching handfuls of his shirt inside them. The sensuous feel of the cloth beneath her fingers made her reckless, and tearing the buttons of his shirt apart, she touched his warm skin. Her hands spread eagerly against his taut flesh, delighting in the response her innocent caresses evoked.

But her mind spun when Armand's fingers slipped inside the torn neckline of her gown. The sensations he aroused by caressing the smooth skin of her shoulder with his lips drove all coherent thoughts from her head, and when his hand slid down between their bodies to touch the hardening mound of her breast, she could hardly breathe.

'Encantadora,' he whispered, drawing back to look at her, and Catherine's blood flowed thickly as he bent his head towards her.

His eyes were like burnished gold, dark and liquid, and eloquent of his emotions. As his tongue laved the swollen nipple exposed to his gaze, she felt an ache beginning between her legs and spreading quickly down her thighs. It was a strange feeling, compounded as it was of the sensations his tongue was arousing and a growing urgency inside herself to respond in kind. She wanted him to go on touching her; she wanted him to go on kissing her and caressing her and arousing her to this high peak of excitement she had not known existed. Although her limbs felt weak and boneless, she found herself arching towards him, wanting to feel him against her. She wanted to know what it was like to be crushed beneath his lean powerful body, and when his hand slid lower, cupping her small buttocks and urging her even closer to him, she felt another pulsating ridge of muscle riding up against the flatness of stomach.

She knew what it was, of course. She was not so naïve, even if a man's naked body was still largely a mystery to her. But the awareness of his thrusting manhood, scarcely confined by the taut material of his pants and the scant protection afforded by her night-gown, did not frighten her. She was too bemused by the hungry pressure of his mouth that had abandoned its sensual suckling of her breasts to return to the parted sweetness of hers. When his tongue plunged familiarly between her lips, seeking and exploring every moist cavity, she met its flagrant invasion with innocent provocation. Her own pink tongue darted to meet his, and Armand moaned low in his throat when he met the startling sexuality of her response.

His lips devoured hers, ravaging her mouth with increasing passion as Catherine's instinctive responses drove him to the limit of his endurance. Her fingers dug deeply into the virile thickness of his hair, her nails raking against his scalp as the flames he was fuelling turned her blood to fire in her veins. She clung to him urgently, her whole body an open invitation, but when one slender leg coiled with innocent sensuality around his, Armand's body stiffened. With a feeling of dismay, she felt his instinctive withdrawal, and she wanted to cry in frustration when he dragged himself away from her.

'*Cristo*, Catarina,' he groaned, putting one hand at either side of her and pushing himself up to the length of his arms. '*Esta é louco!* What am I doing?' He shook his head, as if to clear his stupefied senses and went on: '*Por amor de Deus*, this is not sanity!'

CHAPTER EIGHT

'WHY not?' Although she might later regret her aud-
acity, Catherine was too aroused right now to think
coherently. Making a token effort to hold the bodice of
her gown together, she raised herself on her elbows,
narrowing the space between them and demanding
huskily: 'Didn't you want to touch me? Didn't you
want to kiss me? Oh, Armand—did I do something
wrong?'

'No, I—' Armand's controlled gaze moved rather
less controllably over her flushed face. 'That is—we
both know this should not have happened.'

'Why shouldn't it?' she protested, lifting her hand
and laying it against his cheek. And although he
turned his head aside to try and dislodge her fingers,
he did not force her to remove them.

'I am a man, not a boy,' he said, somewhat indis-
tinctly, concentrating his attention on a point above
her head. 'God knows, I'm old enough to be your
father!'

'Hardly that.' Catherine sighed. 'I'm almost twenty,
Armand.'

'And I'm thirty-seven,' he told her heavily. 'Quite
old enough, believe me!'

Catherine shook her head. 'That doesn't matter—'

'It does matter,' he retorted, looking down at her
through narrowed eyes. 'Desirable though you are, I
don't have the right to take advantage of you.'

Catherine's jaw quivered. 'Don't patronise me!'

'*Meu Deus*, I am not patronising you!' he muttered,

as her hand fell abruptly away from him. 'For pity's sake, Catherine, don't make me despise myself any more than I already do!' He drew an uneven breath, and then continued: 'You're very young, and you're very beautiful, and I am only human. But you are my patient, not my mistress, and I suggest we try and forget this ever happened.'

Catherine hunched her shoulders, looking up at him through her lashes. 'I don't believe you,' she mumbled, reaction setting in like a dull weight over her temples.

Armand sighed. 'What don't you believe?'

She shrugged. 'I'm not beautiful.'

'No?' Armand regarded her half impatiently for a few moments longer, then he got up from the bed. 'What do you want me to say?' he demanded flatly. 'That you are? That these weeks of your illness have given your features a transparency that is quite unique? That any man would be attracted to you—'

'No! *No!*' Catherine put her hands over her ears. 'I just don't believe that that was why you—you kissed me.'

'What do you mean?' Armand gazed at her without comprehension, and Catherine drew up her legs to rest her chin on her knees.

'You're only trying to make excuses,' she said, sniffing. 'You're trying to make me feel better, when—when—when the truth is, I bored you! I'm too young, too naïve, too inexperienced, to interest a man like you seriously—'

'You're crazy!' he interrupted her roughly, raking back the swathe of silky dark hair she had tumbled over his forehead minutes before. 'You—oh, you have *interested* me, to use your words, since that afternoon I encountered you in the convent garden. You had spent the afternoon in the chapel, as I recall, saying prayers for some misdemeanour, I don't remember what.' His golden eyes darkened. 'You looked so meek—so demure; so vulnerable, until I saw your eyes. They were full of fire!'

Catherine's colour deepened. 'That was because Father Donovan made me confess my sin in front of you,' she exclaimed, her tongue appearing in unknowing provocation. 'And you said you were surprised that I was still at the convent.'

'I was,' he responded, tugging impatiently at the hair at the nape of his neck. He grimaced. 'Perhaps it was precognition. Perhaps I had already guessed that you were likely to cause problems, if you stayed.'

Catherine gazed across at him. 'And have I? Caused problems for you?'

Armand looked away from her. 'Of course,' he said tersely. 'You've caused a rift between me and Mother Benedicta which may never be bridged.'

'That's not what I meant,' she exclaimed huskily. 'Oh, Armand, you're not really mad with me, are you? You're not going to send me away?'

'Send you away?' he echoed, turning to look at her again. 'What are you talking about now?'

Catherine pressed her lips together. 'If you're not going to let me work for you, what else can I expect?'

Armand's hand dropped to his side. 'You're not well enough to think about working yet,' he replied shortly. 'When you are, we'll discuss it.'

'You mean—you mean—' Catherine's eyes widened and, with a cry of relief, she scrambled to the end of the bed. But when she would have stumbled off the mattress and gone to him, he caught her wrists, imprisoning them against the iron rail at the end of the bed.

'There are conditions,' he said harshly, avoiding the tremulous face tilted to his. 'This kind of conversation must not be repeated. Do you understand?'

Catherine's face fell. 'But you said—you said you were attracted to me!'

Armand's laugh was without humour. 'I have been attracted to a lot of women, Catherine,' he told her somewhat bitterly. 'However, attraction does not presuppose the kind of relationship you seem to imagine. I have enough problems as it is, without adding to them. Believe me, little one, you will thank me for this one day.'

Catherine's mutinous features were eloquent of her feelings, but Armand chose not to persist with his argument. 'I must go,' he said, releasing her wrists and straightening, ignoring the revealing tremor of her lips. 'I am having dinner with your friend, Major Enriques, this evening—'

'*My* friend?' she choked.

'—and although I do not like the man, I should not wish to be late.'

It was after midnight when he came back, but Catherine heard him. In spite of her tiredness, she had not slept, and her head was aching with the anxiety of worrying about what might happen to Armand if Henri Enriques discovered he was dividing his skills arbitrarily between both sides of the opposing forces. It was a dangerous game he was playing, a game that could so easily go wrong. She had seen what had happened to her father, an innocent individual, in this war of attrition. What more awful punishment might lie in wait for Armand, if he was exposed as a rebel sympathiser?

But it wasn't only this that had kept her eyes open

long after she was normally unconscious to the world. The events of the afternoon were what had kept her tossing and turning on the now wrinkled sheets, and no matter how she tried, she could not dismiss what had happened from her thoughts.

It didn't help that every time she moved, she felt the silken brush of Armand's pyjamas against her skin. Her breasts still tingled with remembrance of the wet intimacy of his tongue, and their sensitised peaks felt tender as they rubbed against the lustrous fabric. The pyjama trousers had felt even more abrasive until she had taken them off. She was unused to sleeping in anything other than a nightgown or her shift, and while she was aware she could not spend her days wearing only the jacket, no one was likely to discover how she spent her nights.

Even so, she was still restless when the sound of the station wagon's engine disturbed the night air. She wondered what he had been doing to keep him out so late, and reluctantly she wondered if he did, indeed, have a mistress. After all, he had left for the major's quarters at seven o'clock. That was five hours ago. What else could have kept him, long after the pleasures of good food, and possibly good wine, were spent?

Turning on to her stomach, Catherine tried to relax herself for sleep. It was nothing to do with her how Armand spent his time, she told herself fiercely. He had made that blatantly clear this afternoon. Just because he had kissed her—just because she had been able to *arouse* him—was no reason to believe that she was the only female who could do so. He had tried to tell her that. He had tried to explain the reasons why he had behaved the way he had, and just because she didn't like it, was no excuse to ignore the truth. He was an attractive man. She wasn't the first woman to have thought so, and she would certainly not be the last. Instead of feeling sorry for herself, she should be grateful he had not chosen to seduce her before revealing his feelings. She would not have been able to stop him: she had acknowledged that fact early in her ruminations. Although none of the boys she had known in England had ever come close to making her lose control, just the touch of Armand's hands on her body had overwhelmed whatever defences she might have raised against him, and she had become a stranger to herself.

Thinking about it now, her blood cooled by the realisation of what might have happened, it seemed incredible that she should have responded the way she had. Remembering the torn bodice of her shift and Armand's lips, suckling at her breasts, a shuddering sensation of disbelief swept over her. How could she face him again after what had happened, she fretted unhappily. How could she pretend nothing had happened, when even thinking about what he had done made every inch of her skin feel as raw as an open wound? Almost involuntarily, her hands crept to the sensitive nipples of her breasts, and she spread her palms against their button hardness. Even now, several hours after he had left her, she could still feel the aching sensation between her legs that had aroused such curious longings inside her. But when her fingers moved to touch that intimate spot, she caught herself up sharply. Dear God, she chided herself disgustedly, what had he done to her? What had she done to herself?

She slept eventually, but it was a shallow oblivion, and several times she awakened, bathed in sweat and shaking from head to foot. She was unutterably relieved when the pale light of morning filtered in through the blinds, and realising that Maria would be here shortly to check on her, she found the pyjama trousers and tugged them on under cover of the sheet. She was perspiring heavily by the time she had achieved this, but happily Maria noticed nothing amiss when she came to assist her patient into the bathroom. She even agreed to the girl's suggestion that she might take a bath, and when Armand made his first visit of the day, Catherine was safely ensconced behind locked doors.

The rapid summons of his fingers against the panels was Catherine's cue to offer her apologies that she was not available for his examination. 'I—er—I'm feeling much better,' she called, holding on to the soap with fingers that shook quite shamefully. 'Really, there's no need for you to wait. I—I'll see you this evening.'

'Was there any reason for you to lock the door?' inquired Armand harshly. 'It was unwise, in your condition, and Santo is unlikely to disturb you.'

'I—I never thought,' murmured Catherine, her tongue circling her dry lips. 'H—habit, I suppose.'

'You mean there were locks at the convent?' inserted Armand, without expression. Her silence was answer enough, and after a moment, he continued: 'Very well. I will assure myself of your progress this evening. *Adeus!*'

'*Adeus,*' she answered in a small voice, and then felt a depressing surge of misery sweep over her at the realisation that it would be at least another eight hours before she laid eyes on him again.

Later in the day, Maria appeared with an armful of clothes. Catherine was sitting by the window, trying to make sense of Armand's copy of the *Ribatejo Jornal,* the local newspaper, when the Indian girl came into the room carrying several garments over her arm.

'*Lá, senhorita,*' she exclaimed, smiling. 'Your clothes!'

'*My* clothes?' Catherine stared at her disbelievingly.

'Some,' said Maria nodding, as the girl got slowly to her feet. '*Espere, senhorita.* Wait—I bring them to you.'

Catherine shook her head. 'But where did they come from?'

'*Qué?*'

Catherine sighed. 'The clothes—where from?'

'Ah . . .' Maria laid the garments reverently over the girl's lap as she subsided again into the chair. 'The *senhor*—he speak to Major Enriques, *senhorita.*'

'You mean Major Enriques has had them all this time?' exclaimed Catherine disbelievingly. 'But why? Why did he keep them? What was he doing with them?'

'*Faz favor, senhorita, não percebo,*' protested the Indian girl apologetically. 'I do not understand. If you speak—more slow, hmm?'

'It doesn't matter, Maria.' Catherine shrugged. She would have to speak to Armand if she wanted to find out how he had rescued her belongings, but for the present, it was so wonderful to have something decent to wear. The shops in Batistamajor were not the kind of establishments that provided clothes she could wear, and in any case she had no money to buy material to make herself what she needed.

'The *senhorita* is pleased?' asked Maria anxiously, and Catherine nodded vigorously.

'Very pleased, thank you, Maria,' she assured the girl fervently. 'I can get dressed now.'

'Get dressed?' inquired Maria frowning. 'Ah, *não*, the *senhor*, he say—you rest today.'

'Oh, I will,' exclaimed Catherine, discovering her

favourite pair of jeans. 'But surely I can put some clothes on?'

Maria hesitated. *'Não sei . . .'*

'I'm going to,' declared Catherine firmly, getting to her feet again. 'I won't move out of this room, I promise, but it's been so long since I wore anything other than shapeless sacks!'

'This not shapeless, *senhorita*,' objected Maria, touching the sleeve of Armand's pyjama jacket. 'Is pretty. Very pretty!'

'Yes, well—' Catherine was already unfastening the cord of the bathrobe Maria seemed to regard as an indispensable part of her attire. 'Maybe I should have said, it will be nice to wear something that is *mine*,' she amended ruefully. She sighed. 'I just can't believe I've got my clothes back again.'

Fifteen minutes later, Catherine viewed her appearance in the mirror with some misgivings. The jeans, which she had pounced on so eagerly, no longer looked as attractive as she remembered. The weight she had lost showed, and in consequence the denim pants did not fit so snugly to her shapely limbs. They looked old, and worn, and she had to rifle through the drawers of the chest to find a belt of Armand's to cinch in the waistband.

The shirt she was wearing with them was less obviously too big for her. Thankfully, her breasts had not suffered in the fining down of her figure, but they did present a problem, nevertheless. Although Maria had brought her pants and shirts and sweaters, and several of the cotton dresses Catherine had brought with her from England, there were no underclothes among the garments, and the thin shirt was more revealing than anything she had worn for months. She thought of asking Maria if she had a bra she could lend her, but the question was never voiced. It was obvious from the sway of the Indian girl's figure that she had never troubled with foundation garments, and Catherine had no alternative but to follow her example.

Her hair, newly-washed, presented few difficulties. In spite of its unruly qualities, it was long enough now to be controlled in the loose braid she had taken to wearing, and it lay silkily over one shoulder, glinting red-gold in the sunlight.

If only her face was not so pale, she thought frustratedly, touching the bones exposed by the hollowness of her cheeks. When she had lived with her father, her skin had taken on the glow of honey, warmed by the hours she had spent outdoors. But months spent mourning her father and confined within the walls of the convent had taken their toll, and her colouring now was as fragile as the magnolias Sister Teresa had nurtured in her garden.

Still, her eyes looked clear enough, she decided firmly. Flecked with silver in this light, they were the only real splash of colour in her face, the gold-tipped lashes that surrounded them as thick and silky as they had ever been. Her father used to say she had witch's eyes, long and green, and slightly tilted at the corners. Catherine thought they were her best feature, particularly now when the rest of her looked so pale and uninteresting.

Maria thought the clothes were a definite improvement. '*Mas*, but you are—*magro*, *senhorita*! So—so slim!'

'Don't you mean *thin*, Maria?' Catherine asked, with a sigh. 'I know. These jeans just hang on me!'

Maria shrugged and surveyed her own generous form. 'Wait until babies come,' she declared philosophically, her hands describing an enormous arc over her stomach. *'Muito gordo!* Very fat!'

Catherine was annoyed to feel the warm colour flood her cheeks at the other girl's words. Heavens, she thought impatiently, she had become as sanctimonious as Sister Angelica. What was wrong with talking about babies, for goodness' sake? Unless—Her eyes turned doubtfully towards Maria. Surely the Indian girl didn't think that she and Armand—that Armand and she—*oh, no!* It was unbelievable! No one could think that Armand had brought her here for any other reason than he had stated: that she had nowhere else to go. What had happened yesterday had not been planned. It had just—happened. And in any case, Maria didn't know about that. No one did.

Her tongue probing tentatively at her upper lip, she asked casually: 'What do you know about babies, Maria? Have you got brothers and sisters who are married?'

Maria smiled, misunderstanding. 'I not married, *senhorita*,' she exclaimed. *'Mas*, is baby boy in village.'

Catherine stared at her. 'You have a baby boy?' she echoed, in astonishment. Maria couldn't be more than sixteen or seventeen years old. Yet, Catherine didn't know why she was so surprised really. She had seen mothers at the school, before her father died, much younger than that. It was just that she had thought of Maria as being like herself, and to discover the other girl had actually had a child was startling.

'The—er—the father of your baby,' she persisted now, unable to leave the subject alone, 'does—does he live in Batistamajor?'

'Qué?' Maria looked confused, and Catherine frowned.

'The baby's father,' she repeated carefully. 'Um—*o*

padre de bebé?' She paused. *'Onde morava o padre?'*

'Ah.' Maria nodded. *'Em Batistamajor, senhorita, sim.'*

Catherine sighed. If the father of Maria's baby lived in Batistamajor, why were they not married? It seemed strange in a community where family life was still so important, and where the church held such sway, that a girl as obviously bright and intelligent as Maria should be left to bring up her child on her own. Unless the child's father was already married, of course. That was always a possibility.

Unable to pursue the subject any farther without feeling as if she was prying, Catherine abandoned the topic. After all, she thought, with an uneasy flutter in her stomach, she, of all people, should be able to understand how such a thing could happen. Remembering the wanton way she had offered herself to Armand, she should have no doubts that passion could overwhelm practicality, and emotions once released were not so easily recaptured.

Armand came home in the late afternoon. Catherine had been in a state of some restlessness ever since Maria had taken her lunch tray away, and by the time she heard the station wagon braking to a halt at the front door, she was no longer capable of remaining demurely in her chair by the window. Hurrying to the mirror, she made another critical appraisal of her features, and then, dissatisfied with what she had seen, she paced fretfully across the floor. If only she didn't have to face him today, she thought, twisting her hands together. If only she could have had a little more time to recover her composure. As it was, she felt as nervous as a kitten, and in no state to handle an interview with him.

She did not have long to wait. The door of the station wagon slammed, the house door opened and closed, and then footsteps sounded in the passageway outside. The firm stride was so manifestly Armand's that Catherine's hands groped urgently for the window-sill behind her, needing its solid reassurance to support her shaking legs. Perhaps she wasn't as strong as she thought, she pondered anxiously. Perhaps she should have remained sitting in her chair. At least that way she might have avoided a face-to-face encounter.

The perfunctory tap he gave on her door before thrusting it open was hardly an adequate warning of intent. He came into the room with the apparent intention of asserting his authority, and Catherine's heartbeat quickened as she met his sombre gaze. He didn't immediately say anything. Instead, his eyes moved searchingly over her slim figure. Then, as if acknowledging the change in her appearance, he inclined his head politely, before gesturing her to her chair.

'I suggest you sit down,' he commented, his hands in the pockets of his white coat. 'In spite of this display of independence, you don't look as if you're ready to walk out on me quite yet.'

Catherine's shoulders sagged, and with a feeling half of relief, she took the few steps that brought her to her chair. Then, sinking down on to the cushions, she looked up at him guiltily, touching the collar of her shirt as she said: 'I—I believe I have you to thank for these.'

'You should thank Major Enriques, actually,' retorted Armand flatly, coming towards her and detachedly studying her features. 'How do you feel? Are you really well enough to get dressed? Just because you have some pretty clothes to put on does not necessarily signify you're fit enough to wear them.'

Catherine hesitated. 'How did Major Enriques come to have them? Does it—I mean, did he—that is, who gave them to him?'

Armand's mouth compressed. 'If you ask him, he will say his security forces rescued them from the hands of the guerrillas who burned the school-house and killed your father,' he replied indifferently. 'So—did you sleep well?'

Catherine bit into her lower lip. 'And if I ask *you* where he got them, what will you say?' she persisted.

Armand took a deep breath. 'Does it matter?'

'Yes.'

'Very well. No doubt they have been in his hands since the day after the attack.'

Catherine gazed up at him. 'You mean—'

'Like I said, they've probably been lying in the quartermaster's stores for the past six—eight months.'

Catherine bent her head. 'You don't think—someone else has been wearing them, do you?'

'Is anything missing?'

'Yes.' Catherine coloured. 'My underwear.'

Armand's lips twitched. 'I see.'

'It's not funny.' Catherine looked up at him again, finding protection in her anger. 'What would anyone want with my underwear?'

'Who knows?' Armand's expression was non-committal. 'It was probably not considered worth saving.'

Catherine absorbed this in silence, and after a few moments Armand continued: 'No doubt Maria will obtain some replacements for you. I'll ask her, if you like.'

Catherine forbore to make the comment that Maria did not wear a bra, and instead she murmured awkwardly: 'I don't have any money to buy any new things. Perhaps you'd better wait, until I've found a job.'

'Oh, I think we can run to a small advance,' remarked Armand drily. 'After all, you have assisted me on two occasions, and even a trainee nurse is paid a living wage.'

Catherine caught her breath. 'You're going to let me work for you then?'

Armand arched one dark brow. 'I'm considering it.' He paused. 'Providing you still want to, of course.'

Catherine clasped her hands together. 'Why shouldn't I?'

'You avoided me this morning,' he reminded her evenly, revealing he had not been taken in by her clumsy attempt at subterfuge. 'If we're going to work together, we have to understand one another.'

Catherine bent her head. 'Do you understand me?' she murmured. 'Did you know why I—why I—'

'—hid in the bathroom?' he inquired bluntly. 'I assume because of what happened between us yesterday.' He paused. 'Evidently, you did not listen to what I said afterwards.'

'I did.' Catherine sniffed. 'You said we shouldn't have that kind of conversation again.'

'And I meant what I said,' averred Armand brusquely. 'There was no need for you to hide away in the bathroom or worry over whether or not I might decide to repeat the episode. Believe me,' his eyes darkened, 'I am not in the habit of—well, of making love to young girls. It was just an unfortunate set of circumstances, and things got out of hand.' He expelled his breath half impatiently. 'I suppose I should apologise. You trusted me and I betrayed that trust. I'm sorry.'

Catherine's face was burning. 'I—oh, there's no

need to apologise,' she mumbled unhappily. 'It—it was as much my fault as yours.' She lifted her shoulders. 'I just feel so embarrassed about the whole affair!'

'Embarrassed?' Armand's expression was taut. 'Why do you feel embarrassed?'

Catherine swallowed. 'I shouldn't like you to think that I—that I've ever—'

'I don't,' Armand retorted flatly, walking towards the door. 'I'm going to take a shower. Perhaps we could eat together later. In the dining room, for a change, if you feel up to it.'

CHAPTER NINE

By the end of the week, Catherine was well enough to look after herself, and with evident regret on her part, Maria made her departure. 'You come one day: see *bebé*,' she invited as she was leaving, and Catherine thanked her and said she would try.

The house was curiously quiet without her. The constant battles she and Santo had waged had become familiar, but it was obvious that Santo preferred a return to the status quo. Catherine was left in little doubt that he would like it even better if she were leaving also, and although she saw little of him, his disapproval of her presence was never in doubt.

Maria's departure did not mean she saw more of Armand, however. On the contrary, now that she had recovered her strength and did not need constant nursing, he left in the mornings generally before she was awake. In consequence, she seldom had any conversation with him during the day, and their relationship was founded on either a few words exchanged before he went out for the evening, or the desultory remarks made over one of Santo's suppers.

It was strange, she thought, how their association had become more distant, instead of less. Seeing him every day, spending at least part of the day in communication with him, should have strengthened their relationship, but it hadn't. Instead, those polite discussions of her health and the weather, of his patients and Santo's cooking, were gradually erecting a barrier between them that Catherine could feel but didn't know how to break down. It was as if he was distancing himself from her, proving perhaps, if any proof was necessary, that what had happened between them had been an unfortunate mistake. At every opportunity, he reinforced the gulf that lay between them, convincing her by his attitude that they could not possibly have anything in common.

The trouble was, the more he tried to detach himself from her, the more Catherine wanted to be with him. Living in his house, seeing him every day, albeit briefly, was having a quite opposite effect on her. Although she told herself it was stupid, although she knew that becoming emotionally attracted to a man like Armand Alvares was madness, she could not deny the excitement she felt every time she saw him. It had always been there, of course, ever since those days at the convent. But now, sleeping in the room next to him, sharing what little of himself he allowed her to share, she found herself living for those moments when they were together. He was unaware of it, she was sure of that. But just occasionally she caught him looking at her in a curiously speculative way, and her heart skipped a beat at the possibility he might suspect her secret.

One afternoon, curiosity drove her to enter Armand's bedroom. Latterly, she had been spending the afternoons in the garden, seated in a chair near the playful fronds of the eucalyptus, reading magazines in an attempt to learn more of the language. But the heat had driven her indoors, and discovering Santo napping in the kitchen, she decided to see for herself where Armand slept.

His room was smaller than the one he had surrendered to her, and its furnishings were much shabbier. Evidently, it had seldom been used before her advent, and apart from the bed and a narrow wardrobe, there was little comfort. There was a rug beside the bed, and the bedspread looked as if it had been locally woven, and a small stool stood close by to support an alarm clock and a photograph frame.

Catherine recognised the photograph as being the one which had occupied a similar position in the other room before she came to stay. She remembered seeing it the night Armand took her to the guerrilla encampment and, feeling a little guilty, she lifted it into her hands.

To her surprise, she saw it was a photograph of Luis, José Rodolfo's son. He was much younger when it had been taken, but the resemblance was unmistakable, and she wondered why Armand should have such a thing in his possession. It didn't make sense, unless he had known José Rodolfo a lot longer than she had imagined, but there was no way she could ask him without betraying her intrusion into his privacy.

A week after Maria had left, when Armand had made no further mention of her desire to work with him, Catherine broached the subject again. They were having supper together in the small dining room, which opened through an archway from the living room. For once, Santo had tried his hand at something other than the spicy stews and *tortillas* Catherine had become used to, and the roast lamb and locally-grown vegetables had been delicious. Catherine waited until the old man had served their coffee before mentioning what was on her mind, but Armand's expression was not encouraging when she ventured her problem.

'It's too soon,' he said, stirring some of the raw cane sugar into his cup. 'You're not strong enough yet. Take it easy for a while. Help Santo around the house, if you must find something to do. We'll discuss this again in a few weeks. After I have convinced myself that you are fit enough to expend your energies on something other than regaining your health.'

Catherine sighed. She had guessed what his answer would be, and she tugged rather frustratedly at a strand of hair that had coiled beside her ear. She had made an especial effort tonight to make herself look as attractive as she could in the hope that Armand might be disarmed, but she ought to have known she was wasting her time. He had not even noticed the pretty lemon-yellow chemise dress that exposed the creamy curve of her throat, or taken the slightest interest in the fact that her hair was loose for once. Its golden beauty curled loosely over her shoulders and fell silkily almost to her waist.

'I am fit,' she persisted now, drawing his unwilling attention to her by the simple means of touching his sleeve. 'You know I am. And as for helping Santo around the house—well, he's as anxious for my assistance as you apparently are.'

Armand's mouth compressed. 'Leave it, Catherine,' he said tersely. 'Be grateful for the fact that you don't have to work in this heat. If this weather continues, I may have an outbreak of malaria on my hands, and I don't want to have to worry about you as well as everyone else.'

Catherine withdrew her hand and looked down into her coffee cup. 'You're never going to allow me to help you, are you?' she murmured bitterly. 'You only said it so I wouldn't feel bad about accepting your charity! Well, I can't go on doing that. It wouldn't be right.'

'*Santo padre!*' Armand expelled his breath on a sound of irritation. 'Don't be a fool! When I consider you are—capable of doing a day's work, I will employ you.

But for the present, it's better that you stay here. Out of danger.'

'What danger?' Catherine looked at him then, trying not to stare too obviously at the brown hollow of his throat, visible above the opened neckline of his shirt. There was a faint film of moisture on his skin that was caught in the flickering light of the lamp, and she knew the craziest impulse to stroke the tips of her fingers across his chest and taste their plunder on her tongue.

Unaware that a little of her feelings showed in her face, she was shocked out of her daydreams by Armand saying harshly: 'Don't look at me like that!' and when he thrust back his chair and got to his feet, she looked up at him with some confusion.

'I—I'm sorry,' she mumbled, unable to sustain his savage gaze, and he strode impatiently through to the living room, leaving her alone at the table.

When she eventually plucked up sufficient courage to follow him he had not, as she had expected, retired to his surgery as he often did after supper. Instead, he was lounging in an armchair, one leg hooked over the arm, and when she came into the room he regarded her with dour frustration. 'All right,' he said, making no move to play the gentleman and get to his feet, 'I had no reason to speak to you like that. I apologise.' He paused, and then continued tautly: 'And surely you can understand the dangers existing in the present situation. No one is entirely safe, so long as the current emergency exists. Conflict could flare up at any time, and I should not wish you to be caught in the cross-fire.'

Catherine wet her lips. 'You take the risk.'

'I'm a man,' he retorted flatly.

'So?'

'So—do you want to get raped?' he demanded, swinging his foot to the floor and observing her with some aggravation. 'For pity's sake, Catherine, have sense! I can't allow you to take risks of that sort. I don't have the right.'

Catherine held up her head. 'You're not my father!'

'I know I'm not,' he muttered, in a driven tone. 'But I am trying very hard to remember my responsibilities, and you don't make it easy!'

'I'm sorry.' Catherine moved across the room to the fireplace, lifting a carved cigar-case off the mantel, examining it, and putting it down again. 'I didn't realise I was such a burden to you.' She took a deep breath, trying to hold back her resentment, but the painful words just kept on coming: 'I'm surprised you haven't written to England, to find out if I have any relatives there who could take me off your hands. Or perhaps you have. Daddy used to say my letters took forever to get here—'

'*Com a breca!* For God's sake, be still!' Armand's incensed tones silenced her, and as she stood there, fighting back the tears she was sure were going to come, she became aware that he had come to stand beside her. 'I have done nothing to warrant this abuse!' he stated grimly. 'But perhaps you are right. Perhaps I should be writing to the authorities in England to ascertain what arrangements can be made for your future. You cannot spend the rest of your life in Batistamajor, that is certain, and England is your home, after all.'

'My home is here!' Catherine turned then, swinging round desperately, her hair clinging sensuously to the sleeve of his brown silk shirt. 'I don't want to leave Batistamajor. I don't want to go back to England. I don't want to leave—you,' she whispered huskily, and Armand sucked in his breath sharply at that innocently phrased confession.

'Catherine—'

'No, don't say anything,' she exclaimed, turning her head urgently from side to side. 'I know I shouldn't have said anything. I know you don't feel the same. But, if you care anything about me at all, don't send me away, *please*! I don't think I could bear it.'

'*Catherine!*' His use of her name was strangled, and almost convulsively his hands moved to grip her forearms, holding her away from him. 'Catherine, you must not say such things! Just because you are alone in the world and I've taken care of you, does not mean you owe me anything!'

'I'm not talking about owing, Armand—'

'But, I am,' he interrupted her fiercely. 'Get things into perspective, little one. You lost your father, in the most terrible way possible. Your adoption by the nuns was a temporary reprieve, at best. Can't you see, my intervention has been magnified out of all proportion because I'm the only person who has treated you as an individual. I've been of some use, I won't deny it, but anyone with a conscience would have done just as well.'

'No!'

'Yes.' Armand met her tremulous gaze without compassion. 'Don't attribute me with virtues I simply don't possess.'

Catherine trembled in his hands. 'So, what are you saying? That you're going to send me away?'

'No. No, I'm not saying that, although God knows perhaps I should.' Armand shook his head frustratedly, and as he did so, she saw the anger in his eyes giving way, and in its place a smouldering warmth turned the tawny irises to a glowing amber. 'We will discuss this at some other time,' he stated roughly. 'I have work to do.'

'Why some other time?' she protested, understanding that for some incredible reason Armand was as disturbed by her nearness as she was by his. 'Why not now?' she persisted and, with a muffled oath, he let go of her arms to brush his palms with shuddering delicacy across the smooth skin of her shoulders. The bootlace straps of her dress presented no barrier to the sensual graze of his fingers, and Catherine shivered involuntarily at the feelings his touch inspired.

'We won't talk about it now because it would not be sensible,' he told her huskily. 'Let it suffice that for the present your position here is secure.' His hands hovered unsteadily over her shoulders for a few moments, and then were withdrawn. 'Now, I suggest you get some rest. It's late, and I—'

'Oh, Armand!' Her cry of exasperation broke into his controlled speech, and her hands gripping the collar of his shirt brought an element of raw emotion into their exchange. 'Why must you always treat me like a child?' she cried helplessly. 'Why can't you accept that I'm a woman?' and with a sob her head drooped against the muscled hardness of his chest, the material of his shirt slipping nervelessly out of her grasp.

'*Deus*, Catherine!' Armand stiffened automatically, but the yielding warmth of her slim body as it rested against his broke through his reserve. With a groan, his arms came around her, and while she turned her face up to his in numbed disbelief, he lowered his head to touch the corner of her mouth with his lips. 'Don't cry,' he commanded roughly, his uneven breathing moistening the hollow of her ear. 'I don't want to hurt you, but this isn't very sensible. You're very sweet, and very desirable, but I don't have the right to do this.'

'If you don't, no one does,' she breathed unsteadily, sliding her arms around his waist. Through the thinness of his shirt, she could feel the damp heat of his body, and the unfamiliar intimacy was marvellously satisfying. She caught her breath. 'I'm just so glad you're not indifferent to me.'

'Indifferent to you?' Armand's voice was tormented. 'Dear God, it would be better if I was.'

'You don't mean that.' Catherine tilted her head to look up at him. 'Do you?' she added uncertainly.

'I should,' he retorted huskily, his fingers sliding into the curling glory of her hair to cup her head in his palm. 'I should be horse-whipped for ever laying a hand on you,' he added, but the searching pressure of his mouth seemed to negate his claims. With a groan of satisfaction, he found the inviting sweetness of her tongue, and the searing insistence of his kiss awakened all the tremulous emotions lying dormant inside her.

His fingers slid down her back, lingering in the hollow at her waist before moving on to her hips. His hands urged her against him, letting her feel the hardening maleness of his body, and with instinctive sexuality, she pulled his shirt free of the waistband of his pants and allowed her small palms to spread against the taut skin covering his spine.

'*Tu quero*,' he muttered, his lips seeking the rounded curve of her breasts rising above the square neckline of her dress. 'I want you—'

The sudden insistent ringing of the telephone arrested Armand's sensuous exploration. As the discordant peal filled the room with its sound, his head lifted, and almost dazedly he looked down into her distracted face. Her somnolent gaze was full of the allure of a woman aroused to passion, and in those charged moments, she sensed his raw impatience at the ill-timing of the call. But they both knew he could not ignore it, and with a smothered oath he let her go and rapidly crossed the room.

'Sim?' His response was curt as he lifted the receiver, and Catherine watched him anxiously, wishing she understood what he was saying. 'Quem é? Qué quer?' His expression hardened. 'Não quero falar consigo, já.'

Unwilling for him to think she was eavesdropping, Catherine moved over to the window, putting as much distance between her and the telephone as it was possible to achieve. Nevertheless, she could not shut out the sound of Armand's voice, or mistake the simmering anger in his tones as he continued with the call. Whoever had interrupted them was being left in no doubt that he resented the intrusion. But while her spirits lifted at this realisation, his grim countenance dispelled the belief that she was occupying his thoughts at the moment. Something must have happened, she decided. The caller had evidently brought him bad news. But what? And about whom? Whatever the answer, the passionate communication between herself and Armand had been severed, and meeting his distinctly brooding gaze she doubted it would be restored.

When the receiver was finally replaced on its rest, he stood for several seconds staring at the instrument as if it had mesmerised him. Then, with an impatient shrug of his shoulders, he turned to survey Catherine, and her faltering hopes wilted beneath his chilling scrutiny.

'I'm sorry you had to be an unwilling party to that exchange,' he said stiffly, after a moment. 'Did you understand any of it?'

It was a curious question, but Catherine hurried to answer it. 'Other than: *Who is it?* and *What do you want?*—no,' she confessed nervously. 'I—who was it? What did they want? Or is that an impertinence?'

Armand breathed out heavily. 'It was nothing that need concern you,' he responded bleakly, effectively cutting off any further inquiry. He sighed. 'I'm afraid I've got to go away for a few days. My—presence is required in Terasina. Will you be all right here on your own? Or would you like me to ask Maria to come and stay with you?'

Catherine moistened her lips. It was difficult to find the right words to say when what she really wanted was to beg him to take her with him. *A few days*, he had said: it sounded like half a lifetime, and the conviction that he would go away without touching her again was agonising.

'I—I'll be all right,' she got out at last. 'W—when will you be back?'

'I'm not sure.' He pushed his hands into the hip pockets of the dark brown corded pants he was wearing. 'Sunday or Monday, I suppose.'

'But that's almost a week!' exclaimed Catherine, unable to prevent herself, and he inclined his head.

'I know it. However, I will try and—execute my dealings in the shortest time possible.'

Catherine gazed at him. 'It's—business, then?'

His eyes darkened. 'Did you think otherwise?'

'I don't know what to think, do I?' she retorted, finding relief in voicing a little of her bitterness, and he bent his head to study the toes of his suede boots.

'I suppose I deserve that,' he said heavily. 'But this

situation between you and me can't go on, and perhaps it's as well we've been given this reprieve. Maybe, by the time I get back, you'll have got things into perspective—'

'*Into perspective!*' Catherine choked, breaking in on him. 'I don't need to get things "into perspective", as you put it!"

'Well, I do,' retorted Armand grimly, lifting his head to look at her, and she made a helpless little gesture.

'You didn't fifteen minutes ago,' she argued painfully. 'You wanted me. You said so. Or was that just to appease me? To satisfy my craving to be treated as an adult human being?'

'Don't be an idiot!' he said succinctly, pulling his hands out of his pockets and rubbing his palms over the seat of his pants. 'For God's sake, Catherine, I—'

'Oh, don't say any more!' she exclaimed emotively, and turning her back on him, she gave way to the tears that had been burning at the backs of her eyes. What was the use, she asked herself miserably. He was impossible. He was determined to destroy whatever feelings might have been between them, and she was only debasing herself by begging for his sympathy. For all she knew, he might have some woman in Terasina he was going to see. He had not said whether his 'business' was professional or personal. And the fact that he had not discussed it with her pointed to the latter.

'You're getting hysterical!' he declared now, and she knew a ridiculous desire to pretend that it was true. She was in a state of high tension, and the idea of letting go completely and screaming at him was an attractive proposition. But she didn't. Instead, she wiped her eyes with the backs of her hands and turned to face him, focussing her gaze on the gold buckle of his belt, and imprisoning all the bitter words inside her.

'When are you leaving?' she inquired, her voice as expressionless as he could have wished, and she sensed the whipcord tautness of his body.

'In the morning,' he responded harshly, returning his hands to his pockets as if he didn't trust them. 'I shall drive to Ribatejo and take the train from there. It's a twelve-hour journey. I should arrive in Terasina before midnight.'

Catherine acknowledged this in silence. Then she said stiffly: 'Where will you stay? Is there—I mean— shouldn't you leave a forwarding address or a telephone number or something? In—in case I need to get in touch with you.'

Armand hesitated. 'Very well.' He moved across to the small bureau set to one side of the fireplace and, pulling out a notepad, he scribbled a few words upon it. 'This is the address of my apartment,' he declared, tearing off the sheet and holding it out to her. 'The telephone has been disconnected, but a message would reach me there.'

'Thank you.'

Catherine took the proffered sheet of notepaper from him, taking care not to touch his fingers as she did so, and then folded it into a neat square that fitted into her palm. She would read it later, she thought; when she had time to linger over the words. Right now, it was important to get through the next few minutes without making an utter fool of herself again.

'You will be all right?' he demanded suddenly, and she was instantly aware that he had not returned to his position across the room. Instead, he was only an arm's-length away from her, staring at her as if he really cared about her answer.

'I'll be fine,' she replied tensely, deciding now might be a good time to examine what he had written after all. Opening out the page of notepaper again between fingers that were revealingly unsteady, she endeavoured to concentrate on the fact that he still kept an apartment in Terasina. But the words wavered hopelessly before her eyes, and she prayed he would leave her soon, so she could let her feelings show.

'What will you do?'

His persistence was forcing her to go on with the charade, and unable to give him a satisfactory response, she lifted her shoulders. 'I'll do what I always do,' she answered at last. 'Wait for you to come back, I suppose. Like—like Santo.'

Armand swore, her unnatural submissiveness getting under his skin. 'Look at me, can't you!' he exclaimed angrily. 'I know you're upset, and I know you think I'm an unfeeling brute, but I can't go away and leave you in this state!'

'Why not?' Catherine made a supreme effort and lifted her head. 'You'll forget all about me when you get to Terasina.'

'Is that what you think?' he demanded savagely, his gold eyes glittering with suppressed emotion, and she swallowed rather convulsively before she could respond.

'I expect—I expect there's a woman in Terasina, isn't there?' she insisted, her throat aching. 'A man like you . . . I realise you must have known—lots of women. You said yourself you'd known English girls when you were in London, and . . . and doctors have always been a . . . a source of attraction to the opposite sex.'

'How would you know?' he demanded roughly, his eyes raking her tremulous features. 'You're talking a lot of garbage and you know it.'

'Well, at least you don't have to worry about me,' she retorted bravely, surreptitiously disposing of a fugitive tear. 'I've got lots to do. I've got newspapers to read—I'm trying to learn the language, you see—and Maria said I could visit her and . . . and see her baby boy—'

'All right. You've convinced me.' Armand's expression had become harsh and controlled. 'In any case, I have no choice in the matter. I couldn't take you with me, even if I wanted to.'

'Which you don't,' inserted Catherine tremulously, and he inclined his head in cold acknowledgement.

'Which I don't,' he conceded grimly, and she caught her breath.

'Because of a woman,' she persisted, driven on in spite of herself, and although she sensed the conflict in him, he nodded once again.

'Because of a woman,' he agreed, without expression, and the sound of the door slamming behind him was the final humiliation.

CHAPTER TEN

CATHERINE did not see Armand again before he left for Terasina. He set off the next morning before she was up, and although she knew he was moving about and could hear his and Santo's muffled conversation as he left his instructions, she made no effort to go and wish him a good journey. Before the sound of the station wagon's engine warned her of his imminent departure, she did entertain the thought that he might come and see if she was awake. But he didn't. Instead, the receding roar as he accelerated away banished any such hopes, and her lips compressed tightly as she contemplated the empty days ahead.

The first day was the worst, of course. Getting up; enjoying a cup of Santo's strong black coffee for breakfast; sun-bathing for a while, before preparing for lunch—these activities were quite normal for her. The crunch came when she considered that Armand would not be home for supper, that he would not even be available to exchange a few words with her before going out for the evening. That was when the whole weight of what his leaving meant struck her, and it was devastating to contemplate she had no one to talk to but Santo, when his few words of English were less comprehensible than Maria's.

However, after going to bed in tears, she awakened the next morning determined that some more positive action was needed. It was feeble to anticipate spending her days just waiting for Armand's return. He would not thank her for it. He had made that perfectly clear. And she had to find something to do if only to rid her mind of the dangers he might be facing in travelling over five hundred miles through hostile territory. It did no good telling herself that as a friend of José Rodolfo he was unlikely to be attacked. Her father had held no political opinions, and look what had happened to him. With dozens of marauding groups active in the countryside around the capital, how could Armand's safety be assured? Desperate men were inclined to act first and ask questions afterwards. What chance did anyone have in such a situation?

And there was still the anxiety in the back of her mind that Major Enriques was not to be trusted. What if he had learned of Armand's affiliation with the rebels? What if that was the reason Armand had been summoned to Terasina? She had heard of what General Montoya's attitude was towards so-called traitors, and her skin crawled at the thought of Armand in that man's hands. They would not kill him; not if they suspected he could lead them to Rodolfo. But the things they might do to him to make him do as they commanded did not bear thinking about.

Who had made that call two nights ago, she wondered for the umpteenth time. Her jealous belief that it had been from a woman was acquiring a decidedly hollow ring, and in spite of his assertion that a female was involved, she was beginning to have doubts. What better way to make her hate him than to pretend there was someone else? He had said he was too old for her, that there was no future in their association, and she had not believed him. Was this his ploy, a way to make or break their relationship by giving her time to have second thoughts? Oh, not that she imagined this trip to Terasina was a ploy. He had not manufactured that. But had he taken the opportunity to test the strength of her feelings, by allowing her to think he had just been playing with her emotions?

It was no answer, but it was a possibility, and one that helped her face the day ahead. It didn't prevent her worrying about him; if anything, it increased her fears. But it was something to cling to when she went to bed at night, a tenuous glimmer of hope that refused to be dispelled.

After discovering Maria's address from Santo, Catherine set off to look for her after breakfast. The village was not so large that she anticipated having any difficulty in finding the cottage, and it was quite a novelty re-discovering her surroundings. When she had first come to join her father at the school, he had encouraged her to go with him and meet the people, most of whom were grateful to Professor Loring for his work in the community. She had become familiar with the bakery and the foodstore, and the small post office where her father used to mail the articles he wrote to specialist magazines in London. They had even visited the small church, where Father Donovan conducted the services, for although Professor Loring had been a non-believer, he had greatly admired the gold and silver artefacts regularly used as altar vessels. It had always amazed him that a church, essentially so poor, should possess such wealth. As a humanist, however, he had been of the opinion that simpler receptacles would have served just as well, and the money acquired by selling the precious artefacts to a museum, could have been spent in providing the hospital the community so badly needed.

Unfortunately, Father Donovan was the first person Catherine recognised as she crossed the village square. He was not the first person she could have wished to see, and she half thought of stepping back into the shadows, cast by the overhanging eaves of the local tavern. But the sight of several old men—some seated on a wooden bench in the shade, and others propped against the adobe wall of the tavern, chewing ruminatively on the root tobacco that had so blackened their teeth—made her change her mind. She had no wish to draw attention to herself, or give Father Donovan the impression that she was afraid to speak to him. But after what had happened, it did take a certain amount of courage to walk out into the middle of the sunlit square, and face the old priest with a semblance of dignity. She wished, rather irrelevantly, that she had been wearing a dress, instead of the knee-length cotton pants and short-sleeved shirt which had looked so suitable when she put them on. Naturally Father Donovan was wearing his black cassock, and her trousers seemed so totally alien to everything he stood for.

'Well, child!' he greeted her sombrely. 'So you decided the life of chastity and obedience was not for you. Dare I say, I was sorry to hear it? Sure, you seemed happy enough at the convent until Dr Alvares chose to interfere.'

Catherine hesitated. 'I'm sorry, Father,' she said, at last. 'But I really don't think it was what my father would have wanted.'

'Your father?' The priest folded his hands inside the sleeves of his robe. 'And tell me, do you think your father would approve of your living with a man out of wedlock?'

Catherine flushed. 'I'm not—living with him, Father. At least, not in the way you mean,' she amended hotly.

'Is that so?' Father Donovan considered her

thoughtfully. 'So he hasn't taken you to his bed yet, hmm? Well—' His nostrils flared disdainfully. 'I suppose it's only a matter of time.'

Catherine held up her head. 'He—Dr Alvares has been very kind to me,' she averred stiffly.

'No doubt he has. No doubt he has.' Father Donovan was evidently not impressed. 'Sure, but I think your father didn't spend time enough, teaching you the facts of life. Alannah, a man like Alvares doesn't take the responsibility for a young girl like you upon himself, without he had a motive for so doing.'

'He did.' Catherine was stubborn. 'He felt sorry for me.'

'Sorry for you!' Father Donovan snorted. 'You were being punished, child. Mother Benedicta told me all about it. You knew you had done wrong. Sure, is your spirit so weak it couldn't stand up to a little healthy castigation?'

Catherine bent her head. 'I wanted to leave the convent, Father. Oh, I admit I was grateful for it once, but I've got over that episode now—'

'Are you telling me you no longer care how your father was killed?' The priest looked horrified. 'Have you forgotten that his murderers are still at large?'

'No!' Catherine made a negative gesture. 'Of course, I haven't forgotten. I'll never forget. But my hiding away behind the walls of the convent won't bring him back, will it?'

'That's not the point.' Father Donovan took a deep breath and tried again. 'As you know, your father was not of our faith,' he declared gently. 'Indeed, he and I had little in common, except perhaps our mutual desire to better the lot of these poor people.' He paused. 'And yet, when he died—so tragically—God sent you to us. A curious anomaly, some might say;

yet I chose to regard it as a small miracle.'

'Father Donovan—'

'No, let me finish.' The priest held up his hand, and Catherine fell silent. 'It was a miracle, child. The gates of hell had opened, but you had been saved; saved, so I believed, to swell our numbers, and to help spread the faith throughout this heathen land!'

Catherine shook her head. 'I don't have a vocation, Father.'

'How do you know? You hardly had time to adjust to our ways before Dr Alvares came and carried you off!'

'I had eight months, Father.' Catherine shifted her weight from one foot to the other. 'Really, I want to lead a normal life. And—and Dr Alvares is going to help me.'

Father Donovan's features hardened. 'And what makes you think you will be allowed to lead "a normal life", as you put it? With the threat of guerrilla war always on our doorstep?'

Catherine straightened her spine. 'Are you trying to frighten me, Father?'

'Of course I'm not trying to frighten you.' The priest heaved a sigh. 'But, when Rodolfo's men discover you are no longer protected by the church, you may be in danger. After all, they don't know that you didn't see the men who murdered Professor Loring. They may fear that you could identify them.'

Catherine felt a momentary frisson of fear slide down her spine. 'Surely, if there'd been any way I could identify them, I'd have done so before now,' she exclaimed, forcing a light tone. 'Besides, it may not have been Rodolfo's men who—who burned the school.'

Father Donovan's brows ascended. 'And who put

that idea into your head?' he demanded harshly. 'Alvares, I suppose. Sure, the man's reckless enough to say anything to save his own skin. Wasn't he there the night your father died? And wasn't it fortunate that he was able to spirit you away, without injury to you or himself?'

Catherine swallowed. 'I'd rather not talk about it.'

'Well, I would.' The priest grunted. 'I think it's time I had a word with him myself.'

'You can't.' Catherine flushed as his scowling expression questioned her denial. 'He's away. Dr Alvares is away. In Terasina.'

'Is he so?'

'Yes.' Catherine expelled the breath she had hardly realised she was holding. 'Is that all, Father?'

He pursed his lips. 'So you're not going to change your mind?'

'No, Father.'

'Hah!'

He made a sound which revealed that he renounced her totally, and with only the most perfunctory of blessings, he strode off across the square. For a man of his age, he moved with surprising agility, his cassock swinging with evident disapproval about his scrawny ankles.

It wasn't easy to continue on her way as if nothing had happened. Catherine stood quite still for several seconds in the middle of the square watching the old priest's progress before realising she was doing the very thing she had not wanted to do: drawing attention to herself. She was suddenly conscious of how vulnerable she was, and the warning she had been given no longer seemed so unthinkable. She was alone here, she was the alien in this community; and with Armand hundreds of miles away in Terasina, there was no one to whom she could turn.

She knew an overwhelming urge to abandon her
search for Maria, to return to the house and stay there,
in comparative safety, until Armand's return. But then
the realities of what she was thinking forcibly struck
her. She was being foolish, utterly foolish; allowing
someone with a self-confessed interest in her future to
manipulate her actions. He wanted her to think about
what he had said; he wanted her to worry; he wanted
her to feel she was under observation every minute
she was out of the house, so that eventually she would
only feel safe within the walls of the convent.

But why? Why was Father Donovan so eager to
return her to the nuns? She couldn't believe Mother
Benedicta shared his enthusiasm. Indeed, Catherine
was sure *she* would be most opposed to her re-entry
into the sisterhood. But where Father Donovan was
concerned, Reverend Mother had been known to be
less inflexible, so perhaps, in this instance, an exception could be made.

But Catherine didn't want an exception to be made.
These past weeks, staying in Armand's house, had
only confirmed her belief that she was not meant to
live a life of seclusion. She admired the nuns and the
work they accomplished, and if she could, she would
have liked to go on helping them. But she was not like
them—she had too many uncontrollably human feelings—and while she was grateful for the kindness
they had shown her, she had no wish to be one of their
number.

With a determined effort, she put these thoughts
aside. It was hot, and she could feel the sun's heat
burning her shoulders. It was also later than she had
anticipated, and if she didn't find Maria's house soon,
it would be lunchtime. If Santo's graphic gestures

could be relied upon, Maria lived only a few yards from the army barracks, whose parade-ground wall backed on to the square, and identifying her surroundings she set out to gain the shade at the opposite side.

'*Senhorita!*' Her progress was arrested by the single word and, although she could hardly believe anyone was speaking to her, Catherine turned.

There was a stone basin in the square, and a barely distinguishable lump of marble which had once been a fountain sprouted from its base. As the uniformed figure stepped out from behind the moss-covered masonry, she thought for a moment Father Donovan had been right, and that she was to be punished for her scepticism. But then she recognised the moustachioed features of Henri Enriques, and her palpitating heart slowed its suffocating beat.

'Major,' she got out weakly. 'You startled me. I didn't see you there behind the fountain.'

'*Desculpe, senhorita,* I am sorry.' The army officer stepped round the basin to her side. 'I did not mean to alarm you. But you seemed rapt in thought, and until you moved I was loath to draw attention to my presence.'

Catherine forced a slight smile. 'I was—wool-gathering,' she admitted, as he fell into step beside her.

'Wool-gathering?' he echoed. 'Forgive me, but I do not think I have heard that expression before.'

'Oh—' Catherine was glad of the diversion. 'It means, thinking—daydreaming.' She lifted her slim shoulders expressively. 'I'm afraid I was miles away.'

'Ah, yes.' Major Enriques gave her a polite smile. 'That I can understand. But what were you thinking?

That is the beguiling question.'

Catherine bent her head. 'Nothing of importance, I assure you, Major,' she responded with determined lightness. 'I—what can I do for you? You wanted to speak to me?'

Henri Enriques regarded her whimsically. 'What better reason could I have than a selfish desire to assure myself of your well-being, Miss Loring,' he averred gallantly. 'Particularly now, as we meet as individuals for the first time.'

Catherine permitted him a sideways glance. 'You've heard what happened, I suppose.'

'From our good friend, the doctor,' he conceded, his footsteps slowing as they reached the dappled shadow of a pantiled roof. 'But, I have to admit to a certain amount of curiosity, and when I saw you here, I could not resist the opportunity of speaking to you myself.'

Catherine took a deep breath. 'I imagine you agree with Father Donovan: you don't think I should have left the convent?'

'On the contrary.' The officer shrugged. 'I was merely intrigued by your reasons for so doing. Could it be that you are to return to England?'

'No.' Catherine sighed. 'At least, not yet. I just— decided I was not cut out for that kind of life.'

'I see.' Henri Enriques absorbed this consideringly. 'And have you made plans? If there is any way I can help you—you must let me know.'

'You're very kind.' After Father Donovan's repudiation, it was quite a relief to find that Major Enriques did not condemn her for what she had done. Even so, she couldn't help the insidious thought that he might well have his own motives for wanting her out of the convent, and she couldn't dispel the feeling that he

was more interested in her future activities than he
was saying.

'You are out for a walk?' he inquired now, glancing
quickly round the square, and belatedly Catherine
became aware of their silent audience. Their conversation had become the cynosure for countless pairs of
eyes, and she wondered, with some misgivings,
whether Major Enriques's appearance had been such a
good thing after all. Obviously, there were people
here who had no sympathy with the military regime,
and if what Armand said was true, they were in the
majority. How might her innocent exchange with the
army officer be interpreted, she wondered, when so
far as they knew, she still blamed the guerrillas for her
father's death?

'I—was going to visit Maria Callea,' she admitted
unwillingly. 'She looked after me while I was ill, and I
promised to keep in touch.'

'Maria Callea.' Major Enriques inclined his head
slowly. 'I know the Callea family. She lives with her
father and her four younger brothers not far from
here.' He paused. 'Will you allow me to conduct you to
your destination? Although all is quiet at the moment,
I do not think Dr Alvares would approve of your
visiting your friend without an escort, and I should be
happy to perform this service for Armand.'

Catherine's brain laboured furiously to try and come
up with some excuse for not accepting his assistance,
but she was powerless to stop him, and her reception
at the Callea house was not the friendly visit she had
anticipated.

For one thing, their arrival interrupted Maria in the
throes of washing, and her red face and equally red
hands were indicative of her embarrassment. She
should have sent a note, Catherine realised belatedly,

feeling worse than ever with Major Enriques at her side, and Maria's mortification was only compounded by her father's sullen taciturnity. Evidently, he did not wish to be seen giving hospitality to a member of the military, and for Maria's sake, Catherine refused the cup of coffee she tendered.

She did see the baby, however. A child of perhaps three months of age was kicking his legs lustily in a wooden bassinet, and as he was not wearing a nappy, his gender was in no doubt. In all honesty, Catherine didn't see much resemblance to his mother in his chubby features. His skin was fairer than hers, for one thing, and his eyes were not brown, but grey. Nevertheless, Maria was obviously very proud of him, and Catherine was glad she had made the effort, even if it hadn't turned out exactly as she had expected.

The next couple of days were uneventful. In spite of Armand's absence, Santo's behaviour towards her was no more friendly, and she was not encouraged to spend too much time in the kitchen. He served her meals, answered any questions she chose to put to him—if he understood them—but otherwise they lived separate lives. Indeed, she wondered sometimes if he blamed her for Armand's being away, but as their exchanges were supplemented by hand signals, she had no way of vindicating herself.

The days dragged, and although there were times when she was tempted to leave the security of the house, mostly she confined herself within its environs. One afternoon, she did summon all her courage to walk to the outskirts of the village, where the ruins of the school-house could still be seen. But, although she crossed the dusty road and stood staring at the smoke-blackened walls and crumbling roof, she did not venture through the iron gate. It was still too painful, too stark a reminder of what had once been to cast it off so lightly. But she was glad she had come, for all that. In a strange way, it helped to exorcise the ghost of her father.

On Sunday evening she was sitting in the living room, flicking restlessly through the pages of an old medical journal of Armand's, when the telephone rang. It had not rung since the call the previous Tuesday evening when Armand had received that summons to Terasina, and for a few moments Catherine sat and stared at it, not at all sure whether she should pick up the receiver.

However, when it became apparent that Santo was not going to do so, she dropped the magazine to the floor and got up from her chair. She knew a quite ridiculous anxiety now as she crossed the room, that it should not stop ringing before she reached it; and when her fingers closed around the instrument she raised it urgently to her ear.

'Yes?'

'Where were you?'

Armand's voice was unmistakable, even over the crackly line, and she clutched the receiver closer, as if it might lessen the distance between them. 'I didn't know if I should answer it or not,' she admitted huskily. 'Where are you? What are you doing?' Her voice faltered. 'I thought you might get home tonight.'

'Did you?' He sounded sardonic. 'Before I went away, I got the distinct impression I would not exactly be missed.'

'Oh . . .' Catherine sighed. 'Well, I have missed you.' She paused, schooling her tone. 'When are you coming back? You said you'd only be away a week.'

'Yes—well, perhaps I was overly optimistic,' he

replied flatly. 'I can't get away before Wednesday or Thursday now.' And at her exclamation of dismay, he added: 'You're all right, aren't you?'

'Apart from having no one to talk to, of course,' she told him tightly, and there was a pregnant silence before he spoke again.

'I've been thinking about that while I've been away,' he remarked at last. 'I know you said you didn't want to go back to England to work, but I really think you ought to give it further consideration.'

Catherine caught her breath. 'You can't make me go!'

'Don't be ridiculous!' His impatience was audible. 'I'm not threatening you with deportation or anything. I'm merely suggesting that perhaps you ought to reconsider your decision.'

'I don't want to reconsider my decision.' Catherine discovered she was trembling. It was so hard to conduct this kind of a conversation without even being able to see Armand's face, and she wished, rather childishly, that she had ignored the call after all. 'I've lost touch with my friends, and I don't have any relations there. I don't want to go to England.'

'Very well.' Armand's tone sounded as hollow as she felt. 'We'll have to make other arrangements. We'll discuss the matter more fully when I get back.'

'Thank you. Thank you very much.' Catherine could not hide the break in her voice, even though her intonation was sarcastic, and Armand made an exasperated sound.

'Stop making me feel like a pig for bringing the subject up,' he exclaimed. 'I'm not suggesting anything drastic. Just a—change of surroundings perhaps.'

Catherine groped for a chair and sat down rather

heavily. 'A change of surroundings?' she choked, and he expelled his breath wearily.

'I know of a job in Terasina,' he began patiently, but Catherine wasn't listening. With precise, controlled movements, she was replacing the receiver on its rest. When the telephone rang again a few minutes later, she was already safely in her bedroom, and although the bell went on and on, she endured the novel sensation of defying him.

CHAPTER ELEVEN

PREDICTABLY, her desire to thwart Armand only lasted as long as it took for the phone to stop ringing. As soon as it fell silent, she was smitten with pangs of remorse and, perched unhappily on the side of her bed, she pressed her palms together.

Dear God, she thought, she had done it now. Armand would never forgive her for hanging up on him. He had taken the trouble to ring and inform her of his movements, and because she hadn't liked what he told her, she had childishly disconnected the call.

She shook her head. Why had she done it? Why had she destroyed any chance of reasoning with him? It wasn't as if she hadn't been prepared for what he said. He had said much the same before he left for Terasina, and instead of dealing with it in an adult way, she had reacted like a spoilt baby. How could she hope to convince him of her maturity if every time he opposed her wishes she either burst into tears or threw a tantrum?

Surprisingly enough, Armand's call did provoke an inquiry from Santo. The next morning, when he served her her coffee, he let it be known that he had heard the telephone ringing, and although she had little desire to discuss it, Catherine was obliged to tell him it was Armand who had rung.

'Esteve em Terasina?' Santo asked curiously, and translating with some difficulty, Catherine nodded, confirming that Armand was in Terasina.

'He should be back by Wednesday,' she submitted, in careful Portuguese, and glimpsed the first trace of a smile in the old man's features.

'*Muito bem!*' he complimented her drily, and she felt her colour deepen at the unexpected praise.

Nevertheless, although Santo's belated approval did boost her confidence, Catherine found herself anticipating Armand's arrival with increasing apprehension. Whereas before, she had been looking forward to his return, eager to make amends and certain that, once he was back, their differences would not appear so insurmountable; now she awaited his homecoming with anxious eyes, her time at Batista-major limited by the troubled awareness of his ultimatum.

On Tuesday night, she couldn't sleep. The knowledge that the following day was Wednesday filled her with dread, even while her pulses raced at the thought of seeing Armand again. Fleetingly, she gave a thought to the reasons that had taken him to Terasina, but they seemed of minor importance compared to the consequences of his return. He was not the kind of man to allow an insult to go unpunished, and she would be lucky if he was even willing to listen to her excuses now.

The unexpected sound of a car's engine broke into her feverish thoughts, stilling her threshing body and arousing an unwelcome remembrance of what Father Donovan had said. Earlier, she had been startled by the unearthly screech of a wild-cat which had seemed to be prowling just outside her window. But right now, she would have exchanged that sound for the ominous purr of a deadlier predator, and she wondered if her father's killers knew that tonight was the last night she would be alone.

It was ridiculous, of course; the logical part of her brain rejected the idea that there had been any truth in the old priest's assertions. But nevertheless, the memory of what had happened to her father wouldn't go away, and when the vehicle stopped outside the house, her breathing seemed suspended.

It seemed hours and not just seconds before she heard the outer door open and close, but when it did her heart leapt into her throat. Santo always locked the doors before retiring for the night, so whoever had come into the house had let themselves in with a key. *Armand?* she asked herself tremulously, coming upright in the bed. Could it be Armand getting back sooner than he had anticipated? He was due back tomorrow. Had he managed to get an earlier train? But then, on the heels of this thought, came the chilling reminder that this had once been an army officer's quarters, and it was reasonable to assume that Major Enriques might have a key, too.

Her mouth felt parched, and every inch of her flesh was bathed in a cold sweat. Although she strained her ears, there had been no sound since the betraying thud of the door closing. Whoever it was was taking his time about revealing his whereabouts, but her vivid imagination could already see someone standing outside her room in the darkness, just waiting for a betraying breath.

The clatter, as a lamp in the living room was overturned, brought her out of bed. It didn't seem credible that a would-be assassin wouldn't even know which room she was occupying, and she pulled the bedroom door ajar and listened intently. There was a bar of light now, shining through the half-open living room door, and she expelled her breath weakly. No intruder would advertise his presence so openly surely, and as if to confirm this conclusion, Armand chose that moment to give out a tired groan.

Her relief that it was him and not anyone else overcame all Catherine's inhibitions. Without stopping to think that the last words they had exchanged had been less than friendly, or considering the wisdom of leaving her room without the enveloping folds of his bathrobe flapping about her, she flew along the passage towards the light. Her fingertips against the panels propelled the door inward, and she paused on the threshold, gazing wordlessly at him.

Armand was stretched out in one of the armchairs. He had shed his jacket and it was tossed carelessly on to the couch, half concealing the canvas holdall lying beneath it. He was in the process of unbuttoning the cuffs of his shirt and loosening the knot of his tie, and to Catherine, who had never seen him formally dressed before, he looked disturbingly dark and alien.

It was only when his eyes moved over her that she remembered the scarcity of her attire. The peacock-blue pyjama jacket, with its brocade braiding, barely covered her hips, the hem resting provocatively at the tops of her legs. She was decent, but only just, and her heart palpitated wildly at the awareness of his forbidding expression. To add to her confusion, she had washed her hair the night before and instead of plaiting it as she usually did, she had left it loose. It had not been properly dry when she went to bed, but now it flowed unrestrainedly over her shoulders and down her back, a bronzed curtain in the subdued light.

'You're—back,' she got out at last, when it became obvious that he was not about to say anything, and with a controlled inclination of his head, he got stiffly to his feet.

'As you see,' he conceded, pulling the knot of his tie halfway down his chest and unloosening the top two buttons of his shirt. 'And having ascertained the fact, I suggest you go back to bed—*imediatamente!*'

Catherine hesitated, anxiety getting the better of discretion. 'You're still angry with me then.'

A muscle was jerking spasmodically in his cheek, and the compression of his mouth did nothing to relieve it. 'Did you expect otherwise?' he queried. Then, breathing deeply, he added: 'We will talk about it in the morning. Now is not the time to indulge in futile recriminations.'

Catherine made a fretful little sound. 'You're not going to forgive me, are you? I know I shouldn't have hung up on you like that, but you wouldn't listen to reason.'

'And you would, I suppose?' he remarked, his lips twisting. 'Oh, go to bed, Catherine! I have no intention of losing any more sleep over you!'

Catherine gasped. '*You* lose sleep over *me*?' She shook her head. 'I don't believe it. I'm the one who loses sleep here. It doesn't occur to you to wonder what I'm doing awake at this time, does it?'

'I assumed you'd heard my clumsy entry into this room,' he responded bleakly. 'Or perhaps the station wagon's engine. At this time of night, either one could have wakened you.'

'Well, they didn't.' Catherine sniffed. 'I was already awake, and when I heard the car's engine, I didn't know who it might be.'

Armand regarded her sceptically. 'Who did you expect?'

'I didn't "expect" anyone,' she retorted. 'But—well, it did occur to me that . . . that my father's murderers

have never been caught, and they might think I could
identify them.'

'What?' Armand's ejaculation was strangled. 'Who
has been feeding you that nonsense? Enriques?'

'As—as a matter of fact, it was Father Donovan,'
Catherine told him, tilting her head a little indignantly. Barefoot, as she was, Armand seemed so
much bigger and more powerful. 'It's true, isn't it?
Daddy's killers are still free. And—and I am their
logical target.'

Armand's eyes had narrowed. 'Donovan told you
this?'

'I've said so, haven't I?' Catherine lifted one discon-
solate shoulder. 'I must say you don't seem very
concerned.'

Armand shook his head. 'Catherine, if it's true that
your father was the victim of a terrorist attack, what
possible reason could they have for caring whether
you recognised them or not?'

Catherine blinked. 'But you said—'

'I know what I said.' Armand considered his words
for a moment, then he went on: 'If, however, your
father was killed by—other forces, then rest assured,
they are no longer around here.'

Catherine frowned. 'What do you mean?'

'No assassin worth his salt is going to stick around to
be identified by you or anyone else.' Armand hesitated. 'Now, I suggest you return to bed before your
imagination leads you into any further flights of
fancy.'

'It wasn't a—flight of fancy!' protested Catherine
defensively. 'Father Donovan did suggest that I might
be in some danger.'

'Did he?' Armand's lips thinned. 'Ah, well—I imagine the good priest was simply indulging a less-

than-priestly desire to make you squirm.'

Catherine blinked. 'I don't understand.'

Armand sighed. 'Donovan is a good friend of Mother Benedicta's, isn't he?' he continued, after a moment. 'It's not unreasonable that he might try to make you regret your expulsion.'

Catherine rubbed her nose with a thoughtful finger, unaware that when she did so the hem of the pyjama jacket rose tantalisingly at her hip. 'He did try to persuade me to go back,' she admitted slowly, and Armand's taut expression eased somewhat.

'There you are then.'

'Yes.' Catherine caught her lower lip between her teeth. 'He—he was quite put out when I said I didn't want to.'

'I can imagine.' Armand's smile was thin. 'Well, as I said a few minutes ago, we can discuss this more fully in the morning. Right now, I'm tired, and I'm sure you are, too.'

Catherine stubbed her toe against the roughly-woven rug that covered the floor. 'You're not really going to send me away, are you?' she probed, returning to the problem that had kept her awake. She took an involuntary step forward and touched his sleeve. 'Armand, I know you don't want to hear this just now, but if you'll let me stay, I won't precipitate any more scenes like—like the one we had before you went away.'

'Won't you?' With restrained deliberation, Armand lifted his arm so that her fingers fell away. 'What are you doing now?'

Catherine sighed. 'I'm trying to be reasonable.'

Armand's expression hardened. 'Are you? And do I have Father Donovan to thank for this, also?'

Catherine wilted beneath his contemptuous stare,

and she shifted a little uncertainly, not altogether understanding his mood. 'He did—mention our association,' she conceded unwillingly.

'I guessed he would.' Armand's lips twisted. 'And did you confess your sins to him?'

'No—'

'Yet he spoke of our . . . association in glowing terms, no doubt?'

Catherine shrugged. 'You wouldn't expect him to approve.'

'No.' Armand was coldly acquiescent. 'It's not a situation any—sane person would approve of. At least we agree on that point.'

The conversation was not going at all the way Catherine had wanted and moving closer to him, she tilted her head appealingly. 'I'm sorry,' she said. 'I know I've made things difficult for you, but I am grateful.' She shook her head and strands of sun-streaked silk lodged themselves on his sleeve. 'Armand, don't be angry with me, please!'

'Not now, Catherine,' he exhorted in a harsh voice, brushing past her to pick up the lamp he had lit earlier and striding towards the door. 'Come: I will escort you back to your room. As I said before, we will talk further in the morning.'

Catherine had no choice but to accompany him. She had the distinct suspicion that if she didn't he would leave her there in the dark, to make her own way back to bed. With a dejected air, she followed him to the door and at his silent command preceded him through it, treading the carpet forlornly along the passage to her room.

His pace was quicker than hers, primarily because his legs were longer, and he reached her door before she did, going inside to set down the lamp he was carrying on the small cabinet beside the bed. Its soft illumination was reflected back by the mirror, giving warmth and colour where there had been only shadow. When she came through the door, he was just straightening from his task, his features taking on a guarded expression when he met her reproachful gaze.

'Sleep well,' he bid her bleakly, intent on quitting the room, and she moved aside obediently as he came towards her.

'Did you—did you see your friend?' she demanded painfully, as he reached the door, and although she sensed from the set of his shoulders that he wanted to ignore her, he reluctantly turned.

'Friend? What friend?' he asked wearily. 'Catherine, can we leave this until tomorrow—*today*—later this morning! I am too tired to play these games.'

'It's not a game,' she retorted, sniffing. 'I only asked if you'd seen the woman you told me about. That's not such a difficult question, is it?'

Armand closed his eyes for a brief moment, and then opened them again. 'Very well,' he said flatly, and she noticed how in moments of stress his speech became very precise. 'Yes. Yes, I saw her. Now, may I be permitted to go to my bed?'

Catherine's jaw quivered. 'Is she beautiful?'

Armand uttered an oath. 'Catherine, why are you asking these questions?'

'Why not?' Catherine schooled her voice with an effort. 'I want to know where I stand. I want to know what you're going to do about me. Is that so unreasonable?'

Armand was silent for so long she thought he wasn't going to answer her, but then, when she was on the point of surrendering her offensive, he said wearily: 'There is a position. In Terasina. It involves taking care of a young child. I want you to take it.'

'No—'

'Yes.' His tone was inflexible. 'You did not really think we could go on living together indefinitely, did you?'

'Why not?'

'Why not?' His echo of her words was incredulous. 'Catherine, you know why not. That is what all this is about. You know it and I know it. Now, I suggest we get some sleep and talk again in the morning.'

Catherine moved her head disbelievingly from side to side. 'Please—please, don't send me away!'

'Catherine—'

'No, listen to me; Armand, please, listen to me!' Stumbling over her words, she rushed on: 'I know I've been foolish. I know you think I'm childish, and I probably am. But I'll grow out of that. I know there's another woman in your life, perhaps more than one, but that doesn't matter. All I want to do is stay here—work here—work with you, for . . . for the people—'

'*Catherine*—'

'I won't ask anything of you. I don't even need much in the way of a salary. What do I need money for? All I need is a couple of shirts and some jeans, and I've got those. Perhaps a little money to cover the personal things I have to buy—'

'Catherine, stop it!' His features contorted by an emotion she could not identify, Armand halted her outburst by stepping forward and grasping both her wrists. The force of his grip interrupted the flow of blood into her hands, but their growing numbness was nothing compared to the numbness his anger was evoking. 'You are crazy!' he told her harshly. '*Por Deus*! I am not suggesting we never see one another again. Terasina is not the end of the earth! You may even come to like it there, once you have recovered from this ridiculous infatuation you seem to have acquired for me.'

Catherine lifted her head. 'It's not an infatuation,' she declared bravely. 'It just pleases you to treat it as such.'

'Oh, for pity's sake!' Armand gazed at her frustratedly. 'You should have listened to Father Donovan. I am sure he defined my character in no uncertain terms.'

'I don't care what Father Donovan thinks,' she responded, concentrating on the loosened knot of his tie and the sweep of brown skin above it.

'Well, perhaps you should,' Armand countered. 'Catherine, listen to me for a change: you know nothing about me. To you, I am the doctor at Batista-major, nothing more, nothing less. But I have a life outside this small valley—a life which you can have no part of!'

Catherine felt a sob rising in her throat, but she swallowed it back and said, albeit unsteadily: 'I don't believe you. You're just trying to make me hate you!' She paused to shake her head and then continued huskily: 'But you won't. You can't. I care too much about you.'

'*Nâo presta para nada*, Catherine.' Armand's roughly-spoken words sent a shiver of anticipation down her spine, and his hands gripping her wrists moved convulsively. 'You do not know what you are saying. You cannot have everything you want,' he muttered, but she felt his gaze raking the averted contours of her face. 'You are just a child, an inexperienced child, to whom the whole concept of a relationship focusses on the emotions involved.'

'And are there emotions involved?' she ventured, her eyes moving up over the strong column of his throat to the taut curve of his jawline. Shaking her hair back, she lifted her head and met his eyes, and the smouldering amber of their depths brought a quivering unsureness to her stomach.

'Do you doubt it?' he demanded at last, the words torn from him. '*Cristo, pequena*, why do you do this to me—to us? Our paths have crossed, but now they must part again. Accept it. Accept the truth of it. Anything else would be—sheer madness!'

With a muffled imprecation, he thrust her hands away from him, intent only on turning aside and getting out of there. But she was close, closer than he had imagined, and when he turned his weight came down heavily on her bare toes.

Her cry of pain was equalled by his own oath of impatience, and stepping back he gazed at her with tortured eyes. '*Mãe de Deus!* What have I done now?' he exclaimed, his gaze travelling down over the revealing hemline of his pyjama jacket: over smooth thighs and shapely calves, to the bruised toes she was presently lifting gingerly from the floor. 'How does it feel?' he demanded. 'Can you move your toes? There is nothing broken, is there? *Santa Maria*, I am a clumsy fool!'

'It's—all right, really,' she got out unevenly, becoming aware of the increased charging of the atmosphere. The small accident had achieved what all her pleas had not, and when he bent to examine her foot, she stepped towards him almost instinctively. The smooth vitality of his hair brushed sensuously against her knees, mocking their quivering vulnerability, and his hands on her foot were incredibly gentle, belying his anger of moments before. He *wanted* to touch her. It was there in his voice, and in the almost caressing quality of his fingers as they probed her slim foot; and when he lifted his head and looked up at her, her whole body trembled in the face of the passion in his eyes.

'I have hurt you,' he said huskily, and Catherine quickly shook her head.

'No, you haven't. It was nothing. Just a momentary twinge. You didn't do it on purpose. It was my fault. I should have stepped away—'

'I am not just talking about your toes,' he cut in on her swiftly, and she didn't know whether she was glad or sorry when he released her from that imprisoning gaze to transfer his attention back to her foot. His hands moved sensitively to her ankles, massaging the skin above her heels with sensuous deliberation. 'You should not have left your bed,' he continued roughly, and the heated scent of his body rose to her nostrils as his hands progressed to the slender muscles at the backs of her legs.

'Armand—' she began, tipping her head back so that the silken curtain of her hair almost touched her waist, but he was not listening to her. With a lithe movement, he came to his feet, and the journey his hands had started continued to the gentle swell of her buttocks.

'Are you wearing anything under this?' he demanded, but she knew he had already found the answer. 'In any case, it is too much,' he added, disposing of the three buttons with insistent fingers, and the exotic jacket fell heedlessly to the floor.

There was a moment when Catherine knew an instinctive urge to cover herself, but the moment passed unchallenged. Instead, her hands went out to him, seeking the loose knot of his tie and pulling it free. The remaining buttons of his shirt soon followed it, and with an exclamation of impatience, he shrugged out of the offending garment.

'*Meu bem, meu formosa*, Catarina,' he muttered, his hands at her waist urging her towards him, and the yielding warmth of her softness was compelled against his hard chest and muscled thighs. 'Sweet, irresistible Catarina,' he breathed, his breath fanning the silken curve of her shoulder. 'By all the saints, I am a man, not a priest! And God knows, I have thought of nothing else since I left for the capital.'

'You still want me?' she whispered, drawing back from where her lips had been pressed against the sharp bones of his collarbone, and his acknowledgement was bitter.

'Yes, I still want you,' he conceded, his teeth fastening on the tender lobe of her ear and tugging painfully. 'But that does not mean I should take you. No, that does not follow at all.'

'Why not?' Her hands cupped his face, guiding him to look at her.

'Because—oh, because you are untouched, and I am not,' he retorted harshly. 'You need someone like yourself: someone young and free, with all his life in front of him. Not a man old enough to have sired you, whose experiences have left him—at best—jaded with his existence.'

'I don't want a *boy*!' she exclaimed scornfully, when he would have released himself from her hold. 'Do you really believe someone without any experience is what I need?'

Armand sighed. 'Stop twisting my words.'

'It's what you said.'

'I said you needed someone younger—'

'Someone inexperienced.'

'Not necessarily.'

'Why?' she allowed her tongue to circle her lips with instinctive sensuality. 'Tell me about it.'

'I am persuaded you know about the—how do you say it?—the birds and the bees,' he agreed unevenly. 'You do not need me to tell you.'

'But I have had no experience,' she persisted, allowing her hands to slide around the back of his neck, her fingers coiling in the silky hair at his nape. 'You said so.'

'*Meu Deus*, Catherine, stop tormenting me! Do you not think it is enough that I must hold you in my arms without kissing you? Is it not sufficient that I should feel your naked body against mine without making love to you?'

'You're not naked,' she pointed out huskily, burying her face in the hollow of his neck, and she felt the shudder that ran through him at her words.

'I am as good as,' he muttered, and she had to admit that the thrusting pressure of his manhood was only thinly disguised by the taut material of his pants.

'I don't want you to go,' she breathed, turning her lips against the side of his neck. 'Stay with me, Armand. Please—stay with me!'

'Catherine, if I stay with you—'

'I know,' she said simply, and with a groan of anguish, Armand found her chin and tilted it upward, seeking her mouth with his.

His lips were tender at first, bestowing a tenuous bounty that left her trembling, but unfulfilled. His kisses were light and exploratory, finding the quivering fullness of her lower lip, before moving with increasing sureness to the slightly shorter upper one, coaxing them apart to allow his tongue to dart between. Catherine felt almost bemused beneath that sinuous exploration, the moist tip of his tongue finding every sensitive cavity of her mouth. It was a delicate operation, eloquent of the control Armand had over his emotions, but Catherine had no such restraint. With her heart palpitating wildly, and the blood rushing hotly through her veins, her legs sagged, and her hands at his nape were all that supported her.

'Do you want me to stop?' he demanded, barely audibly, his hands gliding softly over her hips, and Catherine allowed a shaky sound to escape her.

'Could you?' she countered unsteadily, pulling his mouth back to hers, and with a groan of submission, Armand swung her off her feet.

With a feeling almost of inevitability, Catherine felt the coarse cotton of the bed sheet against the heated skin of her back. But when she attempted to pull Armand down on top of her, his hands firmly disposed of her arms about his neck. Lifting her lids, she was about to make a protest when she saw what he was doing, and her eyes became limpid pools of enchantment to which Armand was no longer immune. Shifting restlessly on the bed, her movements innocently provocative as she turned her legs from side to side, she saw the way his hands trembled as he unzipped his pants and stepped out of them. But then, the sight of his muscled body brought her upwards on her elbows, her eyes lingering sensuously on the fine whorls of dark hair that arrowed down below his navel.

'Com a breca, you should not look at me like that,' he muttered, sinking down on the bed beside her, and her lips parted to acknowledge his hoarse reproof.

'Why not?' she breathed, even though the primitive beauty of his body had instilled a momentary sense of panic inside her. He was so big; so powerful; so obviously experienced in his dealings with her sex. While she—she had only her instincts to guide her, and little confidence in her own abilities to please a man like him.

'You do not know what you do to me,' he answered her now, his hands slipping around her and bringing her up into the circle of his arms. She was between his legs as he half sat, half knelt, on the bed, and the pulsating heat of his manhood throbbed insistently against her stomach. 'I am trying to be gentle,' he added, his low voice, the slumbering sexuality in his eyes, causing her senses to swim. 'But, you do not make it easy.'

'Don't I?' With unknowing allure, Catherine lifted her arms to slide her fingers into his hair, the revealing arousal of her breasts crushed against the muscled width of his chest. 'Perhaps I don't want to make it easy.' She turned her lips against the pulse beating erratically beside his jaw. 'Perhaps I want you to commit yourself.'

'To commit myself?' Armand uttered a shaken laugh. 'Oh, *querida*, if this is not committing myself— to the devil, if nowhere else—I do not know what is!' and with a muffled exclamation, he grasped a handful of her hair to bring her teasing mouth to his.

Now, his possessive tongue plundered her mouth, a fierce catalyst that changed the tenor of his caresses from restrained tenderness to the all-consuming fire of passion. The seductive persuasion of his kisses banished her fears of moments before. Now, she had no thought for anything but the searing hunger of his need, and her arms wrapped themselves tightly about his neck as her emotions threatened to suffocate her.

'You are so beautiful,' he breathed, lowering her back against the pillows and stretching his length beside her. With one leg insinuating itself between hers, his mouth moved from her lips to her cheek and then to her ear, his warm breath moistening its delicate cavities, evoking a voluptuous sigh she had no will to resist.

His lips moved on, following a sensuous path along the curve of her jaw and down her slender throat, hesitating now and then to incite her surrender by nibbling at her tender flesh. He was evidently no amateur in the art of making love, and the blood rose hotly beneath his touch, tingeing the creamy-white skin.

When his mouth found the swollen nipple of one full breast, she experienced the curious ache between her legs he had evoked once before. There was a slick moistness between her thighs that was not unpleasant to feel, but her heart almost stopped beating when his caressing fingers probed that innocent betrayal. His hands slid possessively over the silken curls that nestled there, and then gently, but insistently, parted her legs to allow his exploration.

'Armand . . .' she whispered shakily, but protestingly, and he quickly moved to silence her uncertainty.

'Let me,' he said huskily, covering her mouth with his. Then, burying his face in the scented hollow of her neck, he added softly: 'I want to touch every part of you. Do you not wish to touch me?'

Catherine swallowed convulsively. 'Can I? May I?'

'You may do with me what you will,' he told her unsteadily, rolling on to his back beside her and regarding her with a captivating artlessness. 'Kiss me,' he breathed, as she raised herself on one elbow to look down at him, and his hand behind her head put action to the words.

With her lips on his, her tongue venturing daringly into his mouth, Catherine's fingers made their own exploration, and the shuddering response he gave seemed to point to her success. His body was so different from her own, the fine hair that partially covered the lower part of his chest prickling her palm as her fingertips strayed down to his flat stomach.

'*Valha-me Deus!*' he groaned, when her tantalising touch found his manhood, and unable to sustain that enflaming caress for longer than a few seconds, he uttered an oath and reversed their positions.

'Did I do something wrong?' she asked innocently, as his lean hard body imprisoned hers against the sheet, and his lips moved with momentary amusement.

'*Nada,*' he told her huskily. 'Nothing, *querida*, but I find you much too desirable to permit you to continue.'

'Really?' she breathed, as his tortured breathing fired her blood, and his head scraped positively against her breast.

'Really,' he assured her, his tongue reaching across the hair's-breadth of space that separated their mouths to trace the outline of her lips. 'Sweet Catarina, you have no idea how much I want you.'

'I know what I want,' she whispered against his lips, and the hot invasion of his tongue convinced her that he knew what he wanted, too.

With controlled deliberation, his leg was parting her legs, and any lingering doubts she might have had concerning her own inadequacies were swept away by the searching pressure of his mouth. Even so, when she felt the pulsating length of him nudging the secret recesses of her body, she knew another moment's panic. How could she go through with this, she asked herself desperately, remembering the whispered stories she had heard, the sordid gossip concerning who had done what with whom, and how terrifying it must be? Girl-talk, perhaps, but containing an element of truth just the same, the time-worn uncertainties of those members of her sex who were not yet women.

'Relax, little one.' Armand's reassuring voice beside her ear was calming, but the pressure was increasing just the same, and anxiety flowered anew. It was like dying, she thought fancifully; the whole measure of her life was flashing before her eyes, and she had barely reached the point where she was asking herself what her father would say if he were alive when a stabbing pain swept up agonisingly into her stomach.

Her choked cry of protest was stifled beneath his lips, and, amazingly, with that cry went all her fears. It was done, it was over, she realised tremulously, and the intimacy of Armand's possession drove all other thoughts from her head.

'*Desculpe*, I'm sorry,' he sighed unsteadily, feeling the dampness of her forehead with his, but with a fervent shake of her head, Catherine wound her arms around his neck.

'Love me,' she breathed, eager for him to declare himself. Surely now, he would tell her he loved her, she thought dreamily, arching her body so that there was no breath of air between them.

But, instead of making some equally fervent proclamation, Armand seemed to take her remark to mean something else entirely. With a little start, she felt him moving inside her, swelling, if that were humanly possible, spreading the tight coil of muscle that had closed around him and bringing a curiously breathless feeling to the back of her throat.

'Don't—don't go—' she whispered, hardly understanding what he intended to do, and the passion in his kiss left her weak and gasping for air.

'I have no intention of doing so,' he told her roughly, and unleashing the emotions he had so patiently held in check, he moved against her.

The stillness that had gripped her at his words was only a momentary thing. To her astonishment, he began to drive more deeply into the honeyed sheath that surrounded him, and what was more, instead of hurting her, as she had expected, it became a disturbingly pleasurable sensation. Her body welcomed his invasion, her limbs actually spread wider to accommodate him, curling round his back as her fingernails curled into his flesh.

Dear God, she thought, as he introduced her to the wine-dark world of searing sensuality, and I assumed I knew all there was to know! With Armand, she was scaling the heights of sexual awareness, her body moving with his to facilitate his possession.

Every inch of her skin felt sensitised. Her breasts felt infinitely tender against the taut muscles of his chest, the hair on his belly was tantalisingly abrasive where it brushed her softness. She was alive with every tingling nerve of her body, straining towards a fulfilment she neither knew nor could guess at until a shattering climax sent her hurtling over the brink of ecstasy. Armand reached his climax only seconds later, the shudder that swept through his body matching her own for completeness. With a groan of satisfaction, he spilled himself inside her, and Catherine's nails slid harmlessly down over his hips as his prone weight slumped on top of her.

CHAPTER TWELVE

DAWN was sweeping down over the mountains, pushing persistent fingers through the cracks in the blind, when Catherine heard the insistent tapping at the door.

'Menina! Menina inglesa! Onde está o medico, menina?'

It was Santo's voice that disturbed her. The tapping she could have ignored, but the old man's anxious tones asking for the doctor demanded a response, and although she felt sleepy and lethargic, and curiously unwilling to move, she was going to have to open her eyes. Why was he knocking at her door, she wondered confusedly, at the same moment that she became aware of a warm, alien body beside hers in the bed. Armand! she remembered weakly, the events of the night before instantly crowding her consciousness. That was why Santo was knocking at *her* door. He must have seen—*or heard*—the station wagon, and as Armand was not in his own room, he had come to the inevitable conclusion.

Blinking her eyes, Catherine took a hasty account of their surroundings. Armand's clothes were still strewn about the floor where he had dropped them, as well as the silk pyjama jacket he had stripped from her. It was a revealing sight, and not one she had any wish for Santo to see.

More intimately, there was Armand's present position to concern her. As on that other occasion when she had slept beside him, his limbs were coiled possessively about her. His dark head, his harsh features relaxed and strangely vulnerable in sleep, was once more cushioned on the silken pillow of her hair, one hand resting familiarly on her hip, but this time the leg that lay so naturally between hers was naked.

'Menina, tenho de falar a medico!'

Santo's voice came again, and this time Armand stirred too, frowning at the unwelcome interruption without opening his eyes. He groaned a little, burrowed more deeply into the pillows, and his hand slid intimately over her hip to rest with disturbing sensuality against her stomach.

Catherine didn't want to move. Indeed, even the involuntary weight of Armand's hand in that most sensitive place was enough to rekindle all the unfamiliar emotions of the night before. She didn't want to get up; she didn't want to leave the bed; all she really wanted to do was stir Armand from his slumbers and ignite the smouldering passions that had eventually swept them both to a satiated oblivion.

Briefly, Catherine re-lived those moments, remembering, almost incredulously, how ignorant she had been. Making love with Armand had been nothing like the innocent daydreams she had indulged in, and it was only now, in retrospect, that she could smile at her fears and apprehensions. Certainly, she had never anticipated how *satisfying* making love could be; nor had she had any idea that a man could recover so quickly from one devastating encounter and want more! Yet, her own body had been equally as resilient as his, and in spite of her doubts and uncertainties, twice more before they fell into an exhausted slumber Armand had taken her to the highest realms of human experience.

'Menina, por favor . . .'

This time Santo's call was shrill and impatient, and Armand's eyes opened. '*Qué es?*' he muttered unwillingly. '*Qué quer?*' And then, meeting Catherine's clear green eyes, he turned his face into the pillow and uttered a muffled groan.

'It's Santo,' said Catherine in a low voice. 'He must have guessed you were here. Do you want me to go and speak to him?'

'No.' Armand expelled the word frustratedly, rubbing his face in the silken curtain of her hair before turning rueful eyes upon her. 'No, I'll speak to him,' he declared, making a concerted effort to clear his head. '*Deus*, what time is it? I feel as if I've just gone to bed!'

'It's nearly seven,' said Catherine, twisting her head to consult the small alarm clock on the cabinet beside the bed. The lamp, she saw with some relief, had gone out while they were sleeping, so Santo would not have further fuel for his censure.

'Nearly seven?' Armand repeated wearily. 'Yes, I should be up. No doubt there's been a message to get Santo out of bed. He'll be most put out that he had to answer it.'

With a determined effort he withdrew his hand and pushed himself up on his elbows, shaking the sleep from his head. In the pale dawn light he was disturbingly attractive, the single sheet, which was all that had covered them, falling back to reveal the smooth brown skin of his chest and shoulders.

'Don't go!'

Involuntarily, the words spilled from Catherine's lips, and Armand turned his head towards her just as Santo made one last appeal. '*Muito bem, muito bem, venho*—I'm coming!' Armand responded impatiently, and they heard the old man grunt his understanding, and stump away along the passage, content that he had achieved his objective.

'I have to go,' Armand said now, dragging his gaze away from the innocent beauty of her breasts, clearly outlined beneath the thin cotton of the sheet. There was a note of anguish in his voice that troubled Catherine somewhat, and her hand came out to rest on his shoulder, stilling his instinctive withdrawal.

'I love you,' she said simply, leaning towards him and depositing a lingering kiss on the taut muscles of his upper arm. 'Come back soon.'

'Catherine—' he began roughly, closing his eyes briefly against her unconscious allure, but she was not listening to him. With a confidence she had not possessed the night before, she scrambled on to her knees beside him, and before he apprehended her intentions, she had fastened her mouth to his.

Whatever Armand had been about to say was silenced by the warm insistence of her lips, and he was not yet sufficiently in control of his emotions to prevent the instinctive passion that fused their embrace. Although his hands came to her shoulders to press her away from him, the artless seduction of her tongue in his mouth was irresistible. With a muffled imprecation, he bore her back against the pillows, his own tongue reminding her of the full meaning of his possession.

'Deus!' he muttered at last, when she was weak and clinging to him, 'I have got to go!' He dragged himself up from her and turned aside, groping desperately for his pants. But Catherine had felt the hard strength of him against her hip, and she knew it had taken an iron effort of will to leave her.

'Will you be back for lunch?' she asked hopefully,

after a moment, pushing herself up into a sitting position. Watching him as he pushed the hem of his shirt into the waistband of his pants, she did not realise how desirable she looked, and she was anxiously monitoring Armand's expression. She felt completely shameless sitting there, but after what had happened the night before, she was no longer afraid of Armand's eyes upon her. Drawing up one knee to rest her chin upon it, she wondered just exactly what he was thinking, unaware that with her hair tumbling silkily about her shoulders and her eyes fixed appealingly upon him, she was silent proof of the contempt he felt for himself.

'No,' he said shortly now, gathering up his tie and socks and preparing to leave the room. 'No, I won't be back for lunch.' He paused, as if realising something more was required, and then walked constrainedly towards the door. 'We'll—talk this evening,' he told her over his shoulder, and went out closing the door behind him, without looking at her again.

It was early evening before Catherine heard the station wagon braking to a halt outside. It had been a long day, made the longer by Santo's unvoiced, but apparent, disapproval, and by the time the lamps were lit and the insects had started their nightly cacophony of sound, Catherine was feeling distinctly edgy. She had thought Armand might change his mind and put in an appearance in the middle of the day, but he hadn't. Instead, she had been left to Santo's grudging ministrations, and the unequivocal indication that he did not endorse his employer's behaviour. Not for the first time, Catherine wished she spoke his language. It would have been so much more satisfying to ask him why he disapproved of her so completely, instead of having to suffer the discomfort of his silent condemnation.

Her feelings were not appeased when she discovered Armand had gone straight to the bathroom after entering the house. While she was standing in the living room awaiting his appearance with some agitation, the unmistakable sound of the shower came to her ears, and she expelled her breath frustratedly at the realisation of what he had done.

Moments later, she had herself in control again, and running a nervous hand over the loosely secured fall of silky red-gold hair; she reassessed her appearance. She had chosen a dress Armand had not seen before. Made of emerald-green taffeta, it was a dress she had bought to attend a dinner party she had been invited to by one of her school-friends. The neckline dipped into a vee, both back and front, and the sleeves were full and puffy, ending in a cuff at the elbow. The bodice was tight, the skirt full, and although her sandals let it down a bit, it was still more formal than anything she had previously worn. In truth, she had found little use for it since coming to Surajo, but this evening she wanted to look her best. Nevertheless, Armand's prolonged absence did little to reinforce her confidence, and by the time he did come into the living room, she was convinced her temperature was well over a hundred.

Aware of her flushed cheeks and the persistent dampness of her palms, Catherine thought how typical it was that Armand should appear so cool and unconcerned. Apart from a certain shadow of fatigue around his eyes, he looked very much as ever, and although his swift appraisal took in the green dress and her newly-washed hair, he had little apparent appreciation for the appealing picture she made.

'Hello,' he said, rather distantly, bypassing her to go straight away to help himself to a measure of Scotch from a bottle standing on a tray on the bookshelves. After half-filling his glass, he took a generous gulp before turning to face her, his mouth tightening perceptibly when he realised she had not moved.

'Did you have a good day?' she asked, linking her fingers together at her waist, trying hard to hide her disappointment.

'It was—much as usual,' Armand responded, after a moment. Then, after swallowing the remainder of the liquid in his glass, he added: 'Did you?'

Catherine caught her breath. 'Oh, yes,' she said, angry that she was unable to keep the note of frustration out of her voice. 'It's been so hot, I spent most of the day outdoors.'

Armand inclined his head. 'I noticed.'

'Did you?' Catherine's nails dug into her palms. 'I suppose you've been very busy.'

'I had an emergency appendectomy, and a delivery up in the mountains,' he conceded, toying with his glass. 'The appendectomy was successful. The baby was still-born.'

'I'm sorry.' The awareness of death moved her. 'I—no wonder you had no time to think about—about anything else.'

'About you, you mean?' suggested Armand briefly, but before she could take any comfort from his statement, he had turned away to help himself to another drink.

'You . . . did . . . think about me then?' she ventured, abandoning her attempt at detachment and following him across the room. She put out her hand and stroked her fingertips lightly down the hollow of his spine. His skin was still moist from his shower, and the brown silk shirt he was wearing was clinging to his flesh. She wanted to touch him. She wanted to prove to herself she had the right to do so. But she stepped back automatically when he swung abruptly round to face her.

'*De facto*, as a matter of fact, I have thought about you for much of the day,' he told her roughly, but when she would have stepped towards him, he quickly put the width of the room between them. 'Please,' he said, 'you must listen to me. After what has happened, I realise there is no going back for us, but that does not mean that this situation can continue.'

Catherine gasped. 'You're not going to tell me you're too old for me again, are you?' she cried. 'For heaven's sake, haven't we proved that isn't so?'

'Yes.' He regarded her from beneath lowered lids. 'I think we proved a lot of things last night. Not least that I am a man totally without scruples!' His lips twisted in bitter self-derision. 'Believe me, Catherine, when you hear what I have to tell you, you will not want to stay here. You will never want to see me again. So—allow me to continue.'

'I don't care what you have to tell me,' she exclaimed fiercely, shaking her head. 'I don't care what you are or what you've done.' She sighed. 'I love you! I want to be with you! That's all that matters.'

'No, it is not.' Armand lifted one hand to massage the muscles at the back of his neck, his expression losing none of its intensity. 'You don't understand,' he muttered harshly. 'There is so much you do not know about me—'

'I know all I need to know,' declared Catherine confidently, covering the distance between them, and evading his attempts to keep her at bay, she slipped her arms around his waist and pressed herself against him. 'Hold me, Armand,' she whispered huskily, inhaling the clean male scent of his body. 'I just want you to hold me! Just prove to me that last night was as good for you as it was for me.'

'*Cristo*, you know it was,' he told her shakenly, his voice as emotive as she could have wished, but when she tilted her face to look up at him, anticipating his kiss, he put his hands on her shoulders and compelled her away from him. 'I am married,' he said brutally, as if realising there was no other way to tell her. 'I have a wife in Terasina. And a son, too, *paz a sua alma*—peace to his soul. Now, do you understand?'

It was the worst moment of Catherine's life. Losing her father, as she had, had been agonising enough, but she had never felt so close to her father, having spent at least twelve years of her life separated from him. With Armand, it was different. Time, the few months they had known one another, meant nothing in their relationship. Her whole lifetime seemed to have been condensed into these past few weeks, and she could scarcely conceive of a time when she had not known—and loved—the man who had now exploded all her hopes and dreams.

'It's . . . not . . . true—' she faltered, but she knew it was. There was no way Armand would tell her something like that, without there being an element of truth in it. 'But how? Why?' She caught her breath on a choking gulp of anger. 'Why didn't you tell me before?'

'Indeed, why did I not?' he conceded bleakly, letting go her arms now there was no reason to hold her at bay. Lifting his shoulders in a curiously defenceless gesture, he shook his head. 'I suppose—because I did not want you to know.'

Catherine swallowed. 'I don't understand. You

must have known how I would feel—'

'Of course I knew,' he retorted savagely. 'At best, the only excuse I can give is that I thought I could control the situation. I knew it would not be easy when I took you from the convent, but I could not leave you there, and you had no one else.' He ran unsteady fingers through his hair, and then continued: 'I was arrogant enough to believe I could deal with you without emotions getting in the way. I was wrong.'

'Armand—'

'I am not excusing myself,' he overrode her harshly. 'Believe me, I have nothing but contempt for the way I have behaved. But enough is enough, as they say, and although I realise I cannot undo what has been done, I can take steps to insure it will never happen again.'

Catherine's tongue circled her dry lips. 'By— sending me away, I suppose,' she said tautly.

'By putting you out of reach!' he responded, tugging grimly at the hair at his nape. 'It is what I should have done as soon as you were fit to travel.'

'To Terasina,' said Catherine dully, and Armand hesitated a moment before nodding vigorously.

'To Terasina,' he agreed. 'Although, whether the position I had in mind for you is suitable, after all—'

Catherine turned away, trying to absorb what he had told her. But all she could think of, all she could hear, ringing in her ears, was his bald admission that he was married, and she didn't know how she was going to bear it. She should hate him, she knew. She should despise him for waiting until now to confess this fact that altered everything. But she didn't! She couldn't! Nothing short of the pain of death could change her feelings for him. She was simply going through the motions, because it was expected of her. She was shocked, *numbed*, by what had happened, but her feelings hadn't changed. She was still the same girl who had welcomed him so eagerly into her life—and into her bed—and it was only sympathy for his wife's feelings that kept her from committing the mortal sin of offering him forgiveness.

Forcing herself to consider what was going to happen to her, she glanced at him over her shoulder and said: 'There's a child, you say. An infant. Someone I could teach?'

Armand expelled his breath wearily. 'I do not know. I am not sure.' He paused. 'The position may not be suitable.'

'You mean, I may no longer be suitable to my employers?' Catherine countered, swinging round to face him. 'They are friends of yours, of course? And—and your wife's? You are—afraid—she may find out.'

'That is not what I meant.' Armand's jaw hardened angrily. 'It is not easy to explain.'

'Something else I would not understand?' inquired Catherine bitterly, the unwelcome nearness of tears giving an edge to her voice, and Armand closed his eyes against her unconscious appeal.

'Forget it!' he said abruptly, meeting her tremulous gaze with grim determination, and Catherine's wide brow furrowed.

'Forget what? Forget this position you so *kindly* found for me?'

'No!' Armand thrust his clenched fists into his pockets. 'No, I mean forget I expressed any doubts in the matter. The position still stands. If you want it.'

'Do I have any choice?' demanded Catherine huskily, as the realisation of what she was committing herself to thudded unpleasantly in her temples. Wherever she went, whatever she did, she was going to be living hundreds of miles from him, and did it really matter anyway, when he was so consummately out of reach?

Armand sighed. 'If there is something else you would rather do . . .' He shrugged. 'Tell me!'

The words: 'Stay here,' were never spoken, but as if apprehending her silent plea, Armand made a savage gesture. 'Do you think I want you to go?' he demanded, pacing restlessly across the floor. 'Do you think I am looking forward to the emptiness of this house, once you are no longer in it? You think I am a devil and a brute, a mindless heathen, who has taken your innocence without care or consideration, but it is not so. I have feelings! Believe me, Catherine, I have feelings! You talk about love, and I know you believe that it exists. Me—I am not so certain. All I do know is that when I am with you, I have this need to keep you with me; I wanted you . . . I want you still, and there is little consolation in the knowledge that my selfishness—my lust, if you will—has destroyed any chance of my keeping your friendship!'

'Friendship?' echoed Catherine faintly, at once exhilarated, yet chilled, by his confession. He still wanted her; that was something, surely; but the sting came with the knowledge that he spoke of lust, and nothing else.

'Yes, friendship,' Armand declared now, turning to regard her with grim penetration. 'I wanted to be your friend. I wanted to look after you; to care for you; and instead—' He broke off briefly, and then continued contemptuously: 'Instead, I seduced you!'

Catherine trembled. 'Will—will you tell your wife?'

'About you?' Armand's lips twisted. 'No.'

'I see.' Catherine bent her head, and Armand watched her with growing frustration.

'Do you see?' he grated. 'I wonder. Just what

thoughts are going through your head at this moment? Are you imagining, perhaps, that I make a habit of deceiving my wife? That she is some—long-suffering individual, to whom my affairs are a constant pain and humiliation?' He stared at her grimly, and when she made no answer, he uttered an ugly expletive. 'Believe me, that is not how it is,' he told her harshly. 'And if you are entertaining such thoughts, then I advise you to forget them!'

Catherine lifted her head. 'I only have your word for that, don't I?' she eventually articulated painfully, and he covered the space between them to grasp her by her shoulders.

'Have I ever lied to you?' he asked her savagely. 'Except by omission?'

Catherine quivered. 'I don't know, do I?'

'Will you take my word that I have not?' He shook her a little roughly. 'Will you? Will you?'

Catherine's green eyes were swimming with tears when she turned them up to his harsh face, and Armand's restraint crumbled. With a helpless groan, he gathered her up into his arms, pressing her head against his shoulder. And then, when he felt the wetness of her tears soaking the front of his shirt, he tilted her face to his, and found her tremulous lips.

It was heavenly to be close to him again. Even feeling the hard strength of his arms about her was like awakening from a nightmare, and when his hungry mouth sought hers, she had no will to resist. Besides, she thought fatalistically, this was where she wanted to be, this was what she wanted to happen; and surely his wife could not deny her these few moments out of his life.

'You see how it is with me,' he muttered unevenly, burying his face in the hollow of her neck. 'When I am with you, I cannot think of anyone else, not even my *son!*'

The anguish in his voice brought Catherine a measure of sanity. He had a wife and a *son*, she told herself fiercely, and no matter how she felt about him, she could not destroy his family.

With careful determination, she swept the back of her hand across her tear-wet cheeks, and gently, but firmly, extricated herself from his embrace. 'I'll go to Terasina,' she said, speaking with the toneless enunciation of someone under hypnosis. 'I'll leave as soon as you can make the arrangements.'

CHAPTER THIRTEEN

THE house was set on the last stretch of solid earth before the ground gave way to rolling sand-dunes. It had a wooden frame, set on iron struts to keep it safe from the shifting waters of the bay that Senhor Lopez had told her sometimes swept inland during the winter storms. Its roof was tiled, there were attractively hanging eaves, and the front of the house was composed of sliding windows that gave access to the balcony that faced the ocean.

It wasn't a big house. There were only three bedrooms and two bathrooms on the upper floor, and below them, the living area was planned to take the best advantage of the space that was available. A huge living room took up most of the lower floor, with squashy sofas and armchairs grouped about occasional tables and potted plants. One end of the room was given over to a circular table and four chairs, suitable for more formal dining, but as the kitchen was large, too, Catherine suspected she and her charge would take most of their meals in there.

It was all very practical, but very attractive, its simplicity in no way detracting from its inherent good taste. Whoever Mr Lopez was, he was not without affluence, thought Catherine shrewdly, and the air of opulent, yet lived-in, elegance that surrounded her was exactly what a boy like Ricardo might feel comfortable with in a holiday home.

Not that she had met the boy she was to have charge of yet. He was not due to arrive until tomorrow. For the present, she was to kick her heels, and familiarise herself with her surroundings, so that when he was delivered into her keeping, she would have no difficulty in keeping him entertained. Her duties were to be less than onerous. As they were to stay here for the first six weeks of her employment, she was expected to give Ricardo the most perfunctory of instruction, and that only in the mornings. The rest of the day was to be left to her discretion, and their proximity to the beach seemed to point to lazy afternoons spent bathing, or making sand-castles, or exploring for sea-shells along the shoreline.

The house was taken care of by a pretty Italian girl, who lived in the nearby village of Casca de Mar. Fortunately, Senhor Lopez had told her, Sophia spoke a little English, but in any case, she had her instructions and would carry them out without any problems. She would cook and clean, and do any shopping that was necessary. Any purchases she made were to be accounted for by Senhor Lopez himself, and Catherine's only employment was to be in caring for the child.

It sounded an ideal situation, and in other circumstances Catherine would have considered herself extremely lucky to have found it. She had expected to be living and working in Terasina itself, and it had been quite a relief to discover that she was to spend these first weeks in such beautiful surroundings. The coastline here, only a half-hour's drive from the capital, was almost untouched, and most habitations that there were, were owned by oyster catchers and fisherfolk, to whom the struggle for survival meant more than the struggle for political domination. They had passed one or two other houses, set above the dunes, as this one was, but Catherine had seen no sign of their occupants, and she suspected the properties may have been confiscated by President Ferreira and his government.

This thought left her with the vaguely troublesome question as to what Senhor Lopez's standing might be. Did he openly support the military regime, or was he one of the intellectuals her father had told her about, whose opposition was passionate, but seldom voiced? So far as Catherine was aware, Senhor Lopez was simply a member of the legal profession, a lawyer, with a lucrative practice in Terasina. But he was obviously a man of education and principle; exactly the kind of person President Ferreira would hope to enlist. With his background, Senhor Lopez could talk to his contemporaries in other capitals of the world, and perhaps use his advocatory skills to persuade other governments to support the government of Surajo. Which might make him a dangerous friend for Armand to have with his evident sympathy for the opposition's cause.

The unbidden reference to Armand caused her to leave her present position on the balcony and descend the half dozen or so wooden steps to the beach. She had determined not to think of him, but it wasn't easy, particularly when even the possibility that he might be in some danger filled her with a panicky sense of alarm. *Stop it!* she told herself severely. It was not up to her to wonder where he was or what he was doing. His activities no longer concerned her. He was married! He had a wife and child! How could she be feeling anxiety for someone who had treated all three of them so badly?

The fact remained she was. As she scuffed her bare toes in the sand, she could not dismiss the knowledge that her feelings towards Armand had not changed. In spite of his duplicity, in spite of what he had done, her love for him was still as strong as ever. The pain of his deception had not gone away. She would always remember that terrible moment when he had told her he was married. Even now, three weeks later, she still woke nights sweating from the horror of re-living that scene. But time had blunted her acceptance of the truth. What had, at first, seemed totally unacceptable, was now an everyday part of her existence, and she had even found herself wondering what his wife was like, and how old his son might be.

As Armand had told her he was thirty-seven, she speculated the boy was probably in his early teens, an impressionable youth, who must surely have some opinion regarding his father's continued separation from his mother. Armand's wife lived in Terasina, of course. He had told her that in confirmation of her query as to whether she was the woman he had gone to see. It had hurt then to think that while she was waiting at Batistamajor, fretting on his return, Armand had been spending a pleasant week with his family. No wonder his departure had been delayed, she conjectured bitterly. Who had a better right to monopolise his time than the woman he had honoured with his name?

Armand's reasons for living and working in Batista-major had never been satisfactorily explained. She knew he had a genuine respect for human life, and his sympathy and humanity were two of his most attract-ive characteristics. For all his cynicism in relation to his work, she knew he would never deny anyone his professional skills, and his ability as a doctor and a surgeon was undeniable.

Yet, it had been common knowledge in the village that he had left a lucrative practice in Terasina to go to

Batistamajor. No doubt that was when his separation from his family had begun. Either his wife had not wanted to leave her home in the capital, or he had felt unable to take her. Whatever the truth of the matter, he had freely abandoned his familial responsibilities to take up a position with the military garrison, which seemed an odd thing to do if his sympathies lay elsewhere. Perhaps they didn't, she speculated wildly. Perhaps he really did support the Ferreira regime. By befriending the rebels, he might be seeking to betray them, and Catherine's anxieties increased at the thought of the double game he might be playing.

It was ironic, she thought, that she should still concern herself over his safety. Innocent lives might be in danger, and she could only think of him. It wasn't fair. The past could have no bearing on the future. She had to get on and lead her own life, independent of Armand and the frustrated love she had for him. Whatever happened to him in the future was not her concern. She had been given a chance to start again, and she had to take it, not continually yearn for something that was permanently out of reach.

He did not love her; he had said so. He had *wanted* her, but for how long? If things had been different—if she had been prepared to go on living with him, and he had been prepared to let her—how long would it have lasted? He had never spoken of a commitment. He had never spoken of divorce, or even expressed a wish that she might be his wife. It could be that in spite of his criticism of the church, he still held some religious beliefs; and as Surajo was a Catholic country, and his wife was almost certainly a Catholic, too, divorce was out of the question. But he had not said that. Nor had he made any attempt to justify the omission. Characteristically, he had allowed her to come to her own conclusions, and she thought how sickening it was that she should still have any faith in his integrity.

Pushing her hands into the pockets of the white cotton pants she had bought in Terasina that morning, Catherine trudged disconsolately to the waterline. From here, it was possible to see the curving headland which hid most of the port of Terasina from her view. Only the forest of masts in the marina, which had once hosted the Latin American Yacht Races, was visible from her position, the wide sweep of the newly-named Ferreira Bay stretching to the horizon. It was beautiful. No matter what government was in power, no matter what strictures were put on the people, nothing could spoil the simple pleasures of nature, she thought reflectively. Life went on, whatever the aggravation, and she should remember that in respect of her own problems.

Turning back towards the house, she allowed the memory of the last three weeks at Batistamajor to intrude into her thoughts. It had not been easy, filling the days until her departure. She had had little to do, and scant interest in the pursuits she had followed before that awful scene with Armand. He, she knew, had avoided her company as much as possible, and while she appreciated his discretion, she had ached to bridge the gulf that had opened between them.

But it couldn't be done. Once she had made the decision to take the position in Terasina, Armand seemed to detach himself from the situation, and if it had been hard for him to accept the thought of their separation, he had managed to conceal it. Perhaps he had been relieved, Catherine pondered now, realising how her presence must have complicated his life. He had never wanted that kind of involvement; he had said so. And it must have been a relief when she agreed to make the break.

Pressing her lips together, she halted at the flight of stairs that led up to the balcony again, resting one foot on the first step. Looking about her, she hoped that this peaceful place would have a similar effect on her emotions. She had been wounded, and it still hurt; bruised, and she still wore the scars. Maybe Casca de Mar would act like a salve to her raw feelings, and these days of sun and tranquillity would give her the recuperative strength to face an uncertain future.

The delicious aroma of coffee came to Catherine's nostrils as she passed through the sliding glass doors into the living room. Sophia was just setting a tray containing a jug of coffee, a jug of cream, and a brown earthenware cup and saucer on a low, mosaic-topped table, and the plump Italian girl looked up smilingly as her shadow crossed the floor.

'Did you have a good swim?' she inquired, taking note of Catherine's damp swimsuit and the moist tendrils of hair, which had escaped from the braid she had secured on top of her head, and were now curling about her nape. 'The water is warm, no? And so refreshing at this hour of the morning.'

'It's beautiful,' agreed Catherine enthusiastically, spreading the towel she had wrapped around her on the polished floor, and dropping down upon it beside the low table. 'Hmm, this smells delicious, Sophia. How did you guess I would want some?'

'You had no breakfast, *signorina*, and the *signor*—e—the *signor* who owns the villa, *capísce*,' she flushed, 'he usually enjoys some *caffè* after his swim.'

Catherine frowned. 'You mean Senhor Lopez?'

'Ah, no, *signorina*.' Sophia straightened from setting out the tray to her liking and shook her head. 'Signor Lopez does not own the villa. It—it belongs to Signor de Castro. Ricardo's father, *signorina*.'

Catherine blinked. 'But I thought Ricardo was Senhor Lopez's son!'

'No, *signorina*.' Sophia looked a little discomfited now, and Catherine could tell she was eager to depart.

'Well—thank you,' Catherine murmured, picking up the coffee jug, and Sophia's unguarded expression was a mirror of her relief.

'Will that be all, *signorina*?'

'Oh—yes, I think so.' Catherine filled her cup and gave the girl a reassuring smile. 'I'm not trying to pry, you know,' she added. 'I just—assumed Senhor Lopez had employed me.'

'*Si, signorina*.'

'There is one more thing.'

'*Si, signorina*?' Sophia turned at the archway that gave access to the kitchen and storeroom at the back of the house.

'Yes.' Catherine lifted her shoulders. 'What time do you think Ricardo will arrive?'

'After lunch,' said Sophia positively. 'Always, after lunch, *signorina*.' And now she smiled. 'Do not look so—so *apprensivo, signorina*. Ricardo is a fine boy. You will love him.'

Catherine grimaced. 'I hope his English is as good as yours.'

'It is.' Sophia laughed. 'Ricardo has an English grandmother, no? She made sure he could speak her language.'

'Really?' Catherine was intrigued. 'And does Ricardo's grandmother live in Terasina, too?'

'No!' The Italian girl made a negative gesture, and

once again Catherine had the distinct impression that Sophia wished she had not been so talkative. 'She— er—Signora de Castro, that is—Signora de Castro, *la piú anziana*, the elder, *capísce*—she lives in São Paulo, *signorina*.'

'São Paulo?' Catherine echoed in surprise. 'But that's in Brazil, isn't it?'

'*Si, signorina*. But now, I must get on,' Sophia declared hurriedly and, without waiting for any further inquiries, she disappeared into the kitchen.

Later, showering in the bathroom that adjoined her bedroom, Catherine speculated about how Ricardo might react to having a governess-cum-nursemaid. Senhor Lopez—it was difficult to remember that he was not the boy's father—had said that he had attended a small private school in Terasina until just recently. But a severe cold, and the increasing fear of terrorist violence in the city, had persuaded his parents that a course of private tuition might be more sensible, beginning with this prolonged vacation at Casca de Mar.

Catherine decided his parents must love the boy very much to give so much consideration to his well-being, although she had to admit Ricardo might not see it quite that way. It would depend on his personality, of course, but it was always possible he might regard his removal to the villa as some kind of punishment, particularly if he missed living in the city and being with his family.

She ate lunch in the kitchen, while Sophia ironed the linen she had washed that morning, and kept up an inconsequential chatter about her home and her family, and the two teenage boys she and her husband were struggling to raise.

'Have you lived in Surajo long?' asked Catherine,

picking up a shred of lettuce with her fingers and depositing it in her mouth. 'It's so unusual, an Italian girl living in Casca de Mar. What part of Italy do you come from?'

'*Toscàna*, *signorina*. E—how do you say it?—Tuscany, no? I come from a small town called Certaldo, which produces some wine, which is not unknown in that part of the world.'

'But how did you come to live in Surajo?' exclaimed Catherine blankly. 'Certaldo in Italy is a long way from Casca de Mar.'

'It is.' Sophia laughed. 'But my husband has relatives who live in Brazil and so do I. *Eccolo!*'

'I see.' Catherine smiled. 'It was love at first sight.'

'Perhaps second,' conceded Sophia, with a wry grimace. 'But we have been happy. And that is what matters, is it not?' She paused. 'You have a—boy-friend, *signorina*?'

'I'm afraid not.' Catherine bent over her salad, applying herself to her food with sudden determination. 'Er—what time is it, Sophia? My watch stopped working several months ago, and I haven't been able to replace it.'

Ricardo arrived just after three o'clock. The sight of the sleek black limousine gliding up the drive to the door filled Catherine with an inexplicable sense of panic, and she could only put it down to the fact that this was to be her first real experience of employment. What if she wasn't suitable? she thought anxiously. What if Ricardo didn't like her? What precautions should one take in such circumstances to insure such a disaster didn't happen?

Not quite sure how she should react to the arrival of the car, Catherine took her courage in both hands and did the thing she would have done without knowing the restrictions of etiquette. She went to meet the car, joining a slightly surprised Sophia on the doorstep, and giving her a nervous smile.

'He's a little boy,' she said, in an undertone. 'And he's leaving his mother for the first time. I want him to feel he has nothing to fear.'

Sophia arched her dark brows, but said nothing for, in any case, the limousine was already braking and there was no time to exchange opinions. The uniformed chauffeur at the wheel brought the car to a smooth halt, and then sprang out smartly to take charge of the door. Catherine had only a moment to notice the coat of arms on the panels before a shapely leg appeared, and her eyes widened admiringly as an elegantly-attired female stepped out of the car.

Ricardo's mother, Catherine surmised dazedly, momentarily stunned by the woman's appearance. This exotic vision bore no resemblance to the perspiring matron she had expected, and she wondered if perhaps she had made a mistake.

But, no, Sophia was already greeting her employer's wife with studied effusion, shaking her hand and wishing her well, and gesturing towards the car. It had to be Senhora de Castro, decided Catherine blankly, although she was nothing like the tearful mother she had expected to have to deal with. In her pale blue silk suit and strappy sandals, Ricardo's mother looked more suitably attired to attend a garden party, than to deliver her son into the hands of a stranger. But she was attractive, Catherine had to give her that, and quite young, no more than thirty-five, she guessed. Dark, in the manner of most Latin races, her skin had the texture of a magnolia, and her glossy lips were parted delicately, in just the suggestion of a smile.

'Sophia, Sophia,' she was saying now, her eyes

moving past the Italian woman to alight on Catherine's nervous form. 'Please to introduce me to Miss Loring. This is Miss Loring, is it not? She seems *very* young.'

'I'm Catherine Loring, Senhora de Castro,' Catherine replied swiftly, without waiting for Sophia's introduction. 'And I'm almost twenty, *senhora*. I'm afraid my appearance is deceptive.'

'*Realmente?*' Senhora de Castro arched thin dark brows above eyes so black Catherine could see no pinprick of light in them. Her gaze swept over the younger girl, dismissing the simple cotton shirt and baggy pants with such disdain that Catherine felt a wave of colour rising up her cheeks. '*Pois bem*, we will see,' she said, glancing behind her half impatiently. 'Ricardo! Ricardo, *depressa!* Come: meet your *professora!*'

Catherine forgot the woman's rudeness as her eyes turned back to the car. A boy was climbing obediently out of the back of the vehicle, and she watched him intently, wondering why she had the sensation of having seen him before. It wasn't possible, yet there was something familiar about his thin dark face and narrow-limbed body. She had never met him, she was convinced of that, but she could not dispel the sense of identity that his solemn looks engendered. He was tall for his age, but painfully thin, his bony arms jutting from the sleeves of a dark blue cotton shirt. He wore matching dark blue shorts and knee-length dark blue socks above unscuffed brown sandals. He was like any one of a hundred children one might see every day in the streets of Terasina, and noting his unmarked knees and restrained expression, she wondered if he had ever been allowed to get dirty in his life.

'This is Miss Loring, Ricardo,' his mother declared

briefly, successfully putting Catherine in her place. 'My son, Miss Loring,' she continued smoothly, as Ricardo held out his hand politely. 'I trust you will take good care of him. He is very important to me.'

'Of course, *senhora*.' Catherine determinedly ignored the woman's insolence. 'Hello, Ricardo. I'm pleased to meet you. I'm sure we're going to have lots of fun together.'

'How do you do?' Ricardo was painfully correct and, glancing at his mother, he quickly withdrew his hand again and stood waiting for her to make the next move.

'Carlos, *faz favor de trazer os bagagens*,' Senhora de Castro ordered sharply, gesturing towards where the luggage was stored in the boot of the car, and Sophia stepped aside politely, inviting her employer's wife into the villa.

'Ah, no, I cannot stay,' Ricardo's mother refused, with a tight smile. She took the boy's arm and propelled him forward. 'Mama has an appointment she must keep, *pequeno*,' she declared, running scarlet-tipped fingers over the smooth cap of her hair. 'I will telephone you in a few days, *menina*.' This as she turned her attention back to Catherine. 'Until then, *adeus. Até a vista*, Ricardo.'

The kiss she deposited on the boy's cheek was less than enthusiastic, but Ricardo didn't seem to mind. Perhaps he was used to this kind of treatment after all, reflected Catherine thoughtfully, feeling an unwarranted surge of sympathy for him. He looked so lost and alone, she could almost forget he had a father, too.

The suitcases and trunk containing Ricardo's belongings were soon carried into the villa and up the stairs to his room. His bedroom adjoined the room Catherine was using and overlooked the beach and the ocean. Catherine hoped he liked the seaside more than he appeared to. She couldn't imagine any English boy of his age not charging immediately down to the sea and dipping his toes in the water.

The limousine carrying Senhora de Castro back to Terasina departed a few moments later, and with some relief, Catherine felt, Sophia led the way back into the house. 'I will make some tea,' she announced, disappearing in the direction of the kitchen, and it was left to Catherine to make the first overtures to Ricardo.

She had to force herself to remember he knew this house better than she did. The way he hung back and allowed her to lead the way into the living room, she could have been forgiven for thinking he had never visited here before, and she gazed at him doubtfully, wondering how to gain his confidence.

'You've spent holidays here before, haven't you, Ricardo?' she ventured, struck again by his unsettling resemblance to a person, or persons, unknown, as he looked inquiringly up at her.

'I have spent weekends here,' he corrected her politely. 'With my father.'

'Really?' Catherine was intrigued. She wanted to ask whether his mother had not been with them, too, but it really wasn't her affair, and she stifled her inquisitiveness and asked instead: 'I suppose you can swim then?'

'Oh, yes.' Ricardo smiled, and when he did so that disturbing likeness was actively pronounced. 'Papa always lets me do what I like.'

'Does he?' Catherine was encouraged. 'You know, when I saw you getting out of the car, I thought you had never had sand in your shoes in your life.'

'Oh—' Ricardo's cheeks turned slightly pink. 'Mama does not like the *praia—perdão*, I mean the seaside, Miss Loring. She does not approve of—of improper behaviour.'

'I see.' Catherine's tongue explored her upper lip. 'You mean—your mother expects certain standards of behaviour from you?' she suggested helpfully, trying to make it easier for him, and his features relaxed.

'*Sim, senhorita*. I mean—yes, Miss Loring.' He pulled an apologetic face. 'But please, do not tell Mama what I told you. About Papa, that is. It would only cause a row, and—and perhaps she and Uncle Estéban might not let me come again.'

Catherine frowned. Who was Uncle Estéban, she wondered. Whoever he was, Ricardo evidently thought he had some influence when it came to ordering his life. She presumed he must be Senhora de Castro's brother as their ideas were so similar. It seemed a shame that the boy should feel compelled to protect his father in this way.

'Don't worry,' she said now, putting a reassuring hand on his bony shoulder. 'I don't tell tales. And besides, we have much more important things to do. Don't you agree?'

Ricardo looked doubtful. 'Important things?' he echoed uncertainly, and Catherine allowed her warm laughter to fill the room.

'Like going for a paddle before supper,' she declared, watching the anxiety leave his face. Sophia was right. He was very lovable.

Over the pot of tea and dainty sandwiches Sophia had prepared, Catherine learned a little more about him. He was eight, as Senhor Lopez had told her, but he would be nine in only two weeks. 'My birthday is on the fifteenth, *senhorita*,' he told her proudly. 'Papa says I may have a new bicycle, if I am a good boy.'

'A new bicycle!' Catherine sounded envious. 'How

lovely! We'll have to arrange a celebration of some
sort. Or will you be going home for the occasion?'

'I do not think so,' Ricardo replied swiftly, with no
visible signs of disappointment. 'Papa will not be
there, and Mama is going away with Uncle Estéban,
and I do not know when they will be back.' He
stretched across the table to take a slice of the fruit cake
Sophia had made. 'Can I have this, please?'

'You can, if you eat your sandwich,' declared
Catherine, noticing he had scarcely touched the bread.
'Aren't you hungry?'

'I do not like sandwiches, *senhorita*,' he responded,
his hand returning to his lap without the coveted fruit
cake. 'May I be excused, please? I want to go up to my
room.'

Catherine sighed. 'I thought you wanted a piece of
fruit cake,' she exclaimed frustratedly, not altogether
sure herself how to proceed, and he shrugged.

'I have had enough, thank you, *senhorita*,' he said
politely. 'May I be excused? I have to use the bathroom.'

'Oh—yes. Yes, of course.'

Catherine had no choice but to let him go, and he
trotted obediently across the room and started up the
spiral staircase that gave access to the upper floor. The
momentary glimpse of life she had seen in him seemed
to have been doused, and she cursed her own incompetence for not waiting before setting out her rules.

When Sophia came to clear the tray away, she
looked askance at the plate of scarcely-touched sandwiches. 'No appetite, *signorina*?' she suggested with a
frown. 'Or is ham and shrimp not to your liking?'

'Oh, no. They were delicious, Sophia, really,'
Catherine assured her eagerly, not wanting to offend
her only ally. 'But I'm afraid I've upset our house-

guest. He only wanted cake and I, like a fool, told him he had to eat a sandwich first.'

'Ah . . .' Sophia nodded. 'And that is troubling you?'

'Wouldn't it trouble you?'

Sophia shrugged, lifting the tray and standing with it in her hands. 'Let me say this, *signorina*,' she said confidingly. 'When Ricardo comes here with his father, there is the same problem. At home, he is not supervised at mealtimes, and I think he does not eat.'

Catherine gasped. 'But isn't that rather foolhardy?'

'Of course,' Sophia nodded. 'But when—when the *signor* brings him here, he does not give in so easily.'

'You mean—he makes Ricardo eat?'

'I mean, he makes mealtimes more—how shall I say it?—attractive, no?'

'Attractive?'

'I am afraid he uses a little blackmail, *signorina*.' Sophia swung the tray from side to side. 'You eat this—we do that!' she explained, pulling a wry face. 'Two sandwiches—two ball games on the beach! A bowl of soup—a swim in the sea! A bit of this, and a bit of that, and in no time at all, Signor Ricardo is forgetting that he is not hungry.'

Catherine got to her feet in disbelief. 'But why doesn't his mother do this, too?'

Sophia shook her head. 'Signora de Castro is a busy woman, *signorina*,' she said evasively, moving towards the arch. 'Do not fret. Ricardo will come round. The sea air will do the trick, you will see.'

Catherine wished she felt as confident, but after Sophia had disappeared into the kitchen, she decided to make another effort. Climbing the stairs, she made her way to Ricardo's room, stopping in the doorway when she found him on his hands and knees on the floor. He had opened his trunk and taken out a box of mechanical parts, which he was presently assembling into a creditable facsimile of a crane. But her arrival had not gone unnoticed, and she had to admire his self-control as he got politely to his feet.

'Did you want to see me, Miss Loring?' he inquired formally, his gaze fixed somewhere around her middle, and Catherine expelled her breath in a rush as the desire to take him into her arms and hug him almost overwhelmed her.

'I—thought we were going paddling,' she said, deciding she could play this game by no one's rules but her own. 'I've come up to put on my swimsuit. Don't tell me you've forgotten.'

Ricardo gulped, and his eyes turned almost disbelievingly up to her. 'You mean—you mean we can still go in the water?' he exclaimed, blinking rapidly, and Catherine nodded.

'Why not?' she countered, noticing his eyes were grey, not black. 'Do you know where your swimsuit is?' She surveyed the pigskin suitcases strewn around him. 'Would you like me to help you to unpack?'

'Oh, no, *senhorita*, Sophia will do it,' he responded, with unconscious hauteur. 'And I know where my shorts are. They are here.'

With a triumphant gesture, he bent and pulled a pair of white cotton shorts from the trunk, and Catherine guessed he had packed this particular item himself.

'All right,' she said, backing out of the room. 'I'll meet you downstairs in five minutes.'

'*Cinco minutos!*' agreed Ricardo eagerly, and Catherine knew a ridiculous surge of gratitude to Armand for finding her this job.

CHAPTER FOURTEEN

THAT night, for the first time since Armand had told her he was married, Catherine fell asleep as soon as her head touched the pillow. For days she had lain awake for hours after turning out the light, staring into the darkness, praying for an oblivion which had often been long in coming. Even the night she had spent in Terasina, after the daylong train journey from Ribatejo, had been no different, the knowledge that she had left everything she cared for in Batistamajor burning its way into her consciousness. Senhor Lopez had been kind enough, of course. Armand had telegraphed him the date and time of her arrival, and he had met her at the railway station and taken her to an hotel. Then, he had come for her again in the morning, allowing her a little time to buy the few essentials that she needed, before driving her out to Casca de Mar, and this villa set attractively by the ocean.

But today had been different, somehow. Meeting Ricardo, spending time with him, had eased the persistent ache around her heart, and she had already sensed that he was someone who *needed* her. It was good to be needed, it was good to feel that someone valued her friendship. And she and Ricardo were going to be friends, she knew that quite instinctively.

It was even more of a pleasure the following morning to awake with the sound of the ocean drifting invitingly to her ears. She had noticed the muted thunder of the waves as the tide turned inward the previous morning, but then she had had the prospect of meeting Ricardo ahead of her, and the uneasy anticipation that she might not be suitable. Now, she could face the days ahead with growing confidence, and the idea of spending several hours on the beach was not at all displeasing.

She had told Ricardo that as today was Saturday, lessons would not begin until Monday, at the earliest. The trunk that held his toys also held the books and writing materials she would need for preliminary instruction, but as Senhor Lopez had impressed upon her the fact that rest and recuperation were to be given priority in her plans, she was in no particular hurry to start setting time-tables. She had already gathered that Ricardo was a bright, intelligent boy. His conversation had told her that. Besides which, she would need a few days to study his books and familiarise herself with his progress to date, before preparing a satisfactory schedule. In the meantime, any child who had such a comprehensive grasp of a language other than his own, could afford to take a few days' holiday. She was quite sure Ricardo did not find learning difficult, and it was going to be quite a challenge to exercise his mind.

After putting on her swimsuit—a simple one-piece garment, made of pink polyester, whose colour only just managed not to clash with her hair—she tied a white wraparound skirt about her waist, and slipped her feet into her sandals. With the money Armand had given her before she left Batistamajor, she had bought several items of clothing, including the swimsuit, although the choice in Terasina had not been extensive. She had even bought some shoes: a pair made of plain cream leather, with modest heels and a low-cut vamp. It had been quite a novelty to try on shoes again, and although she had not wanted to take it, she had been glad of the money Armand had given her.

Armand!

Her fingers trembled as she endeavoured to secure her hair in one thick braid. Unbidden, his name had entered her thoughts, and in spite of all her good resolutions, she couldn't prevent herself from seeing the image of his face that was imprinted in her mind. *Oh, Armand!* she thought unsteadily, her fingers fumbling over their task, *however am I going to live without you?* And then, outside her door, she heard the distinctive clatter of Ricardo's feet as he descended the stairs, and she impatiently abandoned her hair and hurried after him.

Sophia had already arrived, and the aromatic smell of coffee filled Catherine's nostrils as she reached the foot of the stairs. Someone had pushed back the sliding glass doors that opened on to the balcony, and the cooler air from outside was invading the living room. The tang of the ocean came to Catherine's lips, pungent and sharp with brine, but there was no sign of Ricardo on the sand, so she turned and walked back to the kitchen.

Ricardo was seated at the pine table that stood squarely on the glazed tile floor. Taking a leaf out of Catherine's book he, too, was wearing the thin shorts he wore for swimming and nothing else, although he did meet her gaze a trifle anxiously as she took in his bare brown torso.

'You did say we would be going swimming again, did you not, *senhorita*?' he ventured shyly, shifting a little nervously on his seat. 'I did not think you would mind. But, if you would like me to wear a shirt—'

He began to get to his feet, but Catherine's hand on his shoulder pushed him down again. 'Don't be silly,' she said, taking the ladder-backed chair beside him. 'Of course I don't mind. There's only Sophia and ourselves, and I'm sure she doesn't mind looking at your muscles.'

Ricardo grinned. 'I do not have any muscles,' he said with a grimace.

'No, I know. But perhaps you will after this holiday,' declared Catherine, resisting the impulse to hug him. 'Hmm, that coffee is irresistible, Sophia. I sometimes wonder how I lived for so long without it.'

The Italian girl set coffee, cream, and a cup in front of her, smiling as she watched Catherine help herself. 'What did you mean—you lived without it?' she queried, a frown giving a serious cast to her plump face. 'Do not tell me they do not drink coffee in England!'

'Oh, no.' Catherine flushed, realising she had put herself in a difficult position. She had either to lie, or admit to having spent nine months in the convent, which was bound to promote questions she did not want to answer.

She was casting about for an alternative when Ricardo unwittingly provided an escape. 'I do not like coffee,' he declared, finishing the orange juice he had been offered. 'Can we go down to the beach now, *senhorita*? You said you would teach me how to make a castle with a real moat!'

'You have had no breakfast, Ricardo!' Sophia objected at once, diverted by his innocent request. 'And nor has Miss Loring. Your papa will be very cross if I do not feed your new governess!'

Catherine sighed with relief, and Ricardo cast her a rueful glance. 'Do you eat a lot of breakfast, *senhorita*?' he asked, clearly hoping she would say no, and she managed a thin smile.

'That depends what Sophia has to offer,' she replied, remembering that the day before she had only had a roll and coffee. 'Are they pancakes I can smell, Sophia? Whatever it is, it smells good.'

'Pancakes,' agreed the Italian girl, turning back to the grill. 'You can have them as they are, with lemon juice or maple syrup. Or how about folded with a few strawberries and some sugar? That's how your papa likes them, is it not, *giovinétto*?'

'Strawberries? You have strawberries, Sophia?' Ricardo asked eagerly, and the Italian girl nodded.

'Especially for you, *píccolo*,' she confirmed, lifting one of the luscious fruits out of a basin and handing it to him. 'So—what is it to be, *signorina*?'

Catherine hesitated. 'Well . . .' She lifted her shoulders. 'Pancakes with strawberries, I think,' she declared, never having tasted such a delicacy in her life. 'How about you, Ricardo? Is it strawberries for you? Or are you going to have maple syrup?'

Ricardo hunched his shoulders. 'Can I not just have strawberries with sugar?' he suggested hopefully. He was watching Sophia take the plate of pancakes out of the oven. 'They look—so big!'

'No pancakes, no strawberries,' replied Sophia, after exchanging a speaking glance with Catherine. 'There you are, *signorina*. Especially for you!'

Contrary to Ricardo's opinion, the pancakes were not big at all. They were small and light, and deliciously fluffy, their juicy filling oozing out over the rim of Catherine's plate. She found herself eating what she had and asking for more and, wiping the grains of sugar from her chin, she found Ricardo watching her with something akin to envy.

But she knew better than to try and persuade him. If he wanted to eat, he would ask for some. Instead, she concentrated on her own enjoyment, giving Sophia the pleasure of having known her efforts had not been in vain.

Even so, it was hard to get up from the table after she had finished, knowing that Ricardo's eyes were on the basin containing the remainder of the strawberries. It was harder still to walk to the door without allowing him even one of the rosy berries, and his lips were pressed together a little mutinously when they returned to the living room.

'Oh, I think I'm going to have to rest a while before going for a swim,' Catherine declared, rubbing her full stomach with a rueful hand. 'Why don't I sit here on the balcony, while you go and build a sand-castle? I'll come and help you later after my breakfast's digested.'

'Yes, *senhorita*.'

Ricardo had definitely lost the sparkle he had had the night before, she reflected impatiently. But the night before he had actually drunk some soup and eaten a little meat at suppertime, and she had foolishly believed the battle was won with only the first skirmish behind her.

Nevertheless, she had to begin as she intended to continue, and forcing a bright smile to her face, she took up her position on one of the comfortable cushioned loungers on the balcony. Shedding her skirt, she stretched her legs and turned her face up to the sun. Even so, she knew at exactly what moment Ricardo decided to leave her to her pursuits, and her eyes flickered open regretfully as he went disconsolately down the steps.

Who did he remind her of, she pondered frustratedly, as his dark head disappeared below the level of the rail. Not Senhor Lopez, that was for sure, and now she knew the dark-skinned moustachioed Surajan was not Ricardo's father she had no paternal resemblance to compare to. Nor did he look particularly like his mother. Senhora de Castro's features were rounder, smoother; less intense. Perhaps she should ask if he had a photograph of his father, she reflected thoughtfully, tracing idle patterns on the arm of her chair, although how she could conceivably expect to know his father—

The photograph!

Almost dizzily Catherine pulled herself upright, her hands closing convulsively over the bleached wood. The photograph! she reminded herself weakly. The photograph she had seen beside Armand's bed! It was not, as she had imagined, an out-dated photograph of Luis Rodolfo. It was a picture of Ricardo; Ricardo de Castro. And as Armand had a son of his own, why would he keep a picture of Ricardo de Castro by his bed? Unless . . .

Her heart palpitated wildly. *No!* she told herself fiercely; no, it couldn't be true. Armand's surname was Alvares, not de Castro. In any case, his son was older, easily thirteen or fourteen. But then she remembered that that was only her assessment of the boy's age, and as she continued to think about it, so many other things fell into perspective.

Senhor Lopez meeting her in Terasina, for example, and not explaining his relationship to the child; the fact that Ricardo had said his father was away; even Sophia's slight discomfort when she discovered she was talking too much. Perhaps she had been warned not to discuss her employer's identity, for it was obvious Armand would not expect Catherine to find out by any other means. She did know very little about him, after all, and he did not suspect she had studied the photograph.

She shook her head. Was it possible? Could Armand Alvares and Senhor de Castro be one and the same man? *Would* Armand be cruel enough to send her here to act as nursemaid to his own son? She licked her dry lips. Recalling the reckless way he had betrayed his marriage vows, she thought it was altogether possible, and her face burned with humiliation at the way he had tricked her.

Why had he done it? she asked herself. What earthly pleasure could he derive from knowing she was here, taking care of his son? Was it some warped way of punishing his wife? Did he intend to denounce her as his mistress at some nebulous date in the future? Or did he simply get enjoyment from keeping them both in ignorance—the woman he had married, and the girl he had seduced?

With thoughts like these for company, Catherine could no longer sit still, and getting to her feet, she walked to the rail on legs that threatened to betray her. That woman, she thought dully, that exotic creature who had delivered Ricardo the day before, was Armand's wife! No wonder he had never mentioned divorce to her. Senhora de Castro was quite exquisite, and his only use for Catherine had been in satisfying a normal sexual appetite.

'*Senhorita! Senhorita!* Miss Loring!'

Ricardo's excited voice drew her gaze, and she looked down abruptly, blinking back the threat of tears.

'Look what I've found!' Ricardo exclaimed, holding up a tiny sand crab for her notice. 'See, he has tiny legs and tiny claws, and he walks sideways just like the bigger ones do!'

'He's—sweet.' Catherine's voice was choked, but she couldn't help it, and sensing something was wrong, Ricardo set the tiny crab free and came racing up the steps.

'Are you crying, *senhorita*?' he asked, slowing his pace as he neared her, and she understood now why she had taken to him from the start. It wasn't so much that he looked like Armand, although, now she had the proof in her grasp, she could see a slight resemblance in the way his hair grew, and in the thin, intelligent features that were watching her so anxiously. But there was a more characteristic likeness, a gentleness and sensitivity Armand could exhibit when he chose, that drew her like a magnet to those qualities in his son.

'No,' she said now, brushing her knuckles across her cheeks and forcing a smile. 'I—er—the sun made my eyes water, that's all.'

'You look hot,' said Ricardo candidly. 'Are you going to come down to the beach now?'

To the beach! Catherine knew an almost uncontrollable feeling of hysteria. How could she go down to the beach with him? How could she go on being his companion, knowing that he was Armand's son? It wasn't fair on her, and it certainly wasn't fair on Armand's wife. His father had put her in an intolerable position, and the only sensible thing to do would be to resign.

'You are still cross about the pancakes, are you not, *senhorita*?' Ricardo suggested, moving closer to her and touching her hand. 'Oh, I know you did not say so, but I knew.' He sighed. 'If I promise to eat something at lunchtime, will you play with me?'

Catherine shook her head, looking down at him. 'I don't make those kind of bargains, Ricardo.'

'Papa does.'

'Yes.' Catherine took a deep breath. 'Yes, I know the

kind of bargains your father makes. But—it's not that simple.'

'If I say I am sorry, will you forgive me?' Ricardo looked up at her appealingly, and the entreaty in those clear grey eyes was almost irresistible.

'You are—incorrigible,' she told him huskily, fighting to control her emotions.

'Is that good or bad?' he asked perplexedly, and she expelled her breath in a rueful sigh.

'A little of both, I think,' she told him, giving in to the impulse to take his hand. 'All right. I'll come down to the beach. If only because I need the exercise to work off Sophia's pancakes.'

In spite of her problems, the morning passed remarkably quickly. As she already knew to her cost, Ricardo was good company, and there was an acute pleasure in seeing his thin face light up with excitement and in hearing the spontaneous shout of his laughter. In much the same way she and Armand had related, right from the beginning, she and his son did the same, and by the time Sophia came on to the balcony to announce that lunch was ready, Catherine was wondering how on earth she was going to face another parting.

Was that what Armand had wanted, she wondered. Had his intention been for her to become so attached to his son that when she did learn the truth, as she ultimately would, she would not be able to leave? It was a plausible explanation, but even he could not have guessed how quickly it would become a reality. In a little less than twenty-four hours, Ricardo had found his way into her heart, and the idea of leaving him now was not one she wished to contemplate.

Who would take care of him if she resigned? she fretted. Not his mother, if what Ricardo had said was true. Did he have any other relatives beside his parents? And if not, how could she leave him to the care of a stranger?

She dismissed the fact that she had been a stranger herself until yesterday. She had not been a stranger to his father, and Armand must have known she would never do anything to hurt a child. *Particularly not his child*, a small voice inside her taunted hollowly, and she knew a futile desire that she had not guessed the truth.

Of course, no one else knew she had, she reflected consideringly, as she tied her skirt about her waist once again. Even Armand himself had no idea she had uncovered his little deception. Ricardo was innocent of any duplicity, of course, and even Sophia could have no idea why her employer should wish to keep his identity secret. She could go on, as before, without anyone but herself being the wiser.

Sophia had served lunch on the balcony, and looking at the mouth-watering array of shellfish and salad, Catherine wondered how she was going to set Ricardo a good example right now. In spite of the exercise she had had, she was still choked by what she had discovered, and it took an effort to help herself to several battered shrimps and a single leaf of lettuce.

To her relief, however, Ricardo did not pay a great deal of attention to her plate. Instead, he armed himself with an appetising slice of seafood quiche and a handful of crisps, and seating himself on the top step, proceeded to feed most of his food to the cormorants.

'Remember what you said,' Catherine was forced to remind him at last, and Ricardo gave her a shame-faced grin.

'I am eating some of it,' he protested, cramming several crisps into his mouth at once to prove the point, and Catherine shook her head defeatedly.

'I suppose you'll eat if you're hungry,' she re-marked, nibbling at the tail of a huge shrimp. 'Doesn't your mother get cross with you at home?'

'I do not take my meals with my mother, *senhorita*,' declared Ricardo carelessly, but he avoided her eyes. Then, almost compulsively, he added: 'Mama spends all her time with Uncle Estéban.'

'Does she?'

Catherine wondered at a woman who could disregard her son's welfare so completely, to play hostess to her brother. But she should not make judgments, she warned herself severely. If Senhora de Castro's husband chose to dally with other members of her sex, what more natural but that his wife should devote her energies towards a brother? Nevertheless, Ricardo's health should take precedence over the resentment she evidently felt towards her husband. He was only a child. He needed a mother's love, and her guidance.

Lunch over, and the noonday sun almost too hot to bear, Ricardo was quite content to disappear to play in his room. Catherine followed him and collected the books she needed to begin her preliminary assessment of his progress. In spite of the fact that Sophia had done his unpacking and put all his things tidily away, the floor was again strewn with modelling bricks and other paraphernalia, but she hadn't the heart to chastise him when he looked up from his knees and gave her a dazzling smile.

'We do not have to start lessons today, do we?' he pleaded, and she thought he was not above a little bribery himself.

'I told you: we'll probably get down to some work at the beginning of next week,' she averred, wondering if her unhesitatingly-voiced words were an indication that, subconsciously, she had already decided to stay.

'Oh, good!' Ricardo was evidently content with her answer. 'So—can we go for a walk later? You did say we could look for some shells when the tide has gone out.'

'Perhaps.' Catherine wrapped her arms around the notebooks and text books he had given her. She paused. 'Do you think you are going to be happy here? With me, I mean?'

Ricardo looked up in surprise. 'But, of course,' he exclaimed. And then, with endearing anxiousness: 'Are you?'

Catherine expelled her breath unsteadily. 'Oh—yes,' she told him honestly. 'Yes, I like it here. I—just wondered if there was someone else—' She broke off abruptly, and then added: 'Who looks after you at home, Ricardo?'

He rumpled his hair, and a silky lock fell across his forehead with a disturbingly familiar lack of discipline. 'At home, *senhorita*?' he echoed in some confusion. 'I do not understand.'

Catherine sighed. 'Do you have a nanny?'

Ricardo frowned. 'What is a nanny?'

Catherine hesitated. 'A—nursemaid, I suppose.'

'You mean an *ama*?' he demanded indignantly. 'I do not need an *ama*, *senhorita*! I am not a baby.'

'I know that,' Catherine hastened to reassure him. 'But if you don't eat your meals with your mother, who do you eat them with?'

It was an impertinent question, she knew, and Ricardo regarded her a little mutinously before giving her an answer. 'With Papa, when he is there,' he responded at last, albeit a trifle defensively, and Catherine knew a momentary sense of wonder. 'And

Violetta, when he is not,' Ricardo added, lifting his hand to dash the control tower of the model airport he had been building to the floor. 'There! There! A plane has crashed!'

His expression should have warned her not to go on, but Catherine could not give up now. 'Who is Violetta?' she asked, determined that this should be the last question, but Ricardo had had enough.

'Why do you want to know?' he demanded, his small chin jutting. 'Why are you asking all these questions?' His grey eyes grew dark and clouded with emotion. 'Do you not wish to stay with me, Miss Loring? As Mama is going away, are you trying to find out if there is someone else to take charge of me?'

He was very astute, as well as very bright, but he was also only eight years old; and even though he could reason like an adult, his feelings were those of a child. Although his words had been delivered with an hauteur his mother would have been proud of, his eyes were filled with tears and, abandoning any thought of leaving him, Catherine dropped down on to her knees beside him and drew his resisting body into her arms.

'I'm staying!' she told him fiercely, resting her cheek against the silky line where his hair parted. But he still fought away from her, his face smudged with tears.

'I am not a baby!' he insisted, but he didn't look very much older as he struggled to restore his dignity. Then, after dealing with his tears with the backs of his hands, he regarded her through the thick lashes that were so like his father's. 'But I am glad you are staying,' he admitted sheepishly. 'Violetta is old, and Papa does not like her. He would not come here if

Violetta was here.' He paused, and then added disconcertingly: 'Papa will not stay away because you are here. Papa will like you. I know.'

CHAPTER FIFTEEN

To her relief, by the time Senhora de Castro rang to inquire about her son's progress, Catherine was able to tell her he had settled down well. She could also have said he was actually acquiring an appetite, had Senhora de Castro given her the chance. But she didn't. After ascertaining that there had been no problems, she announced that she would be out of the country for the next three weeks, and that should Catherine run into any difficulties while she was away, she should refer herself to Senhor Lopez.

'He will contact Ricardo's father, should that prove necessary,' Senhora de Castro declared carelessly. 'You have not seen Ricardo's father, I presume. I am sure you would have told me if you had.'

Catherine only just managed to disguise her gasp of astonishment behind a hastily-produced cough. 'I—should I have seen him?' she asked faintly, and Ricardo's mother made a sound of impatience.

'I suppose it is just possible,' she declared, as if considering the contingency. 'My husband works in the north-west part of the country, *menina*. In a rather remote, mountainous area. I am never exactly sure where he is.' Her voice took on an ironic ring. 'He seldom troubles to tell me.'

Catherine's mouth was dry. 'I see,' she murmured, hoping to conclude this conversation, but Senhora de Castro was not quite finished yet.

'You might as well know, *menina*, my husband cares little for myself and Ricardo. For some years now, he

256

has made a mockery of our marriage, and this reflects badly on the boy, as you may have guessed.'

Catherine could not answer, and without waiting for a reply, Senhora de Castro swept on: '*Não importa*, I am relying on you, *menina*, to insure that Ricardo has some order in his life while I am away. He is a clever child. I should not wish for him to get behind in his studies, *está entendido*?—is that understood?'

'Very well, *senhora*.' Catherine spoke with difficulty, but Ricardo's mother paid little attention.

'*Pois bem!*' she declared, seemingly satisfied with the girl's answer, but behind her voice now Catherine could hear the muffled sound of a man's impatient tones. As if responding to some summons given her by her companion, Senhora de Castro brought the call quickly to its conclusion. 'I will telephone you again on my return, *menina*,' she affirmed crisply, and without asking to speak to her son, without even sending him her love or affection, she replaced her receiver, and Catherine was left listening to the disconnected line.

'It was Mama!' remarked Ricardo behind her, and Catherine turned to find her charge perched on the arm of a chair close by.

'I—yes,' she conceded, replacing the handset carefully, realising there was no point in lying to him. 'She was—in a hurry, I think.'

'Uncle Estéban is very impatient,' Ricardo averred, lifting his narrow shoulders. 'He does not like to be kept waiting.'

Catherine forced a smile. 'I believe that's a masculine failing.'

'I do not mind waiting for you,' said Ricardo generously.

'But you're not a man!' pointed out Catherine lightly, glad of the diversion, and Ricardo shrugged.

'I will be one day,' he replied practically. 'But I will not be like Uncle Estéban. Not ever!'

Catherine expelled a nervous breath. 'How can you be sure?' she countered. 'He is your uncle, after all.'

'He is not my *real* uncle!' retorted Ricardo scornfully, sliding down from the chair. 'Now—can we go for our swim? It will soon be lunchtime!'

It was doubtful how much faith one could put in the contemptuous words of a child, but Catherine had been with Ricardo for over a week now, and she had never known him to lie. Besides which, he was an intelligent child. He would know he could not make that kind of statement without its being the truth.

For her part, Catherine was stunned by his candour. If it was true, and she had no reason to doubt it, it threw an entirely new light on Senhora de Castro's relationship with this man, and on the fact that they were going away together!

Of course, she could be jumping to wild conclusions. He could be a friend of Armand's, persuaded to look after his wife in his absence. He could be her employer. Catherine had no way of knowing how Ricardo's mother kept herself occupied.

But the persistent thought that plagued her was that there might be more to Ricardo's lack of appetite than she had at first suspected. Remembering the way he had looked when she had first met him, she wondered if there might not be some other reason for his starved appearance. She had put it down to his father's prolonged absence, and a lack of interest of his mother's part; but there could be more. Ricardo was an imaginative child. He could be fretting about his mother's relationship with his 'Uncle Estéban', no matter how innocent that might be. If only she could ask him. If only Armand knew what was going on . . .

In the days that followed, Catherine found at least one thing to cheer about. Whatever Ricardo's aberrations might have been, as each day at Casca de Mar passed his appetite improved accordingly. He no longer waited for Catherine to offer him this or that. Whenever possible, he helped himself, and already the hollows in his cheeks were filling out. His condition was definitely emotional, rather than physical, Catherine realised quickly. Was that how Armand had succeeded in the past? Because Ricardo was happiest when he was with him?

Ricardo's birthday was fast approaching, and realising she had no gift to give him, Catherine asked Sophia's advice.

'There is a store in the village that sells many things,' the Italian girl whispered, conscious of Ricardo playing with his cars on the balcony. 'It mostly caters to the *turísti*, you understand, but you may find something there to suit you.'

'But how do I get there?' asked Catherine eagerly. 'Is it far?'

'You walk—like me,' declared Sophia, putting the finishing touches to the cake she had been icing for him. 'His birthday is tomorrow, you know. You do not have much time.'

'I know.' Catherine sighed. 'I should have asked you before, but I forgot.'

'No matter.' Sophia shrugged. 'Why do you not go now? It is early yet, and Ricardo is busy. I will tell him you have gone to buy some candles for his cake.'

'I doubt if he'll believe you.' Catherine smiled. 'Thanks, Sophia. I won't be long.'

It was the first time she had left the villa alone. She

and Ricardo had taken lots of walks together during
the past two weeks, but they had mainly been along
the beach, and she had never felt so conspicuous as
she did now.

Her white cotton pants and short-sleeved shirt were
so different from the long black skirts and enveloping
shawls of the women who passed her. Not even in
Batistamajor had she experienced such a sense of
alienation, and she quickened her step accordingly,
eager to make her purchase and return.

The road to Casca de Mar followed the line of the
shore for some way before curving inland to embrace a
row of cottages, scattered up the hillside. Below the
cluster of dwellings, a small harbour gave protection
to a handful of fishing boats, and men and women
were sitting on the quay in the morning sunshine,
mending their nets and exchanging gossip. There was
a smell of fish and drying nets, and the ever-present
scent of the sea.

Catherine was aware that voices were stilled as they
stared at her, and she wondered how Sophia had
infiltrated this closed community. Perhaps, as she was
married to one of them, it made a difference. Whatever
the Italian girl's circumstances, Catherine felt their
eyes boring into her back as she entered the tiny store,
and she was relieved to discover she was the only
customer.

Cheap plastic toys and garish jewellery filled the
shelves devoted to the unlikely visitor. Tin replicas of
patron saints, painted to resemble bronze castings,
imported pottery from Hong Kong, fans from China:
the quantity of useless keepsakes was amazing, particularly in a place that had had few visitors since
the fighting started.

In a more practical vein, there were tubs of rice and

flour, grain and coffee beans. There were sacks of potatoes strewn about the limited floor space, a huge drum of corn oil, and even one of paraffin, so that Catherine wondered gingerly if they ever confused the two. A slab of strongly-smelling goats' cheese set on the counter, brought a distinctly nauseous flutter to her stomach, and she looked about her hurriedly, eager to escape.

'Sim, senhora?'

As the rather lugubrious individual standing behind the counter prepared to serve her, Catherine realised, belatedly, that her few words of Portuguese might well prove a problem here. 'Er—quero—um presente,' she ventured awkwardly, hoping he would not come back with a long monologue she could not understand. 'Por—um menino, sim?'

'Um menino, senhora?' The man put a thin cheroot between his teeth and lit it from the flickering flame of the lamp that illuminated the rather dim interior of the store. 'Qué quer?'

It wasn't easy, but by means of trial and error, and a considerable amount of sign language, Catherine managed to explain what she was looking for. She had her doubts that she would find anything here suitable to give to Ricardo, and she was rather perturbed when, after several abortive attempts to persuade her to buy one or other of the cheap toys on display, the man disappeared through the curtained opening that led to the back of the store.

Had he given up on her, she wondered, not sure whether she was expected to wait. It was certainly a temptation to abandon her search and get out of there, away from the pungent aroma of the cheese. But she decided to give him a few more minutes, and as she tried to put as much distance between herself and the counter as possible, she saw the pile of newspapers stacked in the corner. Permitting herself a casual glance, she saw it was the *Terasina Gazeta*, the most popular newspaper in the capital according to her father. Professor Loring used to have the Saturday edition mailed out to him from time to time, until the cost of postage became prohibitive.

'*Qué lhe parece?*'

While Catherine had been engrossed in trying to translate the *Gazeta*'s headlines, the proprietor had returned and was asking for her opinion on the article he held in his hands. Collecting a paper to take with her, Catherine turned back to the counter, and then gave a gasp of pleasure at what she saw.

It was a sheepskin rug; just a small one to be sure, but delightful nonetheless. It was exactly the kind of thing Ricardo would like to have beside his bed. It would be soft and fluffy to put his toes on when he got out of bed in the mornings, and she knew, instinctively, he would love it. But it was evidently genuine, and probably much too expensive, and although she admired it, there was a rueful gleam in her eyes.

'You like?' inquired the man hopefully, clearly proud of his business acumen, and Catherine nodded.

'*Quanto é?*' she asked enviously. 'How much?' And the man puffed thoughtfully on his cheroot before giving her his price.

It was, amazingly, within her reach, and she handed over her money eagerly, watching as he wrapped the skin inside a scrappy piece of paper. Ricardo would be so excited when he saw it, she thought, anticipating his reactions. With his parents away, and no brothers or sisters to share his celebration, she and Sophia must try their best to see that he was not disappointed.

It was an enormous relief to get out in the fresh air again. Still, the success of her outing more than made up for the discomfort she had suffered inside the store, and the proprietor had been kind, after all, giving her the newspaper free of charge, as a gesture of goodwill. She could even face the barrage of curious eyes that followed her progress back towards the villa without flinching. They were not hostile eyes, she realised; only inquisitive.

She was still some distance from the villa when a car, travelling in the opposite direction, slowed beside her. Oh, no! she thought. Not someone trying to pick her up on this quiet road, surely! But the car had stopped and she automatically quickened her pace.

'*Bom dia, senhorita. Como está?*' she heard, in disturbingly familiar tones, and although she knew it could not be him, the temptation to prove it was too great.

Stopping, she turned, and then caught her breath. '*Armand!*' she gasped, clutching the untidy parcel to her chest like a shield as the tall dark man, in mud-coloured Levis and a matching cotton shirt, uncoiled himself from behind the wheel of the cream Mercedes. And then, remembering his deception: 'What are you doing here?'

'Are you not pleased to see me?' he inquired, his English not half as cordial as his Portuguese had been, and Catherine took an unsteady gulp of air.

'Surprised,' she amended, reminding herself of the coolness of their parting almost three weeks ago. 'I—what are you doing in Casca de Mar? Do you—do you have friends here?'

'Don't you know?' he responded tautly, holding her gaze, but when she refused to sustain that brooding

appraisal, he ran a careless hand into the opened neck
of his shirt. It was a casual gesture. She doubted he
was even aware of what he was doing. But it drew her
eyes to the muscled column of his throat, and the
associations it evoked made a mockery of her attempts
to appear detached. Remembering what they had
once shared, it was incredibly difficult to hold on to the
image of his wife, and although she guessed he was
not in Casca de Mar for her benefit, she could not deny
she wanted him still.

But wanting was not having, she reminded herself
fiercely. Loving a man did not change his character.
He was still the man who had betrayed his wife and
taken her innocence, and she should remember that
instead of gazing, open-mouthed, at his lean body and
harsh good looks.

'How are you?' he asked now. 'Are you happy
here?'

Catherine schooled her features. 'I am very happy,
thank you. This is a beautiful place. Who would not be
happy here?'

His mouth compressed, as though her words had
irritated him. 'You like your job?' he persisted. 'It lives
up to your expectations?'

'I like my job very much,' she replied honestly. 'I
like working with children. They are so . . . uncom-
plicated. And Ricardo—'

She broke off abruptly, unwilling to talk about his
son with him, and Armand made an impatient
gesture. 'Yes? Yes? And Ricardo—what?' he urged,
waiting for her to continue. 'You find the boy un-
complicated, too?'

Catherine held up her head. 'Of what interest is it to
you, *senhor*? I'm sure Senhora de Castro would not
approve of my discussing Ricardo's progress with an

outsider. Even if you are a doctor and, possibly, a friend of the family!'

Armand's nostrils flared as he met her scornful gaze. 'You know.' It was a statement, not a question. 'How did you find out?'

'I assume from your attitude that you expected me to find out,' Catherine temporised carefully. 'Why did you do it?'

'You needed a job.'

'Not this job!' Catherine's anger came to her rescue. 'There must have been something else I could do.'

'I wanted you in a safe place; so I knew where you were,' he retorted, glancing impatiently up and down the road. 'Look—can we get into the car and discuss it? I don't like feeling this conspicuous.'

'I have no desire to get into your car,' responded Catherine tensely, hugging her parcel closer. 'Sophia is expecting me back. She'll worry if I'm late.'

Armand's expression hardened. 'I could remind you that both you and Sophia are my employees,' he remarked. 'Come along. I'll drive you back.'

Catherine looked mutinous. 'I prefer to walk.'

'Nevertheless.' Armand inhaled deeply. 'Don't make me threaten you, Catherine.'

Catherine scuffed the toe of her sandal in the dirt path. 'You're going in the wrong direction,' she protested.

'I was on my way to the house when I saw you,' Armand explained briefly. 'I turned back because I wanted to speak to you privately.'

'I bet you did.' Catherine pursed her lips. 'Oh—all right.' With ill grace, she gave in, and walked back to the car. 'You can be an absolute pig when you like,' she muttered, hoping he wouldn't hear her, but the expression on his face was not promising, and she subsided into her seat without another word.

Armand closed her door with a distinct click, and then walked round the car and got in beside her. 'This is nice, isn't it?' he remarked, with cutting sarcasm, and she turned her head to the open window to avoid his mocking gaze.

'What do you want, Armand?' she asked, staring out at the sloping fields that edged the dunes at this point. It had been incredibly difficult to maintain her indifference to him out in the open. It was virtually impossible in the close confines of the car.

'It's Ricardo's birthday tomorrow,' he said simply, abandoning his biting humour. 'I promised him a bicycle. It had to be delivered.'

'Oh.' Catherine's fingers closed convulsively around the parcel in her lap. She should have thought of that. Ricardo's birthday! Ricardo's *father*! She took a breath. 'You've got it then?'

'In the trunk,' he agreed, half turning in his seat towards her. 'Now—tell me how you knew?'

Catherine shrugged, concentrating on her hands. In the car, she was intensely aware of his nearness, and the heated scent of his body drifted irresistibly to her nostrils. It was so warm and clean and *male*, and she could not ignore it. She wanted to press herself against him; she wanted to throw her arms around his neck and cover his face with kisses. And she had to steel herself not to reveal this in any of the things she said.

'You—did expect me to find out,' she said, and he made an indifferent gesture.

'You're an intelligent young woman. It was on the cards.'

'So why didn't you tell me?'

She looked at him then, and Armand's lips twisted. 'Would you have come?'

Catherine expelled her breath in a rush. 'You admit it then?'

'Admit what?'

'That you deliberately tricked me!'

Armand shrugged. 'Don't be so melodramatic. I knew if I told you you'd be taking care of my son you wouldn't want to do it. So—I didn't.'

Catherine gasped. 'Just like that!'

'It was no big deal.' Armand's mouth thinned. 'How did you discover Ricardo was my son? Did he tell you?'

'No.' Catherine looked away from him again, disturbed by his manner. He was making her feel as if she was to blame, not him, and she resented the arrogant way he had disposed of her objections. 'I—saw the photograph,' she admitted at last. 'The one of Ricardo that you keep beside your bed. It wasn't difficult after that.'

Armand shook his head. 'But you only saw it fleetingly, the night I took you up to José's camp.'

'No, I . . . afterwards—' Catherine found it very difficult to admit it '—afterwards, I saw it in your bedroom. One day when you were working.' She flushed. 'I thought it was a picture of Luis. He—he looks a lot like him, don't you think?'

'He should,' said Armand, after a moment. 'They're cousins. But perhaps you should tell me what you were doing in my bedroom?'

Catherine shook her head. 'José Rodolfo is *your* brother?'

'Half-brother,' Armand corrected her impatiently. 'His father died soon after he was born. When he was four, our mother married again. I was the son of her second marriage.'

Catherine moistened her lips. 'And your mother is English!'

'How do you know that?' Armand was diverted.

Catherine shook her head. 'Something Sophia said,' she exclaimed. 'About—Ricardo's grandmother. She said she was English and lived in São Paulo.'

'That's right.' Armand inclined his head. 'But I am Brazilian, nevertheless. As is my father.'

'And José's father?' Catherine was curious.

'He was Surajan,' said Armand levelly. Then: 'He was a member of the civilian government here. He was killed in the coup that put a military regime in power. Oh, not President Ferreira's government,' he added drily. 'This was more than forty years ago. Before either you or I were born.'

Catherine nodded. 'Is that why José . . . ?'

'I suppose so.' Armand bent his head. 'He left home to join the army when I was thirteen.'

'The Surajan army?' asked Catherine in surprise, but Armand made a negative gesture.

'The Brazilian army initially,' he said. 'Then, when I was twenty-two, he disappeared. It's only been a matter of two or three years since we discovered what had happened.'

'So long!' Catherine's lips parted. 'Your mother must have been frantic!'

'Yes. She was.' Armand hesitated, and then continued tolerantly: 'She never stopped trying to find him. She initiated inquiries all over Latin America, without any success. Then, quite by accident, really, we learned he had been living in Terasina for several years. Prior to a warrant being issued for his arrest as a dissident.'

Catherine was intrigued. 'How exciting!'

'Not really.' Armand shifted his position, his arm dropping carelessly along the back of the seat behind her. 'José must have been pretty scared to take off like he did. To be arrested in Terasina is as good as signing your own death warrant.'

'Were you living in Terasina then?'

'No.' Armand shook his head. 'Look—you can't want to hear all this. It can be of no interest to you.'

'But it is.' Catherine put her hand on his knee, and then withdrew it again sharply. 'I—I'd like you to go on,' she murmured. 'How did you come to Surajo?'

Armand frowned. 'I suppose it was a little over two years ago,' he responded. 'I was working in Rio, and when my mother came to me with the news that José had been living in Terasina, I offered to try and get a transfer here. It wasn't difficult. Many doctors were leaving, if they could get a visa. My coming here was seen as a gesture of support for the Ferreira government.'

Catherine shook her head. 'But it wasn't.'

'Hardly,' said Armand drily.

'And your—your wife and Ricardo: they came with you?' she offered tentatively. 'Wasn't that rather—dangerous?'

Armand looked at her steadily. 'Will you believe me if I tell you, I didn't want them to come.'

'But they came.'

'Yes.'

Catherine swallowed. 'Why shouldn't I believe you?'

'Oh, I don't know.' Armand lifted one shoulder. 'You don't have a very high opinion of me, do you?'

Catherine avoided his eyes. 'We weren't talking about me.'

'No. That's right.' Armand conceded the point. 'And now I think we have spoken enough of me, no? Tell me about Ricardo. Do you like him?'

Catherine smoothed the rough paper of her parcel. 'You knew I would.'

'I hoped,' he amended quietly, his fingers brushing her collar, almost involuntarily, she thought. 'So— what is your opinion of him?'

Catherine quivered. 'I don't think I'm equipped to judge.'

'But you know him. No doubt he has talked to you. Do you think he has been irreparably damaged by what has happened?'

Catherine was disconcerted. 'Your going away, you mean?' she ventured awkwardly, and Armand muffled an oath.

'No, I do not mean as a result of my absence,' he said, harshly, 'although I suppose I am responsible, too. But I could not take the boy to Batistamajor, even if Estella would have let me. It was too dangerous. I couldn't take the risk.'

'Estella?' Catherine's tongue circled her upper lip. 'That—that's your wife?'

'Yes.' The lines that bracketed Armand's mouth gave his lean face a bitter look.

'She's very beautiful,' said Catherine impulsively, forcing herself to speak of the other woman without exhibiting any of the painful jealousy she was feeling. But Armand's reaction was violent.

'You have seen her?' he demanded, his hand behind her head turning her face towards him. 'When?'

Catherine trembled. 'When—when she brought Ricardo to the villa, of course.'

'*Estella* brought Ricardo to the villa?'

'Yes. Yes.' Catherine twisted her head. 'Armand, you're hurting me!'

But it was more the emotions his hard grasp was promoting that caused her to offer the protest. His action had brought them closer; the imprisonment of his hold was forcing her to face him, and although she

could avoid his eyes, she could not avoid the awareness of his arm along her cheek, the hair-roughened
skin abusing her soft flesh.

'What did she say to you?' he adjured, ignoring her
pleas. 'Did she ask you any questions?'

'What about?' Catherine winced as his impatient
fingers tugged the hair from her scalp. 'What could
she say?' she exclaimed, defensively. 'We—we just
talked about Ricardo, that's all. As you'd expect.'

Armand's fingers relaxed, but he did not let her go,
and his penetrating stare was almost tangible. 'Have
you seen her again?' he persisted, his controlled tones
deceptive, but Catherine was not beguiled.

'No,' she said honestly, though she refrained from
mentioning the phone call. 'Now, will you let me go?
Sophia will be worried.'

Armand did not move, and his warm breath fanned
her forehead with disruptive consequences. 'Where
have you been anyway?' he demanded. 'I am not sure
that I approve of your walking to the village alone.'

Catherine gasped. '*You* don't approve!' she echoed
indignantly. 'I don't think it has anything to do with
you, *Senhor de Castro*!'

Armand regarded her intently for a moment, and
then he let her go. 'I did not like deceiving you,' he
declared flatly. 'It was not my intention to deceive
anyone. But there were circumstances . . .'

'Did it make it easier for you to forget the fact that
you were married?' inquired Catherine scornfully,
lifting her hands to smooth her tender scalp. 'As
Armand Alvares, no one would connect you with Dr
de Castro, or with Dr de Castro's wife and child,
would they?'

'*Basta assim!* That will do!' grated Armand angrily,
his hands moving swiftly to imprison her hands

against the back of her head. 'What kind of monster do you think I am? My reasons for keeping my identity private had nothing to do with any perverted desire to shun my responsibilities. Whatever you may be thinking, whatever opinion you have of me, I do not take my marriage vows lightly.'

'No?' Catherine's response was barely audible, but he heard it.

'No,' he averred harshly. 'If that were so, I would not be hurting you now; I would not be holding you away from me, when what I really want to do is take you in my arms; I would not be killing this thing there is between us, when my body aches to feel every inch of yours, naked beneath me!'

'Armand!'

Catherine spoke his name breathily, the air in her lungs scarcely sufficient to expel the single word. Her breathing felt constricted, suspended, her chest rising and falling shallowly with the tremor of her emotions. If he was hurting her, she could scarcely feel it. His words were a potent intoxicant that numbed her brain to anything but the devastating sensibility of his nearness. Somehow, even the space between them had become sensitised, and when her eyes lifted to meet his tormented gaze, she saw her hunger reflected in his face.

And then, when she was sure that he was going to kiss her, when his gaze had dropped sensuously to her parted lips, and from there to the thinly-protected fullness of her breasts, their peaks provocatively outlined against the fabric of her shirt, the parcel she had been holding on her lap fell noisily to the floor of the car. The crumpled paper rustled aggravatingly against her legs before subsiding in a heap beside her feet, and although Armand closed his eyes for a moment, as if to blot out the sound, the damage had been done.

'What the hell is that?' he muttered frustratedly, releasing her to rescue the loosely-wrapped bundle from below the glove compartment, and Catherine envied him his iron control.

'It's a gift for Ricardo,' she answered, expelling her breath unsteadily as his son's name seemed to thicken the wedge the falling parcel had driven between them. 'It's a rug; a sheepskin rug. That was why I went to the village.'

Armand's features tightened as the soft skin, freed from its confinement, opened on his lap. 'You got this at Rodrigo's?' he inquired tautly, his tone indicative of the restraint he was putting on himself, and she nodded.

'If—if that is the name of the man who keeps the store, then yes,' she replied, licking her lips rather nervously. 'Do you—do you think he'll like it?'

Armand's mouth compressed. 'I am sure he will love it,' he murmured, folding the skin up again and wrapping the paper rather more expertly around it. 'I suggest you leave it in the car for now. If you want to keep it a secret, that is.'

'Well—yes, I do.' She looked at him a little uncertainly as he reached for the ignition. 'Armand—'

'Not now, Catherine!'

His terse words silenced her abruptly, the chilling emptiness of his tone making any response futile. He had withdrawn into the impenetrable shell where she could no longer reach him. Gathering the parcel he had thrust at her into her arms, she hugged it tightly to her. But for comfort this time, not protection.

CHAPTER SIXTEEN

CATHERINE took especial care as she dressed for supper that evening, though she knew it was an unnecessary gesture. It wasn't as if she and Armand were dining alone. And even if they had been, there was no guarantee that he would notice her. But, as it happened, Ricardo had already gained permission to stay up later than usual because his father was here, and watching them together earlier, Catherine had been left in little doubt that consideration for his son was the only reason Armand had left Batistamajor.

Not that she begrudged Ricardo his excitement. On the contrary, she was delighted he was to have at least one of his parents present on his birthday. But the realisation that Armand was staying over, that she would have to conceal her feelings for more than twenty-four hours, was a daunting prospect.

Armand's attitude should have made it easier, but it hadn't. For some reason, she resented the fact that he seemed capable of turning his feelings off and on at will. What manner of man was he, she wondered, to speak to her so passionately one minute and then treat her as a casual acquaintance the next. No one, hearing his casual explanation of how Catherine came to arrive home in his car, would have doubted his sincerity, and she wondered with a sinking heart if he had been lying to her, after all.

Ricardo had been so thrilled when his father's car turned up the drive to the villa. Before Catherine had time to extricate herself from the car, before she had time to concoct any explanation, Ricardo had been out of the house and tearing at the door, crying: 'Papa! Papa!' at the top of his voice.

Armand's expression was indulgent as he thrust open his door and swept the boy up into his arms. With Ricardo's arms clasped tightly about his neck, he patiently tried to answer the almost incoherent babble of questions being hurled at him, and Catherine opened her door and walked unnoticed into the house.

'*Dío, signorina*, what is going on?'

Sophia met her in the doorway, drawn by the shrill sound of Ricardo's voice. But at the sight of the sleek Mercedes, her expression softened dramatically, and Catherine guessed her explanation was unnecessary.

'Er—Senhor de Castro is here,' she declared offhandedly, wishing she could simply go to her room and leave them to it, but Ricardo had seen her and was beckoning excitedly.

'*Signor!*'

Sophia hurried down the steps to greet her employer, speaking to him first in her own language, alienating the girl still further. But then, as Armand's eyes moved to Catherine over Ricardo's head, Sophia realised her error, and her excited, halting words in English gave the younger girl her first intimation that this might not be just a flying visit.

'You are staying, *signor*?' she demanded. 'But yes, of course, you must be. It is not the little one's birthday until tomorrow!'

'Of course Papa is staying!' Ricardo declared fiercely, giving Sophia an impatient look. 'Perhaps this time he will stay for good!'

'Perhaps you should introduce your father to Miss Loring,' suggested Sophia drily, not put out by his indignation, and Ricardo frowned.

'But—Miss Loring came with Papa,' he declared, as if just recognising that fact. He turned to look at his father. 'Why was Miss Loring riding in your car, Papa? Sophia said she had gone to the village to get some candles for my cake.'

Aware that Sophia, too, was looking somewhat bewildered now, Catherine wished the ground would open up and swallow her. She should have known Ricardo would remember she had been in his father's car. She should have spent these past few minutes inventing an explanation why. If Ricardo was to discover she had known his father all along, it could well jeopardise the progress she had made with him. Besides which, she had no desire for Sophia to start speculating upon their relationship. Whatever interpretation could be put on Armand's wife's association with Ricardo's 'Uncle' Estéban, Senhora de Castro evidently cared about her husband. Why else would she show such dismay when she spoke of Armand's attitude? Why else would she be hurt by their continued separation?

As Catherine struggled with her conscience, Armand answered his son's troubled inquiry. 'I encountered Miss Loring just a few yards from the gate,' he declared crisply, a tight smile defusing the situation. 'I was very clever, don't you think? Identifying her?'

Ricardo pursed his lips. 'How did you do that, Papa?'

'Ah, well . . .' Armand hoisted him further so that Ricardo's legs were around his neck and the boy was settled comfortably on his shoulders. 'There are not too many fair-haired ladies in Casca de Mar, no? And Miss Loring is very—fair, don't you think?'

'Oh, Papa!' Ricardo's laughter rang out happily, and following Armand's lead, they all went into the house.

Remembering the scene now, Catherine's hand shook a little as she applied mascara to her gold-tipped lashes. It had been such a simple explanation, no one had doubted its sincerity, and she envied Armand's ability not to overstate his case.

Nevertheless, it had not been easy for her to maintain the pretence that she and Ricardo's father were strangers. Armand's impersonal questions about the work she had been doing with his son left her feeling unpleasantly disorientated, as if she had only imagined their previous association. He was so cool, so polite, so completely in control of the situation. His concern for Ricardo's welfare really seemed to be the only point of contact between them, and the golden beauty of his eyes held nothing but an enigmatic urbanity.

She thought Ricardo noticed nothing amiss. If he had thought his governess was perhaps a little withdrawn in her employer's presence, no doubt he put it down to a natural awe of his father, and Catherine's abstraction reinforced this belief. For himself, he was obviously riding on cloud nine, now that he had Armand's undivided attention. He looked for no ulterior motives. He was content to bask in his father's love.

For the first time since Catherine had come to the villa, lunch was served at the round dining table. It had been something of an ordeal for her, her appetite, never robust, disappearing completely as Armand continued to ignore her. Fortunately, Ricardo and his father were too wrapped up in themselves to notice, she thought, and she was glad when the meal was over and she could escape to her room.

Then, in the late afternoon, when the sun had passed its zenith and the shadows were lengthening on the balcony, Ricardo came to ask her if she would like to join him and his father for a walk along the beach.

'Please come,' he said simply, when she looked as if she might refuse. 'Papa said to tell you, he is not such an—an ogre as you might think. He says you have spent long enough indoors. A walk in the fresh air will do you good.'

Catherine wondered how much of what Ricardo had said Armand had, in fact, instructed. The comment about his being an ogre had to have come from him. She doubted Ricardo would have known the word otherwise. But the rest—the part about being indoors long enough and enjoying a walk in the fresh air—sounded more like Ricardo than the man she had felt so uneasy with at lunchtime.

Deciding that the boy's happiness was worth more than her foolish resentment, Catherine accepted his invitation. Without giving herself time to have second thoughts, she merely ran the brush through the loose strands of hair that framed her anxious features. The rest of her hair was still reasonably securely ensnared within the single braid that fell over her shoulder, and grimacing at her expression in the mirror, she followed the boy down the winding staircase.

Armand was standing by the long windows in the living room as they entered, staring broodingly out towards the distant horizon. He turned at the sound of Ricardo's voice, however, and for an unguarded moment, over the dancing head of his son, his eyes met Catherine's. His intense gaze stopped her dead in her tracks, the naked hunger in his face bringing an uncontrollable trembling to her knees. She was glad she

was wearing trousers so that the revealing tremor of
her legs should not be noticed, but her palms felt
damp and sticky as they sought the wrought-iron rail
of the banister.

'You see!' exclaimed Ricardo excitedly, intent only
on drawing his father's attention back to him, and
with a faintly bemused shake of his head, Armand
dragged his eyes away. 'I told you she would come,'
the boy added, tugging at his sleeve. 'Did I not?'

'You did.' Armand's lips twisted a little mockingly
as he acknowledged his son's success, and Catherine
expelled her breath in an uneasy sigh. She didn't need
to be told the spell was broken. She didn't need to see
the impersonal mask which had once again settled
over Armand's face to know he regretted that in-
cautious appraisal. Whatever he was feeling, he had
no intention of forgetting his responsibilities again.

Remembering the walk along the beach now,
Catherine wondered why she was taking so much
trouble over her appearance. It wasn't as if Armand
had shown her any special attention. He was kind and
polite, but he had not spoken often to her, and when
he did it was always about his son. Even on those
occasions when Ricardo had dashed away from the two
adults, to rescue a particular shell from the dappled
pools that edged the shoreline, or to race with boyish
fearlessness into the shallows, he had not allowed his
guard to drop, and Catherine's head ached with the
effort of sustaining a matching detachment.

Rising from the mirror now, Catherine reached for
the apricot silk blouse, which had been her one
extravagance during that shopping excursion in
Terasina. Its buttonless mandarin neckline and full,
leg-of-mutton sleeves were very flattering, as was the

colour, which brought out the red-gold lights in her hair and accentuated the honey-beige tan she was acquiring. With the blouse, she wore her one and only skirt: a plain brown sheath, with a wrapover waistline, that hinted at the contours of her slim legs as she moved.

After considering her hair for several minutes, she decided to leave it loose. But she did secure it behind her ears with two combs, allowing the curling strands to fall unhindered over her shoulders.

It was quite dark when she went downstairs again, but Sophia had turned on the lamps and slid the mesh screen across the open french doors. This way, whatever breeze there was could lightly enter the room, while less welcome visitors were kept out. Already several moths, of the variety Catherine disliked most, were beating their velvet wings against the mesh, and she shivered a little apprehensively at the vehemence of their attack.

She had thought the room was empty, but as she walked rather uneasily across the polished boards, Armand rose like an avenging angel from the depths of an armchair. In dark pants and a white silk shirt, unbuttoned half down his chest for coolness, he looked arrestingly attractive, and Catherine found herself searching his face for some remnant of the emotion she had glimpsed earlier.

'Not very pretty, are they?' he remarked, gesturing with the half-filled glass in his hand, and Catherine blinked in confusion. 'The moths,' he added helpfully, as she endeavoured to pull herself together. 'Hairy legs, and all.'

'What? Oh—oh, yes.' Catherine coloured and made an effort to act naturally. 'I don't like them at all.'

'No.' Armand finished the Scotch in his glass and

HIDDEN IN THE FLAME

then indicated the trolley Sophia had wheeled in earlier. 'Can I get you a drink? Some sherry, perhaps?'

'I'd prefer a glass of white wine,' said Catherine at once, recovering a little of her composure. 'Where is Ricardo? He is going to join us, isn't he?'

'He's just gone to find Sophia.' Armand paused. 'I've asked her if she will spend the night here.'

'Sophia!' Catherine couldn't keep the surprise out of her voice. 'But—why?'

'I think we both know the reason why,' Armand replied levelly, handing her a stemmed glass. 'Now—why don't you sit down and enjoy your wine. I'll go and tell Sophia we're ready.'

He was gone before she could offer any objection, and besides, what could she say? It was obvious he wanted to protect himself and Ricardo from any gossip which might ensue if it got around that he had spent the night at the villa. Nothing she said would dissuade him. And besides, why should she want to? He was still a married man. She ought to remember that.

When he came back, Ricardo was with him and there was no further opportunity for private discussion. The little boy monopolised the conversation, even when he expressed a rather rueful admiration for his governess's appearance.

'Does she not look pretty, Papa?' he exclaimed, regarding Catherine with some misgivings, and she was briefly diverted from her own problems. Ricardo had not seen her in anything but pants or shorts, or her swimsuit, and evidently the transformation was not entirely to his liking. She guessed he had thought of her as a contemporary, in spite of their teacher-pupil status; someone not so much older than himself, to whom he could relate. Tonight, his erstwhile companion looked like a woman, and Catherine guessed he wasn't sure whether he approved of the metamorphosis.

'Very pretty,' Armand answered, his endorsement coolly polite. 'But now, I think we should have supper. It is long past your bedtime, young man, and you want to enjoy your birthday tomorrow, don't you?'

Supper was an especially delicious meal of crispy pancakes, filled with cheese, a spicy stew of meat and beans with rice, and slices of fresh pineapple served with a sprinkling of cinnamon. There was a bottle of red wine for Catherine and Armand, and a jug of iced lemonade for Ricardo; and afterwards, some of Sophia's freshly ground coffee, to drink with tiny glasses of a potent local liqueur. Catherine was tempted to refuse the alcohol when it was offered. She had never tasted anything quite so intoxicating. But the thought that it might help to relieve her nerves was appealing, and she swallowed the raw spirit without really savouring its content.

She had noticed Armand watching his son from time to time throughout the meal, and guessed he had observed Ricardo's improved appetite. Indeed, in spite of the excitement of his father's visit, Ricardo actually seemed to be enjoying his food, and Catherine felt a sense of achievement for having accomplished this, at least.

With the meal over, Catherine imagined her company was superfluous, but Ricardo had other ideas. 'Can we all play cards, Papa?' he pleaded, clearly afraid he was about to be banished to his room. And although Armand looked sombre, he eventually gave in.

'For thirty minutes only,' he conceded, and his son gave a delighted whoop. 'But perhaps Miss Loring will not wish to join us. She may prefer a little privacy.'

The golden eyes were turned in her direction, and Catherine knew an instinctive desire to thwart his calm deliberation. But how? By going to her room, and in so doing disappointing Ricardo? Or by staying, and running the gauntlet of Armand's possible displeasure? Which did he really want her to do? How could she tell?

'You do not wish to go to bed yet, *senhorita*, do you?'

Ricardo's hopeful entreaty was irresistible, and Catherine forced a faint smile. 'I'll stay,' she said, earning an enigmatic glance from his father. 'You get the cards, Ricardo, while I help Sophia clear the table.'

'There is no need for you to do this,' Armand declared somewhat impatiently, as his son went to find the playing cards and Catherine began loading the coffee cups and liqueur glasses on to a tray. 'Sophia!' His summons brought the Italian girl from the kitchen, and Catherine stepped back stiffly as the housekeeper took command.

He really was the most infuriating man, she thought, controlling her temper with difficulty. Why should he care whether or not she chose to act as maid sometimes? It was as if he wanted to control her as effectively as he controlled his feelings, and she knew a frustrated longing to tear down his cold façade.

Ricardo returned with the playing cards, and, after some discussion, a simple game of knock-out whist was devised. It was a game he and Catherine had played on several occasions, when the sun had been too hot to go outdoors, and Ricardo was quite good at it. He was soon chortling delightedly at his own success, and even Armand had to laugh when for the second time he was knocked out at the first hand.

'When my father and I used to play, we always let the first person to lose have a second chance!'

Catherine exclaimed, forgetting for a moment her determination to ignore Armand, and Ricardo frowned.

'Did you?' he asked, looking at her thoughtfully. Then, turning to his father, he added irrelevantly: 'Do you think Nana will ring tomorrow? Mama rang last week and Nana and Poppa know where I am, don't they?'

Armand sobered. 'Your mother rang here?'

'Oh, yes.' Ricardo began to deal the cards to himself and Catherine, totally unaware of the silent exchange going on between her and his father. 'She rang on Tuesday, did she not, *senhorita*? Before she and Uncle Estéban left for their holiday.'

Catherine's mouth went dry at Ricardo's carelessly-spoken announcement. Her eyes darting away from Armand's, she tried to concentrate on the cards in her hand, but the boy's innocent revelations had created an atmosphere of tension in the room. What must Armand be thinking, she wondered achingly, her own anger forgotten as she suffered his betrayal with him. Whatever he had done—and he was by no means blameless—he did not deserve to learn of his wife's indiscretions like this: *from his son's lips!*

'Is this true?' Armand inquired now, his voice as chilled as dry ice, and Catherine was finally compelled to look up at him.

'That your wife rang?' she temporised. And then, as he continued to regard her with a degree of malevolence, she recalled his anger in the car when she had told him his wife had brought Ricardo to the villa. What did he object to, she wondered painfully. His wife's associating with *her*?

Gathering her composure, she lifted one shoulder. 'Yes,' she answered him now. 'She—she rang to check on Ricardo's progress. I—I told her he was doing very well.'

'Did you?' Armand's mouth compressed. 'And why did you not tell me my wife had gone away?'

The precision of his words should have warned her, but she was still too absorbed with her own feelings to notice. 'I—I never thought of it,' she lied, responding to the boy's lead with a lower card of the same suit. 'Er—what did you say were trumps, Ricardo? I'm losing track of the game.'

'To hell with the game!' Armand grated, pushing back his chair and getting up from the table with thinly-controlled violence. 'I should have realised she was up to something! *Sangre de Deus!* And you kept this to yourself!'

Catherine's lips parted in consternation and her gaze moved with dismay to Ricardo's small face. No matter how angry Armand must be, he should not speak like this about his wife—*and the boy's mother*—in Ricardo's presence. Yet, she had to admit, his son seemed more concerned about other things.

'Do you think Nana will ring, Papa?' he persisted, drawing his dark brows together. 'It is a long way from São Paulo to Casca de Mar. Perhaps she will not want to spend so much money.'

Armand turned back to the table, controlling his own feelings beneath the careless smile he gave his son. 'I am sure Nana will consider the end well worth the means, Ricardo,' he reassured him tautly. 'Has she—or Poppa—ever forgotten your birthday?'

'Well—no.'

'*Por isso*—therefore—you have nothing to worry about.'

Ricardo sighed. 'I wish it was here.'

'*Qué?* Your birthday?' Armand leant forward to rest

his palms flat on the table. 'It would come that much sooner if you were to go to bed.'

Drawing back from Armand's disturbing nearness, Catherine added her endorsement to his father's suggestion. 'It is getting late, Ricardo,' she murmured. 'Why don't I take you upstairs, and then your father can come and say good night, hmm?'

Ricardo grimaced, torn by the twin desires to finish the game, and bring his birthday that much more quickly. 'I will not be able to get to sleep,' he declared at last. 'I am too excited. Could I not stay up a little bit longer?'

'And get more excited?' Armand's tone was ironic. 'Ricardo, I did say half an hour only, and it is past that now.'

Ricardo hesitated. 'Perhaps, if I slept in your bed, Papa,' he ventured hopefully. 'Then, I might find sleeping easier, and you would be there in the morning to wish me a happy day.'

Armand straightened, pushing his hands into the narrow pockets of his pants. 'Very well,' he agreed, after a moment. 'You may share my bed. But only if you agree to go at once, without making any further conditions, no?'

Ricardo smiled. '*Sim*, Papa. As you say.' And giving his father an endearing smile, he left the cards and thundered up the stairs.

Following him, Catherine did not look back at Armand. She knew there would be time enough later for him to express his opinion of her, and her heart was beating rather quickly as she helped Ricardo with washing and cleaning his teeth.

'This is Papa's room,' he announced, after he had put on the pale blue cotton pyjama trousers he wore to sleep in. He led the way into the room next door, switching on the lamp and indicating the pale green curtains that matched the sheets on the huge bed. He was like a salesman demonstrating the advantages of this room over his, not least of which seemed to be the absence of toys shrewn over the floor, and Catherine flushed in embarrassment when Armand suddenly appeared in the open doorway.

'Not in bed yet, Ricardo?' he commented, his eyes moving inquiringly from the boy to Catherine, and then back to the boy again.

'I was just showing Miss Loring your bedroom, Papa,' Ricardo declared undaunted. Diving on to the bed, he tucked his toes beneath the sheet. 'Are you coming to bed soon? It is nearly nine o'clock.'

'I thought we agreed there were to be no more conditions,' remarked Armand, bending down to kiss his son. 'I wish to speak privately to Miss Loring, and I expect you to be fast asleep when I come to bed.'

'*Sim*, Papa.'

Ricardo grimaced, and then held up his arms for Catherine to give him his usual night-time hug. It was a practice she had started the very first night she had put Ricardo to bed, but it was a little different hugging him now with Armand closely watching their performance.

'If I do not wake up early, you will wake me, won't you, Papa?' Ricardo added, as he settled down, and Armand nodded.

'Something tells me it will not be necessary,' he averred drily, moving towards the door. '*Boa noite, pequeno. Veja se de manha.* See you in the morning.'

Downstairs again, Catherine gathered the playing cards together and pushed them back into their box. Then, aware of Armand's appraisal, she turned nervously to face him. 'You had something to say?'

'Did you doubt it?' With a gesture of impatience, Armand subsided on to the couch nearest to him, and lounged comfortably against the cushions. 'You are going to tell me everything Estella said to you, and then perhaps we may concern ourselves with more important things. How soon I can remove Ricardo from the country, for instance!'

Catherine stared at him. 'From the country? I don't understand.'

'You should.' He shrugged. 'You knew the revolution was coming. *Pois bem*, it seems it is here.'

Catherine blinked. 'What do you mean?'

'What do I mean?' Armand echoed, as if irritated by her obtuseness. Then, grimly, he explained: 'There have been—incidents in Terasina. How serious, I could not tell until now. Taken by themselves, they are not important, but I cannot take the risk that reprisals will not be forthcoming. They have happened before. They may happen again.'

'You're taking Ricardo away?' Catherine shook her head. 'Is there likely to be fighting? Surely not here!'

'Don't be naïve!' Armand frowned. 'Ricardo could be in danger. There are worse things than fighting, I have told you before.'

Catherine tried to absorb what he was saying. 'But—surely, if there had been any danger—'

Her voice trailed away and Armand's lean features took on a sardonic expression. 'Yes?' he prompted. 'If there had been any danger—what?' He waited, and when she did not go on, his lips twisted. 'What do you think, Catherine? That if there had been any danger Estella would not have allowed Ricardo to remain here? Do you think if she believed his life was at risk, she would not have gone off with her pretty general!'

Catherine gasped. 'You knew?'

Armand's golden eyes darkened. 'Knew what? That Estella had gone away? No. This was news to me.'

Catherine sighed. 'I didn't mean that.'

'Then you mean, did I know of her close liaison with General Montoya?'

'General Montoya!' Catherine was appalled.

'Estéban Montoya,' agreed Armand flatly. 'Yes. I knew.' He paused. 'Now, tell me what she said when she rang.'

Catherine ran her damp palms down over her hips. 'Oh—I can't remember. It was days ago. Like I said, she wanted to know if Ricardo was making progress.'

Armand regarded her dourly. 'Is that all?'

'What more could there be?'

'You tell me.' He moved to rest his ankle across his knee.

Catherine probed her memory. 'I—I think she said she would only be away for three weeks,' she ventured, after a moment. 'Yes. She—she said she would ring me on her return.'

'Anything else? Did she say where she was going, for example?'

'No.' Catherine could be quite sure on that score. 'I remember because she said I should contact Senhor Lopez if I had any problems. He—he was supposed to contact you in that event.'

Armand inclined his head. 'I see.'

Catherine shifted a little uncomfortably. 'I'm sorry if you think I should have informed you about the call,' she murmured. 'I didn't think it was important.'

'No?' Armand's heavy lids lifted. 'Yet you knew I was angry that Estella had brought Ricardo to the villa.'

'Well, yes. But I didn't understand that either.'

Catherine flushed. 'You needn't worry. I won't tell her, you know.'

Armand uttered an oath and got abruptly to his feet. 'You think that is what I am afraid of?'

Catherine flinched. 'I thought it might be.'

'It was not.' A muscle in Armand's jaw worked furiously. 'Oh—what does it matter? Go to bed! We will talk again tomorrow. I need some time to think, and your being here does not make that easy.'

'I'm sorry.'

Cheeks burning, Catherine swept across the floor. How had she ever imagined she loved him? she asked herself bitterly. He was totally unfeeling, and she hated him. Whatever he said, she could not believe he did not care about Estella. He had seen her—probably even lived with her—during the visit he had made to Terasina. He had said she, Catherine, could not go with him because of a woman. If only she had known it was his wife!

She had reached the foot of the stairs when Armand came after her, capturing a handful of her hair when she evaded his attempt to grasp her arm. The sickening jolt of her scalp brought unwilling tears to her eyes, and when he jerked her back against him, she beat frustratedly at the encircling protection of his arm.

'Let me go!' she seethed, twisting helplessly from side to side, but his resistance was unshakeable.

'Do not fight me, *querida*,' he breathed, pressing his face into the hollow between her shoulder and her nape. His tongue moved sensuously against her soft skin. 'I do not mean to hurt you, but you are such a sensitive creature! *Por piedade*, for pity's sake, you must not take what I say so personally!'

'I hate you!' retorted Catherine tremulously, determined not to be seduced by his persuasive words, and with a muffled exclamation he impelled her round to face him.

'You do not hate me!' he contradicted harshly, the hard bones of one long-fingered hand imprisoning her face and turning it up to his. 'You do *not* hate me!' he repeated, his voice thickening, as his gaze lingered on her drowned green eyes and quivering lips. 'God knows, it might be better if you did—'

His last words were spoken against her lips, his warm breath filling her mouth with a suffocating intimacy. His mouth moved on hers, gently at first, but as it met with no resistance, the pressure increased, plundering her lips with a bruising force. Over and over, he kissed her; her eyes, her cheeks, her throat, every inch of her tingling with a delicious ecstasy, so that when he drew back to look at her, her expression was as slumbrous as his own.

'What do you want me to say?' he demanded hoarsely. 'That I came here as much to see you as to see my son? You know I did! That every minute I am with you, I can think of nothing else but making love with you? That, too, is true.' He shook his head, his thumbs moving caressingly at her waist, warm through the fine silk of her blouse. 'But these are difficult times, Catarina. It is not possible for me to—well, to follow my instincts; to make promises I may not be allowed to keep. You have to understand that. You have to trust me.'

'I do trust you,' she protested huskily. 'But why do you get so angry when we talk about—about your wife?'

Armand sighed, stepping back from her, his hands falling wearily to his sides. 'Estella,' he said flatly. 'It all comes back to Estella, does it not?'

Catherine trembled. 'But why can't we talk about it? If the only reason you left your wife and son was to look for José—'

'What did you say?' Armand's face darkened.

Catherine shook her head. 'I—oh, nothing—'

'You are lying!' Armand's nostrils flared. 'Estella spilled a little poison, did she not? I guessed she would, given half a chance!'

'You are her husband!'

'Yes, I am.' His mouth compressed. 'Do you think I ever forget it?'

'Oh, Armand!'

Unable to deny the wanton needs he had ruthlessly exposed, Catherine put out her hands towards him, but Armand turned away. Moving stiffly towards the trolley, he half filled a whisky tumbler with Scotch before turning back to her, and when he did, his expression was not encouraging.

'I imagine Estella told you I abandoned her and Ricardo,' he said tautly, before swallowing a mouthful of the undiluted spirit. 'Well—in effect, I did. I left them in Terasina and took myself off to Batistamajor. My reasons were my own. I did not share them with her.'

Catherine blinked. 'You mean—you didn't tell your wife *why* you were going away?'

'No.' Armand's dark brows arched. 'Any further questions?'

Catherine shook her head. 'I don't understand.'

'No, you do not. And being a woman, you are half inclined to believe Estella, are you not?'

'*No!*'

Catherine's cry was desperate, but Armand had heard enough. 'Go to bed, Catherine,' he said wearily.

'I meant what I said: I want to think. If Terasina erupts into conflict, I need to know that the people I care about are safe.'

CHAPTER SEVENTEEN

IN spite of Catherine's fears that the events of the previous evening might cast a blight over Ricardo's birthday, the day proved to be as happy as he could have wished. He had both his father and Catherine out of bed at an unheard-of hour to view the new bicycle his father had brought for him, and hugging her cotton wrapper about her, Catherine came downstairs to find Armand and his son admiring the glossy red machine.

Armand, a pair of disreputable denim shorts his only attire, looked younger than she had ever seen him, in defiance of the faintly hollow shadows around his eyes. His chest bare, the dusky arrowing of hair that disappeared beneath his waistband reminding her insistently that she had seen him without even the benefit of this scant covering, he exuded simple animal magnetism, and she was not immune to it. He was here, they were together—albeit poles apart; and whatever happened after, she could not ignore him.

The sheepskin rug turned out to be a hit, too. Ricardo draped it around his shoulders, in imitation of the shepherds he had seen in his geography book, and not until his father suggested a swim did he take it upstairs to spread beside his bed.

'You'll come, too, won't you, *senhorita*?' he invited, when Catherine took the opportunity Armand's suggestion created to go back upstairs.

'I—well—'

Catherine hesitated, unsure how Armand would take this, and he lifted his head from his task of lowering the seat on the bicycle. 'Yes. Why don't you?' he conceded, his golden eyes revealing nothing but a mild inquiry, and Catherine expelled an uneven breath.

'Thank you,' she said, turning to hurry up the stairs, and when she looked back, she saw he had returned to his previous employment.

But it was fun on the sand, playing ball in the shallows, and trying to jump over the creaming rivulets of foam as the tide began its foray up the beach. It was still so early, there was a trace of chill in the air, and Catherine was glad of the excuse this gave for the goosebumps that came out over her flesh. Armand had never seen her in a swimsuit before, and although hers was fairly modest, it did display her arms and legs and the swelling curve of her bosom. His appraisal made her ridiculously self-conscious, particularly as he knew her body as well as she knew his, but that didn't prevent her breasts from responding in a way she was unable to disguise.

Thankfully, his eyes did not linger for too long. Ricardo, as usual, demanded his father's attention, and Catherine's colour subsided as the game progressed. It was impossible to act any other way than naturally when one was racing madly along the beach or leaping for the ball. In no time at all, Catherine became as uninhibited as Ricardo, and she was sweating freely when Armand suggested they cool off in the water.

Only once during their swim did Armand come close enough to touch her. Generally, he stayed beside his son, encouraging the boy to extend his range, and reacting good-humouredly when Ricardo resorted to playful splashing. But when the boy had returned to the shallows to continue his search for shells, Armand swam out to where Catherine was floating, the slick length of his body brushing hers as he surfaced beside her.

'I like your tan,' he said casually, his expression enigmatic. 'Are you coming to have some breakfast?'

Catherine trod water. 'Where's Ricardo?'

'He's gone back to the beach.' Armand regarded her intently. 'Did you sleep well?'

Catherine's colour returned. 'Did you?'

'No,' he admitted, before striking out towards the shallows. 'Come on: I'll race you.'

He didn't even try and he won easily, Catherine coming in a late second. She walked slowly up the beach after the others, wringing the water from the braid she had worn to sleep in, and thought how alike they were. Both so brown; both so dark; the two people she cared most about in the world, she thought, with a shattering realisation.

Sophia had breakfast ready, and a small gift from herself and her family. It was a miniature silver medallion on a silver chain, with an engraving of Saint Christopher on one side and Ricardo's initials on the other. He was delighted with it, and insisted on wearing it right away. For the rest of the day, he was constantly to be seen fingering it, and it was no surprise to Catherine when at teatime he discovered it was missing.

'I must have dropped it on the beach,' he exclaimed, half tearfully, his natural resilience giving way to an equally natural exhaustion. It had been a long, tiring day, and his activities had just about worn him out. From the time he got up that morning, which had been incredibly early, he had seldom been off his feet, and now he was hot and fretful, and unwilling to listen to reason.

'We'll look tomorrow,' Catherine reassured him, wondering how on earth they were going to find one silver medallion among so many silver grains of sand. But Ricardo was not content.

'I want to look now,' he said, ignoring the cake which Sophia had prepared for him, and the tiny candles that formed the figure nine. 'I want my medallion. I want to wear it to go to bed like Uncle Estéban does. Let go of my hand, *senhorita*. I have to go down to the beach!'

'That will do, Ricardo.' Armand's crisp tones brooked no argument, and the boy's small face crumpled.

'But I want my medallion,' he mumbled, burying his wet face in the cushions of the sofa, and Catherine, meeting Armand's eyes above his head, wondered if it was Ricardo's behaviour—*or what he had said*—that brought that look of sudden savagery to his face.

'Miss Loring has told you. We will find the medallion tomorrow,' Armand commented now, lifting Ricardo out of the cushions, and permitting him to bury his face against his chest. 'Now—come and see the cake Sophia has prepared for you. You would not wish to hurt her feelings, would you?'

'N—o.' Ricardo sniffed. 'I am sorry, Papa.'

'*Não importa.* Come: say you are sorry to Miss Loring, too. She does not deserve your anger.'

Ricardo hesitated, and then held out his arms to Catherine, and she went into them. In so doing, she was unbearably close to Armand, but the hug lasted only a minute.

'Can I blow the candles out now, Papa?' Ricardo

asked, unaware of the tension between his father and his governess, and Armand nodded.

'Why not?' he acceded evenly, and Ricardo's subdued face brightened.

The telephone rang as they were having tea, and after a moment's hesitation, Armand went to answer it. Watching him, Catherine saw the way his expression softened as he identified the caller.

'Mama! How are you? I was beginning to think you had forgotten.'

'*E Nana; é Nana!*' exclaimed Ricardo, bounding out of his chair and across the floor to tug excitedly at his father's shorts. 'Please, let me speak to her, Papa. It is *my* birthday.'

Deciding she could not sit there, eavesdropping on the call, Catherine left the table and went into the kitchen, surprising Sophia as she was taking a well-earned rest with the newspaper Catherine had brought home the day before.

'Is something wrong?' she asked, her plump face showing her concern, and Catherine shook her head as she subsided on to the edge of the table. 'I think—Senhor de Castro's mother is on the phone,' she said, straightening the folds of the wraparound skirt she had donned over her bathing suit. 'I didn't want to be in the way.'

'Ah.' Sophia nodded. 'The little one's grandmother has not forgot his birthday. That is good.' She grimaced. 'A pity his mother is not so considerate.'

Catherine bent her head. 'Don't you like Senhora de Castro?' she asked, giving in to an irresistible impulse to discover Sophia's opinion.

'I hardly know her,' retorted the Italian girl carelessly, putting the newspaper aside and getting to her feet. Then, as if relenting, she added: 'But what I know, I do not like, if that is any consolation.'

Catherine's head lifted. 'Consolation?'

'*Si.*' Sophia regarded her levelly. 'I have seen the way you look at the *signor*.'

Catherine's face burned. 'Oh, but I—I—'

'I know.' Sophia gave a typically continental shrug of her shoulders. 'It means nothing. Do not worry. I am not accusing you of anything. Many women have been attracted to the good doctor. But, regrettably, he is not attracted to them!'

Catherine swallowed. 'How do you know?'

'I know.' Sophia frowned. 'He is not a man like that. Believe me, *signorina*, I have been around, and the *signor*, he does not notice I exist. You can always tell. It is in the eyes, I think.'

Catherine caught her breath. 'I see.'

'There was a young woman one time.' Sophia smiled. Now that she had started, she seemed loath to abandon the subject. 'I think she was a doctor—at the hospital in Terasina, where the *signor* worked when he first came to Surajo. She came here. She was quite beautiful!' Sophia spread her hands expansively. 'Dark hair, dark eyes, and such a figure!' Her actions were expressive. '*Bene*, she had some reason for coming here, of course. Something to do with their work, you understand? She—how do you say it?—she made the fool of herself! The *signor* was most courteous, *naturale*. It is his way. But, I realised then, the *signora's* activities—Signora de Castro, that is—they have hurt him, more than words can say.'

How Catherine would have responded to this, she was not to find out. Even as her brain absorbed what Sophia had been telling her, Ricardo burst into the room, and his excited announcement drove all other thoughts from her head.

'I am to go to stay with Nana and Poppa!' he declared, wrapping his arms around Catherine's waist and almost overbalancing her. 'Is it not *maravilhoso! Fantástico!*'

His use of Portuguese expletives showed how truly excited he was, but Catherine only stared wordlessly at him. He was going away; he was leaving her! After what Armand had said, she should have been prepared for this, but she had not imagined he would act so quickly.

'When? When are you going to stay with Nana?' Sophia demanded, her unguarded response covering Catherine's shocked reaction. 'Does your Papa say you can go to São Paulo? Remember, Nana has asked you before, but it has not been possible to let you go.'

'I have said he can go.'

Armand's low attractive tones entered the conversation at this point, and glancing over her shoulder, Catherine saw that he had joined them. For a fleeting moment, her eyes met his, and to her shame she was unable to hide the bitter sense of rejection Ricardo's news had evoked. But then, the boy's impatient jostling demanded her attention, and she tried to show the enthusiasm she knew that he expected.

'When do you leave?' she asked, forcing a smile to her lips, and Ricardo glanced expectantly at his father.

'At the end of the week,' said Armand, watching his son with gentle toleration. 'And now, I suggest we go and finish our tea. Let Miss Loring go, Ricardo. We still have the birthday cake to cut.'

For Catherine, the remainder of the meal was something of a trial. It wasn't easy trying to act as if nothing had happened when she knew, at the end of the week, her small world was coming to an end. But for Ricardo's sake, she put on a brave face, avoiding

Armand's eyes as often as possible, and sharing in the boy's delight of blowing out his candles.

By the time the cake had been cut and everyone, including Sophia, had had a piece, Ricardo was almost asleep on his feet. With an exquisitely tender smile, Armand lifted the boy into his arms and carried him off to bed. 'Leave him to me,' he said, when Catherine would have followed them, and it was another turn of the knife that he should not wish to share the task with her.

Sophia wanted to go home for an hour or two during the evening, and it had been arranged that Armand should take her, and fetch her back again. In consequence, after Ricardo had gone to bed, his father and the housekeeper departed in the Mercedes, and Catherine was left with unwanted time on her hands.

She spent almost an hour searching the house for Ricardo's medallion, and it wasn't until she had given up this activity she realised Armand had not come back. She guessed Sophia had invited him in to meet her family, and as they would probably not be back for some time, she decided to go to bed.

Since coming to Casca de Mar, she had adopted Armand's example and taken to sleeping without a nightgown when it was hot. She did have a simple cotton gown, which she had bought in Terasina to replace Armand's pyjama jacket, but tonight she slipped between the sheets without any covering whatsoever.

But she did not sleep. Even though, like Ricardo, she had been up at six, she did not feel tired. Like the night before, the adrenalin in her blood kept her body in a fine state of stimulation, and she could not relax, no matter how she tried.

It must have been after ten o'clock when she heard

the Mercedes return, and the muffled sound of
Armand's and Sophia's voices in the living room. No
doubt Armand expected her to be in bed, she thought
bitterly. By staying out of the way, he had achieved the
dual purpose of avoiding a *tête-à-tête* with her, and
ensured that such an event was unlikely to occur
before he left tomorrow. She knew he was leaving
soon. He had said as much to Sophia the day before.
She might not see him alone again before Ricardo left
for São Paulo. She could not expect him to treat her as
he might treat his son.

What she was going to do after Ricardo had left, she
had yet to consider. She supposed it might be possible
to get another job, similar to this. But if Terasina was in
a state of turmoil, how could she apply? It seemed she
was going to have to go back to England, after all. With
the money Armand had given her, and the salary she
had earned thus far, she should be able to afford an air
ticket. But the prospect of returning to an English
winter did not appeal to her, even without the obvious
drawbacks of leaving Surajo.

At midnight, she abandoned any idea of trying to
sleep and got out of bed. Pulling on the white cotton
nightgown that lay at the foot of her bed, she left her
room and went downstairs. To her surprise, there was
still a lamp glowing in the living room, but although
she hesitated halfway down the spiral, apprehensive
that Armand might be waiting for her as he had been
the night before, the room was quite empty.

Crossing to the windows, the curtains of which
were seldom drawn, she gazed out at the stretch of
beach and the ocean beyond. It was a beautiful night; a
little cooler than of late, but with a crescent moon
riding on the breeze, so that it was not absolutely dark.
Catherine breathed deeply, envying the stars their

place in the ebony-brushed velvet of the night sky. She seemed to have no place where she could settle down, she thought unhappily. Perhaps she should have stayed in the convent, after all. Some of the nuns must have taken their vows out of a basic need for sanctuary, hadn't they?

The french doors were not locked and, on impulse, Catherine pushed the glass aside and stepped out on to the balcony. The air was intoxicating, crystal clear and only lightly tinged with the smell of seaweed. She knew a ridiculous sense of relief to be out of the house at last, and ignoring the nagging suspicion that she was behaving recklessly, she descended the steps to the beach.

The sand ran between her toes as she walked towards the ocean, the grains cool now that the sun had gone. The breeze whispered against her nightgown, moulding the thin cotton against her over-heated skin. The peaks of her breasts stood out sharply against the cloth, but she was not ashamed tonight. There was no one here to see her lonely vigil, no golden eyes to witness her silent obeisance to the moon.

Yet, as she stood there, staring out over the silvery swell of the tide, and her eyes became accustomed to the shadows, she thought she saw a darker silhouette in the water. It came, and went, and then came again, and almost before her disbelieving brain could acknowledge what she was seeing, a dark, dripping figure rose up out of the water, and came towards her through the shallows.

The instinctive surge of panic that gripped her was quickly controlled. Armand's lithe frame was recognisable to her, even in shadow, and although she knew a momentary desire to put off what he must say to her, she quelled it and stood her ground.

It was not until he was almost upon her that another realisation came to her: he was nude. Watching him walk up from the sea, like some ancient statue come to life, she had not considered he might have taken advantage of his isolation. But as he grew nearer, the barely perceptible lightening of the skin stretched taut across his hip bones, brought the disturbing awareness that he had eschewed his shorts.

Her own presence was unmistakable. The white nightgown saw to that. If she had wished to disguise the fact that she had seen him, it would have been well-nigh impossible. As it was, she was obliged to stand there, waiting for him to reach her, fully prepared for his anger when he realised who she was.

His first words were not of anger however. Without any trace of embarrassment, he acknowledged her presence with a faint nod of his head, and then bent to retrieve the towel, which she now saw had been lying on the sand all the time. Then, as he towelled the moisture from his chest, he said softly; 'I thought you were tired.'

'Tired?' Catherine found she was absurdly resentful of his infuriating detachment. He should be the defendant, not her. Yet, he just stood there, drying his body, as if he was used to having a woman's eyes on him as he did so. Perhaps he was, she thought miserably. He was married, after all. She *must* not forget that. 'I—why should you think I was tired?'

'You went to bed,' he reminded her simply.

'Yes—well, you went out and didn't come back—'

'Sophia's husband insisted I join them for a drink,' Armand explained levelly. 'Naturally, with the country in a state of flux, he is concerned for his family, too.'

'Naturally.' Catherine could not keep the bitterness

out of her voice. 'Although it seems quiet enough here, doesn't it?'

'Sometimes it is like that,' agreed Armand, without rancour. 'The eye of the hurricane can almost convince you that the storm is over.'

Catherine sighed. 'So you stayed.'

'As Sophia was coming back, it seemed a reasonable thing to do,' he responded, his eyes enigmatic in the half light. 'Surely, you were not worried.'

'Worried?' Catherine looked down at her toes, watching as she scuffed them in the sand. 'Why should I be worried? What you do is nothing to do with me, is it?'

He let that go, continuing to dry his arms and legs with a complete absence of self-consciousness. And why should he be self-conscious? Catherine asked herself frustratedly. His body was beautiful: all muscled curves and angles, without an ounce of spare flesh anywhere. She badly wanted to touch him. She desperately wanted to throw caution to the winds, and take the chance of his repulsing her. But the habits of a lifetime were not easily broken, and her reserve had only once betrayed her.

'So why are you here?' he asked now, and she belatedly realised how her innocent expedition might appear to him.

'I—I didn't know you were here!' she exclaimed, the colour running hotly into her cheeks. She was glad he couldn't see it. She must look as guilty as she felt. And her voice quavered a little as she hurried on with her denial. 'I—I just felt like a walk,' she said. 'I couldn't sleep, and—and so—'

'And so?' he prompted, and she clutched at the first thing that came into her head.

'And so I thought I might look for Ricardo's

medallion,' she declared, knowing as she said the words, he would not believe her. 'He—he said he lost it on the beach, so—'

'I found it,' Armand cut in quietly. 'When we got back. I saw something glinting in the glare of the headlights, and that was what it was. Ricardo must have lost it while he was playing on his bicycle. I did look on the drive earlier, but it was easy to miss.'

'Oh!' Catherine's response was hardly enthusiastic, but she couldn't help it. 'I didn't know.'

'How could you?' he conceded drily, and she lifted her shoulders helplessly.

'I didn't know you were here,' she insisted, avoiding the almost overriding impulse to look at him. 'If I had, I wouldn't have come. Surely, you believe that.'

'If it is important to you,' he granted evenly, his eyes on her profile, averted from his. 'Why should I object to your presence? I have nothing to hide from you.'

'No—well—' Catherine moved her head jerkily from side to side. 'I just wanted you to know.'

'And now I do,' he responded brusquely. 'So, do you think you could stop behaving like an outraged spinster and look at me?'

Catherine did not obey him. 'Why should I?' she countered childishly, his impatient words stirring the pain of rejection inside her. 'Ours is a futile relationship. You told me that yourself. Not in so many words, perhaps, but as good as. And last night you didn't seem to care what I thought!'

Armand groaned. 'Last night—last week—you know how I feel!'

'Do I?' Catherine looked at him from the corners of her eyes.

'Yes. *Yes!*' Armand tossed the towel impatiently

aside, and took her wrist between his hands. 'What more must I do to convince you?'

Catherine quivered. 'You're sending Ricardo away from me—'

'What!' Armand gazed at her blankly. 'What in God's name are you saying now?'

'You're sending Ricardo to São Paolo, aren't you?'

'Yes.' Armand nodded vigorously. 'Yes, I am sending Ricardo to São Paulo. *With you!*'

Catherine caught her breath. 'You never said that.'

'I thought it must be obvious,' he retorted, shaking his head. 'Catherine, I sent you here to look after my son. His life—well, his life has not been easy of late and, until recently, Estella would not listen to any suggestions from me.' He paused, massaging her wrist almost involuntarily. 'You have to understand, she is his mother, and I was torn between my need to help my son and my promise to my mother.'

'José,' ventured Catherine, almost inaudibly, and he nodded.

'José,' he agreed. '*Bem*, to return to your position: I naturally assumed that as Ricardo's—companion; governess; *friend*, you would remain with the boy until this situation in Surajo is resolved, one way or the other.'

Catherine looked down at their hands, entwined together, and brought her free hand to join them. 'You should have said,' she whispered huskily. 'I thought I might have to return to England.'

'Oh, Catherine!' he muttered, lifting her hands to his lips. 'Something tells me I am not going to be able to let you return to England, whatever happens between Estella and me.'

Catherine trembled, and with a tortured sound he leant towards her, caressing her mouth with his. Her

lips parted automatically, the wine-dark sweetness of
his kiss liquefying all her bones. She felt amorphous:
fluid—her limbs melting beneath the demanding
onslaught of emotion. And when he pushed her
hands down between them, so that she could feel the
pulsating heat of his manhood throbbing against her
stomach, her fingers closed quite possessively around
him.

 · With exquisite tenderness, Armand drew the straps
of her nightgown off her shoulders, pressing the
resisting cotton down over her breasts. The rosy peaks
of those creamy swellings burst eagerly from their
confinement, and Armand's mouth followed his
hands, delighting in their innocent provocation.

Freed from any restriction, the nightgown pooled
about her feet, and Armand's hands moved to her
hips, urging her against him. The hair on his stomach
was deliciously abrasive to her smoother flesh, her
nipples taut against the cooler skin of his chest.
Arching herself nearer, she moulded her body to his,
and her hands slid convulsively about his neck as his
mouth returned to hers.

Now his tongue slipped between her lips, possess-
ing her with sensuous insistence. It was a leisurely
invasion, a measure of the enjoyment they were taking from the simple touching of their bodies. But such
controlled restraint could not go on indefinitely, and
the quickening of their breathing was an indication of
that fact.

'Meiga—tu quero,' he whispered, drawing her down
on to the beach, and there was no question of her
denying something she wanted just as much.

With unhurried indulgence, Armand lowered her
on to the sand, his hands brushing sensuously over
her taut flesh. He was eager to satisfy the hunger that

raged within him, but he was evidently loath to precipitate his pleasure, and Catherine trembled uncontrollably beneath the intoxicating sweetness of his lips.

With infinite sensuality, his mouth moved from
hers, trailing urgent kisses across her shoulder and
down, over the creamy expanse of her throat to her
breasts. His tongue teased her nipples, arousing them
to an almost unbearable peak of frenzy, before suckling at their tender tips.

His lips moved lower, caressing her stomach and
the silken skin of her belly that quivered beneath his
touch. His lips seemed to be everywhere; nibbling at
her skin, nuzzling the secret places of her body, parting her legs to explore the inner contours of her thighs.
She suspected she ought to stop him. His love-making
was destroying every shred of conscience she had
clung to. But his touch inflamed her; his hungry
mouth drove any thought of hesitation from her mind.
Her lips turned urgently against his throat, against his
hardened nipples, so different from her own, and
when his mouth returned to hers, she could think of
nothing but the need he had evoked inside her.

As his hands slid possessively down the sides of her
body, the whole weight of him cushioned on her
softness, she lifted her hips, as if seeking his entry.
Armand, his own senses swimming with the instinctive sexuality of her response, could delay no longer.
Her legs fell apart as he nudged the moist triangle of
curls that hid her sweetness, and he penetrated her
gently, gliding smoothly into a silken sheath that
tightly closed about him.

He moved on her slowly, and the fleeting anxiety
she had had that perhaps he might hurt her again, was
quickly dispelled. Even though that night in Batistamajor he had made love to her more than once,

inexperience had left her wondering whether it might always be the same, the first time; but Armand's body fitted itself to hers with unbelievable ease. There was an unquestioning joy in feeling him inside her, in knowing his body in this most intimate way. But most of all, she wanted to please him, as he was pleasing her, and she moved instinctively with him, savouring every moment.

In spite of himself, Armand's gentle luxuriation in her body soon became a hungry possession. Her innocent responses to his demands, the delicate caress of her hands across his back and down to the thrusting curve of his hips drove him almost out of his mind.

For Catherine, the plunging urgency of his body was an unreasoning pleasure. Her body ached with anticipation of the ecstasy he was building, a growing expanding surge of emotion, that made her clutch him closely, her nails digging urgently into his hips. It was like being inside his skin, she thought fancifully. She could feel his emotion, sense the moment when his release mirrored hers. They were like two halves of a perfect whole, meeting and fusing together with the intensity of their feelings. Armand buried his face between her breasts as they scaled the heights of enchantment, and his shuddering sigh of contentment enveloped her in its folds.

CHAPTER EIGHTEEN

São Paulo was a state as well as a city, Catherine discovered, and Ricardo's grandparents lived some distance from the metropolis. With some of the richest farmland in Brazil, the area apparently produced sufficient coffee, fruit and vegetables to supply half the country's population, and it was by no means only an agricultural community.

From the air, Catherine had been amazed at the wealth of towering skyscrapers and many-laned highways leading into the city, and she was almost disappointed when she learned they were not to drive to their destination. They landed at Viracopos, the city's international airport, but from there, a helicopter transported them to Congonhas field. The smaller, internal airport was not their final stop, however. A twin-engined Cessna was waiting to take them on the final leg of their journey.

It had been a long, tiring flight from Terasina, and Catherine had been glad Senhor Lopez had accompanied them to answer some of Ricardo's interminable questions. For her part, she had been too sick at heart at leaving Surajo to pay much attention to the boy's excited chatter, and not until they were actually preparing to land in Brazil did she force herself to take an interest in her surroundings.

Ricardo's decline in spirits since his father's departure four days ago was now almost forgotten. The excitement of the plane journey and his anticipation at seeing his grandparents again helped to make up for

his disappointment that his father could not go
with them, but Catherine did not know Armand's
parents, and she was apprehensive of their reactions
to her.

It was all very well for Armand to insist that they
would make her welcome, but Catherine was not so
sure. What did they know of her, after all? How did
they regard her? So far as they were concerned, she
was Ricardo's governess, nothing else. How could
they treat her as he did, when they already had a
daughter-in-law?

The night Armand had made love to her on the
beach seemed so very remote from this beautiful corner of Brazil; and not only in distance. Those idyllic
moments on the sand might never be repeated, and
while being with his son was some compensation, the
knowledge that Armand might be in danger was not.
If only he could have come with them, she thought
wretchedly, pressing her forehead against the cool
curving frame of the Cessna's window. If only she
could be sure he would not take any unnecessary
risks. But she could not forget he was José Rodolfo's
brother, and she wondered with an anxious pang
whether General Montoya knew it, too.

She and Armand had talked little before his departure. There had been so little time, and she knew
Armand had been loath to make any promises he
could not keep. He did not speak of Estella. Even
though Catherine had longed to ask him about his
wife, that subject had remained dauntingly taboo. It
was as if he could not speak of his wife without
remembering how she had betrayed him with Estéban
Montoya, and Catherine could not deny the sneaking
suspicion that in spite of everything Estella had done,
he still had some feeling for her.

Armand had left the morning after Ricardo's birthday. Catherine had still been asleep, the result of not seeking the comfort of her bed before the fingers of dawn lit up the eastern sky, and when she learned he had gone, her desperation knew no bounds. If only he had told her, she fretted. If only he had warned her that that night would be their last together.

Yet, as the hours passed, she had to admit he had probably done the only sensible thing. How could she have concealed her feelings from Ricardo, had Armand told her of his plans in the boy's presence? It was hard enough to maintain a composed façade in the face of Sophia's speculative eyes, and Ricardo was very perceptive when it came to hidden emotions.

As it happened, Ricardo's tearful reaction to his father's departure helped Catherine to bear her own grief. He was such a lovable child, and she was never sure where comforting him ended and comforting herself began. She only knew that in the days that followed Armand's leaving, she and Ricardo drew that much closer together, and it was no surprise at all when he started calling her Catarina, instead of *senhorita*.

It was dark when the Cessna landed at their destination. As the plane made its approach, Catherine stared out of the window, trying to identify a little of their surroundings, but apart from a few airport lights, there was little to see.

As if perceiving her dilemma, Senhor Lopez leaned towards her. 'This is the small landing field owned by the de Castro coffee plantation, *senhorita*,' he explained, as they bumped along the runway. 'The home of Ricardo's grandparents is only a short distance from here; near the village of Aguas de Seda.'

'I see.'

Catherine swallowed her apprehension at the realisation that Armand's family owned a coffee plantation, and endeavoured to sustain a polite interest. But the knowledge that her future had never seemed less secure was demoralising, and when Ricardo tucked his hand into hers as they left the plane, she gripped it with unknowing tightness.

It was a warm evening, a little fresher than Catherine had become accustomed to during her stay at Casca de Mar, but not cool enough to require a jacket. In her usual attire of shirt and pants, Catherine was suitably equipped for the climate, and she was glad she would not be required to buy more clothes from her dwindling money supply. She supposed she should have mentioned the fact that she had not been paid any salary to Armand. But money seemed to have no part in their relationship, and not until he had gone did she realise she did not have the fare to England should circumstances demand it.

A limousine was waiting at the edge of the airstrip, and as they walked towards it, Catherine could smell the rich aroma of tropical vegetation and moist earth. There was no distinguishable odour of coffee beans as she had expected. Just the scent of grass and sun-warmed foliage, and the delicate fragrance of some night-flowering blossom.

Their suitcases were loaded into the boot of the car by Senhor Lopez and the uniformed chauffeur. Then, after Catherine and Ricardo had got inside, Senhor Lopez closed the rear door upon them.

'Adeus, senhorita. Adeus, Ricardo,' he declared, as the dark-skinned chauffeur settled himself behind the wheel. 'Até a vista—'

'Wait!' Catherine put a nervous hand on the opened

window frame and gazed out at him. She blinked rapidly. 'Aren't you coming with us, *senhor*?'

'Regrettably, no,' the lawyer responded, with a shake of his balding head. 'I must return to Terasina, *senhorita*. My work is done. You are here, as Senhor de Castro requested, *não é verdade*?—isn't that so?'

'But—' Catherine licked her lips. 'Not tonight, surely!'

'I return to São Paulo tonight, *senhorita*,' Senhor Lopez told her gently. 'I will spend one—maybe two days in the city. Then . . .' He shrugged. 'I return to Terasina.'

'I see.' Catherine felt as if every familiar face was being withdrawn from her.

'*Fique descansado, senhorita*,' he assured her gently. 'Don't worry! Senhora de Castro is English, like yourself. She will understand.'

'Yes. You will like Nana,' exclaimed Ricardo eagerly, jumping up and down in his seat. 'And now, can we go, Catarina? It is getting late, and I am hungry!'

Catherine turned and gave him an affectionate glance. In the muted illumination of the airport lights, his eyes sparkled excitedly, and she thought inconsequently how much happier he looked since they had been together.

'Hungry?' she echoed, forcing her own anxieties aside, and touching his nose with a playful finger. 'That's a healthy sign, at any rate.'

'So, can we go now, please?' he pleaded, leaning past her to wave to Senhor Lopez. '*Adeus, senhor. Adeus!*'

The man hesitated a moment longer, as if aware of Catherine's uncertainty, and then he bent towards her. 'I shall be staying at the Hotel Avenida, *senhorita*,' he informed her gently. 'If you should wish to get in

touch with me during the next twenty-four hours, a
message left with the concierge will reach me. *Muito
bem?'*

'Thank you.' Catherine looked up at him gratefully.
'And—and goodbye.'

Senhor Lopez bid the chauffeur drive on, and then
lifted his hand in farewell. As Catherine settled back in
her seat, she had the satisfaction of knowing that she
still had one last link with Armand. It was a tenuous
connection, due to be broken very shortly, but
welcome nonetheless.

Catherine's room was situated across the hall from
Ricardo's. She had never seen a room quite like it, nor
indeed a house like Armand's parents' house, and for
all her troubled misgivings, she was woman enough to
appreciate her surroundings. The room was all cream
and gold: a huge square bed, with polished brass
bed-posts; a massive clothes-press and matching
cabinets in honey-coloured wood; a soft cream carpet
that flowed into every recess; and a heavily brocaded
bedspread, made of silk, that matched the flowing
curtains at the windows. Adjoining the bedroom was
a bathroom of similarly generous proportions, and
similarly equipped with every modern convenience.
The first thing Catherine had done was take a bath in
the sunken circular tub, and it was quite a novelty to
find scented bath gels and perfumed oils provided for
her use on the glass shelves above the vanity.

It was all so new and not a little intimidating, in
spite of Senhora de Castro's welcome. Catherine
was simply not used to wealth on this scale, and
she couldn't help feeling she was here under false
pretences.

The house itself was predictably large, and designed

in the style of the old plantation houses, which she supposed it was. But certain modernisations had evidently taken place, not least the installation of air-conditioning to benefit its inhabitants and protect the valuable furnishings.

Catherine's first sight of the house had been from the back of the limousine, as the chauffeur drove between the stone gateposts which marked the boundary of the estate. The front of the building had been floodlit, so although it was early evening, she had no difficulty in distinguishing her whereabouts. Its white, pillared portico had been daunting; the columns that supported the balcony above giving it a regal air. Even the gardens surrounding the house were magnificent, the artificial light only dimming their exotic array.

A stone-flagged terrace ran the whole width of the building, reached by three shallow steps, which likewise spread out to either side of the double-panelled doors. There were lights glowing from many of the windows that flanked the imposing entrance, and Catherine's nerves had tightened as their arrival was perceived.

Across the terrace and through the panelled doors, she discovered the vaulted roof of a reception hall that arched above her, two floors high. But Catherine was only distantly aware of her surroundings. Her attention was held by the woman who had crossed the hall to greet them, and her resemblance to Armand, which was unmistakable. While the chauffeur and another servant attended to their luggage, Ricardo uttered a squeal of delight and ran into the woman's arms. Hugging her excitedly, he made any further introductions unnecessary, and Senhora de Castro smiled as she straightened and held out her hand to Catherine.

'Miss Loring,' she said, her voice clear and un-accented. 'Or may I call you Catherine? It seems Ricardo has fallen in love with you, and we must all do the same.'

Catherine's smile was nervous. 'How do you do?' she murmured, grateful for the older woman's tact. 'And please, do call me Catherine. But I'm sure you know, Ricardo exaggerates.'

Senhora de Castro said nothing for a moment, merely regarding her with an unhurried appraisal. Then, with another hug for Ricardo, she dismissed the suggestion. 'Whatever the truth of the matter, my dear, you're very welcome to Aguas de Seda. Armand has told me all about you, and I want you to know we are delighted to meet anyone who has made Ricardo's life a little easier.'

'Thank you.' Catherine coloured, wondering ex-actly what Armand had told his mother about her. Not that she was his mistress, she surmised a little bitterly, and then rejected the thought as unworthy. He had done so much for her, and it was useless pretending she had not invited his attentions. No matter how innocent she had been when he first made love to her in Batistamajor, the consequences of their second encounter could not be put down to him. She had known what she was doing. There was no excuse for that.

'And now, I'm sure, you would like to see your room,' Senhora de Castro suggested, summoning a dark-skinned maid-servant. 'Lucetta: take the *senhorita* upstairs. You have a little over an hour, my dear, and then we will eat dinner.' She paused, glanc-ing affectionately down at her grandson. 'Ricardo will join us. As he has had his birthday, I am sure a special concession can be made for once.'

'Do you have a present for me, Nana?' Ricardo exclaimed, with characteristic candour, and his grandmother smiled.

'You will have to wait and see,' she declared, exchanging a knowing glance with his governess. 'Come: Poppa is waiting to see you.'

As Catherine began to climb the curving staircase that led up to a circular gallery, Armand's mother made one last remark. 'Come downstairs when you are ready, Catherine. Someone will direct you to the library.'

And now, here she was, Catherine thought apprehensively, viewing herself in the long mirror that was hidden on the inner side of the clothes-press. Bathed and changed into the dress she had folded on the top of the clothes in her suitcase. It was not her favourite dress, the emerald green taffeta reminding her too painfully of the scene she and Armand had had the night after he had returned to Terasina, after seeing Estella. But then, she thought dejectedly, most of her clothes reminded her of Armand, and thrusting his disturbing image aside, she determinedly attacked her hair.

Fifteen minutes later, with her hair neatly wound into its braid and secured on top of her head, she pronounced herself satisfied with her appearance. She was not content. The dress was still creased, and she thought her hairstyle was too severe. But she was employed as Ricardo's governess, and she wanted to appear that way to Armand's father; not give the impression that she was barely out of school.

Downstairs again, yet another maid-servant pointed her in the direction of the library. She crossed the hall, with its imposing ceiling and dauntingly Catholic icons, passed through a gallery, lined with the portraits of a bygone era, and finally reached the leather-bound doors she was seeking.

Her tentative knock was answered by a man in his sixties, his thick thatch of grey hair distinctly reminiscent of his son's. He was as tall as Armand, but more heavily built, and the moustache that etched his upper lip gave him an infinitely less familiar appearance.

'Miss Loring, I presume?' he remarked politely, inviting her into the room. 'I am delighted to make your acquaintance.'

'Thank you, *senhor*.'

Catherine allowed him to take her hand, and was most taken aback when he raised it almost to his lips. It was a chivalrous gesture, a courteous observance of her womanhood, and looking up into his twinkling brown eyes, Catherine could understand why Senhora de Castro had so quickly abandoned her widowhood.

The library was just as imposing as the rest of the house. Tall shelves, lined with books, formed a backcloth for comfortable leather sofas and chairs, the solid mahogany desk standing against one wall the only indication that the room was used for a more professional purpose.

But the room was empty, and Catherine turned in some confusion to confront her host, wondering if by some accident she had misunderstood Armand's mother.

'My wife will join us shortly,' Senhor de Castro inserted swiftly, comprehending her distress. 'And Ricardo, too, of course. Now, may I offer you a drink? I have mixed some martini cocktails, or perhaps you would prefer some wine.'

'I would like a glass of white wine, please, if you

don't mind,' Catherine accepted rather nervously, seating herself on the low squashy sofa he indicated. She had not expected to have to deal with Armand's father on her own, and she couldn't help the suspicion that his wife's absence was no accident.

'So . . .' After handing her the wine she had chosen, Senhor de Castro disconcerted her still further by seating himself on the sofa beside her. '*A sua saúde—* your health,' he declared, raising his glass, and Catherine swallowed a mouthful of wine obediently, wishing Ricardo would make one of his unannounced entrances.

'Tell me,' her host prompted, settling himself more comfortably beside her, 'how long have you lived in Surajo, Miss Loring?'

'Please: call me Catherine.' She flushed. 'I suppose—about eighteen months.'

'So little time.' Senhor de Castro frowned. 'Forgive me, Miss Loring, I had received the impression that your parents used to live in Surajo.'

'My father did,' said Catherine quickly. 'He—well, he was killed almost a year ago.'

'Really?'

He was evidently expecting her to go on, and realising that, as their employee, she was obliged to give an account of herself, Catherine continued: 'He was a student of ancient civilisations, *senhor*. He had worked in South America for as long as I can remember. My mother was dead, you see, and I was in school, and I suppose his work became the most important thing in his life.'

'Next to you, Miss Loring, I am sure,' Senhor de Castro said gallantly, but Catherine shook her head.

'Anyway,' she added, 'when I left school, I came out

to join him, and for a time I helped him run the small school he had founded. Then—then—'

'Then he was killed,' put in her host gently, and Catherine nodded, and took another sip of her wine. 'This school,' he probed, after a moment. 'It was at—Batistamajor?'

Catherine's eyes widened. 'Yes. How do you know that?'

'Oh—' Senhor de Castro shrugged. 'My son had to have met you somewhere, and that seemed a likely location.'

'I see.' Catherine's cheeks flamed anew. 'I—what did—what did your son tell you about me, *senhor*?'

'*Touché!*' He smiled, and then made a negative gesture. 'Very little, I regret. I was hoping you would fill in some of the gaps.'

Catherine bent her head. 'There's not a lot to tell, really.'

'No?' Armand's father regarded her expectantly for a few moments, but when she said nothing more, he ventured: 'What is your opinion of the situation in Surajo, *senhorita*? Armand told me you know about José.'

'Oh, yes.' Catherine glanced swiftly at him. 'I suppose it must be nerve-racking for you, having two sons caught up in the—in the turmoil.'

'*E verdade.*' The man's expression sobered. 'It has been much worse for Elena, of course.'

'Elena?' Catherine swallowed convulsively.

'Elena—*Helen*; my wife,' explained Armand's father reassuringly. 'She had been searching for news of José for so long.'

Catherine acknowledged this in silence. Then she asked: 'What do you think will happen, *senhor*?'

'In Surajo?' He swallowed a little of the wine he had

poured for himself and considered her question. 'I think perhaps Presidente Ferreira has imprisoned his last dissident.'

Catherine's lips parted. 'You think there will be a coup then?'

'If Montoya has left the country, it seems likely,' agreed her host thoughtfully. 'Did you meet General Montoya, Miss Loring? Did my daughter-in-law bring him to Casca de Mar?'

Catherine gulped. 'No.' She shook her head. 'No, she didn't.'

'Hmm.' Armand's father ruminated for a moment. 'You know of their affair, of course.'

'I—well—' Catherine was nonplussed. 'Ricardo said something about—about *Uncle* Estéban.'

'Ah, yes.' Senhor de Castro nodded, though she had the strongest feeling that he didn't entirely believe her. 'Well, no doubt you have seen the effect it has had on Ricardo. The boy has had to live with it for so long.'

Catherine inclined her head. 'I—could he not have stayed with you, *senhor*?'

'Regrettably, no.' Armand's father rose to his feet to get himself some more wine. 'You would like some? No? Well, then—let me explain: in Surajo, Armand had no choice but to leave the child with his mother.'

Catherine frowned. 'You mean—because of his work in Batistamajor?'

'From his point of view, yes. But Elena and I would have had the boy here, and Estella knew that.'

'I see.'

Catherine wondered why he was telling her all this. It wasn't really her concern, except insofar as it affected Ricardo. But it was so intriguing she hoped he would go on. For so long she had pondered Armand's actions herself.

'You probably think I am very bitter, Miss Loring,' her host declared now, reseating himself beside her. 'But it was a great shock to my wife and me when my daughter-in-law took up with that—that butcher, Montoya.'

'Yes, *senhor*.'

'At first, we used to blame ourselves, for influencing Armand's decision to leave the hospital in Rio. But when I learned that it was through Estella's association with Estéban Montoya that Armand discovered José's whereabouts, how could our involvement be entirely responsible?'

Catherine gazed at him. 'You mean—your daughter-in-law knew Montoya before—before she and—and Dr de Castro moved to Terasina?'

'Apparently.' He sighed. 'I suppose you find all this very boring.'

'Oh, no.' Catherine shook her head. 'I—I just wonder why you are telling me.'

'Do you?' He regarded her through his lashes, as Armand had sometimes done, and her heart contracted. Did he know? Had he guessed? Was she such a transparent person? Or was he simply unloading his worries on to sympathetic ears in the hope that she herself might reassure him.

Moistening her lips, she said cautiously: 'I still don't really understand why Ricardo had to stay in Surajo. Not if he would have been happier here, with you.'

'Do you not?' He regarded the wine in his glass with studied concentration. 'Well, my dear, it was a simple matter of blackmail. Estella knew of José's identity, you see. So long as Armand was willing to dance to her tune—and incidentally, that of General Montoya— Estella was prepared to keep his relationship to José Rodolfo to herself.'

Catherine gasped. 'But—you can't mean he worked against José!' She couldn't believe it, not remembering Armand's gentleness when he had tended his brother's injuries.

'Oh, no. No!' Senhor de Castro spoke impatiently. 'But doctors are scarce in Surajo, as I am sure you know, and Armand was—persuaded to donate his services to the military garrisons at Batistamajor and Ribatejo.'

'Oh, I see.' Catherine's expression was very revealing, though she was not aware of it. 'So that was why Arm—I mean, *Dr* de Castro left Terasina.'

'Essentially, yes.' He nodded. 'Although, as it turned out, that was exactly where Armand wanted to be.'

'Because of José?'

'Because of José,' he agreed. 'I believe you, too, were instrumental in saving José's life.'

'Hardly.' Catherine made a dismissive gesture. 'It was Dr Alvares.'

It was only as she finished speaking, Catherine realised what she had said, Dr *Alvares*, not Dr *de Castro*. But why?

As if understanding her confusion, Armand's father regarded her gently. 'Perhaps you are pondering why Armand called himself Alvares and not de Castro?' he suggested. 'I imagine this is not the first time you have queried his intentions.'

'Well . . .' Catherine had to be honest. 'I—did wonder.'

'But, of course.' Senhor de Castro nodded again. 'You can see no reason for it. Did you think Armand wanted to conceal his identity?'

'It did cross my mind.'

'Ah.' He gave her a considering look. 'Well—it was

an idea Armand had. You see, you have to understand, it was many years since José had seen his brother. How was he to recognise him? For Armand, it was different. José's identity was unmistakable. Armand's was not.'

Catherine frowned. 'The name—meant something then?'

'When they were children, they used to play a game. Even in those days, Armand wanted to be a doctor. He was always Dr Armand Alvares, which happened to be the name of our doctor, here in São Paulo. It is as simple as that.'

Catherine's lips parted. 'And—and Armand thought José might recognise the name,' she breathed softly, unaware of using Armand's name, or of the light that came into her eyes when she did so.

'Só certo. Exactly.' Armand's father smiled. 'Our name, de Castro, is not uncommon in Surajo. There would be no reason for José to question the identity of a Dr de Castro. But Dr *Armand Alvares*! *Bem*, Armand hoped it might—how would you say?—ring some bells, no?'

'And did it?' Catherine was intrigued.

'Not initially, no.' Senhor de Castro grimaced. 'After all, why should it? It was more than fifteen years since they had seen one another. But, eventually, José learned that the doctor in Batistamajor had been treating some of his men at the convent hospital, and when he was wounded, he sent a message to Armand. It was signed with the distinctive mark of *O Tigre*, which is how José is known to his men. It was a calculated risk. Had Armand not been the man José expected him to be, the results could have been disastrous. But, it was a risk he had to take. He knew he would die without treatment, so . . .' He shrugged.

'You know what happened.'

Catherine shook her head. 'It's quite incredible!'

'Some might say foolhardy,' remarked the old man reflectively. 'Armand took risks, too.'

'But—his name?' persisted Catherine, returning to their original theme. 'Didn't—didn't General Montoya suspect?'

'Why should he? He did not know Armand and José were brothers. When Armand suggested using an alias, he used Montoya's own tactics. He suggested that, living in such an isolated community, he might inadvertently learn something to Montoya's advantage. But, if everyone knew of his—close association to the military regime, they might not be prepared to trust him.'

Catherine stared at him in disbelief. 'But surely, General Montoya must know that Armand has no love for the Ferreira regime!'

'Why?' Senhor de Castro held her gaze. 'Do not confuse personal issues with national ones. It is not Presidente Ferreira who is sleeping with Armand's wife.'

Catherine blinked. 'But, you said—'

'Armand *does not* support the regime,' Senhor de Castro told her patiently. 'I am merely pointing out to you how Montoya's mind works.'

'I see.' Catherine's shoulders sagged. 'So what happens now?'

'I suppose that depends on José,' said Armand's father heavily. 'I pray to God he will succeed, without too much bloodshed.'

Catherine trembled. 'You know—you know José has a son, too?' she ventured, trying to dispel the image of Armand caught up in the fighting.

'So Armand tells us, yes.'

'You've never met him.' It was a statement, not a question.

'How could we?' asked another voice, and turning, Catherine saw Senhora de Castro standing in the doorway. 'Forgive me,' she added, 'but I could not help overhearing what you were saying, my dear.' She paused. 'Do I understand that you have met Luis?' And at Catherine's nod: 'Will you tell us about him? We would so much like to know him.'

CHAPTER NINETEEN

IT was a curious evening with Catherine finding herself doing most of the talking. Instead of her learning more about Armand from his mother, she spent the time before and during dinner telling Senhora de Castro as much about José as she could remember, and about Luis, and his resemblance to Ricardo.

Ricardo, for his part, seemed quite content to listen for once, though his eyes began to droop as the dessert was served. It had been a long day, for all of them, and Catherine was quite relieved when a smiling maid-servant took him off to bed, relieving her of that duty for this evening at least.

Catherine made her excuses after dinner. 'I am very tired,' she murmured apologetically, needing time herself to mull over everything Armand's father had told her. She had learned so much, and yet so little, about the man she loved so desperately. What were Armand's feelings for Estella now? If the coup succeeded and she left Estéban Montoya, would Armand take her back? Remembering his determination to respect his marriage vows, Catherine was very much afraid he would. For Ricardo's sake, if for nothing else.

In her absence, one of the maids had entered her room and turned down the bed. Her suitcase, too, had been unpacked, and its contents neatly hung away in the clothes-press. The bag containing her few items of make-up had been set on the chest of drawers, and the newspaper she had bought almost a week ago in Casca de Mar—and which Sophia had stuffed into the side of her bag—was laid neatly on the table beside the bed.

Sophia should have thrown it away, Catherine reflected impatiently now, picking up the offending item to drop into the waste bin. Just because she had not had time to read it was no reason to hang on to it. It was out of date, and nothing was more stale than yesterday's news!

But, as she was about to discard the paper, one article caught her attention. Sophia had been reading the paper, and it was folded at the place she had reached. In consequence, the piece that caught Catherine's eye had probably escaped her notice. It was headed: *Oficial Militar prendido em Batistamajor*; and it was the name of the village that sprang out at her.

Cursing her fumbling Portuguese, Catherine perched on the side of the bed and made a concerted attempt to read what the article said. It wasn't easy. There were lots of words she didn't understand, and she considered going to find Armand's father to ask him to translate it for her. But, gradually, as she stumbled through the unfamiliar words and phrases, one salient fact was made known to her: she should *not* show this piece to Armand's parents, for the army officer who had been arrested was *Henri Enriques*!

Dry-mouthed, Catherine struggled to gain the gist of what the reporter was saying. That Major Enriques had been detained, there was no doubt. He had been arrested almost a week ago, for crimes against the state; but what those crimes were, and how he came to be involved in such an unlikely event, she could not make out. All that kept ringing in her brain was that Armand was involved with Henri Enriques; they had spent a lot of time together, time Catherine had resented when she was living in Armand's house. What

if Major Enriques's detention had something to do
with Armand? What if Armand's involvement with
the rebels had been discovered? What if *Armand* was
arrested, too?

Unable to sit still, Catherine got up and paced
restlessly about the room. A little less than a week ago,
at the time this newspaper was being printed, Armand
had been in Casca de Mar. Oh, she thought futilely, if
only she had read it then? If only she had taken the
time to scan its pages, surely she would have noticed
an article about *Batistamajor*?

She sighed. Sophia might have seen it, of course,
and not even connected it with Armand. Did Sophia
know where Armand had been working? It was a
question she had no way of answering, and besides, it
was too late now to hope she might have said something. Surely, if she had, Armand would have told
her. *Or would he?*

She shook her head. It was all her fault. If she had
not been so foolishly overwhelmed at seeing Armand
again, she might have remembered the newspaper the
night she had been unable to get to sleep. How much
more sensible it would have been to prove herself
some use to him; instead of putting herself in his way,
and seducing his instincts for self-preservation.

Her tiredness left her. Whereas before, she had been
looking forward to crawling between the sheets and
allowing exhaustion to claim her, now she was wide
awake and restive. Her mind was darting in all directions, trying to find an avenue of escape. But all she
could think of was that Armand had returned to
Batistamajor; Armand might be in danger; Armand
might, already, be lying in a prison cell.

She had to go back, she decided at last. She had to
return to Surajo, and Batistamajor. She would never

have a moment's peace until she knew whether
Armand was safe or not, and it was useless to pretend
her life was worth anything if he was dead.

Pushing back her hair with a trembling hand, she
tried to think. It must have been providence that
persuaded Senhor Lopez to give her his address in São
Paulo. He was her only chance of getting back into
Surajo. Without his protection, she doubted she
would be granted a visa to land. But if she went back
with him, if the officials at the airport could be persuaded that she had accompanied him to Brazil for
purely personal reasons . . .

She shook her head. Senhor Lopez was in São
Paulo, but the city of São Paulo was probably a hundred miles away. How on earth could she get to the
city without enlisting anyone's aid? And even if she
confided in Senhor de Castro, how could she be sure
he would let her go?

Pacing back across the carpet, she surveyed her
appearance without favour. One thing was certain:
she could not go anywhere in green taffeta. But she
could do nothing before morning, she reflected
realistically, and taking off her clothes, she slid
disconsolately between the sheets.

She hardly slept, and at first light she was up again,
cleaning her teeth and sluicing her face before
dressing in the clothes she had worn the day before.
She brushed her hair and secured it again in the single
braid, this time leaving it loose down her back. She did
consider putting it up, as she had done the previous
evening, but she discarded the idea. She looked
younger—and therefore less conspicuous—as she
was.

When she drew back the curtains, the view was a
momentary diversion. Her room faced east, down the

valley, and in the pearly morning light the gardens below her windows were a glowing mass of colour. She had never seen so many different varieties of flowers, and although there were lots she didn't recognise, there were many she did. Camellias; begonias; fuchsias; hibiscus—the list was endless. Tiny dog-eyed daisies rubbing shoulders with delicate rose mallows; morning glory and foxgloves, lobelias and sunflowers; there was even Catherine's favourite, the delicate calla lily, whose creamy white petals were opening to the sun. Her lips parted in admiration, and she thought how delightful it would be to go outdoors and smell so many different fragrances. But then, depression closed around her when she remembered what she had to do.

With no satisfactory plan of how she was going to get to São Paulo, Catherine left her room and descended the stairs. Perhaps some miraculous idea would occur to her, she thought, without much confidence. Perhaps Armand would appear and put paid to all the anxieties she was suffering. But the chances of this were virtually non-existent, and unless she thought of something soon, it might be too late.

She tried not to think about what she would do if she arrived in Batistamajor to find Armand had been arrested. She would face that problem when she came to it. For the moment, the actual physical effort of finding a way to get back to Surajo was more than enough to cope with.

As she hesitated in the hall, unsure of the time, and of what arrangements might be made for breakfast, Senhora de Castro emerged from the room to her right. Dressed in a long, flowing caftan, which served the dual purpose of morning robe and dressing gown, Armand's mother looked as regally elegant as she had done the night before. Though, as Catherine looked more closely, she perceived a certain weariness in her expression, as if she, too, had found it difficult to rest.

'Catherine!' she exclaimed, when she saw her young house guest. 'My dear, if you had wanted anything, you should have called one of the maids. It's barely six thirty! You should still be asleep.'

Catherine sighed. 'You're very kind, but—well, I was restless.'

'You, too?' Armand's mother grimaced. 'I must admit, I didn't find sleeping easy either.'

Catherine's arched her brows. 'You're worried about your sons?'

'Wouldn't you be?' Senhora de Castro shook her head. 'Particularly Armand. I sent him into this, and now I'm afraid something awful has happened to him.'

Catherine paled. 'Why?'

'Oh—' Senhora de Castro glanced impatiently about her. 'Just an old woman's intuition, I suppose. Look—' She gestured towards the room she had just left. 'Let's go in here. I'll ask Anita to bring us some coffee.'

Five minutes later, Catherine was admiring the appointments of a sunlit morning room, whose long windows were open to the garden. At this hour of the morning, the air was deliciously cool and fresh, and the buzzing of the insects among the flowers was soothing. Armand's mother was seated beside her on a chintz-covered sofa, whose pattern was repeated on the walls, busying herself with coffee cups while her young companion looked around.

'Terribly English, isn't it?' Senhora de Castro asked, handing Catherine a cup. 'André says I'm hopelessly patriotic, but I just love this style of decoration. And I suppose it does remind me of home.'

Catherine sipped her coffee. 'Were both your sons educated in England, *senhora*?'

'They both went to school in England,' Senhora de Castro amended. 'But José was never an academic, and he did not complete his education.'

'I see.' Catherine nodded. 'You must have missed them.'

'Yes, I did.' Senhora de Castro bit her lip. 'Particularly Armand.' She shrugged a little defensively. 'He was such an adorable little boy. Exactly as Ricardo is now.'

Catherine looked down into her cup. 'You—you were saying earlier, about—about your being worried about—your sons.'

'You mean Armand, don't you?' Senhora de Castro watched her closely. 'Tell me, my dear, how long have you been in love with my son?'

Catherine's face flamed. 'I beg your pardon—'

'Oh, don't get upset, my dear.' Armand's mother patted her hand. 'I don't mean to pry. Just put it down to a mother's curiosity.

'*Senhora*—Armand is married—'

'I know.' Senhora de Castro inclined her head. 'But his marriage to Estella has been a sham for many years now. As I'm sure he told you.'

Catherine bent her head. 'Armand has told me nothing.'

'No?' Senhora de Castro snorted. 'Well, that's typical, I suppose. Armand was always absurdly honest—scrupulous—*loyal*; call it what you will. He's taken a lot; for Ricardo's sake. But he's a fool if he thinks his father and I are going to sit back and allow Estella to ruin the rest of his life!'

'I—don't think Armand will allow you to interfere,' said Catherine quietly.

'No. Perhaps not.' His mother pressed her lips together impatiently. 'But enough is enough, as they say, and no man should be forced to bear the burden of guilt for a lifetime!'

'The burden of guilt?' Catherine was confused. 'I don't understand . . .'

'Oh—José was going to marry Estella,' explained Armand's mother wearily. 'He was twenty-six, Estella was twenty-one; the same age as Armand incidentally.' She paused. 'Well, a few weeks before the wedding, Armand came home from England, for a holiday. He was at university there, you see. Estella had never met him. And, as soon as she saw Armand, she wanted him. You can guess what happened.' She sighed. 'I'm not saying Armand was blameless, you understand. Estella was—*is*—a beautiful woman: outwardly, at least. And he was used to the admiration of women, much more than poor José was.'

Catherine moistened her lips. 'She broke her engagement.'

'Estella? Yes,' Senhora de Castro lifted her shoulders. 'Shortly afterwards, José—went away.'

'I see.' Catherine was beginning to understand so many things. 'So—so Armand married Estella instead.'

'Oh, no. At least, not immediately,' Senhora de Castro frowned. 'I'm afraid, so far as Armand was concerned, it meant little.' She pressed her palms to her cheeks in bitter remembrance. 'It was a terrible time. You can have no idea. Armand tried to persuade José that he was sorry; that Estella cared nothing for him. But José wouldn't listen; and Estella only aggravated the situation by insisting she was in love with Armand.'

'And—was she?'

'I don't know.' Senhora de Castro sighed again. 'To be charitable, I suppose she could have been. But Armand had to return to England to continue with his studies, and Estella remained here.'

'Then how—?'

'I suppose it must have been about six years later, when Armand had qualified,' said Senhora de Castro bitterly. 'He returned to Brazil to practise here, and he met Estella again. I don't know what possessed him to ask her to marry him, except perhaps that she was still unattached and he felt responsible. Anyway, the marriage took place, he obtained a post at a hospital in Rio, and you know the rest.'

Catherine put down her coffee cup. 'Perhaps he did care for her, after all.'

'Who knows?' Senhora de Castro looked bleak. 'In any event, Ricardo was born almost a year after their marriage, and perhaps a year after that, she met Estéban Montoya at a diplomatic function.'

'And—fell in love with him?'

'And became his mistress,' responded Armand's mother caustically.

'So why didn't she just—leave Armand?'

'Huh!' Senhora de Castro's lips twisted. 'Estella was never one to give up anything she owned. Besides, she still wanted him; Armand, I mean. I remember on one occasion they came here—' She broke off abruptly to take a shuddering breath. 'It was so—embarrassing! She taunted Armand all through dinner—boasting about the men she had known, questioning his masculinity! Then, later, when she discovered Armand had requested a separate room for himself, she began throwing herself at him, urging him to forgive her, *begging* him to make love to her!' She closed her eyes for a moment, as if to dispel the images her words had evoked, and then continued flatly: 'They were already living separate lives, you see. Only Armand had never told his father or me. Afterwards, she never came here again.'

Catherine's tongue circled her upper lip. 'I'm sorry.'

'Yes. So are we,' said Armand's mother heavily. 'She has certainly caused this family a great deal of distress.' She paused. 'Were it not for Ricardo . . .'

'But surely—' Catherine caught her lower lip between her teeth. 'I mean—couldn't Ricardo live with his father?'

'He could. If Estella would let him,' declared Senhora de Castro harshly. 'But, you see, she knows that so long as she can say she is prepared to resume relations with my son, no Catholic court is going to take the child from her.'

Catherine's throat felt tight. 'And she'd do that?'

'Unless Montoya is prepared to marry her,' said Armand's mother bitterly. 'Estella knows that so long as she has Armand's ring on her finger, she has security, and so far Montoya has not offered her that.'

Catherine gazed at her helplessly. 'Poor Armand!'

'Yes. Poor Armand,' agreed the old lady wryly. 'So, you see now why I was curious about your relationship with my son.'

Catherine bent her head. 'I do love him.'

'And does he love you?'

'I don't know. He—wants me. But that's not the same, is it?'

'I imagine to Armand it might be,' murmured his mother softly. 'So much misery has been accomplished in the name of love. I can understand his reluctance to commit himself again.'

Disturbed by what Armand's mother had said, Catherine got to her feet and walked tensely over to the window. 'If only he was here,' she said tremulously. And then, turning: 'Senhora de Castro, I want to go back to Surajo!'

The Latin American Airlines DC 10 landed at Ribatejo in the early hours of the morning.

Catherine, who had spent the flight staring blindly out of the darkened window, had been startled out of her apathy by the pilot's announcement an hour and a half ago that the airport at Terasina was closed to all traffic. Their flight was being diverted to Ribatejo, he said, because it was the only other airport in the country which could take a plane of its size.

Catherine could scarcely believe her good fortune. She had not been looking forward to the long train journey north, and although she was not exactly afraid, she had been apprehensive of the difficulties she might have to face. Now, the problem had been resolved for her.

'It seems we may be flying into a hornet's nest, senhorita,' Senhor Lopez remarked beside her, and Catherine gave him a rueful smile as she remembered his opposition to her plans.

The elderly lawyer had been most surprised to find her waiting for him at his hotel the previous afternoon. When he returned from the business meeting he had been attending, and learned of Catherine's intentions, his reaction had been predictably bleak. She could not be serious, he informed her. Had she not heard the news? Had she not read the newspapers? Surajo was in the throes of the worst civil disturbances for ten years! Only that afternoon, news had come through of aircraft being shot down over Surajan territory. She would be risking her life if she was even allowed to set foot in the country.

But Catherine had been adamant, and with Senhora de Castro's written support, she was eventually able to convince him she was not about to change her mind. Even if she suspected Armand's mother was more concerned about her son's safety than that of the girl who had offered to go and find out if he was still alive, she was determined to have her way and Senhor Lopez had reluctantly given in.

As they emerged from the plane, however, it soon became apparent that this part of the country was no longer in the hands of the military government. Placards and posters depicting images of José were pasted over the airport buildings, and slogans proclaiming *O Salvador Rodolfo* and *Rodolfo por Presidente* were everywhere.

'So: it is done,' murmured Senhor Lopez obliquely, as they entered the modest Arrivals Hall under the watchful eye of an armed guerrilla. 'You would have done well to remain in São Paulo, *senhorita*. Your involvement with the de Castro family is unlikely to mean much to these desperate men.'

In all honesty, Catherine was inclined to believe him, and she did experience a few anxious moments when their luggage was searched and their passports confiscated. As an alien in the country, her allegiance to either Ferreira's or Rodolfo's regime could be suspect.

Beyond the control point, a uniformed officer was waiting to speak to them. Catherine thought she recognised him as one of the men who had been present the night Armand operated on José, but she couldn't be absolutely sure. In any event, he would be unlikely to remember her, or recognise her as the nurse from the convent. She could only hope they were to be allowed to go free. Surely if the guerrilla forces were in command, they had nothing to fear.

She did notice, however, that several of the passengers from the plane had not been allowed to proceed beyond the control point. They were men, for the most part, some in civilian clothes, others in military dress. Catherine guessed they had affiliations with the Ferreira regime, and were being detained for questioning. Thank goodness Senhor Lopez had not been arrested, she thought gratefully.

With the nervous attention of most of the passengers fastened on him, the officer began speaking. Although Catherine did not understand all the address, she was able to pick out a few words here and there. It soon became evident that although they were not being arrested, they were being detained, and Catherine knew a helpless sense of frustration at the realisation she was not to be allowed to complete her journey.

'It is for our own good, apparently,' Senhor Lopez assured her in a low tone, when she expressed her disappointment. 'There are still soldiers loyal to President Ferreira hiding out in the hills, and General Rodolfo does not wish to see any more bloodshed.'

Catherine shook her head. 'But surely—if you are prepared to take the risk—'

'They are not,' retorted Senhor Lopez firmly, and when the remaining passengers were ushered into the tiny waiting room, Catherine was obliged to go with them.

The hours before dawn passed slowly and fretfully for Catherine. To be so near and yet so far from Batistamajor. It wasn't fair. *It simply wasn't fair!*

She considered asking to speak to the commanding

officer, and demanding that she be set free to go and find *General* Rodolfo's *brother*, but her courage was not so great. Besides, she had no way of knowing whether, if she drew attention to herself, she might not be despatched elsewhere as a possible dissident, and that would be disastrous. So, like all the other passengers, she was forced to wait out her sentence, inwardly seething with a mixture of anticipation and fear.

It was getting light when the door to their imposed cell opened and the officer appeared again. 'Food will be brought to you,' he said, in words that Catherine could understand, and the uneasy silence which had fallen was broken by his voice.

Several of the passengers had questions to ask, not least when they were to be allowed to leave, but the officer parried all direct inquiries. '*O mais cedo possivel,*' he assured them briefly, which Catherine took to mean they would be released as soon as their identities had been endorsed.

A meal of coffee, cheese and oatbread was produced some thirty minutes later, and although Catherine wasn't hungry, she accepted a plastic beaker of coffee gratefully. '*Nada de açúcar, obrigado,*' she averred, refusing the sachet of sugar the young soldier was holding out to her, and then, as her gaze lifted to his face, she gasped: '*Luis!*'

Her involuntary exclamation attracted the attention of most of the other passengers, and Catherine's face reddened. But it *was* José Rodolfo's son who was helping serve the coffee, and his eyes narrowed uncomprehendingly as he looked at her.

'*Perdão, senhorita, mas não o conheco!*'

Catherine sighed frustratedly. 'You do know me, you do,' she insisted, speaking in English. 'Don't you remember?' She didn't want to be too explicit. 'The— operation? On your father?'

'*Senhorita*—Loring?' he ventured, gazing disbelievingly at her. 'Is it really you?'

'Yes, oh, yes!' Aware that Senhor Lopez was regarding their exchange with something akin to astonishment, Catherine gave him a rueful look. But she couldn't explain yet. Returning her attention to the boy, she forced a tight smile. 'I've come back to find your uncle. Do you know where he is?'

'Ah!' Luis inclined his head, glancing thoughtfully towards the guard on duty at the door. 'Yes.' He hesitated. 'Wait a moment, *senhorita*. I will be right back.'

Leaving her, he crossed the room, apparently unaware that he was the cynosure of all eyes. But after he had disappeared outside, Catherine herself learned what it was like to have so many pairs of eyes upon her.

'Do I understand you correctly?' Senhor Lopez demanded hoarsely in her ear. 'That boy—*that youth*—is José Rodolfo's son?'

Catherine nodded. 'You don't know him?'

'Obviously not.' Senhor Lopez shook his head. 'You are a constant source of amazement to me, *senhorita*. I thought, for one moment, you had taken leave of your senses!'

Catherine smiled, albeit nervously. 'I must admit, I had my moment of fear,' she conceded. 'I thought he wasn't going to remember me.'

When Luis came back, however, he was not alone. An older, sterner-looking individual was with him, and with polite formality, Luis requested that Catherine accompany them. She hesitated at first, tempted to suggest that Senhor Lopez be allowed to go with her. But the look in the older man's eyes deterred her and, giving Senhor Lopez an apologetic look, she accompanied them out of the room.

'*Por aqui, senhorita,*' the guide directed, taking her arm and urging her towards the exit, while Luis lifted his hand in farewell.

'Filipe will take good care of you, *senhorita,*' he told her as she cast him a rather desperate glance. '*Até a vista.* Until we meet again.'

There was a distinctly sinking feeling in Catherine's stomach when she emerged into the parking area to find a mud-smeared station wagon waiting for them. An unshaven driver was behind the wheel, and he gave her an insolent appraisal as her companion forcibly helped her into the back of the car. Then, after he had joined her, the car was set in motion, and Catherine clung desperately to her seat as they swung out on to the dusty highway. She hoped Luis knew what he was doing. She hoped he really did remember her. It was frightening to think he might have mistaken her for some kind of spy, masquerading as a nurse in order to worm her way into his confidence.

Dawn was breaking over the high sierras, the stark beauty of the landscape reminding her of the morning she and Armand had returned from José's encampment. Then she had been apprehensive, too, though not as apprehensive as she was now. Where were they taking her? What were they going to do?

The outskirts of Ribatejo came into view at that moment, and Catherine saw the checkpoint ahead, guarding the entrance to the city. Their car was stopped and searched, even though its occupants were evidently known to the armed sentries, and Catherine herself was subjected to another speculative appraisal. Obviously, the vibrant colour of her hair set her apart from her captors, but they could be no more curious than she was to learn exactly where she was headed.

Within the city there was chilling proof that fighting had taken place. Some buildings had suffered from mortar attacks, and others had had all their windows blown out. Shops in the city's main street were boarded up and empty, and the streets themselves were strewn with the debris of an army in retreat.

The army barracks had taken the worst of the gunfire. A severe explosion had ripped apart the heavy gates that protected the entry, and the crumbling walls of the guardhouse were silent witnesses to the battle which had ensued.

Yet it was between the gates of the army barracks that the station wagon turned, and for one awful moment, Catherine wondered whether she had been mistaken: that perhaps the army of General Montoya was still in control. It was inconceivable to think that she had made an error over Luis's identity, but her palms moistened all the same as the vehicle came to a standstill before the remaining block of buildings.

'Venha comigo, senhorita,' her escort ordered, and although her brain was in a turmoil, Catherine knew that he wanted her to go with him. Wasting no time, she scrambled out of the station wagon to join him on the parade ground. Then, at his direction, she preceded him up the steps and into the building.

There was an unpleasantly acrid smell in the air, which Catherine suspected might be cordite, and the corridors were thick with soldiers, dressed in green fatigues. The man with her was saluted several times, which seemed to point to his being someone of importance, but to Catherine it was all too harrowing for her to try and identify anyone.

At the end of the corridor they were progressing along was a flight of stairs, and her escort indicated that she should climb them. With her heart beating rapidly, Catherine complied, aware of an increasingly nauseous feeling in the pit of her stomach. It was fear, she knew; fear of why they had brought her here; fear of all these armed men; fear of the unknown. But most of all, it was a growing fear that somehow Armand was dead, and she was being brought here to identify his body.

A closed door guarded by two more sentries confronted her at the top of the stairs. This was evidently her destination, she guessed, as her escort exchanged a few words with his subordinates. She was being left here, abandoned to their uncertain mercies, and her knees almost gave out on her as she was ushered unceremoniously through the door.

She found herself in a kind of ante room, the sort of room a secretary might occupy, she thought, but which was presently inhabited by a young man, perched on the side of the desk, talking volubly into the telephone. He looked surprised at her entrance, but one of the men with her quickly explained her purpose. Or at least, that was how it seemed to Catherine, as her nervous gaze took in the haphazard piles of paper files tumbling over the desk, and the filing cabinet, forced open, its contents allowed to spill in all directions.

In any event, her escort departed, and the door was closed again. She was left to cope with the situation as best she could, and her mouth watered unpleasantly at the thought of what was to come. If only he would stop talking into the telephone, she fretted, shifting her weight from one foot to the other. She was feeling increasingly queasy, and she didn't know how long

she could control her churning stomach. Was this the
person they had brought her to see, she wondered,
praying he understood English. Or was there someone else beyond that other door, which seemed to lead
to an inner sanctum?

Then, two things happened simultaneously. The
young man completed his call, and the door to that
inner room opened. Catherine dragged her gaze away
from the young man in time to see another man
entering the room. Tall, dark, bearded, his gaunt
features bearing witness to some inward strain he was
suffering, he was nonetheless recognisable for all that.

'José!' she breathed, an immense feeling of relief
enveloping her. So, Luis had not betrayed her after all.
He had sent her to his father.

José had heard that barely audible whisper of his
name, and now his face took on a look of arrant
disbelief. 'Miss—Loring!' he exclaimed. 'It is—
Miss Loring, *não é? Meu Deus*, what are you doing
here?'

Conscious that she had the attention of both men,
Catherine took an involuntary step towards him. 'I
came—oh, I came to find Armand,' she blurted impulsively, not trying to justify her reasons for doing so.
'We—I—was detained by your men at the airport.
That was when I saw Luis. I managed to speak to him,
and he—he sent me here—'

'*Um momento, senhorita.*' José advanced towards her,
taking the hand she had extended and enfolding it
between both of his. His actions were jerky, convul-
sive; the hands gripping hers almost numbing her
circulation. 'What are you saying, *senhorita*?' he demanded harshly. 'I thought you were safely in São
Paulo.'

'I was, I was,' exclaimed Catherine impatiently. 'But

your mother—that is, Senhora de Castro—had a premonition that something was wrong.'

'You mean—Armand is not with you?' José interrupted, his grip tightening even more. 'Armand is still in São Paulo?'

Catherine swallowed, scarcely understanding what he was talking about. 'Armand did not go to São Paulo,' she replied, shaking her head. 'But you know that. *Don't you?*'

But she suddenly realised he didn't, and as the implication of his words swept over her, she became aware of a curious buzzing noise in her head.

'Ar—Armand's not here?' she articulated blankly, groping for the back of the chair to support herself, and José slowly shook his head.

'He—he left for Terasina over a week ago,' he said heavily. 'No one has seen him since. I had told him to get out of Surajo; to take you and Ricardo to São Paulo at the first sign of trouble, but I had no way of knowing if he had gone. Since the coup, I have been trying to convince myself that he took my advice, but now you say he did not leave the country. I should have known. Armand always insisted I would need him more than his family would, when the fighting started.'

CHAPTER TWENTY

IT was quite a relief to discover that at first sight Batistamajor looked little different from when she had left it. Although José's men had taken the place of the military garrison, there were few outward signs of violence, and Catherine wondered if Henri Enriques's arrest had had anything to do with the ease with which the guerrilla forces had evidently taken control.

Sitting beside Luis in the front of the station wagon, Catherine was desperately trying to come to terms with the news of Armand's disappearance. She didn't remember much about what happened after José's announcement that Armand was not here. For only the second time in her life, she had fainted dead away, and by the time she came round, José was preparing to leave. Obviously, he had spent more time with her than he could really afford, and she had to be satisfied with his terse assurance that as soon as he had any news, she would hear it. He was shattered, too, she knew that, but he had had to put his personal feelings aside. He was José Rodolfo; his people's saviour; how could he waste valuable time searching for one man, albeit his brother, when the war he was fighting was only partially won?

Luis's reappearance had been another relief. At least he understood English, she thought gratefully. It had been thoughtful of José to have his son brought from the airport to take care of her in his absence, though she somehow doubted Luis welcomed the privilege.

Her decision to go back to Batistamajor had been greeted with some misgivings. The purpose for her journey to Surajo was no longer relevant and José, she knew, would have preferred to put her on the next flight out. He had enough problems as it was, without worrying over a useless English girl, who fainted at the first hint of danger.

But, in this, Catherine had been adamant, and short of overruling her decision and despatching her forcibly back to the airport, José was obliged to give way to her. Leaving Luis instructions to stay with her, he departed about his own business, and as soon as a vehicle could be requisitioned, Catherine and her escort had left the barracks.

Luis was to drive her, too, she discovered, when he climbed behind the wheel of the Land-Rover. 'I am sixteen, *senhorita*,' he declared flatly, noticing her doubtful expression. 'Boys grow to men very quickly in this climate.'

'I'm sorry.' Catherine got obediently in beside him. 'I didn't mean to question your ability.'

'But you did wonder if I was capable,' Luis responded, with unconscious cynicism. 'Relax, *senhorita*. My father would not have placed you in my hands, if he had not believed I was competent.' He smiled, and then said obliquely: '*Tio* Armand would never forgive me, no?'

It was the first time Armand's name had been mentioned since her ignominious collapse on the floor of the office upstairs. But Catherine waited until Luis had started the Land-Rover's engine and driven through the gates before asking, tensely: 'What do you know about your uncle's disappearance? Has your father any idea where he might be?'

'No.' Luis shook his head, and a wave of absolute

desolation swept over her. '*Senhorita*, if my father had known anything, he would have told you. All we know is, Armand left for Terasina over a week ago, and he has not returned.'

'You know he came to Casca de Mar?'

'We knew that was where he was headed,' Luis nodded, without taking his eyes from the road. 'And my father assumed that as you said you had come from São Paulo, my uncle sent you and Ricardo there. Was he correct?'

Catherine inclined her head. 'Armand made the arrangements,' she conceded; and then, remembering, she added: 'A Senhor Lopez escorted us. He was the man I was with at the airport, when I saw you.' She paused uncertainly. 'How long does your father intend to keep those people there? Couldn't they be allowed to leave now?'

'Arrangements are being made to transport all passengers to their destinations as soon as possible,' said Luis equably. 'Do not worry, *senhorita*. So long as your friend has not been actively involved with the Ferreira regime, he will be treated fairly.'

Catherine sighed. 'I can hardly believe it.'

'What?' Luis permitted her a brief glance. 'That the forces of the revolution do not treat people fairly?'

'No!' Catherine bent her head. 'That Armand is missing.' Her voice broke. 'Do you think he is still alive?'

Luis was silent for a few moments, and then he sighed. 'I do not know, *senhorita*. It is possible he has been taken prisoner. There are still forces loyal to Ferreira active in the countryside. My father knows that. If my uncle was arrested—*identified*—' He shrugged. 'It is perhaps fortunate his name is not the same as my father's.'

'But mightn't it work the other way?' protested Catherine tremulously. 'I mean, if some of your father's men arrested him, for example?'

Luis's mouth twitched. 'It is possible, I suppose,' he admitted reluctantly. '*Senhorita*, I advise you not to think about what *might* have happened. My father will let you know as soon as he has definite information. Until then, you must not worry.'

It was good advice, but impossible to follow. Until she knew exactly what had happened to Armand, Catherine knew she would do nothing else but worry. She refused to consider what she might do if he was dead. That was a contingency she would face if—or when—she had to. Until then, she intended to stay in Armand's house, whether Santo approved of her or not.

But all that was left of Armand's house was a smoke-blackened shell. Catherine could hardly believe her eyes when the scorched walls and exposed eaves came into view. The heedless destruction was a chilling reminder of the night her father had been killed, and she caught her breath in horror at the images it evoked.

'*Com a breca!* Who has done this?' demanded Luis angrily, stopping the army vehicle on the grass verge and vaulting out of his seat.

'Don't you know?' asked Catherine dully, pushing open her door.

'Know? How could I know?' responded Luis, momentarily arrested in his advance. '*Senhorita*, you do not believe we did this!'

'Then who?' Catherine stepped out of the vehicle, wrapping her arms closely about her. She moistened her lips. 'Do you—do you think Armand might have been—'

She could not finish the sentence, and Luis pressed his lips tightly together. 'No,' he said at last, fiercely. 'No, my uncle is not dead. I *feel* it. But,' he turned back to the burnt-out building, 'someone perhaps wants us to think so.'

'What do you mean?'

Forcing back the memories, Catherine accompanied Luis towards the house. But with every step she relived the dreadful terror of the night her father died, and rekindled all her guilt that she should have survived. If Armand had not been there—if Armand had not found her hiding under the verandah, would they have killed her, too?

Her father had certainly thought so. It was he who had sent her running for cover, as soon as he had opened the door to his murderers. He must have guessed why they had come. They got few visitors at the schoolhouse, and his staunch protest that he was alone in the house had warned Catherine that something was wrong. But even then she had not understood the harsh choking sound that had followed her father's statement. That came later, while the men were looting and firing the house, when she had crawled out of her hiding place to find out what was going on.

Shivering now, in spite of the heat of the day, Catherine could not thrust away the memory of finding her father's body. Edging along the verandah, she had stumbled against it, and her involuntary cry had almost betrayed her. Unwilling to believe that he was dead, she had somehow managed to drag his body down the steps and into hiding with her. It was only when she discovered her hands were caked with some warm, sticky fluid that she realised what they had done.

She didn't remember much after that. There were footsteps on the verandah above her head, a knife thrust savagely between the slats, and then the welcoming roar of the station wagon's engine that warned the men someone else was coming. By the time Armand dragged her out of her self-imposed prison, the roof of the verandah was smouldering, and her father's blood had soaked her to the skin. She was shaking so much, her teeth were chattering, and she could neither move nor speak.

Armand had lifted her up and carried her to safety, and then gone back and dragged her father's body away from what could have been his funeral pyre. Then, he had driven them both to the convent, and delivered her into Reverend Mother's hands.

Remembering Reverend Mother now, Catherine turned away, feeling the blessed relief of a breeze against her hot cheeks. It was pointless thinking about the past. It was the present that should concern her. And if anyone knew what went on in the village, Reverend Mother was that person.

'I think someone deliberately fired the house,' Luis said now, walking back to join her. 'I have seen buildings which have been set alight by mortar fire or incendiaries, and they are not like this. Always the fire is worst at the point of the explosion, but in this case, it does not seem so. Besides which,' he grimaced, 'there is a strong smell of gasoline.'

In spite of the seriousness of the situation, Catherine had to smile. 'Oh, Luis!' she said, touching his sleeve. 'I'm so glad you came with me.'

Luis smiled, too, albeit a little ruefully, and then looked again at the house. 'This must bring back painful memories, *senhorita*,' he said, after a moment. 'I am glad I am here, too. To share it with you.'

Catherine frowned. 'You know—about my father?'

'My uncle told us,' agreed Luis, turning back to her. 'He cares about you very much, I think. And you care about him, *não*?'

Catherine sighed. 'Is it that obvious?'

'You do not search here for an employer, *senhorita*,' replied Luis reasonably. 'And I do not think my uncle will be too dismayed to learn that his wife may have died with General Montoya.'

Catherine hastened after him. 'What did you say?'

'Estéban Montoya is dead,' declared Luis, climbing back into the Land-Rover. 'The plane bringing him back to Terasina was shot down by his own forces. Presidente Ferreira's generalissimo was caught like the rat he was, in his own trap!'

Catherine pressed a hand to her throat. 'And—and Estella was with him?'

'Well—she boarded the plane with him,' remarked Luis unfeelingly, gesturing for Catherine to join him. 'Unless she had a parachute, which I doubt, she ended her life as she had lived it: without honour or dignity.'

His words were harsh; but he had not known Estella, Catherine reminded herself. So far as Luis was concerned, she had been the enemy, one of the hated few who had benefited from Ferreira's corrupt regime. The fact that she had also been his uncle's wife meant nothing, except in providing another reason for his hostility.

'She was a beautiful woman,' Catherine murmured, as she got in beside him, feeling the need to defend Estella now that she was dead. 'You never met her. How do you know she had no honour or dignity?'

'She lived with Montoya, did she not?' Luis was unrepentant. Abandoning the subject, his face lost its bitterness. 'Now where, *senhorita*? Back to Ribatejo?'

'No.' Catherine caught her lower lip between her teeth, and made a decision. 'I'd like to visit the convent first. You know about the convent, don't you?'

'I should.' Luis nodded. 'Though I have to admit, when you spoke to me at the airport, I could hardly believe you were the same person. You used to be so thin!'

Catherine gave him a rueful look. 'That's not exactly a compliment, Luis,' she said reprovingly, trying to lighten their mood, but it wasn't easy. They were both too conscious that someone had seen fit to destroy Armand's house—and maybe Armand, too, who could tell?

Fifteen minutes later, Catherine was sitting in Reverend Mother's office, facing the convent's superior across her desk. How long was it since she had last been seated here, Catherine found herself wondering irrelevantly. It seemed like a lifetime since she had departed from the convent in the back of Armand's car.

And there was a difference; she could sense it. Half expecting Mother Benedicta to refuse to see her, she had been pleasantly surprised when she had been ushered into her presence. Instead of regarding her with the contempt she had expected, Mother Benedicta had greeted her arrival with an unexpected show of compassion, and her voice was not disparaging when she asked how Catherine was.

'So child,' she went on, encouraging the girl opposite with a faint smile, 'you have come back to Batistamajor after all.'

'Yes, Reverend Mother.' Catherine's fingers closed convulsively over the arms of her chair. 'I came back to find Dr—Alvares. Un—unfortunately, he seems to have disappeared.'

Watching her erstwhile superior's face, Catherine could have sworn she saw a flicker of emotion at this news. Just for a moment, Mother Benedicta's mask of urbanity slipped, and a curious look of speculation took its place. But then, the older woman lifted a hand to adjust her wimple and when she lowered it again her expression was as bland as ever.

'You have seen the remains of the doctor's house, I presume?' she remarked smoothly. 'Such needless devastation! I understand valuable drugs were destroyed.'

'And Dr—Alvares?' Catherine moistened her lips. 'What happened to him? Do—do you have any idea?'

Mother Benedicta looked down at her hands, folded on the desk in front of her. 'I understand you have been working for Dr Alvares's wife, in Terasina,' she remarked, without answering Catherine's question. 'Things must be difficult there at the moment.'

'I believe they are. I don't know.' Catherine could feel a rising sense of frustration. 'Arm—I mean, Dr Alvares—arranged for his son and myself to fly to São Paulo before the airport was closed.'

'São Paulo?' Reverend Mother sounded impressed. 'I see.'

'His parents live there,' Catherine added, before the question could be voiced. 'Reverend Mother, do you know where Dr Alvares is? Have you seen him since he left for Terasina almost two weeks ago?'

'Well . . .' Mother Benedicta paused to consider her words before going on. 'I did see him approximately a week ago—'

'*A week!*' Catherine couldn't wait for her to finish. 'Where? Here? In Batistamajor?'

'In Batistamajor, yes,' agreed the nun evenly. 'He—came to the hospital. To check on his patients. He—

well, it was natural that he should do so. He had been away for several days.'

'In Terasina,' agreed Catherine, shifting impatiently in her seat. 'Where did he go afterwards? Did he tell you what he intended to do? Oh, please, Reverend Mother, try to remember! It's terribly urgent, believe me!'

'Who was that young man who brought you to the convent, *senhorita*?' inquired the nun imperturbably, once again sidestepping Catherine's questions. 'He looked like one of Rodolfo's men. The—uniform, you see; or rather the lack of it. There was something faintly familiar about him.'

Catherine sighed. 'Luis is not just one of Rodolfo's men. He's his son.' She took a deep breath. 'Now, can you tell me if you know what Armand was going to do?'

Reverend Mother looked thoughtful. 'José Rodolfo's son,' she murmured, revealing she was not giving any attention to Catherine's inquiries. 'Does he know you are looking for Dr Alvares, *senhorita*? Is it for him you are so anxious to trace the man who saved you?'

Catherine blinked. 'I—Luis knows I'm looking for Armand, yes.'

'I see.'

'Why shouldn't he?' Catherine gazed at her uncomprehendingly. 'It isn't any secret.'

'You feel no—loyalty then? No sense of shame?'

'No sense of shame?' repeated Catherine, totally confused. And then, as a dawning realisation came to her, she added: 'You mean, because Armand is married.'

Reverend Mother's nostrils thinned. 'Dr Alvares's personal affairs are nothing to do with me, *senhorita*.

But I would remind you that the war is not yet over. Does your—Senhor Rodolfo know that the good doctor was helping the military regime?'

Catherine shook her head. 'You mean because he attended the soldiers at the garrison?'

'What else?'

Catherine expelled her breath wearily. 'Armand is a doctor, Reverend Mother. He would never consciously deny anyone his professional services.'

Mother Benedicta held up her head. 'Are you implying he was treating members of the guerrilla forces, too?'

Catherine met the woman's gaze without flinching. 'Don't you know, Reverend Mother?' she asked quietly. 'Haven't you seen them in your hospital yourself?'

There was a moment when she thought the old woman was going to deny it, but then her shoulders sagged, and her elbows supported the weight of her body on the table. 'Yes, yes,' she admitted tersely, 'I suppose I have. But that does not mean Dr Alvares's life is safe. If a man like Father Donovan could—'

She broke off abruptly, realising she had said too much, but Catherine had sensed that there was still something Mother Benedicta was concealing. 'Please,' she said, 'what were you going to say about Father Donovan? Does it—does it have anything to do with Major Enriques?'

'How do you know that?'

Reverend Mother's involuntary ejaculation gave Catherine sudden hope. 'I—I read that he had been arrested,' she explained hurriedly. 'Surely Father Donovan hasn't been arrested, too?' Her stomach plunged. 'Don't tell me that's what happened to Armand!'

'Oh, no. No!' Mother Benedicta was surprisingly adamant on that score. 'I—*only* Major Enriques has been arrested. He was taken away only days before Rodolfo's men occupied the village.'

'Poor Major Enriques!' Catherine shook her head. 'Do you know why he was arrested? Had he done something wrong?'

Reverend Mother regarded her silently for a moment, as if assessing the advisability of being completely honest with her; and then seemed to give in. 'You know about the child,' she said. 'Of course, you must do. Maria looked after you while you were ill. Well, I am afraid the boy was his undoing.'

Catherine blinked. 'The child? Maria's child?' She caught her breath. 'Are you saying Major Enriques was the father?'

'You did not know?' Reverend Mother shrugged. 'No—well, perhaps it was wiser not. Although, in the circumstances, it hardly mattered.'

'Why?'

'Our good priest, Father Donovan,' said Reverend Mother flatly. 'He informed the major's superiors that he was—how do they put it?—consorting with the enemies of the state. I believe, for some time, the major had been having doubts about his political affiliations. The child's identity was simply an endorsement of that.'

'Father Donovan reported him!' Catherine was appalled. 'I can hardly believe it.'

'No.' Mother Benedicta composed herself. 'Nor could I. But it appears the *padre* was not above a little corruption himself. As a pillar of the community, he was in an ideal position to avail himself of its secrets.' She paused. 'Even Dr Alvares was not immune from his treachery.'

Catherine's face paled. 'What do you mean?'

Reverend Mother frowned, and then, reaching across her desk, she touched Catherine's hand. 'My dear, it appears that Father Donovan had something to do with your father's murder.'

'What?' Catherine felt so sick, she wondered if she was going to faint again. 'I—how could he be involved?'

Reverend Mother hesitated. 'Do you remember how your father used to like to go to the church, to admire the vessels?'

'Yes . . .'

'Well, we shall never know for sure, of course, but it seems possible he discovered—or perhaps was only thought to have discovered—something the *padre* wished to conceal. Perhaps he overheard a conversation, intercepted a message, there are any number of ways it could have happened. But it seems obvious that your father inadvertently learned something incriminating, whether or not he connected it with the right man.'

Catherine swallowed convulsively. 'And you think Father Donovan sent—those men—'

After her experiences that morning, she could not go on, but Mother Benedicta seemed to understand. 'It is possible,' she affirmed gently. 'And eventually, Dr Alvares suspected what had happened.'

Catherine pressed a hand to her churning stomach. 'Are you trying to tell me Armand is dead, too?' she choked.

'Not dead, no.' Reverend Mother shook her head firmly. 'Thanks to Maria Callea he is still alive. But only just.'

Catherine's hands gripped the desk. 'He's injured?'

'He—was—dying,' declared Mother Benedicta

softly. 'He went to see Father Donovan, you see. Then he disappeared, as did Father Donovan. Apparently, Donovan left him, imprisoned in the cellar below the church, without either food or water. If Maria had not heard his feeble hammering, when she went to pray for the safety of Henri Enriques, he would now be dead.'

Catherine caught her breath. 'So where is he?'

'This boy,' said Reverend Mother irrelevantly, or so it seemed to Catherine at that moment, 'this son of José Rodolfo's—he is to be trusted?'

'Of course.' Catherine nodded urgently.

'Even with the life of this man you apparently care so much about?'

'Yes! Yes!' Catherine's breathing felt suspended. 'José—Armand and José are half-brothers! Luis is Armand's nephew.'

'Ah!' Reverend Mother expelled her breath on a long sigh. '*E verdade! Seu sobrinho*—his nephew.'

'Reverend Mother, please!' Catherine could contain herself no longer. 'If you know where Armand is, you must tell me!'

'Why—he is here, of course,' replied Reverend Mother calmly, rising to her feet. 'In the hospital. Come: I will take you to him.'

CHAPTER TWENTY-ONE

THEY had put Armand into Sister Cecilia's office, a tiny cubicle that lay midway between the male and female wards. When Catherine entered the room on Reverend Mother's heels, she found he was lying on his back in an attitude of deep unconsciousness, and her heart missed a beat at his coma-like stillness.

'He is asleep, only asleep,' said Mother Benedicta drily, observing Catherine's agitation. 'We have been waking him up and feeding him at intervals, but as you can see, he is exhausted.'

Catherine moved closer to the bed, the nun's reassurance giving her little respite from her anxieties. Armand looked so pale, so drawn; his skin stretched taut across the bones of his thin face. Even the growth of beard that appeared as a dark stubble on his chin gave little colour to his appearance, and she badly wanted to touch him, to assure herself he was still alive.

'I will leave you for a little while,' said Reverend Mother, moving towards the door again. 'Do not expect him to waken. No doubt Sister Felicia will advise you when next he can be disturbed.'

'Yes, Reverend Mother.'

Left to herself, Catherine knelt down beside the bed and tentatively ran her knuckles down Armand's cheek. His skin was still warm, she discovered with some relief, but his breathing was so shallow it was scarcely discernible.

The outline of his body was visible beneath the thin

sheet, which was all that covered him, and she thought his bones seemed more sharply defined than she remembered. How long had he been locked in the cellar before Maria found him, she wondered achingly, taking the hand that was lying so limply on the sheet between both of hers. Was that ugly contusion on his temple Father Donovan's doing as well? He looked so defenceless suddenly, so *vulnerable*. If only there was something she could do to help him.

Bending her head to press her lips to the back of his hand, she was startled out of her preoccupation by a sudden movement in the bed, a restless stirring that brought her face up anxiously so that she could look at him.

'Armand,' she ventured, hardly daring to whisper his name, and almost compulsively his eyes opened.

'*Catarina?*' His expression underwent a quite amazing change, though the sudden whitening around his lips was hardly an improvement. '*Meu Deus! Sou morto!*'

'*Dead?*' Catherine understood his final words very well. 'You're not dead, Armand. You're here. In the hospital at the convent.' She pressed his hand to her cheek, fighting back the tears that were suddenly very near. 'You're alive! Very much alive, thank goodness!'

'Catarina,' he said again, disbelievingly. 'But what are you doing here?' His voice quickened with emotion. 'You are supposed to be in São Paulo!'

'I know, I know.' Catherine sniffed convulsively. 'And I was. But I came back.'

'You're crazy!' Armand's breathing quickened, and he shifted restively beneath her hands. 'Do you not know how dangerous the situation has become?

Catherine, when you left Surajo, you knew I did not want you to come back! Law and order, such as it was, is breaking down! There was fighting in Terasina when I left.' He forced himself up on to his elbows, his breathing ragged now. 'Lady, all over this country—'

'Armand, please!' Alarmed at the extent of his agitation, Catherine got up from her knees and seated herself on the side of his bed. Then, putting her hands on his sweating shoulders, she compelled him back against the pillows. 'Darling, relax,' she told him huskily. 'You don't have to worry about me. I don't know what the nuns have told you, but the fighting in this area is over! José and his men have control of the airport at Ribatejo, and Luis drove me here to find you.'

Armand blinked. 'Are you serious?'

'Never more serious in my life,' she assured him softly, unable to prevent herself from smoothing back his damp hair from his forehead. 'All you have to do is concern yourself with getting well again.' She shook her head. 'You've no idea how worried I've been about you.'

Armand gazed up at her blankly. 'You have seen—José?'

'Yes.' Catherine nodded, suddenly remembering how worried José had been. 'I must let him know you're safe.' She shook her head wonderingly. 'I can hardly believe that it's all over.'

'What is all over?' Armand was regarding her guardedly, and with a little sigh, Catherine bent her head and brushed her lips across the bruise on his temple.

'That you are here; that you are alive and well,' she answered unsteadily. 'Oh, *Armand*—' and ignoring the dictates of her conscience that warned her not to over-excite him, she brought her mouth to his.

His lips parted powerlessly beneath that slight pressure, the shallow warmth of his breathing an impossible relief. Close against his chest, the dampness of his body was moistening the material of her shirt, and drawing back, she gazed at him with tremulous emotion.

'I shouldn't do this,' she breathed, trying to catch her breath, but with unexpected strength, Armand compelled her down to him again.

'Do not believe it,' he groaned, his hand behind her head deepening the urgency of their embrace. 'I do not know why you are here, and when I am stronger I shall, no doubt, be very angry with you for disobeying me. But for now, it is enough that we are together.'

Their lips clung, fused by a passion no force on earth could resist. Catherine almost forgot how ill Armand still was as she cupped the harsh beauty of his face, uncaring that his growth of beard was abrasive to her fingertips.

But eventually, the trickle of sweat from his forehead reminded her of his weakness, and when she drew back this time, she was appalled to see how drained he looked.

'I'll get Sister Felicia,' she exclaimed, but when she would have got up from the bed, his hand on her forearm detained her.

'I am all right,' he insisted huskily, his pallor receding slightly as he got his breath back. '*Querida*, do not go. Stay with me.' He expelled an uneven breath. 'Please. I want to keep you in my sight.'

But he didn't. Seconds later, he was asleep again, his breathing less shallow than before. When Sister Felicia appeared to check on her patient, Catherine had resumed her position on the floor beside the bed, and she looked up in some embarrassment at being caught in such a revealing attitude.

'Relax, *senhorita*,' the elderly nun advised crisply, as Catherine sprang to her feet. 'I would hazard a guess that when our patient wakes, he will not be disappointed to find you here.'

Catherine licked her lips. 'He did wake—a little while ago. He knows I'm here.'

'Ah.' Sister Felicia nodded. 'That is good. And did you speak with him?'

Catherine flushed. 'Briefly.'

'Hmm.' The elderly nun laid her fingers on his forehead. 'Well—it seems he is sleeping quite comfortably now. Do you want to remain?'

'Yes. Oh, yes. But—' Catherine caught her lower lip between her teeth. 'A young man brought me here. In a Land-Rover. Do you know if he has returned?'

'I think perhaps he has,' Sister Felicia replied thoughtfully. 'Do you wish me to give him a message?'

'No. No—' Catherine looked anxiously at Armand's sleeping form. 'I will speak with him.' She hesitated. 'Can I come back?'

'Could I stop you?' inquired Sister Felicia drily. 'Yes. Yes. Come back. I have the feeling we have found the reason why you decided the religious life was not for you.'

Luis was waiting in the Land-Rover at the gates, but he got out at her approach, aware of something different about her. 'You know where my uncle is?' he demanded, catching the hands she held out to him and, nodding vehemently, Catherine struggled to explain what she had learned.

'He is here!' Luis gazed up at the fluted cupola above the gateway. 'But why was my father not informed?'

'It's a long story.' Catherine shook her head. 'It seems that Reverend Mother didn't know who she could trust, and Armand himself was too ill to question what was going on. He didn't even know that José had gained control of this area.'

Luis's mouth compressed. 'And where is this—bastard—Donovan now?'

'Who knows?' Catherine shrugged. 'Obviously, it was he who set fire to Armand's house. He probably hoped people would think Armand died in the fire. That way, he could come back without fear of exposure.'

Luis looked grim. 'But—my uncle's body would have been found eventually.'

'And Father Donovan could deny all knowledge of it,' declared Catherine bleakly. 'Who would there be to contradict him?'

Luis expelled his breath savagely. 'I hope my father catches up with him.'

'Yes. So do I,' agreed Catherine, with a taut smile. 'But now, I suggest you go and tell your father the good news. Armand's sleeping at the moment, and I want to be there when he wakes.'

Luis smiled then. 'Okay,' he said, climbing back behind the wheel of the Land-Rover. 'Give him our love, will you?' He grimaced. 'Though he could probably get well on yours alone!'

It was late in the afternoon, after Catherine had helped Armand to swallow some of the beef soup Sister Margarita had brought for him, that they were able to talk again. In spite of Sister Margarita's warning that Armand should not be overtired; that Catherine should ask Reverend Mother if she might spend the night in one of the beds in the female ward, and come back again tomorrow, Armand had been adamant. She should stay, he averred harshly, holding on to Catherine's hand like a lifeline, and Sister Margarita eventually went away, muttering over doctors who refused to follow their own advice.

'Come here,' he muttered, as soon as they were alone, and the hungry pressure of his mouth left little doubt of his returning strength. '*Deus*, I have been wanting to do this ever since I opened my eyes,' he added huskily. 'I thought Sister Margarita would never leave.'

'I don't think she approves of me at all,' remarked Catherine ruefully as Armand drew her hands to his lips. 'She hasn't forgotten it was you who took me out of here. And now, our being here together offends all her sensibilities.'

'Poor Sister Margarita,' said Armand, looking anything but repentant. 'Now—tell me how you came to be here. Do you have any idea how I would have felt if I had suspected you might come back looking for me?'

Catherine sighed, settling herself more comfortably on the side of his bed. 'Don't be cross,' she said, her fingers straying irresistibly to the fine whorls of hair that covered the lower half of his chest. 'Your mother understood how I felt.' She paused. 'She was worried about you, too. She had had this premonition, and it seems that she was right.'

'Premonitions!' Armand was scathing. 'Catherine, you could have been killed!'

'But I wasn't.'

'That is no thanks to my mother!'

Catherine's lips twitched. 'Darling, she couldn't have stopped me. So—' She shrugged. 'She helped me.'

Armand turned his head impatiently from side to side. 'But what possessed you to come back?' he exclaimed. 'I told Senhor Lopez; I made my instructions very clear—'

'I'm sure you did.' Catherine inclined her head. 'But after I read that Major Enriques had been arrested—'

Armand frowned. 'Where did you read that?'

'In the paper I bought in Casca de Mar.' Catherine looked defensively at him. 'If I'd read it before we boarded the plane, I should probably have refused to go at all. As it was, I read it that first night we arrived in São Paulo.'

'But why should Henri Enriques's arrest mean anything to you?'

Catherine lifted her shoulders. 'He spent a lot of time with you, didn't he? I was afraid—I was afraid you might have been arrested, too!'

Armand regarded her incredulously. 'But what could you have hoped to do if I had been detained by the military?' he demanded.

'I don't know.' Catherine's fingers found his nipple and caressed it almost involuntarily. 'I just wanted to be near you, wherever you were. If—if you had died, I wouldn't have cared what happened to me,' she added simply.

The pressure of Armand's hand on hers prevented her from continuing her exploration, and his voice was thick with emotion as he said: 'You really mean that?'

At her nod, his mouth compressed, and then, after a moment, he continued softly: 'I had much time for thinking while I was incarcerated in Donovan's crypt. They told you about that, did they not?' He shook his head. 'I thought I was going to die, and it is strange how, when one is faced with the prospect of death, everything in life suddenly becomes clear.' He paused, his thumb massaging the tips of her fingers. 'I did not believe in the love of a man for a woman. I did not think I had it in me to care for anyone more than I cared for my son—but it is not true.' He brought her fingers to his lips again, his tongue warm against her palm. 'I love you, Catarina,' he told her huskily. 'I love you so much it hurts when I am away from you. I want you to know that, whatever happens, I will never— *ever*—stop loving you.'

'Oh, Armand!' Suddenly, Catherine's heart was beating wildly, and she bent to lay her cheek against his chest. 'I haven't told you, have I? You don't know!'

'Know? Know what?'

Armand was confused, and lifting her head again, Catherine regarded him with troubled eyes. 'It's Estella,' she said, her lips faltering over the words. 'She's dead! Luis told me. The plane carrying her and—and General Montoya back to Terasina, was shot down by his own forces.'

'Dead!' Armand closed his eyes for a moment, and then opened them again to look at her. 'Does Ricardo know?'

'No.'

'I must tell him.' Armand's face was sombre. 'Poor Estella! She did not deserve to die.'

Catherine drew a steadying breath. 'No.' His expression was unreadable, and all of a sudden she was afraid.

'I must inform her family, too,' Armand continued grimly. 'Her mother is dead, but her father is still alive. He will need to be told.'

'Yes.'

Catherine bowed her head, but when she would

have got up from the bed, Armand's hand prevented her once again. 'Where are you going?'

Catherine hesitated. 'I thought you might—that is—would you prefer to be alone for a while?'

Armand's eyes darkened. 'No. Why should I?'

'I thought—' Catherine lifted one shoulder helplessly. 'She was your—wife.'

'Oh, *God*!' With a muffled oath, Armand slid his hand behind her nape, cradling her head against his palm. 'I wondered why you looked so anxious suddenly.' His thumb probed the cavity of her ear. 'My sweet Catarina, Estella and I have not lived together for more than five years. I should have told you, I know, but she was always there, between us. How could I ask you to share my life when all I could offer was myself?'

Catherine trembled. 'It would have been enough.'

'Not to me,' declared Armand fiercely. 'I had already destroyed my brother's life. I could not destroy yours as well.'

Catherine bent her head. 'Your mother told me, you know. About you—and José—and Estella.'

'Did she?' Armand's lips twisted. 'And were you suitably disgusted by my behaviour?'

Catherine shook her head. 'She doesn't blame you.'

'She did.'

'Once perhaps. When José disappeared. But, having known Estella—having lived with her—do you think she would have made José any happier?'

Armand gave her a rueful look. 'How can I answer that? Maybe José would have made her happy.'

'She didn't have to marry you.'

'No.' Armand conceded that. 'The same could be said of me.'

Catherine rubbed her cheek against his hand. 'Why did you marry her? Did you love her?'

Armand hesitated. Then he said: 'I am afraid I was very cynical of love in those days. And I was past the age when my mother thought all decent God-fearing men should be married. So—' He shrugged. 'I selfishly took what Estella was offering.'

'You had Ricardo,' said Catherine, allowing him to draw her face into the hollow of his neck.

'Yes. I had Ricardo,' he agreed softly. 'And because of him, Estella has always had a hold on me.'

'Yes. Your father told me.'

Armand gave a rueful laugh. 'It seems to me, my mother and father told you a lot,' he remarked. 'It seems they are more perceptive than I thought.'

'What do you mean?'

Armand nuzzled his chin against the silky softness of her hair. 'Oh—when I told them you would be accompanying Ricardo, I suppose I must have sounded more protective than I had intended.' He paused. 'Do you think they suspect about us?'

'Your mother does,' said Catherine, turning her lips against his neck. 'She guessed I was in love with you.'

'I see.' Armand threaded his fingers into her hair, and systematically loosened it from the braid.'

'Do you mind?' Catherine lifted her head to look at him, and his eyes gave her answer.

'How could I?' he muttered, propelling her mouth insistently to his, and with a groan of satisfaction, he rolled her over so that she was lying beneath him.

His kisses became deeper, more urgent, eloquent of the need that was overwhelming even the weakness of his body. He wanted her, she knew that. She could feel the insistent pressure that was swelling against her hip, and she longed to be able to satisfy that need. But this was a hospital; any one of the Sisters could appear at any time.

'We can't!' she got out at last, when he released her mouth to seek the perfumed hollow, visible above the opened neckline of her shirt, and he gave a shudder of acquiescence.

'I know, I know,' he said, breathing in the scent of her. 'But as soon as I get out of here . . .'

Catherine's lips turned upward. 'As soon as you like,' she agreed huskily, and he was about to seek her mouth again when a discreet cough from the doorway interrupted them.

'José!' Armand's exclamation caused Catherine no little embarrassment, and wriggling off the bed, she struggled to her feet.

She managed to disguise the first wave of giddiness that swept over her. José was coming into the room, making some comment about Armand always falling on his feet, and the two men's attentions were fixed on each other. But, to her dismay, the dizziness did not subside, and as she groped groggily for the door, Armand noticed something was wrong.

'Catherine!' he muttered, his smile of welcome for his brother forgotten, and thrusting back the sheet, he swung his feet to the floor.

But he was weaker than he thought, and José regarded him impatiently for a moment before going to Catherine's assistance. 'Sit down,' he said, helping her to the end of the bed, and Armand dragged himself towards her, his eyes running over her with professional deliberation.

'I'm all right,' murmured Catherine unhappily, hoping José did not think she was trying to monopolise Armand's attention. 'I—I just felt giddy for a moment. It must be because I haven't eaten anything today.'

'You had some soup,' Armand reminded her, his face dark with concern. 'Has this happened before?'

'She fainted in my office this morning,' put in José briefly. 'I thought it was because I had just told her you were missing.'

'It was.' Catherine looked at him defensively, before turning her attention back to Armand. 'I'll be fine, really,' she insisted. 'It—it's been a long day.'

Armand's mouth tightened, and his eyes moved down, over the burgeoning fullness of her breasts to the slight mound of her abdomen. 'If you say so,' he acceded at last, his golden gaze returning to her face, and José tactfully changed the subject.

'I suggest you either get back into bed or put on some clothes,' he advised his brother drily. 'You don't want to give the nuns a heart attack, do you?'

Three weeks later, Catherine was reclining lazily on the balcony of the de Castros' apartment on Guaruja. The lush little island, just across the water from the coastal resort of Santos, was the holiday home of many *Paulistas*, as she had discovered the people of São Paulo liked to call themselves, and the de Castros' apartment overlooked waving palms, pure white sands, and the creaming surge of the ocean.

She and Armand had been at the apartment for the past three days, and to begin with they had done little else but make love, swim, and make love again. It was the first time they had been completely alone together; the maid, who took care of the apartment, only appearing at certain hours of the day. In consequence, they were seldom out of one another's arms for long—bathing together, eating together, sleeping together, learning everything there was to know about one another, without anyone to interrupt them.

Ricardo had not come with them. He was quite content to stay at Aguas de Seda, and his grandparents were spoiling him terribly. But both Catherine and Armand thought he could do with a little spoiling after the uncertain life he had lived these past two years.

He had taken the news of his mother's death with some emotion, but the realisation that he was to live with his father from now on seemed to reassure him. What he needed now was a period of readjustment, Armand had told Catherine gently, when she expressed her worries about him. It was natural that for a time he should experience a sense of insecurity. It was up to them to show him that so far as they were concerned, he was an integral part of their lives. 'He already cares about you,' he assured her softly. 'And once we are married, he'll know what it can be like to have a proper family life.'

Now, hearing Armand's footsteps crossing the tiled floor of the living room, Catherine turned her head to see him emerging on to the balcony with the can of iced beer he had been to fetch. In white cotton shorts, that hung low on his hips, she thought he had never looked healthier, or more attractive, and her lips parted in a provocative smile when he came to stand over her.

'What time is it?' she murmured, shading her eyes with her arm, and dropping the empty can on to the floor, Armand came down on the cushioned lounger beside her.

'I think it's time you came indoors out of the sun,' he

murmured, his thumbs probing the bra strap of her bikini.

'*Armand!*' Affecting disapproval, Catherine glanced in mock-apprehension about her. 'Someone might see us!'

'So? Let them,' he responded carelessly, bearing her back against the soft cushions. '*Deus*, you smell of coconuts! What have you been putting on yourself?'

'Only sun-tan lotion,' protested Catherine, sliding her arms around his neck nevertheless. 'Armand—not here!'

'Then let's go take a shower, hmm?' he breathed into her nape, and with a jack-knifing movement, he got off the lounger and swung her up into his arms.

Standing together beneath the cooling spray, Armand soaped the offending lotion from her body, his hands lingering in those places he considered exclusively his. 'Let me,' she offered huskily, taking the soap from him, but Armand was not immune to such blatant seduction.

Without bothering with a towel, he carried her into the bedroom, and although she protested that the satin quilt would get wet, he ignored her pleas. 'It will dry,' he assured her thickly, covering her body with his, and Catherine had no will to gainsay him.

As always, the pulsating power of his body drove them both to the outer limits of human experience, the sensual pleasure they found in one another never diminishing. They were made for one another, thought Catherine dreamily, lingering in the glowing aftermath of his lovemaking. They fitted together so perfectly, and she was always loath for him to draw away from her.

Now, when he moved, she wrapped her arms more tightly around his neck, making little nuzzling sounds of protest. 'Don't go,' she breathed, one leg sliding sensually down the length of his. 'I don't want you to.'

'No?' he murmured, capturing the lobe of her ear between his teeth and biting it gently. 'But I think we have to talk, and if we stay like this you know what will happen.'

'So?' she prompted, and he stifled a low laugh as he firmly detached himself from her.

'So, we have to talk,' he insisted, while not being able to resist keeping her close within the circle of his arms. 'Catherine, *querida*, when are you going to marry me?'

She looked up at him. 'You still want me to?'

'You are joking, of course,' he muttered, his face sobering even so. 'Yes, I want to marry you. The sooner the better, I think.'

'But Ricardo—'

'Ricardo is not a baby. He knows we care about one another,' Armand assured her firmly. 'I suggest three days from now, if that is suitable to you.'

'Three days!' Catherine touched his cheek. 'But, won't people think it is too soon?'

'Because of Estella, you mean?' Armand inquired softly. 'My darling, I am not suggesting a grand affair. Just a simple ceremony, in the company of my parents and Ricardo.' He paused. 'Well?'

Catherine pressed her face against his chest. 'You know I'd marry you this minute if you asked me. I—I just don't want you to feel—well, you made a mistake once—'

'But not this time,' Armand averred huskily. 'You are everything I have ever wanted in a woman, and I adore you.'

There was a satisfying interlude while Armand convinced her he meant what he said, and then, stretching luxuriously, Catherine escaped from his arms to do a pirouette across the room. The dizziness that assailed her as she did so was confusing, and uttering a little cry, she sank helplessly down on to the soft carpet.

Armand was off the bed in a second. Half squatting, half kneeling beside her, he gathered her up into his arms, and she caught her breath as the sickening feeling gradually disappeared again.

'I must have had too much sun,' she mumbled, feeling a fool, but Armand carried her back to the bed and laid her very gently on the coverlet.

'*Querida*,' he said softly, 'is there something you should have told me?'

Catherine blinked, a faint trace of colour running into her cheeks. 'I—I didn't want to worry you,' she admitted, as he ran expert fingers over the slight thickening at her waist. 'Is—is it true?'

'That you are going to have a baby?' he inquired wryly. 'Oh, *querida*, I did not mean for this to happen!'

'Why not?'

Her eyes were anxious, and he lifted one leg to rest on the edge of the bed, running his hand round the back of his neck. 'Oh—because it's too soon,' he muttered. 'It's not fair on you. You're not yet a wife, and already you're going to be a mother!'

'Do—do you mind so much?' Catherine propped herself up on her elbows and looked at him with troubled eyes.

'Do I mind?' he echoed, gazing at her. 'Well—only for you. You are so young.'

'I'm almost twenty,' she reminded him fiercely. 'And—and as a matter of fact, I did suspect that was what it was. Only—only I didn't want you to marry me just because I was expecting your child!'

Armand looked thunderstruck. 'You can't be serious!'

'Why not?'

'Oh—because you cannot,' he muttered savagely. 'I am incapable of thinking of a life without you, and you are making foolish statements like that!'

Catherine's tongue appeared. 'Then, you don't mind about the child?'

'Mind?' Armand raised his eyes heavenward for a moment. '*Querida*, I can think of nothing more satisfying than knowing my child is growing inside you,' he told her emotively.

'That's all right then, because I feel the same.' Catherine slipped her arms around his neck. 'I hope Ricardo won't mind.'

'Ricardo! Ricardo!' muttered Armand frustratedly, burying his face in the silken curtain of her hair. 'Ricardo has always wanted brothers and sisters. And, be assured, my mother will be delighted.'

'Will she?'

'Of course.' Armand grimaced. 'It was a great disappointment to her when Luis decided he would rather stay in Terasina with his father, than come to live with his grandparents.'

Catherine lifted her shoulder to his caressing lips. 'I suppose he wants to enjoy a little of the kudos of being *General* Rodolfo's son,' she murmured contentedly. 'And as his mother is dead . . .'

'Hmm.' Armand was reflective. 'One more reason for José to hate the Ferreira regime. You know Montoya had her killed when she refused to tell him of José's whereabouts?'

'Yes.' Catherine was silent for a moment. 'Thank goodness Major Enriques managed to escape.'

'Indeed.' Armand rested his chin on her shoulder. 'Particularly for Maria's sake. I owe her a lot.'

'So do I,' said Catherine fervently. She lifted her head. 'You never did tell me how long you were imprisoned in that cellar.'

'I'm not absolutely sure,' replied Armand honestly. 'Four—maybe five days. Without water, I soon lost track of time.'

Catherine shook her head in remembered horror. 'Does anyone know what happened to Father Donovan?'

'José suspects he may have fled the country. Who knows?'

Catherine heaved a sigh. 'Well, at least he didn't kill you.'

'No.' Armand's tone was dry. 'I suspect even Father Donovan drew the line at actual assassination, although he did deliver me one hell of a blow with one of the altar candlesticks!'

Catherine closed her eyes against the images his words evoked, opening them again to ask more optimistically: 'Who do you think will become president, now that Ferreira's government has been deposed?'

'I don't know.' Armand shrugged. 'José says there are to be democratic elections at last. But I favour my brother, don't you?'

Catherine smiled mischievously. 'He is rather impressive,' she agreed. 'And very handsome, don't you think?'

'I think we've talked enough about José and his problems for the moment,' declared Armand, allowing her to subside back against the covers before tickling her unmercifully. Then, when she was weak with laughter, he looked down at her, the light of love gleaming in his golden eyes. 'You know, I sometimes wonder how I lived all those years without you,' he said in a shaken voice, and with her arms around his neck, Catherine showed him she knew exactly what he meant . . .

ABOUT THE AUTHOR

ANNE MATHER began her career by writing the kind of book she likes to read—romance. Her first novel was published by Harlequin in 1970, and she has recently celebrated the publication of her one hundredth book. The excitement of having her novel WILD CONCERTO hit the NEW YORK TIMES Best Sellers list is but one highlight in Anne's career. With more than one hundred million copies of her titles in print in over ninety countries and in fifteen languages, Anne Mather is a model for many aspiring romance writers.